By Peggy Hanchar
Published by Fawcett Books:

THE GILDED DOVE
WHERE EAGLES SOAR
CHEYENNE DREAMS
FANCY LADY
WILD SAGE
SWAN NECKLACE
THE SCOTTISH BRIDE

THE SCOTTISH BRIDE

Peggy Hanchar

FAWCETT GOLD MEDAL • NEW YORK

A Fawcett Gold Medal Book
Published by Ballantine Books
Copyright © 1996 by Peggy Hanchar

ISBN 0-449-14866-1

Manufactured in the United States of America

Prologue

"**F**LEE, CHILD. THE hounds of hell are upon us!"
Rough hands shook Lillias from her slumber.
Mumbling a sleepy protest, she rubbed her eyes and sat up.
Had she been dreaming? Fine gold hair swirled in silken
disarray over her small face.

"They've come, my lady—the MacLeods, those bloodthirsty wolfhounds from the North." Lillias leapt from her
bed and ran to the window with all the excitement of a
fearless nine-year-old. From here she had a clear view of
the drawbridge and front gate. Crawling onto the stone seat,
she threw open the glazed windows and peered out. From
below came the sounds and fury of battle, steel clanging
against steel, and men's voices raised in harsh battle cry.

"Is faither below fighting the enemy?"

"Aye, that he is, child." Hannah sighed, snatching up a
fur-trimmed cape to throw over the girl's linen nightshift.
"Come, we must flee while we may."

Lillias leapt down from the window seat, her eyes flashing with excitement more than fear. Suddenly the heavy
window tapestry was rent by the point of an arrow delivered from below. It lodged, quivering and deadly, in the
oaken bedpost. Lillias stared at it open-mouthed. If she
hadn't obeyed Hannah, the arrow would be in her own
back. For the first time since being wakened, fear washed
over her, so that when Hannah grabbed her hand and
tugged her toward the corridor, she followed willingly.

1

"Will they kill us, Hannah?" she asked fearfully.

"Nay, child. Not wi' Sir Robert below to fight them off." Hannah whisked her toward the narrow spiral stairwell that led to the kitchen, the vaulted basements below, and finally to a postern opening in the curtain wall where they might leave the castle undetected. But before they gained the kitchen with its barreled ceilings and huge fireplace, they heard a commotion in the great hall.

Suddenly the castle was swarming with wild, fierce-looking men dressed in saffron shirts of linen and vests of quilted leather, with belted tartans thrown over all, not unlike that which her father's own men wore, save for the colors of the plaid itself. Lillias was confused as to whether these men were really their enemies, then she looked at their savage faces, made more fearsome by the iron headpieces they wore. These were the demons that lived in her dreams, the monsters of which Hannah had told her, the slavering beasts of Cullayne. She screamed with fright and hid behind Hannah's ample skirts.

One man came forward. Beneath his black-and-red plaid he wore a shirt of chain mail; his headpiece bore a camail of the same and carried the markings of a chief. He was covered with coarse red hair. Red eyes, filled with a light of vengeance, gleamed from beneath his helmet as he regarded Lillias.

"The red devil himself!" Hannah cried, and turned, trying to herd Lillias up the stairs to the chambers above. At a signal from the fierce bearded chief, one of the young soldiers sprang up the stone steps after them, his hairy legs flashing beneath his short plaid, his step surefooted and quick. Lillias screamed as he reached for her.

"Hannah!" she cried, dodging away. From below came the sound of deep-bellied laughter as the clan chief regarded their futile attempt at flight. He must surely be the devil, Lillias thought, to laugh so at someone else's misfortune. At the end of the long kitchen, she caught a glimpse of her cousin, Garth McGinnis. His sword was sheathed. He made no effort to fight off the invaders.

"Garth, help me!" she called frantically, but he cast her

a sly glance and left the kitchen without looking back. No enemy stepped forward to stop him.

"You'll na' take the bairn," Hannah cried, striking at the warrior's broad shoulders. He raised a large hand and slapped her away as one would a child. The old woman fell heavily against the stone steps. Before Lillias knew what he was about, the warrior plunged his dirk into her chest.

Her own fear forgotten at seeing Hannah so wounded, Lillias leapt forward, scratching and kicking. Startled, the young soldier tried to hold her away from him, but she swung at him with her small fists and finally sank her teeth into his thumb—so hard that she tasted blood and he dropped his dagger. The warrior howled with pain and leapt away from her so that he lost his balance and tumbled down the steps, crashing on the floor below. The laughter had stopped.

Sobbing from exertion and fear, Lillias knelt beside Hannah. Blood gushed from the wound in the old woman's chest. Her face was unearthly pale, her plump cheeks waxen. Lillias used the tail of her nightshift to staunch the flow of blood.

"Hannah," she whispered through her tears, "you mustn't die. Dinna leave me." From behind, two pairs of hands plucked her from the steps so quickly she had no time to reach for the dagger again.

"Leave me!" she cried, kicking out with all her might, her long coltish legs giving discomfort wherever her small heels landed. She was carried down the steps and dumped on the floor, at the feet of the chief. When she tried to rise, a rough kick sent her down again. She crouched where she was, staring up at the red devil, seeing his girth and strength and the evil red lights of his black eyes.

"Aye, she's a bonny lass, and she has more fight than her faither and his men. Bring her."

Her mother appeared at the top of steps, solitary and motionless. The chief paused and stared up at her as if mesmerized by her fine beauty. His stance was strangely tense. Finally he bowed slightly, a surprisingly elegant gesture in one so coarse.

"Red Rafe MacLeod at yer command, Lady Margaret," he called in a jeering tone. "I have what I came for, yer daughter. D'ye na' wish to join her in her captivity?"

At first, when there was no response, Lillias thought the silhouette was only a shadow after all. Then Margaret spoke as if from some distant place—far removed from the strife surrounding them—for not even the veil that hung from her headdress moved.

"I wait for Robert," she answered quietly.

"Yer husband lies yonder in the bailey near the dovecote, where I have left him." The MacLeod chief sneered. "When next ye walk there, remember that the grass beneath yer feet is greener because his blood has spilled there. My revenge is complete, Lady Margaret."

The veil jerked as if she were in a spasm. Lillias heard the words of her father's death and whimpered.

"Mither!" Lillias cried, reaching out her arms to the aloof figure, but Lady Margaret had already slumped to the stone floor in a dead faint.

Outside in the bailey, all was pandemonium. Torches flared, lighting the mangled limbs of the McGinnis men who had fallen in defense of Dunbeath Castle. Lillias glanced toward the dovecote, hoping to pick out her father, but too many bodies littered the ground.

"Rafe!" someone shouted. "Lord Robert's escaped."

With a curse, Red Rafe MacLeod thrust Lillias from him and signaled to a man. Someone placed a hood over her head, drawing the string tight, so all light was shut out. Such darkness was frightening, so she grew still and whimpered. She felt herself being lifted and settled on a horse.

"Back to Cullayne," Red Rafe shouted, and the horses were kicked into a fast gallop. The sounds and smells of Dunbeath were left behind her. Within the dark, suffocating confines of the hood, she whimpered, terrified.

Abruptly her abductors reined in their horses and waited. From the distance came the sound of other riders approaching at a fast gallop.

"So, lad, ye've deigned to join us, after all," Red Rafe shouted to some unseen clansman. "I dinna see ye in the thick of battle. Did ye find a place to hide while better men than ye fought the hated McGinnises?"

"I was there, Faither," someone answered. His voice was lighter, younger than Red Rafe's. "If ye'd but cleared the blood lust from yer eyes, mayhap ye'd have seen me."

"Aye, lad. I've na doubt ye fought and well, for ye've the blood of the MacLeods running in yer veins," Red Rafe growled. "Therefore, I've brought ye a prize." Rough hands lifted Lillias from her perch and held her aloft. Feeling nothing but air beneath her, hampered by the darkness of the hood, Lillias screamed with terror, kicking her feet wildly.

"God's teeth, have ye taken to making war on bairns, then?" the young voice cried.

Rage rumbled in Red Rafe's chest. "Take care, Iain," he cried. "Ye've become *bool-horned*, but ye're not too big for me to knock ye from yer horse."

"Aye, Faither. Ye kin do that, right enough." The young voice was steady, without a show of fear. "But I'll get up again and ye'll have to deliver me another blow and yet another."

There was a moment of uneasy silence and Red Rafe filled it with a bellow of laughter. His men joined in hesitantly. They'd often been witness to the goading of Red Rafe to his son, and each of them knew his taunts were untrue, for they'd ridden with Iain MacLeod and knew he could be savage against his enemies, so he'd already earned the nickname the Black Beast of Cullayne. None could touch him with the *claidheamh mor*, the two-handed sword, or the lighter-weighted basket hilt sword. Despite his fierce prowess in battle, Iain had a gentler side to him that would not allow for cruelty and unwarranted killing. And Red Rafe saw this as a weakness.

"Aye, my son is not a *cutcher*." Red Rafe shouted the rare praise, ignoring the fact that he'd just accused him of such. "No MacLeod has ever been a coward."

"Nor will I ever be, sire," came the cool reply from Iain MacLeod.

"Then, bigod, I gi' ye a bride!" Red Rafe cried, and delivered his kicking, screaming burden to his son.

"I'll not take another human being as a gift, Faither," Iain protested. The child dangled between them, helpless and passive. Her limbs were delicate, her skin almost translucent in the moonlight. Only an occasional hiccuping sob testified that she was alive.

The laughter had left Red Rafe's eyes. Dark, dangerous lights glittered there. "If ye have no need of her, then neither have I. She dies beneath the hooves of my men's horses," he warned. The girl heard his words and screamed, lashing out again with her feet.

"Aye, she's a sprightly one, Iain. She's a bit young now, but gi' her time to age and she'll liven yer bed. Make up yer mind, lad." Though his words were spoken in jest, his gaze was cruel and unrelenting.

"I'll take her," the young warrior said, and reached for the pitiful package. Red Rafe's triumphant laughter rang out.

Lillias felt herself pulled from his rough grasp and settled on a horse in front of someone. Once again she tore at the confining hood.

"Let me out!" she demanded, and the strings were loosened and the bag jerked from her head. Pale golden hair spilled around her face, so she couldn't see who'd freed her, and by the time she'd brushed it back, she was clasped against the chest of her abductor. She angled her head back, trying to see who'd rescued her from Red Rafe's hands this time, but could make out only the slashing blade of an unshaven jaw and a tangle of black, tumbling hair. Red Rafe's laughter rumbled again, and she squirmed around to face him.

"Aye, she'll make a bonny bride," he called. He moved his horse closer and peered at her. "What think ye, little bride, of the groom I've given ye?"

She stared at him in silence, while fury unfurled in her small chest. The sound of a horseman, riding fast, came to them, all heads turned in that direction.

"Lord Robert and a small group of his men are coming," the rider shouted even before he'd reached them.

Lillias's heart leapt. "My faither's coming to kill you!" she shouted at the chieftain. "He's going to cut off your head!"

Red Rafe considered her for a moment, then turned back to the messenger. "How many men?"

"Less than a dozen," the man replied.

"Likely, 'tis Hugh and that ferret, Garth." Red Rafe fingered his beard and hissed in disgust. "Let's ride to Cullayne."

Iain lagged behind the main body. A fine mist had fallen around them. Lillias shivered, and Iain pulled his woolen plaid around her. It smelled of rain and damp earth. She tugged it closer, grateful for its warmth, yawned, and fell asleep against the hard bulk of her captor.

When she woke they were in the bailey of a strange, dark castle. It loomed black and foreboding against the night sky. Steam rose from the sweating flanks of the horses and their hooves struck sparks against the cobblestones. Men dismounted and cursed as blood flowed through their cramped limbs. Dawn streaked the distant horizon. They'd ridden all night.

"Take her to the tower," Red Rafe called.

Sleepily, Lillias was aware of being lifted down from the horse and carried inside and placed on a pallet. Left in the dark, she lay rigid, listening to the howl of the wind against the tower walls. A shutter rattled, making her pull the plaid over her head and bite her lips to keep from sobbing. At last, fatigue claimed her.

Rough hands shook her awake. A harsh voice ordered her to get up. She was ushered down the steep spiraling staircase, with its yawning black drop, to the floor of the tower. Without pausing, the sour-faced serving woman led her across the bailey, toward a small stone building.

"Hurry up now, get inside," she ordered, flapping her apron at Lillias. "They're waitin' for ye."

"Who's waiting?" Lillias asked, but the woman simply

turned and made her way back across the bailey toward the castle.

"I tell ye, Faither, I'll not go through wi' this farce," Iain MacLeod shouted.

"And I tell ye, ye've no choice," Red Rafe declared. "She's the daughter of our mortal enemy. Ye'll take her as yer bride, for to do so will bring back MacLeod land—and I'll have our land returned or blood will be shed."

"Not hers. She's but a child."

"Hers first, then the rest of the thievin' McGinnis clan," Red Rafe declared. Lillias stood on the cold stone floor in her bare feet and her tattered, bloodstained nightshift and began to weep. Tears rolled down her grubby, round cheeks.

"Ach, ye've frightened the poor bairn," someone cried, and gentle arms encircled her slim shoulders. Lillias turned to her comforter and gave a start at the familiar face of Aggie, Hannah's oldest daughter.

"Bah, enough of this coddling." Red Rafe stepped forward. Imperiously, he waved to the priest. "Let's be about the wedding."

The man of cloth stepped forward and nodded his head. Red Rafe turned to his son and the serving woman. "Bring the child," he demanded.

"Nay!" Lillias cried, straining away from them. Iain picked her up in his strong arms, restraining her.

"Lillias," he said, cutting through her panic. "I'll not harm ye, lass. Can ye trust me for that?" She ceased struggling and lay limp in his arms. Slowly she nodded.

"Ye'll become my wife, Lillias," he explained, noting her tear-streaked face. "Then ye'll be safe. None will harm ye, ever, or they'll answer to me." He turned toward the altar. His face was in shadow, but Lillias sensed the anger and challenge as he faced his father.

"Aye, lad. If she's yer wife, none will harm her," Red Rafe answered. "I give my word on that, and no man has ever dared gainsay Rafe MacLeod on his word."

Iain carried Lillias forward. Her small bare feet dangled below the hem of her nightshirt. Her pale golden hair lay in a tangle against his sleeve. Her eyes were overly large in her small, tear-streaked face. They were blue as the sky over the loch on a clear summer day, he noted. She was a pretty, delicate thing, and he felt sorry for her. She was but a child—caught as a pawn in the game between greedy men.

The words were said, the vows given in Iain's steady voice and her childish pipe. Then they filed out of the church to the open bailey.

"It is done," Red Rafe shouted, raising an arm. "Iain has taken a bride." The gathered men raised a rousing cheer, and when it had died away, Red Rafe spoke again, his mood expansive and jovial. "The wedding banquet is served in the hall. Food and drink for everyone." The people in the bailey cheered again.

"I'll not come to that," Iain snapped, his words heard only by his father. "I'll not continue this mockery ye've forced on me." Red Rafe's smile died away.

"I am hungry," Lillias said in her light silvery voice, holding her head close to Iain's, so he might hear.

He looked down at her. She gazed back at him steadily, noting the glint of torchlight against his black hair. She caught a gleam of green in his eyes, but couldn't be certain in the unsteady light. His face was stern, unyielding, and her lips trembled to think she might have angered him.

"I'm not very hungry," she said quickly.

He smiled then, white teeth flashing against sun-browned skin, eyes sparkling. "We'll go to the wedding banquet. My lady is hungry." With long strides he carried her into the hall, where ladened trestle tables awaited them.

"Ye'll sit in the place of honor," Red Rafe said, indicating the chair to his right. Iain placed Lillias on the cushion Red Rafe had indicated. Red Rafe nodded to a servant, who brought forth a large platter with a beaten-silver dome. Eyes snapping with excitement, Red Rafe rose.

"This is my wedding present to my son," he announced, and lifted the silver dome. Lillias's eyes widened in shock as she took in the contents of the platter and shrill, helpless screams emitted from her mouth.

Iain leapt to his feet, his face twisted with outrage as he looked at the severed head of Robert McGinnis resting on the silver platter. "God's blood, ye're surely mad that ye would do something so barbarous!" he cried.

Red Rafe laughed. "Ye'll never have to fight for that piece of land again, lad."

"I'll not have land drenched in another man's blood!" Iain shouted, and stalked toward the door. The heavy portal closed with a resounding thud that echoed throughout the castle. In his anger and horror, he gave no thought to his child bride.

Lillias didn't see him leave. Her gaze was still pinned on the severed head of her father. Her thin chest rose and fell with every shrill cry she gave. Only when Aggie had wrapped her strong arms around the small twitching body and covered the glazed eyes with her hand did a merciful darkness claim Lillias.

Chapter 1

"*L*ILLIAS, YE'LL NA GO on the shieling. I forbid it."

"Ye're my servant, Aggie. Ye kinna forbid me anything," Lillias answered blithely. She flipped her long golden braid over her shoulder, so it fell against the middle of her back, reaching nearly to her hips. When the golden tresses were undone, they flowed well past her buttocks, but no one knew that but Aggie.

The old woman sighed with exasperation as she watched the slender girl reach for the *arisaid*, a shift made of thin, coarse woolen checked plaid, which most of the village women wore. Lillias settled it around her shoulders, and with nimble fingers knotted the ties that held the shapeless garment in place. She had grown taller during the winter past and the gown was far too short, revealing trim ankles and slim, delicate feet laced in unwelted shoes. The slippers were made with soles of single leather, such as the servants wore.

"Ye'll na go out dressed like a common milkmaid," Aggie snapped. Her pale blue eyes sparkled with impatience. The fact that she was a servant, as Lillias had so ungraciously reminded her, mattered not one whit. Nine years of caring and guiding Lillias had given Aggie a certain impunity where class distinction between mistress and servant was concerned.

" 'Tis na fitting for a woman of position," she grumbled,

11

knowing her words would have little effect on this head-strong girl.

"What position is that, Aggie?" Lillias inquired, impatient herself with the restrictions placed upon her. "I am a woman of noble birth, but without position or status. Since Red Rafe has died, even the servants do not respect me, if they ever did. At least before his death they dared not show their contempt."

"Mayhap they would respect ye if ye dressed as a lady and stayed within the castle as a genteel woman should," Aggie said rather lamely, for she, too, had witnessed the growing arrogance and laziness of the castle servants since the clan chief's death.

Lillias made a scoffing noise. "This castle has never seen a genteel lady," she snapped, "so they'd ha' no idea how to treat one! Why should I bother myself with them? Besides, things will never change if Hugh MacLeod makes his claim as chief."

"That one!" Aggie scoffed, for she had no liking for the sly young chieftain who had assumed authority within the castle and over the clan. "He'll ha' ye as his wife or mistress if he can." Aggie shook her graying head and tried another tack. "He'll be put in his place fast enough when Iain MacLeod returns."

"If he returns," Lillias said cynically. She hadn't set eyes on Red Rafe's son since the time of her kidnapping and had no memory of him, except those things told to her by others.

"He'll return, right enough," Aggie insisted, "and when he does, ye'll take yer place as chatelaine of the castle."

"Dinna put too much faith in Iain MacLeod," Lillias snapped. "He's far too busy in the service of the French king. We've na heard one word from him in the past nine years."

"Aye," Aggie replied. "But there's them that say Iain would na come back as long as his faither was alive and chief of the clan. Now he'll return to claim his inheritance."

"I've heard the rumors among the clansmen," Lillias retorted. "They say the French king has granted him land in France and offered him the hand of a French noblewoman."

"Bah. 'Tis nothing, only the blathering of those who wish Hugh to take his place as clan chief," Aggie answered fiercely. "What true Scotsman would give up his own clan and holdings for land in a foreign country?"

"What true Scotsman would exile himself from his own people to fight for a foreign king who thinks us savage and uncivilized?" Lillias demanded, patting an errant strand in place over her ear. "Nay, Aggie. Iain MacLeod has no wish to be here among us. And I"—she paused and gazed out the window at the blue-green water of Loch Arkaig—"I ha' no place else to go. My own clan has forgotten I exist."

" 'Tis na so, lassie," Aggie said hastily. "They've na forgotten ye. When yer faither died, the new chief agreed to let the marriage stand between ye and Iain MacLeod. Ye belong to the MacLeod clan and MacLeod lands."

"I belong and yet I don't belong," Lillias said pensively. Her troubled blue eyes were dark as sapphires, their sparkle dimmed by her tumbling emotions. Shaking herself, she reached for a large triangle of cloth and threw it about her shoulders, pinning it in place with a round brass brooch.

"I won't be back till the morrow, Aggie," she said, turning toward the door. "Mayhap na even then. I've promised Mary and the others I'd help with the shieling."

"Ach, and it's na proper for a lady such as yerself to traipse about the hills herding goats and milking cows," Aggie replied, returning to her original complaint.

" 'Tis mostly the women and children who go," Lillias replied. "And well ye know that, Aggie. The men are busy fishing for the salmon run. It can't be unseemly for me to go among our own tenants."

"Ye should na' rub elbows with the likes," Aggie said stubbornly.

"They're good people, Aggie," she replied. "And they're the only companions I've had here at Cullayne." Lillias drew down her eyebrows at Aggie's snobbery, but the servant nodded her head in agreement, her rigid principles fading in the face of Lillias's reality.

"Aye, true enough, they are. 'Tis a poor lass ye've been, taken from yer own home. Yer mither, God rest her soul, would turn in her grave to think how ye've lived yer life in this forgotten, uncivilized place."

"My mither knew," Lillias replied pensively. "She chose to ignore what happened to me."

"Ach, 'tis not true, lass." Aggie stoutly defended her old mistress. "Yer mither was a gentle, brokenhearted lady. She hid herself away in a convent to mourn yer faither's death."

"And ignored the fact that she still had a child who needed her help," Lillias flared. "If she'd appealed to other clan chiefs they would have marched on the MacLeods and rescued me."

"They wanted peace, lass," Aggie said sadly.

"And sacrificed me to get it!" Lillias cried. Angry tears rolled down her cheeks.

Aggie's heart contracted at the pain on the young face. The lass hadn't had a happy youth, and try as she might to make up for the loneliness and fear and sense of abandonment Lillias had experienced over all these years, Aggie knew she could never take the place of Lillias's father and mother. She sighed heavily and put her arms around the girl she'd stood by and loved all these years. Strong young arms came up to return the embrace.

Lillias rested her head on Aggie's plump shoulder and let the hot, angry tears flow unchecked. She still grieved for the strong, impulsive father she'd adored so much—and yes, even for the aloof, ethereal woman who'd mothered her. At Dunbeath she'd known every freedom, every comfort. Here, at Cullayne, the warrior stronghold for the MacLeod clan, there'd been little comfort. After that disastrous night when she'd been summoned to supper and found her father's head served on a platter, she'd been sent back to this tower room, which had become her prison and her sanctuary. A bed and stools had been added for their comfort, but the room was stark and barren.

Lillias pulled away from Aggie and crossed to the window overlooking Loch Arkaig. Besides Aggie's plump shoulder and gentle, strong touch, this had been her comfort, this view of the crystalline blue waters and the sky and mist on the horizon. How often had she stood here over the years, straining to catch a glimpse of a curragh emerging from the mist, filled with her clansmen come to rescue her? She had searched in vain for such a sight, and only years later did she learn the truth of her clansmen's revenge for her father's death and her abduction.

A minor MacLeod chief and seven of his men, said to have dealt Robert McGinnis the deathblow and to have taken his head, had themselves been killed, then King James had negotiated a peace between the two clans. The McGinnis clan retained the disputed land—and Lillias had remained a MacLeod bride. Even now, her hands knotted into fists of helpless rage to think of how easily she'd been bartered away, and all for naught.

Red Rafe had continued to purge the McGinnis clan holding, raiding cattle, burning crops and villages. His men had planted their seeds in many a resisting McGinnis maiden, so they often joked that more MacLeod offsprings would be born on McGinnis land than McGinnises.

Lillias felt strongly that if her mother had appealed to King James herself, she might have swayed the final outcome, but Margaret McGinnis had retreated into that shadowy half-world of her own making; she'd never again emerged from the convent walls. Years before, word had come of her mother's death—and Red Rafe had been the one to deliver the news. For a moment, she'd imagined a glimmer of regret in his eyes, then he'd raised his cup and drunk a toast to her mother's death. Lillias had hated him then almost as much as when she thought of her father's ig-nominious death.

A wind rippled the water; suddenly the sunlight and beauty of the day replaced the unhappiness that had claimed her briefly. Hers was a sturdy nature, and she'd long since learned to survive. There had been few enough rules. Stay out of sight and sound of Red Rafe MacLeod when he was in the castle—and should he remember his son's captive bride and summon her, assume a role not un-like that of her mother's, aloof and untouchable.

But Red Rafe was sly if not subtle. He remembered her tempestuous outbursts and knew beneath the calm exterior she was still that impulsive, hotheaded girl, and he'd delighted in baiting her until she threw aside her resolve and railed at him in vain. When she was prodded to tears and angry words, he was amused, and then the amusement was gone and his dark eyes would stare at her with such chilling detachment that although she longed to be brave, she visibly quaked before him. At such times, she was sent back to her tower room.

Red Rafe had never laid a hand on her, nor had anyone else at the castle, but she remembered too well the bloodied remains of her father's head on the beaten-silver platter—and terror nipped at her heels that such a fate awaited her on but a whim of Red Rafe MacLeod's. Her childhood dreams had been filled with nightmares; only in the past few years had she found surcease from their torment.

Red Rafe was dead now, an appropriate fate, for he was killed in a cattle raid against his neighbors, the McCulloughs. His wild clansmen had mourned him these many months, for he'd been a popular and charismatic leader. The wild clansmen had delighted in his daring and irreverent thumbing of his nose at the king's authority. Only their love for their old chief had held them so long in waiting for his son's return to claim his right as *Ceann Mor*.

Some had grown tired of waiting, and even now there was openly talk of a council meeting to name Hugh as their new chief. He was the next of kin, Red Rafe's nephew, and he'd served the old chief well. Lillias shuddered to think of what her fate might be then, for Hugh MacLeod had made no secret that he coveted his cousin's wife as well as his title. Other men had no liking for the hot-tempered young chieftain who'd yet to prove himself courageous enough to lead them. Biddy MacEwan predicted trouble was brewing, and Lillias knew the old woman was right.

So they awaited Iain MacLeod's return and the rumors grew. Lillias wondered what Iain must be like after all these years of fighting in France. Once he'd been kind to her, but in the end, he, too, had left her to Red Rafe's tender mercies. He'd probably become as barbarous and warlike as his father. Sighing, she turned from the window, unwilling to think what would happen to her if Iain *should* return to claim his right as clan chief and as her husband. She must not think of such things, she told herself, else she'd go mad. Once again, she was caught between two ruthless men, the helpless pawn in a struggle for power and wealth.

She turned to Aggie, who hovered nearby, her expression filled with concern for her charge. Lillias forced a smile.

"At any rate," she said lightly, raising her chin proudly, "I've decided that should Iain MacLeod return to Cullayne, I shall do as my mither has done and hie myself off to the nearest convent."

There was a chortle of laughter, quickly subdued, and Lillias swung round to glare at Aggie.

"Ha' I amused ye then, Aggie?" she demanded, narrowing her eyes catlike.

"The thought of ye in a convent amuses me, lass," Aggie said, with a barely concealed grin. "Such an arrangement was well suited for yer mither, but ye've more of yer faither in ye. Ye'd niver last in a convent."

"Do ye truly think me like my faither?" Lillias demanded, her anger as quickly forgotten as it had been roused.

"Aye, lass. Lord Robert was na a man to tolerate things na of his liking and neither are ye. Ye've the fire and courage and steel of yer faither." Lillias was momentarily speechless at the compliment, then she noted the tired lines around Aggie's eyes and her young heart warmed with concern.

"Come with me into the hills for the shieling," she cried impulsively. "Ye used to go and ye loved it as much as I do."

"Aye, that was before my bones became too old and my joints disagreed with the damp nights."

"We'll take thick pads for ye to rest on, and during the day, ye can sit in the shade and tell stories to the children the way ye used to tell me."

Slowly Aggie shook her head. "Aye, lass, I'd like to go,

but I kinna. Ye go along. Never mind what anyone else might think that a lady such as ye runs about through the hills like a hoyden. Ye've little enough happiness in yer life."

"I dinna need much happiness. I have ye," Lillias answered softly. "No matter what I may think about Iain MacLeod, I will always be grateful for his kindness in bringing ye to me."

"Aye, I'm beholding, too, child," Aggie said.

"Even though ye had to leave behind yer own kinsmen?" Lillias asked, knowing beforehand what the answer would be.

"Ye're all the kin I need, lass." They embraced fiercely. How many times had they drawn comfort from each other over the past lonely years? Aggie drew away first. "Now go on wi' ye. Go run the hills like a bleatin' goat. Mayhap the sun will put color in yer cheeks after the hard winter."

"I love ye, Aggie," Lillias said, and hurried away in a rustle of skirts before her nursemaid could change her mind and offer further argument.

Skipping down the steep, narrow spiral steps and out into the sunlit bailey, she hummed softly and paused to draw a deep breath. Never mind that the air was tainted with smells of men and animals housed in a close space. Beyond the odor of uncleaned stables and cesspits was the bracing clean air from the loch and the hills all golden with gorse. If she were truly the wife of the clan chief, with all the power that implied, she'd change many things here in the castle, but she was not—and she'd long since learned not to dwell on those things in life over which she had no control. Instead she took joy in the majestic hills and the clear blue sky that sometimes seemed so close, that, as a child, she'd often tried to touch it.

"What be ye staring at like a goose gone all daft?" a rough voice demanded, and Lillias started. Hugh MacLeod had come out onto the castle steps and stood scratching his crotch. Lillias glanced away, flushing at his crudity.

"I was looking at the light in the morning sky," she answered stiffly. "A sight rare to ye, I'd wager."

"Dinna be sassy wi' me, lassie," he warned, glowering at her. He'd spent a good portion of the night drinking with his friends and his head ached.

Lillias raised her chin defiantly. "What's roused ye from yer drunken stupor so early in the morning?"

Hugh scowled at her insult. "I've come out to relieve m'self," he sneered, and fixed her with a baleful eye while he fumbled beneath his tunic and sent a hot stream of urine into the already foul courtyard.

Color rose to Lillias's cheeks, but she would not let him see how he'd insulted her. "At least, ye've come into the courtyard to do that," she retorted, and strode away.

"Ha' a care, lassie, for when I become chief, ye'll feel the weight of my displeasure."

Lillias made no answer. Her pleasure in the morning was dimmed by his loutish behavior and dire warnings. Pushing away her worries over Hugh MacLeod and his ilk, she ran across the bailey toward the gate house, crossed the moat, and hurried through the village, where poor cottages labored beneath sagging roofs. Even here was evidence of neglect.

Red Rafe had liked best to raid and make war on his neighbors and he'd often lured away the men to this pastime, leaving the tasks of caring for home and hearth to the women. And although the women were diligent and hardworking, tending crops and livestock from dawn to dusk, there were things that needed a man's hand. Thatch roofs needed replenishing, dry-stone walls needed redaubing, and kegs and pails needed restaving.

Since Red Rafe's death, the raids had stopped, for Hugh seemed disinclined to stir himself from the comforts of Cullayne's wine cellars and willing serving wenches to engage in such dangerous pastimes. Slowly, the men who had families had halfheartedly returned to their crops and fishing, but few real improvements had been made. The men were too distracted by the loss of their chief and too unmotivated by the lack of a new leader, so the women carried on as women do in times of peace and war, prosperity and want.

Lillias hurried through the village, returning the greetings of those women who hailed her, for if she was treated with contempt by the castle servants, she was well liked by the village women. Mayhap for the very reason the castle servants hadn't respected her—she put on no airs. She'd worked beside the village women, stood at their elbows learning to milk a cow or birth a calf, mix a poultice for a sick child or weave a fine piece of cloth.

She might be the unclaimed wife of the dead chief's son, but here in the village, no one belittled her for it, though she guessed they whispered about it behind her back. She'd come among them as a child, so they'd pitied her, then admired her, and, finally, had come to accept her as one of them.

She, in turn, treated each woman with respect and deference, for she saw among them a kind of nobility and clarity of purpose. They were strong, good women who kept their families and the village itself intact. They'd become her mentors, her friends, her sisters. Now they hurried out of their cottages to greet her, to show her their baby's first tooth or the new piece of plaid they were weaving, or to invite her in for a cup of tea.

Lillias exclaimed over the children, admired the new plaid, and declined the tea, for she was in a hurry to reach the cottage of her dearest friend of all, Mary McFerris. A tall, dark-haired girl with rounded cheeks and limbs, Mary was considered the village beauty, and the single young men went out of their way to gain her attention. John McFerris, Mary's father, had despaired of her ever choosing a husband and had threatened to find one for her himself if she continued to be so finicky, but Mary was not to be rushed, no matter what the custom.

" 'Tis I who must live wi' him for a lifetime," she declared pertly, "and I'll be doing my own choosin', thank ye." So John McFerris shook his head and accepted the drafts the young swains pressed upon him at the village pub and declared any man Mary chose was all right by him—as long as he was of the clan and a good fighter, by God's teeth! Now, as Lillias neared the McFerris cottage, Mary saw her coming and rushed out to meet her.

"So, ye've come then," she exclaimed. "I feared yer Aggie wouldna let ye come."

"She kinna stop me," Lillias exclaimed, falling into the common speech of the villagers. "I'm my own woman."

"Aye, that ye are," Mary replied, "but does the goody Aggie know that?" The two young women chuckled.

"Would Aggie na come wi' us for the shieling, then?" Mary asked when their mirth had passed.

"Nay, her joints trouble her some," Lillias replied, a frown furrowing her brow. She hated to think of her beloved Aggie suffering.

" 'Tis just the years, Lilli," Mary reassured her. "Biddy MacEwan is na comin' this year."

"At least there'll be less grumbling then," Lillias replied, and once again the girls suppressed giggles and hurried to gather the food and bedding they'd need for their trek into the hills. When they left the cottage with their packs, other women and children had assembled in the lane, their milk cows lowing or munching clumps of new grass in the corners by the fence gates.

Every spring at this time, the women and children drove the livestock into the green hills, where they grazed on new grasses, fattening themselves after the lean winters when their fare had been meager at best. The small children danced ahead of their mothers, weaving in and out of the cattle and around their mothers' skirts until the women scolded them and sent them ahead on the path, challenging them to be the first to sight the new spring pastures. With the children racing ahead, the women proceeded at a more leisurely pace, chatting easily as they drove their cattle with hickory switches.

"Go along wi' ye, Blarach," Helen MacEwan called to her cow, for so important was each milk cow to its family, that it was named and addressed with some affection. Blarach was a dun-colored beast, and so her name reflected this trait.

Mary on the other hand had named her milk cow

Sealbhach, which meant fruitful one. This had occasioned much laughter among the women, who teased Mary that her choice of names reflected her own near future. Despite her reluctance to wed, many of the village women wagered she'd choose a husband before the summer was out.

"Ah, Mary. I've heard Jaimie MacEwan has been around the cottage door," Helen teased. She was not adverse to having the spritely Mary as a kinswoman.

"Jaimie MacEwan, ye say?" Mary retorted, fanning her hickory switch across Sealbhach's haunches. "I've not seen him slinkin' about or I would turn my faither's claymore around and swat his great behind."

"Whoo, Mary. I should like to see that," cried Beitris MacDougall. "Jaimie would na stand still for a woman to treat him thus." She was of the MacLeod clan, but of some distant relation to the mighty MacDougall clan as well. Such bloodlines made her arrogant, so she often affected an air of superiority over the other young women. Now she spoke with an air of personal knowledge concerning Jaimie MacEwan, for he was a handsome lad and well sought after by the young women of marriageable age.

"Mayhap it depends upon the woman," Mary replied archly, and Beitris's face colored. Her pale, darting gaze fell on Lillias and she pursed her lips before launching another barb.

" 'Tis rumored that Iain MacLeod is na coming to claim his title as clan chief."

"Aye, I've heard the rumor, too," Helen exclaimed. " 'Tis well past the time for him to do so, if he's a mind. If he dinna wishes to be chief, he should send word. Then the council can choose a new one."

"My Doug swears he'll return," Kendra McFerris exclaimed. Doug McFerris was Mary's brother. Kendra was a quick-witted woman, not unlike her sister-in-law, and Lillias could see why Doug had chosen her. Although Kendra did not possess the beauty of Mary and some of the other village maidens, she had fine blue eyes and lovely flaxen hair.

"Was na Doug a friend to the new laird?" Nora

MacEwan demanded, giving Iain his proper title despite his absence.

"Aye, they were great friends," Kendra confirmed.

"A pair of devils, they were," Mary exclaimed. "Always in trouble over something."

"If they were such great friends, why did Doug na go to France with Iain?" Beitris asked, with a spiteful grin. Her blue eyes flashed with malice. She had no liking for Kendra, whom she considered smug and altogether too satisfied as the wife of Douglas McFerris. If the village women thought Jaimie MacEwan a handsome lad, they had agreed long before that even he could not light a candle to Douglas McFerris, with his tall, well-muscled body and tousled dark hair and twinkling gray eyes. Despite his married state, many a young woman swooned when he chanced to glance her way.

Secure in the knowledge of her husband's affection and of the passion they shared in their bed even after eight years of marriage, Kendra was merely amused at the reaction of women toward her handsome husband. Now she shrugged, her lips curving in a demure smile that told more than it could ever hope to conceal.

"Doug dinna choose to leave his mither," she said sweetly.

Helen and Mary hooted with laughter. Beitris flushed as if fearing they laughed at her.

"My brither had set his sights on Kendra," Mary said, with some amusement. "And Kendra led him a merry chase before she gave in and became his wife."

Kendra's smile broadened at the memory. Ah, those were glorious times, but not nearly so glorious as the act of climbing into bed and wrapping her limbs around her husband's strong body. Her blush prompted the women to tease her for her thoughts.

"I don't believe Douglas McFerris stayed behind because of Kendra," Beitris snapped, irritated by the affectionate attention the older girl was claiming. She herself had been too young for Doug when he chose a wife, but she'd had a terrific crush on him and had been absolutely certain, if she'd been but two years older, he would have chosen her over Kendra.

"D'ye call us a liar, then, Beitris MacLeod?" Mary demanded.

"Nay," Beitris said hastily, for when they were girls Mary had often taken offense and wreaked a physical retribution that Beitris had no wish to witness again soon. " 'Tis puzzled I am that Doug wouldna go wi' Iain to France. They were always together. 'Tis more of a puzzle why Iain should have left when he'd just acquired a bride."

The women were silent for a while, casting sidelong glances at Lillias, who had remained silent throughout their lively exchange. Now, Mary spoke up in defense of her friend.

"Lillias was but a child and well ye know that, Beitris," she exclaimed.

"But she's been a woman full grown for some years now. Why has he na returned to claim his wife?" Beitris demanded, and seeing the look upon Mary's face, spread her hands upward and affected an innocent demeanor. "I but ask what all of us wonder."

The other women looked away. For it was true, they'd often wondered why Iain hadn't returned to his clan and his wife.

"If Iain but came and gazed at Lilli, he would never leave her side again," Mary said, "for Lilli stands heads above mortal women in her beauty."

"Aye," Helen said, shaking her head. " 'Tis often I've wondered if she was one of the fairy queens come to live among us. 'Tis always been so. Now the fairy child has become a beautiful woman and her husband dinna come to see."

Lillias blushed at their words. "I barely remember m-my husband," she said. "I was but nine years old. I remember that he tried to be kind when his faither was not, but even he could not withstand Red Rafe's cruel tauntings."

"D'ye wish him to return to ye, Lilli?" Helen asked.

Lillias paused, searching for a diplomatic answer, and

knew only truth would do, for these women seemed to ferret out the most secret thoughts of one another.

"He is a stranger to me," she replied. "I have no wish for a stranger to return and—" She ceased speaking, her thoughts all jumbled, for even here among her friends, she could not voice her worst fears. Immediately they understood.

" 'Tis na so bad as ye might think, Lillias," Kendra said in her quiet, firm voice. "To lie with yer husband can bring much pleasure." Her fair cheeks blushed as she realized how much she had revealed. The other women grinned at her revelation.

"Aye, Kendra's right," Helen said, and the other women stared at her in surprise. "Well ye might look at me that way. I am old now and my man is long dead these many years, but on those long, cold nights when the wind's a-howling down from Beinn Bhan, I draw comfort from my memory of our hours in bed. Sean was a goodly man, but when the light was out he had a bit of the divil in him." She raised her chin and the rest of the women looked away at the pain and loneliness they read in her face. Such was the lot of a woman. They loved too well and gave too much of themselves—and in the end were rewarded with their widow years.

"I remember Iain was a handsome lad," Kendra replied. "Nearly as handsome as Doug."

"If not more so," Helen said, "for he had about him the wild, savage look of his father."

Lillias shivered as she remembered Red Rafe MacLeod's black eyes staring at her, unblinking and inscrutable. If Iain MacLeod looked like his father, then he could not be handsome; she feared his return more than anything else in life.

Chapter 2

"**M**ITHER, THERE ARE strangers on the trail ahead," one of Kendra's sons called, rushing back along the path.

"Strangers?" The women exchanged troubled glances. They were wary of any men not known on MacLeod land, for they remembered too well the feuds that brought death or maiming to any hapless body seized by a warring clan—man, woman, or child. Now that Red Rafe was dead, many of his enemies had taken the opportunity to invade his lands and raid his villages. The McCulloughs had been the most relentless. The women raised their voices and called their children back to them.

Suddenly the sound of stampeding hooves and wild howling cries came to them. Men galloped toward the women so swiftly they had no time to climb the stone fences and escape.

" 'Tis the bloody McCulloughs!" Helen MacEwan cried.

The men leapt from their horses with dirks drawn and began binding the women's hands behind their backs while other raiders rounded up the cattle.

The women were too stunned to fight back. They stood as though stupefied while the intruders herded the cattle across the fields. Some of the men clasped the comeliest young maidens around the waist, intent upon carrying them away. Seeing their prized milk cows, goats, and sheep endangered, the women recovered themselves and with an-

26

swering cries used their hickory sticks to beat the armed
intruders about the heads and shoulders.

One man, his dark eyes flashing with cruel purpose,
leaned from his horse to reach for Lillias. She leapt aside.
His great fist closed around her flying braid and with a
lusty yell he yanked her up until her feet no longer touched
the ground. His dark eyes and cruel mouth reminded her of
Red Rafe, and such was her hatred of her cruel captor, that
a black rage rose within her, nearly blinding her sight.

Memory returned of the cruel taunting and the helpless,
impotent rage that had spurred her to defy the chief at
every opportunity. Once she'd even been driven to raise a
claymore against him, though her childishly thin arms had
barely been able to lift it. The sight had occasioned such
merriment in Red Rafe that he'd ordered her to be trained
in the handling of it—and he'd often amused himself humiliating her in a woefully uneven battle before his
smirking retinue. When he raised his own claymore and
waged it against hers, the vibrations of steel against steel
had numbed her arms and she'd been forced to let her
weapon fall from hands gone numb.

Still, the lessons had continued at Red Rafe's perverse
whim, and she'd learned something of parrying and thrust.
Now she used her hickory switch much like a sword,
thrusting at the attacker who had set upon her. The man's
sneers quickly turned to anger as she aimed the end of her
stick at his eyes.

"Ye bitch!" he bellowed, and grabbed the switch from
her. His meaty hand drew back and slashed her across one
cheek, so she fell to the ground, momentarily stunned.
Thinking her subdued, he straddled her, fumbling with his
trews.

Lillias had little doubt as to what he intended, for she'd
often listened to the drunken tales of Red Rafe's men.
Bringing up her feet, she lashed out and had the satisfaction
of feeling them land in the soft pouch between the oaf's
legs. Howling with pain, he stumbled away from her, cradling his injured groin in his hands. Lillias snatched up her

hickory switch and leapt to her feet, whirling to face her next adversary.

The man who stood before her was tall and broad-shouldered, without the added bulk of the first man. His face was keenly drawn, his lips firmly chiseled, his cheeks lean and tanned. Hair as black as the devil himself blew across his brow and fell to his shoulders. His eyes were the torch that held her. Green fire seared her soul, so she caught her breath. All around her the sound of battle, the outraged cries of the other women, and the lowing protests of cattle faded from consciousness. Something stirred within her breast, some long-forgotten memory, and she stood still, her head tilted, her eyes studying him as she struggled for an image, a remembrance that eluded her.

"Are ye all right, lass?" he called, and she was snapped from the spell that held her. She raised her hickory switch and with all her might swung it downward, aiming for the black head of the man before her. His hand clamped around the stick, staying it in its downward plunge.

"Nay, lass!" he cried. "I'm not yer enemy. I've come to help ye."

She halted in her struggle to free her stick and stared into those silvered-green eyes, searching for the truth of what he said. In the smoky depths of his eyes, she saw amusement—and something else that brought a flush to the roots of her hair.

Someone swung a club at him, barely missing his broad shoulders. In a lithe movement, he ducked and swung around, facing his attacker. One of the McCullough raiders had dropped his knobby wooden club and was reaching for his claymore. With a howl of triumph, he faced the dark-haired man. If as he said the green-eyed warrior was their friend and not their enemy, he stood alone and unarmed.

Suddenly Lillias feared for his life and took a step forward, as if in some way she might offer assistance. The McCullough man's club lay at his feet; she darted forward, snatching it up before leaping out of reach of his claymore.

With his attention fixed on the dark-haired man, the raider paid her scant attention. Only when she ran to offer the club to her defender did he give voice to his rage. Emitting a great caterwaul, he swiped at her with his sword. The stranger raised the club. Muscles bunched beneath sunbrowned skin and the blow was turned from her. With a roar of temper, the McCullough man turned on her protector. Lillias leapt out of the way of their struggle, her heart hammering.

All around them, men struggled while the women gathered their children to them and huddled out of the way. Where had their defenders come from? Lillias wondered briefly, then turned her attention to the battle between her attacker and the stranger. He used the club as effectively as the clumsy McCullough used his claymore, parrying each thrust.

Using both hands, the attacker brought his claymore down in a stunning blow that split the wooden club, rendering it useless. Now he brayed with laughter, and Lillias trembled, reminded of Red Rafe and his triumphant roar when he'd bested someone in their war games. Once she'd watched in tears as he'd cut off the ear of one of his opponents.

Now, with the same cruel anticipation, the McCullough attacker advanced on the green-eyed stranger. His small black eyes gleamed with hostility.

"This is for bloody Red Rafe," he shouted, "and all the sorrow that devil brought upon us." He lunged forward, his great weapon aimed at the stranger's chest. Lillias screamed. The black-haired stranger danced to one side.

A wild Highland cry rang out and a sword sailed through the air. It was lighter weight than the two-handed claymore used by the raider, but it was a weapon. Deftly the stranger caught it and turned on his attacker. The intruder sneered at the thin blade.

"Tell me yer name, sir," the stranger asked lightly.

"What's it t'ye?" the intruder sneered.

"That I might send condolences to yer widow," the stranger answered. The intruder's eyes darkened at the challenge.

"So ye may know the man that cuts the life from yer

body, I'll tell ye my name's Goraidh McCullough," the attacker cried. His face flushed with anger and he lunged forward, letting his weight and girth drive the claymore with even more thrust. Once again the stranger danced aside, then brought up his blade, neatly slicing the lumbering attacker along his forearm and shoulder. The clansman stopped and blinked at the welling blood as if unable to believe he'd been wounded. Lillias drew in her breath, awed by the lightning precision of the stranger's sword.

"D'ye reckon to do that again, Godfrey McCullough?" He saluted his clumsy opponent with a small flourish. McCullough looked confused. "Are ye bedundered, man?"

"How d'ye know me as Godfrey?" McCullough asked, his voice thick.

"Are ye not Godfrey, the lumbering ox of Ardgour?" the stranger asked lightly.

Godfrey McCullough gnashed his teeth. "Ye nameless whore son will answer for that with yer life." He raised his claymore and charged. The stranger danced away; his sword flashed yet again, and this time, a long gash was opened on the attacker's other shoulder. Blood gushed forth, so Lillias knew the wound was serious.

Godfrey McCullough dropped his claymore, clamped a hand over the gash, and with a bawling cry to his men headed toward the charger left standing on the path. The stranger made to follow, but a horseman prodded his stallion forward, effectively cutting off pursuit of the wounded McCullough. Godfrey McCullough sounded his war cry, and of one body his raiders spurred their horses away.

"After them, lads," the stranger called, and several men gave chase, driving the raiders before them. They soon disappeared into the woods, and the sound of clashing steel and men's cries came to them. Only the green-eyed stranger and the man who'd tossed him the sword remained with the women.

Now that the danger was past, the women crowded round them, their voices shrill with relief. They'd recognized the tartan plaid the men wore and breathed easier, for it was that of the MacLeod clan.

Now that their concern of an enemy in their midst was past, more than one young woman noted the broad shoulders and rugged, handsome features of the two strangers and jockied forward, so she might turn a winsome glance their way.

Beitris MacDougall was positively shameless, Lillias decided, and stayed to one side, her eyes demurely downcast. Mary stood beside her, but her frank gaze took in every detail of the two travelers' appearance.

Both men were clad in *aketons*, vests of quilted leather. Their tartans had been belted at the waist, forming a long skirtlike affair that fell nearly to their knees, while the other end had been draped over their left shoulders. Lillias knew if the weather grew bad, the draped end could be arranged over their backs and shoulders much like a short cape. Such was the common practice of all Highland men with their tartans.

Unlike local Highlanders, whose legs were bare beneath their belted skirts, these travelers wore plaid hose over their strong calves. All these details were not lost on the women.

"Ye wear the MacLeod plaid, yet I've na seen ye before," Helen declared. "Have you come from far?"

"Aye, woman, and we were hungering to walk on MacLeod land again." The green-eyed stranger answered. He was the tallest—and by far the handsomest of the two. His bearing spoke of authority and a self-assurance that bordered on arrogance. In a land of rugged, handsome men, he took one's breath away. His eyes sparkled with the green lights that had enthralled Lillias in that brief pause during the skirmish. He was clean shaven and his lean cheeks creased when he smiled. His nose was sharp as a blade, his lips firm and well shaped. Black curls lay across his brow, and when he threw back his head and laughed, his teeth flashed white against sun-darkened skin. Lillias found his smile so enchanting she couldn't resist studying him from beneath her lashes. She looked away lest he catch her watching him.

Beitris pushed forward, drawing attention to herself. "Then ye've na need to hunger further, sir," she answered pertly, "for yer feet are planted on MacLeod·soil." Everyone laughed at her sassy reply.

The man shifted his glance to the cheeky young woman, who straightened her back so her shift might show the outline of her small hard breasts.

"Is it wee Beitris MacDougall then?" he asked in amazement, and Beitris put aside her posturing to look at him directly, trying to determine who he might be.

"Aye," she answered reluctantly. "I have na the privilege of ye'r name, sir."

"Have ye na?" he repeated in the same thick brogue. His amused gaze moved over the other women. "Mayhap Nora remembers me," he said, "or Mary McFerris." His gaze fell on Lillias as she stood with her gaze cast down. "Ah, I've no memory of this maiden. What is your name, lass?"

Lillias raised her head and met his gaze head-on. The dark-haired stranger felt the jolt of her glance to his very toes. His eyes had been drawn by her comeliness, but now, with the urgency of battle gone from him, he was able to fully study her. She fair took his breath. She was as beautiful as any French noblewoman he'd seen, her features finely drawn, her rounded brow and pouty full lips adding a promise of sensuality beneath the look of innocence. Yet, she stood mute. Was she a *bluntie* then, or just shy? he wondered.

"Is it that ye have na name, lass, or has the goose taken ye'r tongue from ye?"

"No more nameless than ye, sir," she answered, and one delicate golden eyebrow arched prettily above flashing blue eyes. "I do but follow yer example."

The dark-haired stranger threw back his head and laughed heartily. "Aye, Peadair. 'Tis why I've missed the Scottish women. None else have such wickedly barbed tongues. Sharper than the blade of the finest dirk, they are."

His eyes flashed with humor, drawing amusement from her in spite of herself. She scowled to cover the wild rush of excitement that brought color to her smooth cheeks.

"I've still na heard *yer* name, sir," she replied tartly.

"Ha' none of ye no clue, then?" he asked, glancing

around at the other women. They remained silent. The light made his green eyes silvery. " 'Tis a clue ye're needin'. I've been away in France for these many years. And so has my friend here, Peadair McDermott."

The second man stepped forward and swept an exaggerated bow to the women. They tittered in amusement, which was what he'd intended.

"At your service, fair lasses," McDermott said, and his gaze moved over the women and stopped at Mary. "If ye should ha' need of my protection, ye ha' but to call." Lillias heard Mary draw in her breath sharply, as if she'd been startled.

"Are ye one of the fainthearted Scotsmen who run off with Iain MacLeod to fight for a foreign king?" Helen snapped. The plainspoken Scotswoman stood with her hands on her ample hips, her head cocked to one side, her sharp eyes narrowed suspiciously.

The stranger glanced around the circle of women. He sensed the air of disapproval among them. "Aye, I'm one of them," he admitted. " 'Tis not a warm welcome we're receivin'."

"Better than ye deserve!" Lillias spoke up.

"Why is that, fair lass?" he asked, pinning her with his green gaze. She shivered in spite of herself, for gone was the lighthearted amusement; in its place was implacable anger.

"Ye see what we must endure without a chief." She nodded toward the woods through which the raiders had retreated. "The McCulloughs would not attack us if we had a strong chief again."

"Does this happen often, then?" He looked around the circle of women and children.

"Too often, since Red Rafe's death," Lillias said.

"The men dinna protect ye, then?"

"Bah, they are like pups wi'out a teat," Mary McFerris declared. "They quarrel among themselves as to who will lead them next. Hugh MacLeod claims the privilege and is content to stay at Cullayne, wenching and drinking without tendin' t'our borders."

"What of the chief's son?"

Some of the women scoffed. The stranger looked around at them. "Ye have na liking for yer kinsman?"

"He has na liking for us, otherwise, he'd be here," Helen snapped. "He's developed a taste for French soil over his own land."

All lighthearted humor had vanished from the stranger's eyes. "And ye think he'll na return?" he inquired.

"We dinna ken," Helen replied. "He left his faither, his clan, and his wife nine years ago and we've na seen hide or hair of him since. Some believe him dead. Some believe he's fought on the side of the French king so long, he's forgotten his Scottish blood."

"Aye, and if thet's so, we'll find a new chief and the deevil take Iain MacLeod."

"The devil may already have done that," the stranger answered. "But in case he does return, ye'd do well to give him a better welcome than we've received."

"We still dinna ken yer name," Helen reminded him. She squinted her eyes to peer up at him. The stranger's expression was pensive.

"I have been called Hunter," he replied. His gaze moved back to Lillias. The pensive scowl lifted and once again his lips parted in a rakish grin. "Now, fair maiden, ye know my name. 'Tis only fair I learn yers."

"I made no such bargain with ye, sir," she replied coolly, and thwacking Sealbhach with the hickory switch, drove the cow forward. Now all the other milk cows and goats followed, as did the women and children and the sheep behind.

Lillias cast the two men a scowling sideways glance as she passed them and was incensed to see that the dark-haired stranger was laughing, his green eyes sparkling as his gaze met hers. She struck Sealbhach again for good measure and hurried up the path. She didn't look back, but she felt the silvered-green heat of his gaze until they were far down the road. Her skin tingled and her chest rose and fell in an effort to draw a breath, but she told herself it was simply a reaction to the skirmish they'd had with the McCulloughs.

Once the women and children reached the shieling site, where small stone huts had been erected for shelter, they drove the cows out to pasture, unpacked their bundles, and built fires, over which they hung iron caldrons, and began a pottage. Later, thin bannocks of oatmeal and water would be baked on a griddle laid in the coals. The meal was skimpy, but no worse than they were used to after the winter's rations. Soon gardens would produce fresh vegetables. Soon the deer in the hills would fatten and the men could hunt them again. Deer killed at the end of winter were often too thin to be palatable, and with the loss of their best hunters in Red Rafe's last raid, other game had been scarce, as well.

Soon the cows would calve and their milk would flow strong again. Cheese and cream could be had, and the children would grow sleek and fat and brown. In the meantime, they must content themselves with goat's milk. So when their bedding was stored, Lillias and Mary gathered up staved pails and set off toward the pasture to round up the goats and milk them. The sun had moved beyond its apex and sent slanting shadows over the meadows. Mountain blackbirds chirped from the branches of a juniper tree. The air was fragrant with the scent of wildflowers. Lillias could not contain her curiosity a moment longer.

"D'ye know those strangers on the path, Mary?" she asked as they walked along.

"What strangers?" the dark-haired maiden asked, with deliberate casualness.

"Dinna tease with me, Mary," Lillias scolded. "I saw how your eyes locked with the man called Peadair. Ye could not tear your gaze away."

"How could ye tell where I was looking, Lilli? Ye were starin' so at the tall one, I thought ye meant to devour him."

"I never!" Lillias denied. "Ha' ye forgotten I am a married woman?"

"I hadn't, but I feared ye had." Mary's eyes twinkled and

she relented. "Of course, the one known as Hunter was lookin' back at ye."

"He was not," Lillias said, but her cheeks burned bright red at the memory of the stranger's bold gaze. "D'you know either man? Are they from our village or another? Is he—? Are they married?"

Mary laughed. "Why would that matter t'ye? Ye're taken, yerself."

"Perhaps I'm looking for a suitable husband for ye. 'Tis sad to think ye may become an old maid," Lillias retorted, and leapt away when Mary swung her pail.

The girls made their way across the meadow and up the hills, their shifts blowing in the fresh wind, their laughter running ahead of them. Suddenly Lillias spotted a figure on the hillside and came to an abrupt stop.

"What is it?" Mary demanded upon seeing her face.

Lillias nodded. Mary put up her hand to shield her eyes against the sun. Peadair McDermott stood bold and arrogant against the blue sky.

"D'ye mind, Lilli?" Mary asked, and her voice sounded tight in her chest.

"Dinna mind me," Lillias said quickly. "I'll milk the goats."

"Dinna tell the others that he's here."

"Never would I tell," Lillias called over her shoulder as she made her way around a stone cairn and set off alone.

She wasn't surprised that Peadair had sought out Mary, for he'd looked at her too closely on the path, but Lillias couldn't repress a shiver of envy. She thought of the tall, broad-shouldered man whose rakish grin and dark green eyes had captivated her so. How she longed to be a carefree young maiden like Mary McFerris, able to flirt with a handsome stranger and mayhap taste the forbidden pleasure of a stolen kiss.

Then a thought came to her. If Peadair McDermott had followed them to the shieling, perhaps the dark stranger known as Hunter had as well. Which maiden had *he* chosen to woo? she wondered idly. Beitris MacDougall, no doubt, for the girl had flirted shamelessly with him.

Lillias made a face and hurried on. The thought of Beitris's pretty, simpering face turned to the dark stranger made her simmer with irritation. Her legs flashed beneath her short skirts as she climbed higher, seeking the nimble goats. Suddenly a sound made her whirl and look about. A deep shadow beneath one of the stunted birch trees gave her pause, but after a moment, when nothing moved, she shrugged away her concern and continued up the slope.

Ahead of her a covey of young pipits flew up from a tree. Lillias stopped and watched them in flight against the cloudless blue sky. When she lowered her gaze, the man known as Hunter stood before her.

Lillias gasped with surprise. He seemed larger than before, filling the whole path with his powerful body. Involuntarily, she took a step backward.

"Dinna be afraid of me, fair lass. I'll na harm ye," he said, and his cheeks creased as he grinned down at her. His eyes were darker than she'd at first imagined and the green fires were like water moving over a stone in the bottom of a stream. She couldn't look away—and feared she might drown in their green splendor.

"You startled me is all. I'm not afraid," she lied, for her heart hammered in her chest so, she feared he might hear it. Her breath was quick and shallow. She'd climbed too high, too fast.

He stared at her intently, a half smile of amusement upon his firm lips. "Mayhap ye should be frightened, lass," he said. "For of a sudden, I'm fearful myself."

"Well I'm not!" she declared, and raised her chin. Her blue eyes flashed from beneath golden lashes. Her small rounded breasts rose and fell in a quick rhythm.

"Ah, lass. Ye let me see the fire beneath the beauty and my heart's lost t'ye. Are ye not as moved by my nearness as I am by yours?"

Lillias didn't know what to answer, but her heart twisted at his pretty words.

"What are ye called, lass?" he coaxed, leaning close, so she felt the hot fan of his breath across her cheek. She clasped her arms over her breasts and drew back—at least she thought to draw back, but her feet were rooted to the ground.

He studied her fair face with the pale golden hair sweeping back into a braid and the slight flush on her rounded cheeks. Her skin was like the finest porcelain, he observed. Her gaze was downcast, so her lashes lay perfect and gleaming along her cheeks and her pink lips trembled enticingly. She bore a scent of wildflowers and Highland air, a heady mixture for one so long from his home.

"If ye will na tell me ye'r name, will ye not give me a kiss, then, lass?" he teased. Her blush deepened and a fine sheen rose on her skin. With a sharp movement, she turned her head away from him. She was an innocent, he discerned, and cursed himself for not moving on. He had no taste for an untried maiden, yet there he stood, watching the emotions play across her face. Then she raised her lashes and looked directly into his eyes, as she'd done on the path earlier, and his breath caught. There were fathoms of innocence and wisdom in those gray-blue depths, the innocence of a virgin, the wisdom only a woman carries from her cradle to her deathbed.

"I dinna know ye, sir," she said softly. "Why would I give ye a kiss?" She swayed like a full-headed flower caught in a wind.

"Because, my pretty lass," he whispered. "Yer soft, pale lips would drive a man to madness if he dinna taste them." His hands came out to clasp her shoulders and he pulled her toward him. She did not resist, nor did she come willingly. She simply let him pull her into his arms . . . and all the while those great blue eyes studied him.

She wet her lips with the tip of her tongue just before his mouth claimed hers, a coquettish gesture done so innocently. He felt the heat rise up in his loins and he claimed her mouth hungrily, his tongue sweeping across her primly closed lips, stabbing at the sweet portals until she opened her mouth under his assault and he was free to plunder the moist sweetness beyond. She stood still within the circle of his arms, neither responding nor repulsing his kiss. Disappointed at her lack of enthusiasm, he drew away, but when he gazed into her eyes, he felt the jolt of shock clear to his belly.

Her cheeks flamed with color at his effrontery, but her eyes ... ah, her eyes blazed with a fire so newly kindled. His lips quirked to one side in a slight smile. When she swayed toward him a second time, her arms came up to his shoulders and her lips parted of their own accord. He gasped and molded her mouth to his. Her small, sweet tongue touched his, danced away, then touched again; her lithe body melted against his so that he felt the firm full breasts thrusting against his chest. Too many weeks had passed since he'd last relieved himself with a French whore and his body thrummed with desire. Instantly his shaft hardened. Groaning, he shifted his clasp on her, his large brown hands closing around the sweetly rounded buttocks, lifting and positioning her against him, so she must feel the stiffness of his hardened rod against her mound.

She pulled away, her eyes enormous and bright with surprise as they gazed into his. He'd seen such a look in other women's eyes before. She was not so innocent as she had at first seemed, he decided, and was relieved that he might yet taste the womanly pleasures she offered. Still, he would play the game with her, treating her as the innocent young maiden she pretended to be. She was every bit the practiced courtesan as any French noblewoman.

She moved as if to pull away from him.

"Nay, lass," he murmured, capturing her in the circle of his arms. " 'Tis the way between a lad and lassie." He rained kisses over her eyes and cheeks and down the smooth column of her throat. Now that she was positioned back where he wanted her, he moved a hand upward to cup the fullness of her breast.

"There's a sweet lass," he crooned. He claimed her mouth again, swallowing the honeyed breath that hissed between her teeth in coy surrender, and slowly lowered her to the grass beside the path. She made no protest, and he chuckled silently. Good. She'd thrown away her pretense at innocence.

He'd wager they'd have a rollicking good time here on

the hillside. To think he'd nearly passed up this tasty wench, meaning to rejoin his men and continue their journey, but Peadair had clearly been smitten by the dark-haired one—and he'd not been able to drive the vision of this fair milk maiden from his mind. Now he felt the warm sun on his back, the warm womanly flesh beneath him, and decided this was the best homecoming of all.

She should stop this, Lillias thought wildly. She'd never been kissed before, never known a man's wooing or his passion, and she'd been stunned by the storm of feelings that claimed her. With the first brush of his hardened rod against her belly, she'd felt a pleasure so intense it brought pain to her breast and loins and left her weak, unable to resist.

Now, as his large hand cupped her breast and his tongue plundered her mouth, she thought she might go all *barmy* from the searing power of his touch. She pressed against him, feeling the solid hardness of his body. She'd never known a man's body could feel like this, could awaken such longings within her. She lay in the young grass, smelling the sweet crush of it beneath her head, feeling the unyielding body of the man above her, and some instinct made her move her legs apart, so he could couch himself between them.

"Ah, lass. 'Tis good to feel a woman beneath me again," he murmured. His shaft was hard against her mound, pressing against her swollen flesh until she felt feverish. Only the cloth of her shift held them apart—and she longed to tear it away. He thrust against her, each contact bringing such a measure of pain and pleasure that she feared she might swoon and be helpless against his ravishment. She opened her mouth to cry out against his onslaught, but he captured her lips in another kiss that left her breathless.

From the distant hill came the sound of a tiny bell. A goat was there just above them. The world returned to her, dashing away all the pleasure so newly discovered. She tore her mouth from his.

"Please, sir!" she cried. "I must go."

"Not yet, lass. We've but begun," he muttered huskily. His lips seared a path across her chin.

"Release me!" she cried. "I demand it of ye."

Her tone reached through his haze of passion; he raised his head and stared into her eyes.

"Are ye serious, lass?"

"Aye. I kinna lie here wi' ye like this."

" 'Tis a poor thing to discover now," he said, pulling his eyebrows together in a black line of frustration, but he rolled to one side, releasing her. "I've never taken a lass against her will and I'll na start now, but 'tis a bitter game ye play."

" 'Tis na a game," she gasped. "Ye caught me unawares." For a moment she lay in the grass beside him, thinking of all the unknown, forbidden delights she must turn her back on. She was tempted to stay. The women of the village would shun her if they knew she'd given this much of herself to a stranger. She'd behaved shamelessly. Still, she lingered. Would she ever have the chance again to know a man's rough kisses, to feel his hot passion?

He saw the indecision in her eyes and reached for her, but the goat's bell sounded again and she rolled away from him, her eyes wide with alarm. She leapt to her feet, but before she could be off, running up the hillside, leaving the shame of what she'd done behind her, he took hold of her wrist and halted her flight.

"Will I see ye again, lass?"

"Nay, nay!" she cried urgently, pulling against his grip.

"What is ye'r name then? Tell me that much, at least."

"I kinna." She looked around frantically, and he perceived that a husband might be searching for her.

"Are ye married, then, lass?" he demanded. "Is that yer husband on yonder ridge with the bell?"

"Aye," she blurted out, then bit her tongue to still it from telling more. Let him think what he would. "Please, sir—if ye've any kindness in ye . . ."

"Ye'r name or I'll na let ye go."

She tugged against him, then realized the futility of her struggle. He was far stronger than she. She must answer.

"Do ye promise to let me go?" she bargained.

"Aye." His green eyes sparkled with laughter.

"Lilli. My name is Lilli." She yanked her hand from his and sped away, pausing only long enough to retrieve the pail she'd dropped.

"Wait, ye dinna tell me ye'r whole name," he cried, but she did not pause or look back. The man stood watching her go.

"Lilli," he repeated under his breath in some puzzlement. It was a rare name; he couldn't remember any clansman choosing it for his daughter. Yet it rang a bell. He repeated it to himself, then out loud.

"Lilli . . ." It had a ring of beauty, like the lass herself. Who could she belong to? What clansman had had the good fortune to capture such a prize? Then he remembered her soft yielding in his arms and his envy vanished. "Pity the poor blighter who married her," he muttered, "for she has na a faithful bone in her body."

He headed down the hill, haunted by the memory of her, soft and pliable beneath him, and of her eyes, wide and frightened as she tried to tug free of him. To his mind came the memory of a long-ago day in the courtyard of Cullayne and a child in his arms. His wife! Her eyes had held that same look of fear; the blue depths had darkened in that same manner. He stopped and looked back up the hill, while comprehension roared over him like a runaway river in spring. His eyes grew dark with rage.

It couldn't be. She wouldn't dare! But he knew she had.

"Lillias!" he bellowed, shaking his fists at the distant crags, but she was no longer in sight.

"Damn ye, Lillias MacLeod!" His cry of wrath could be heard over the hillside and down into the next valley.

Chapter 3

"**T**HERE SHE IS, Iain—Cullayne Castle, just as ye described her."

Iain sat his black stallion and stared down on his home. The sturdy stone walls, the tower rising against the sky, and the gleaming waters of Loch Arkaig behind it was a picture he'd carried in his mind for nine years. Joy at his homecoming had been tinged with regret that his father had passed away without their ever having resolved the conflicts between them.

"Where are the men?" he demanded tersely. Peadair looked at Iain quizzically. Something had set him in a foul mood. Obviously the little milkmaid with the honeyed hair and sweet breasts had not succumbed to the famous MacLeod charm—as did most women who fell into his path.

Peadair grinned. Nor had he, himself, enjoyed a roll in the meadow grass as he'd anticipated when he persuaded Iain to follow the women to the shieling huts, for once Mary McFerris had climbed the hill to him and stood with her cheeks all glowing from exertion and her black hair blowing in the wind, he'd felt something turn over inside himself. She was not the sort of lass a man could tumble and forget. Her fine gray eyes had regarded him boldly, from head to foot, frankly assessing him. At first, he'd been needled by her boldness, then he'd puffed out his chest, knowing she'd find naught but a perfect specimen of man-

43

hood. Then she'd laughed at him and he'd let his air out in a great *whoosh*, like a sheep's belly when it's been pierced, and somehow he'd found himself laughing with her. When she finally allowed him to kiss her, he'd felt he'd been given a priceless gift. Even now, he could taste her kiss upon his mouth, a mingling of tartness and sweetness, like wild berries on a hot summer day. He licked his lips at the memory of her, then felt like laughing at his own daftness.

"I asked where are the men?" Iain repeated harshly.

"Sorry, I was but daydreaming about my dalliance with Mary McFerris," Peadair said. Iain's lips tightened. "The rest of the men are resting on the other side of the village." Peadair glanced over his shoulder at the sound of approaching horsemen. "Everard and Leith are joining us now. D'ye want me to send for the rest?"

"Leave them. I'm going down alone." He pulled the hood forward, casting his face in shadows, and buried his chin in his collar, hunching his back, so he looked shapeless and harmless. He might have been mistaken for a monk, save for the vest of woven leather, which only a soldier would have worn.

"But if what the women say is true, there could be danger for ye at Cullayne Castle," Peadair protested.

"Mayhap. If I'm t'be the new chief, then I must know for myself what's occurring. I'll ride in alone." Lucifer stomped with impatience beneath him. "If I have not placed a signal from the tower window yonder in one hour, gather the men and come in." He raised his voice, so Everard and Leith might hear his words. "I appoint ye Tanist, Peadair."

Peadair was stunned. "Are ye sure, man? I'm not of the MacLeod clan. My own clan is broken."

"Aye, and because of that I adopt ye into my own. Ye're as much a MacLeod as any man here, including yon castle. If I die, ye'll be the new chief of the MacLeod clan."

Peadair was deeply moved by his words. "I gladly bear the title of Tanist, my lord, but only until yer firstborn, after which I step down for the true born leader of the clan."

Iain clamped his friend on the shoulder. "Such is the reason I have chosen ye, Peadair," he said. "Ye would never play me false." So saying, he turned Lucifer toward the castle.

His thoughts went back to that last fateful day here at Cullayne, when he'd ridden across this causeway with a frightened young girl huddled in his arms. Wrapped warmly in his plaid, her small golden head resting against his chest, she'd slept trustingly, but as his steed's hooves struck the wooden planks of the drawbridge, she'd opened her eyes and sat up, her small back rigid, with fear or defiance, he hadn't been certain. One thing was certain, he'd been impressed by her courage that day. His mouth tightened into a grim line.

No one challenged him at the drawbridge or at the gate. He rode into the nether bailey and sat looking around. The courtyard was littered with garbage and offal. Weapons lay forgotten and rusting in the mud. There was no sign of men practicing their archery or swordplay. A man staggered from the stables, fastening his trews. His hair was shaggy, his clothes dirty and unkempt. When he got closer to Iain, he halted, blinked his eyes as if to clear his vision, and peered up at him dumbly.

"Good day, my good man," Iain called in a pleasant voice, although inside he felt an anger rising like a red tide.

"G'day tae ye, and who be ye?" the man mumbled, coming closer.

"I'm a traveler in need of shelter for the night. Is your laird at home?"

Slowly the man's head swiveled around to peer at the newcomer. "Aye, he is, but na t'the likes of ye," he answered rudely. "Who's calling on him?"

"They call me Hunter," Iain said, keeping his voice even. "And ye might tell your laird"—the half-drunk man missed the sarcasm in Iain's voice when he uttered the title—"that without waits a man who can be enemy or friend. The choice is his."

The man eyed him warily. "Aye, I'll tell him, right enough. Stay here." He stumbled up the steps to the door, leaving it open when he entered. Iain waited impatiently. Lucifer tossed his mane. The late afternoon sun slanted

across the stone walls and Iain was smote with grief and
anger. It seemed any moment Red Rafe would come roaring from the castle to clasp his errant son in a bear hug, and
within minutes would curse and shout, even cuff him for
some imagined failure. Father and son had always clashed.
Iain swallowed the thickness in his throat. The time for
mending the gap between them was long gone. He'd loved
his father best when they were on separate continents.

The door was flung open and two burly men stalked out
onto the stone steps and stood regarding Iain. Silently he
waited. They exchanged glances and together walked down
the steps and approached Iain. Lucifer whinnied nervously.

"Whoa, boy." Iain quieted the horse. Warily he studied
the approaching men. One was a stranger to him, but the
second one was Kenneth Sinclair, his father's military commander.

"Laird Hugh says he'll see ye." The burly younger man
grasped Iain's arm and yanked, trying to unseat him.

Instinctively Iain's foot lashed out, landing a blow in the
man's chest and sending him reeling backward into a mud
puddle foul with animal dung. Cursing, the man struggled
to get up. His feet slipped on the muddy grass and he
crashed face forward. Iain paid him no further mind, but
turned his attention to the man on his right.

"Ye need not bother to help me dismount," he said in a
conversational tone. "I can handle it m'self."

"Well enough then." Sinclair stepped back, but his keen
eyes studied the traveler closely. His stoic expression gave
no hint to what he thought. Kenneth Sinclair had recognized Iain MacLeod almost at once, despite the disguise.
Hadn't he taught the boy to handle a broadsword and claymore until the pupil's skill had far surpassed the teacher's?
But he'd learned to keep his counsel until the appropriate
time, and so he said nothing of greeting to this stranger.

"Follow me," he advised. "I'll take ye to the MacLeod."

Iain wondered at how swiftly Sinclair had changed his
allegiance to Hugh MacLeod. Silently he followed after the
man, his eyes keenly observant behind his shadowy disguise. Kenneth Sinclair led him straight to the great hall,

where men sprawled around a trestle table, drunken and boastful, ready to spring up to fight at the slightest offense—and there were many, for tongues loosened by too much ale uttered careless obscenities. This was not an unfamiliar scene to Iain, for such was the way of Red Rafe's company when he lived.

At the head of the trestle table was a man with flaming red hair and beard. His dark tunic was stained with food and drink, his large hands bunched around his horn cup. Iain drew a breath, certain he was seeing an apparition, for it seemed Red Rafe himself lolled there. The man turned to stare at Iain and the image was broken.

"Who be ye?" declared Hugh MacLeod. His manner was belligerent.

Iain remembered Hugh well. He had been an unimportant chieftain of one of the smaller branches of the clan, but he'd always swaggered and given himself an air of self-importance. Now Iain added *crafty* and *lazy* to his attributes—crafty in that he'd clearly angled himself into a position to be named Red Rafe's successor, lazy in that he'd lolled here in the questionable comforts of the castle while the women and children toiled unprotected. Iain's lip curled in disdain.

Impatience was another obvious trait of the man who would be leader, for he lurched to his feet and glared at Iain. "Well, man, speak up. Who be ye?"

"My name is Hunter," Iain replied, keeping his voice low and deep.

"And what say ye? Are ye my enemy or friend?"

"I bring news t'ye, Laird MacLeod," Iain replied evenly. "The McCullough clan attacked your villagers as they made their way t'their shieling huts this afternoon."

"The murderin', thievin' McCulloughs," Hugh muttered, and flopped down on his bench, sloshing wine from his cup onto his filthy coat.

"Let's go after them, Hugh," Sinclair said. "They'll not be expectin' us t'strike so quickly."

"Nay, nay." Hugh waved his hand limply. "We need to muster the men."

"We've men aplenty. If we wait, it will give them time to rally more support and prepare for our attack. We must strike quickly, man."

"Nay, I tell ye." Hugh hiccuped. One hairy, dirty hand caressed the cheek of the young serving wench who simpered up at him. "We'll na go tonight. Tomorrow or the next day is soon enough, if we go at all."

"If we go? Hugh, we kinna let this pass. The McCulloughs and the McBains grow more bold every day, certain we're too weak to retaliate when they raid us. We've already lost half our herds, villages have been burned and women debauched."

"Nay and nay again!" Hugh roared, leaping to his feet and pulling his dirk. He held it against Sinclair's throat. "D'ye dare to question my decision?" he demanded, then looked around the room at the other men. "Do any of ye here question my decision?"

Quickly the men looked away, shame mingling with unease in their expressions. Sinclair stood silent, his gaze never wavering from Hugh's. The blade had broken the skin; a thin line of blood ran down Sinclair's neck, a sheen of sweat bathed his face. Hugh read the fear in his eyes and laughed. Sinclair's hands doubled into fists, but he held his temper.

"Ye are not yet declared chief by the council, Hugh," he said in a stubborn tone.

Rage swept across Hugh's face, and for a moment, Iain thought he meant to drive the point of his dirk into Sinclair's throat. Iain's muscles bunched, ready to knock aside Hugh's arm.

"Leave him be, Hugh." A young man stepped forward. "If ye kill my faither, I'll bring an army of men against ye. Ye'll never live long enough for the council to name ye head chief." Hugh's eyebrows twitched, the hand holding the knife trembled, then slowly he laughed and drew back.

"Ye're son dinna ken a jest when he sees one," he declared. Grinning, he looked around the room, and when no one shared his humor, the grin died away and his face grew ugly.

"Soon the council will meet, Sinclair," he threatened,

waving the blade of his dirk in Sinclair's face, "and when I've been appointed chief, ye and that whelp of yers will feel the weight of my power."

"Until then," Sinclair said, "I suggest we ride out t'fight the McCulloughs."

Hugh sat back in his seat, propped a muddy boot on the table, and looked around the hall. "If ye've a desire to fight, then go," he said. "I appoint ye leader of an expedition of men. Who wants t'go with Sinclair?" Immediately the young man who'd spoken up before stepped forward. Another young man, hardly more than a boy, followed.

"My brither and me," he said stoutly. Kenneth Sinclair's face reflected the pride he felt in his sons.

"Anyone else?" Hugh asked, and the other men looked at one another uneasily, all too aware that this was a test as to where their loyalties were placed. Though few of them cared for Hugh, they feared his temper, and of offending him, when it seemed likely he would be named head chief.

Smiling magnanimously at Sinclair, Hugh shrugged. "It seems ye have only yer sons to go wi' ye," he declared. "That's na much support against the McCulloughs, unless, of course, ye plan t'send for some of yer own men, in which case it will be days before they arrive and ye can make the attack."

"By God's teeth, I'll not see McCulloughs go unpunished for attacking our women and children!" Sinclair swore in frustration. "My sons and I will go alone."

"Not quite alone," Iain said, stepping forward. "I offer my sword and those of my men who wait just yonder on the other side of the village."

"I ask ye again, who be ye?" Hugh thundered in anger. "We will na take the help of a man we dinna know."

Iain threw back the hood and squared his shoulders. "Ye should know me well, Hugh MacLeod, for I know ye for the cowardly fool ye are."

Hugh leapt to his feet at the insult. Kenneth Sinclair was staring at Iain.

"I know ye, lad!" he cried. "Many's the time I've seen ye stand and defy Red Rafe." He turned to the other chieftains around the hall. " 'Tis Iain MacLeod, home again, lads!" he cried.

Stunned silence fell around the room as the men took in this news, then of one accord they raised their voices in shouts of cheer. Hugh MacLeod's face flushed red, his neck swelled, and he reached for a sword.

"Look out, Iain!" Sinclair's son cried out a warning. Iain whirled in time to see the blade aimed at his heart. Leaping aside, he threw off the cloak and drew his own sword.

"Have a care, Hugh MacLeod," he called. "No damage has been done, but if ye raise yer blade t'me again, I'll have t'kill ye for the traitor ye are."

Hugh's answer was a maddened snarl. He rushed forward, his blade extended awkwardly. Once again Iain nimbly danced aside, parrying with his own blade. The battle was one-sided. Hugh was clumsy and unschooled in the finer points of swordplay—and out of shape from too many idle days spent in drinking and wenching. Iain's blade seemed to be everywhere, first on one side, then the other, flashing faster than the eye could see, bringing blood in several small cuts over Hugh's chest and shoulders. A final thrust and Hugh's sword went flying across the stone floor. Winded and sweating, Hugh fell to his knees. The point of Iain's blade rested against his neck, much as Hugh had pressed his dirk against Sinclair's neck. Iain bent to look the man in the eyes.

"I kinna blame a man for being ambitious," he said in a low voice, "but I blame a man who would be chief and will na' protect his people. Ye aren't fit t'take my faither's place."

"I—I dinna ken ye were coming back," Hugh blubbered. "We thought ye was dead."

"Take a good look at me, man. I'm not dead—and I'm back t'take my rightful place as head chief. If ye cannot accept that and declare fealty t'me now, say so and ye can leave MacLeod land and make yer way elsewhere. Otherwise, I expect yer loyalty or yer life."

"I was always loyal to Red Rafe," Hugh cried, his eyes rolling. "Why would I na gi' it t'ye?"

"Why, indeed?" Iain said, and drew back.

"Kill him, Iain. He'll stand always a blade at yer back."

"Nay, I'll kill no man who declares his proper loyalty t'me," Iain said, sheathing his blade and looking around the hall. "Be there any among ye who kinna or will not follow me?"

"Nay," they answered of one voice.

"Good." Iain nodded. "We ride within the hour to fight the McCulloughs." A cheer went up around the hall and the men scrambled to retrieve their weapons and horses. Iain turned to Hugh, who still knelt on the stone floor, his face wet with sweat. "D'ye ride wi' us this night, Hugh?" Iain demanded.

The man got to his feet and looked around. He'd lost face with his comrades. "Aye, I will," he said, and hurried out of the hall.

Sinclair stood watching him leave. "Ye must not trust him, lad," he cautioned.

"Dinna worry," Iain exclaimed, clamping Sinclair on the shoulder. "I owe ye my gratitude. I feared my faither's chieftains had all lost their courage and were naught but mewling kittens."

"Nay, my lord," Sinclair answered. "The Sinclairs will always stand at the side of the rightful MacLeod chief. So will my sons, Adhamh and Uilliam." The two young men nodded somberly.

"I've need of men like ye," Iain said, shaking the hands of all three. The young clansmen blushed with pleasure to be treated with such respect by the *Ceann Mor* himself.

"Ye've other brave men, my lord," Adhamh said. "Logan MacCuag, and others who are at their own holdings. They have no taste for Hugh MacLeod and his ways."

"We were uneasy that Hugh might be appointed by the council," Kenneth Sinclair said. "He seemed the favored one. And when Douglas MacLeod declared he'd heard Red Rafe name Hugh MacLeod as his Tanist, I dinna believe it. Yer faither was angry wi' ye for leaving and staying away so long, but he would na have taken away yer birthright to head the clan."

"Aye, 'tis true," Iain observed. "How did my faither die?"

"We raided the McCulloughs one dark night. Red Rafe was in rare form, declaring he could kill three McCulloughs for every one the rest of us killed. I tried t'talk him out of the killing. I declared if we just raided them for cattle, not much would happen, but if we continued killin' we'd have a full-scale war on our hands."

Sinclair shuffled his feet. "Yer faither just laughed and said we had more men than the McCulloughs and there was naught the McCulloughs could do t'us." He bowed his head for a minute, tightening his lips as if he hated speaking about the next part.

"The McCulloughs were waitin' for us. They knew we was comin', and they'd called on the MacBains t'join forces wi' them. We didn't take many men wi' us. Red Rafe was so contemptuous of the McCulloughs. He said he didn't need men to whip them and send them runnin' wi' their tails between their legs. I saw him fightin' two McCulloughs at once, then Angus McCullough himself struck Red Rafe down from behind wi' his claymore."

Tears formed in the old man's eyes. "He went down like a bull, bellowing his rage and defiance. They fell on him like jackals and hacked him t'pieces." He paused for a moment to swallow and wipe at his eyes. "I could hardly believe he was dead. The men were stunned. They seemed to lose heart when they saw Red Rafe was dead. The McCulloughs were cutting our men down like reapers in a field. We lost six men that night and two more were maimed. We rallied, forming a wedge around Red Rafe's body until we could get him back on his horse and flee."

Sinclair stopped speaking and scrubbed at his eyes with the heel of one hand. His sons stood with their heads bowed.

Iain gripped Sinclair's shoulder. "I did ye wrong t'even consider ye'd switched alliance t'a man like Hugh Mac-Leod," he said. "I'm beholden for what ye did for my faither."

"He was a hard man, Iain. Aye, and he could be cruel, but he was a man t'make other men follow."

"Aye, he was that," Iain said, and turned toward the stone steps leading up to the second floor. "I've a need t'see my wife before we ride out."

"Ye'll find her chambers in the tower," Sinclair called.

Iain paused on the stairs and looked back at him in consternation. "In the tower? Ye mean she's still there?"

"Aye. Yer faither was a hard man," Sinclair repeated, and his lips thinned in unspoken disapproval.

Iain strode out of the castle, taking up a banner as he crossed the bailey and entered the tower. Once inside the rounded tower, he could hear the wind howl from off the loch and he was reminded of the tales of his boyhood. Once prisoners had been hanged from the rafters of the first floor and their spirits were said to still haunt the tower. He thought of a small girl who had grown up here and his mouth tightened. He turned to the steep spiral staircase that wound upward. At the top was a narrow passage and an oaken door that opened onto a single chamber.

Iain paused, wondering what would greet him on the other side. Was his child bride there waiting for him—or was she even now running free in the Highland meadow with her slim bare legs flashing and her sweet mouth raised invitingly to some other man? He gripped the door and flung it open. A woman gasped and leapt to her feet, knocking over the stool where she'd sat near the fire. Iain stepped inside the room and stared at the woman. She was not old, but neither was she young. Her round face showed alarm.

"Ye've come t'the wrong place, my—my lord," she stammered. "There's naught here."

Iain continued to stare at her, his mind going back to that night so many years before when he'd ridden back to Dunbeath Castle to kidnap a kinswoman for the child, Lillias. "Be ye Aggie?" he demanded.

The fear was replaced with puzzlement. "Aye," she said hesitantly. "Do I know ye, my lord?"

"Ye should," Iain replied. "I've come t'see my wife."

"Yer wife?" she repeated in amazement, then understanding dawned and she took a step backward. "Ye've come back?" she whispered.

"Aye, I've come back," Iain declared. "Where's my wife?"

"She's—she's na here, my lord," Aggie stammered.

"Where is she?"

"She—she's gone t' the village t'tend a sick child," Aggie lied and could not meet his gaze. She was at heart an honest woman. "I—I'll send someone t'fetch her, my lord."

"She'll return tonight, won't she?" Iain demanded.

"Aye, my lord. She dinna run about the countryside like a—a gypsy." Aggie feigned indignation. Her worst fears had come true—and she herself had sent Lillias off to the shieling with her blessings!

"Then I'll await her return, Aggie. Dinna disturb her works of charity." He stalked out of the room as abruptly as he'd come. At the arrow-loop window in the passageway, he hung his banner, so it was in full view of his men waiting in the hills, then made his way down the stairs to await their arrival.

Aggie had noted the grim expression on his face and her heart pounded with agitation. When she was certain he'd left the tower, she hurried down the stairs and made her way across the bailey to the castle kitchens. She noted the men gathering in the bailey, some of them strange to her, but did not pay attention to the man in a dark hood standing among them. Inside the castle, she quickly sought out Glenda, one of the castle servants.

"The new chief's come home," Glenda babbled. "He set that Hugh MacLeod on his heels and sent him packing. In the kitchen they're telling of how he handles a sword as if it were part of his hand. They say he was always ferocious. They called him the Black Beast of Cullayne when he was a youth."

"Oh, do be quiet, woman!" Aggie snapped. "I've need of ye to travel into the hills t'the shieling huts t'fetch Lillias."

"Aha! She does not know the chief is back," Glenda crowed. "Now she won't be running about the countryside

like a common milkmaid. She'll have t'stay home like a respectable married woman— Ouch!" She stood rubbing the
reddened arm where Aggie had pinched her.

"She is a respectable woman," Aggie snapped. "I sent
her t'the shieling m'self with herbs for Kendra McFerris's
wee bairn what's turned ill wi' a fever."

"And the fool woman is takin' her baby into the mountains when he's fevered?" Glenda inquired derisively.

" 'Tis her affair and none of our own," Aggie reprimanded. "Ye must go quickly and tell no one."

"It will soon be dark." Glenda pouted. "I've na wish t'go
into the mountains after dark."

"Take Niall wi' ye, then," Aggie ordered. "Only go
quickly. If ye bring her back before Laird Iain discovers
she's not about, I'll gi' ye my best brooch."

"The round one wi' the flower carvings?" Glenda asked
greedily.

"Aye, that one. Now, go along wi' ye. Hurry, hurry."

"All right. Just let me get my cape," Glenda declared,
and hurried away.

She returned shortly, and at Aggie's urging hurried from
the castle and crossed to the stable. As she entered and
looked around, a hooded figure came from behind and
clamped a hand about her mouth, pushing her into an
empty stall. Throwing back the hood, Iain fixed the woman
with a stern gaze.

"D'ye know who I am?" he demanded.

Mutely, Glenda nodded.

"I'll release ye, but ye must na scream." Glenda shook
her head. Iain stepped back. "Where d'ye go, wench?"

"I—I have an errand, my lord."

"And what is it?"

"I—I kinna say, my lord." Glenda gulped and tried hard
not to tremble before him. She longed to pull her courage
about her and appear dignified, even beautiful, for the new
chief was a fiercely handsome man.

"Ye'd better say and quickly, wench," Iain declared.
"Have ye forgotten in a breath that I am *Ceann Mor* here?
Where d'ye go?"

"I—I'm t'go t'the shieling huts t'fetch Lilli—yer wife."

"So, it *was* her," he muttered under his breath. His visage changed, growing ferocious, so Glenda no longer thought him handsome, just fearsome-looking.

"The Black Beast of Cullayne?" She gasped despite herself.

Iain looked back at her. "I'll not harm ye. Are ye t'return t'night?"

"Aye, my lord. Aggie said t'fetch her, at once. I'm t'take the smithy, Niall." She nodded her head at the tall, broadshouldered man who worked the bellows.

Iain studied her choice. "Aye, take him and three horses from the stables."

"Aye, my lord."

"And say nothing of our conversation to anyone, not even my wife."

"Aye, my lord," Glenda whispered, nearly weeping with nervousness.

"Be gone now," he commanded. "The light will be fading soon."

"Aye, my—"

"Go!"

Glenda scurried away. When she'd conveyed her instructions to Niall, he looked at Iain MacLeod and hurried to comply.

The courtyard was filled with men and horses. The steeds seemed to anticipate the coming raid, for they stamped their hooves against the stones and reared their heads, nostrils flaring. Iain gave the order and the men mounted, nearly forty in number. With a single curt command, Iain rode out of the castle, across the causeway, and through the village. Dogs barked as they passed and children ignored their mothers' calls to bedtime and hung over stone fences to watch them pass.

They rode hard, reaching the border between MacLeod land and McCullough holdings well after dark. From there on they traveled carefully, taking care to ride around villages and farms until they reached McCullough Castle itself. Clouds rode low in the sky, blocking the moonlight.

Iain positioned his men, surrounding the castle, but no one called out a warning.

"They're not expectin' us," said Peadair.

"They've grown lazy and careless since Red Rafe died," Sinclair observed, with satisfaction.

"They'll pay for that mistake," Iain said. "We'll take Angus McCullough himself as prisoner. Take him alive, if ye can, for I'll have him stand before the council for killing my faither."

"Aye," Sinclair said, and sent the word back among his men.

Leith and two men of his choosing were dispatched to cross the moat and lower the drawbridge. In less than half an hour, the signal came; Iain and his men rode across the drawbridge and into the courtyard of McCullough Castle. Those watchmen who'd dozed, now stirred and made to call out a warning, but were quickly silenced.

Stealthily, MacLeod men took possession of the castle. Only those men sleeping in the great hall needed subduing. Without having shed a drop of blood, Iain climbed the stairs to Angus McCullough's very chamber. When the door was flung open, the sounds of fighting below roused the elderly chief from his sleep. Flinging aside his coverlet, Angus pushed aside the wench he'd chosen to warm his bed that night, and, mindless of his nakedness, reached for his claymore.

"Nay, if ye wish t'live another day," Iain warned. The point of his blade pressed against Angus's neck as he crouched at the foot of his bed. Iain waited for the man to accept defeat. Slowly Angus withdrew his hand from his claymore.

"Ye're a stranger t'me, man," Angus gasped. "Wha' d'ye want wi' me?"

"I've come to avenge my faither's death," Iain said. Angus's face blanched.

"Iain MacLeod, the Black Beast of Cullayne," he muttered. "We heard ye were dead in France." Suddenly he felt afraid of the man standing before him. This then was Red

Rafe's son, and he remembered how fierce the lad had been as a youth. His raids had always been bold and daring, his fighting the most fierce.

Iain shrugged. "I'm here in the flesh and ready to make ye answer for the murder of my faither."

"It was not murder," Angus howled. "I fought him in a fair battle."

"Three men against one?" Iain jeered. "Mayhap it was fair enough, a MacLeod being worth three McCulloughs."

Angus's muscles jerked as if barely held in check at the insult. "My men will cut ye down," he snarled.

"I think not," Iain declared. "It's been surprisingly easy to invade yer castle. The McCulloughs have grown soft attacking only women and children."

The McCullough chief roared at this additional insult and lunged upward with his powerful legs. Iain had anticipated such a move and now his blade spoke well, driving deep into Angus's shoulder. The man staggered against the bedpost and stared at the blood pouring from his wound. The woman on the bed screamed over and over. Iain ignored her.

"Silence, woman!" Angus roared. "Leave a man t'die in peace."

"Ye'll na die, McCullough, 'tis a harmless wound," Iain informed him. "Ye'll live t'dangle at the end of a rope from Cullayne's towers."

"Blast ye, MacLeod," McCullough growled. "I'll see ye in hell first!"

"That well may be," MacLeod said calmly, "but ye'll answer for my faither's murder." He motioned the man toward the door. Clasping a hand to his wounded shoulder, Angus McCullough did as he was bid, pausing only when they reached the stairs and he gazed upon the fallen bodies of his men below.

"This is not the end of the McCulloughs," he declared. "My sons will gather the clan and march on Cullayne Castle. Ye'll pay for this night."

"Aye, and consider the price worth it to capture the murderer of my faither." Iain's blade point urged Angus down the stairs.

The MacLeods howled with laughter when Angus appeared naked. The shaggy-haired chief clamped his teeth together and marched stoically out the door and into the courtyard, where there was more laughter. Spirals of fog rose in the chilled night air.

"Aye, 'tis cold out here," Sinclair called. "Gi' the man a covering." Someone tossed him a MacLeod plaid, which Angus bunched and threw to the ground with contempt. A murmur of anger went round the men at this show of disrespect for their tartan.

"Leave it, then," Iain ordered, "so there will be no doubt whose work this was. It will make a handy calling card for yer sons."

Angus's face suffused with color. Even yet, his oldest son, Godfrey, bore the scars of an encounter with this man. "Curse ye, Iain MacLeod," he shouted. "I'll see ye dead."

"Not this night," Iain reminded him. "Take him back t'Cullayne Castle, tend his wound, and imprison him in the tower."

"Why bother? Kill him now," one of the MacLeod chieftains called out.

Iain faced them all, knowing this was a test. They would either think him soft, or find him a worthy leader to follow. "Sinclair has told me the way of my faither's death. Angus McCullough was afraid t'meet Red Rafe head-on in honest combat. He'll na die at the point of my sword in battle like a man, but hang from the rafters at Cullayne like the foul coward he is." A rough cheer rose from his men at these words. "Furthermore, he'll be an example to every other McCullough and MacBain who thinks to raid our lands." Another lusty cheer rose.

They tied Angus into the saddle, so there was no chance of his escape on the rough ride back to Cullayne, and without bothering to offer him any further covering against the cold, galloped away.

Iain had won over their hearts once and for all. Each man there was ready to pledge his undying support, and in the days ahead, as the tale of this deed spread throughout the bens and glens, other MacLeod men rejoiced to know they had a new chief and he was worthy of their fealty.

Chapter 4

"**A**RE YE ANGRY wi' me, then, Lilli?" Mary McFerris stood before Lillias, her brow creasing in puzzlement. Ever since they'd returned from milking the goats, Lillias had kept to herself and remained stubbornly silent. Mary had longed to tell her about Peadair McDermott, but Lillias's distraction had made that impossible. Now, Mary leaned forward and touched her friend's shoulder. "Will ye not be speakin' wi me?"

"Of course I will, Mary," Lillias said in a voice husky from weeping. She did not look at Mary. She'd come to this grassy ledge high above the shieling camp, seeking solitude while she tried to sort out her feelings, but she couldn't turn her back on Mary. "Why would I be angry wi' ye, Mary?"

"Because I left ye to be with Peadair McDermott," Mary explained. "Do ye think me wicked for leaving ye?"

Lillias's head jerked around, and Mary saw she'd been crying.

"Why, what's wrong, Lilli? Why do ye weep?"

" 'Tis *I* who is wicked, Mary." Lillias turned her face away and studied the valley below. In her misery, she did not see its beauty. The face of a dark-haired stranger who called himself Hunter was ever before her. Mary stared at her in stunned silence.

"Ye're not wicked, Lilli. Why d'ye say such bad things

61

about ye'rself? Ye're one of the least wicked people I know."

"Ye wouldna say that if ye'd been in the high meadow wi' me today." Lillias scrubbed at her cheeks, but the tears spilled from her eyes as quickly as she wiped them away.

A feeling of dread washed over Mary. Something harrowing had happened to her dear friend in the high meadow and she, Mary, had not been there to help her.

"Tell me what terrible fate has befallen ye, Lilli?" she cried softly.

"I canna tell anyone," Lillias cried. "I'm that ashamed of my actions."

Mary's heart sank. She could only think that one of the Lowland raiders had returned and ravished Lillias upon the hillside, and, though the fault would not be hers, Lilli would bear the brunt of scorn at being a ruined woman. Mary's heart beat faster and she remembered that some women, so taken, had ended their lives rather than bear their shame before their loved ones. That couldn't happen to Lillias.

"Lilli," Mary cried, gripping her friend's hands and forcing her to look into her eyes. She struggled to still the sobs that welled in her chest. Somehow she must protect Lillias. "Ye need not speak of what has happened," she whispered. "I'll not tell a soul. No one must ever know. We'll pretend nothing has happened and I'll go down on my knees every night and pray ye'll not bear a child from this."

Lillias listened to her friend's outpouring in growing horror. Her eyes grew wide with indignation. "Nay, there'll no be a child. I dinna lay with him."

Mary drew back, astounded that her heroic effort to protect Lillias was not needed after all. "Ye mean the McCullough man dinna ravish ye?"

"There was no McCullough," Lillias said in puzzlement.

Mary's eyes snapped with exasperation. "Then, pray, what are ye *blathering* about?"

Lillias looked away. "I kinna say."

"Ye'd better say, or I'll sock ye with my fist," Mary warned in some exasperation.

Reluctantly Lillias began her tale of what had happened on the hillside with the dark-haired stranger. Long before she was finished, Mary's fist had unfurled and she had settled herself on the grass beside Lillias, a bemused smile on her face. When Lillias finished, Mary laughed outright.

"Ye laugh at my sinfulness?" Lillias inquired, somewhat affronted that Mary took her downfall so lightly.

"Nay." Mary chuckled, then grew serious. " 'Twas only a few stolen kisses, Lilli," she reasoned. "If ye've been wicked, then so have I, for I gave Peadair McDermott more than a few kisses."

"Ye did?" Lillias gasped. Mary had spoken so blithely of what she'd done. Cheeks blushed with embarrassment at the memory of the dark-haired stranger's kisses, she lowered her lashes and stared at the ground. "Mayhap Peadair's kisses dinna stir ye as Hunter's did me?"

Mary hooted with laughter, then observed her friend's pinkened cheeks. "Peadair's kisses dinna lack fire," she observed mildly. "I felt the same way as ye, Lilli. 'Tis not wicked to feel this way."

"It is if ye're married as I am," Lillias said, and could hold Mary's gaze for only a moment. Mary's amusement vanished and she nodded.

"Aye," she said.

She sat pondering for a while. To think that Lillias had felt this same rush of joy and hot passion as she and could not revel in it, could not anticipate more of it to come, but must sit in abject misery recounting her feelings as sinful, seemed incomprehensible to Mary. To think of Peadair returning to claim yet more stolen kisses made Mary's blood run hot and quick through her veins. He'd been so bold and daring, and she had been hard put not to surrender to his demands. She thought of his hard body pressed against hers and felt her nipples harden beneath her shift. Lillias moved beside her, and, reluctantly, Mary pushed away such seductive imaginings, her joy temporarily tampered by her friend's dilemma.

" 'Tis na yer fault, Lilli, that yer husband does na return home and claim ye as his wife. Ye're young and in need of a man's touch."

"Mayhap." Lillias sighed. "But will the rest of the clan understand that? Will the council forgive me for my wickedness or will they order a punishment too terrible for any woman to bear?"

Once again Mary sank into silence, knowing Lillias's words were true. There would be little forgiveness for a woman's infidelity, even if her husband had remained away at war and was never likely to return. Lillias was in an untenable position.

"Ye could petition the council for a divorce," she offered tentatively, for such a step was seldom taken.

"Nay." Lillias sighed. "Such a recourse is not open to me. I have had no say in this matter from start to finish, Mary. I've never felt like a married woman."

"Because ye're not one—not wi' Iain MacLeod away in France. Why, Lillias, he's never even claimed his husbandly rights."

"Aye, I know, and I've not minded that, until now. Oh, Mary! I wish I had na spoken those vows so long ago! I was but a child and knew na' what they meant," Lillias whispered.

Mary nodded in understanding. Many a time she had heard the village women speculate on the marriage that had never been consummated. Nor would it ever if Iain MacLeod never returned. Mary shook her head with sadness thinking of Kendra and Douglas's fiery relationship and her own newly awakened passion for Peadair McDermott. To think that Lillias might always remain an unclaimed wife, a virgin, and never experience such emotions seemed imminently unfair, but Mary could offer no solution. She could only offer her support.

"If the dark-haired man known as Hunter returns, then be wi' him, Lilli," she advised in a rush of words.

Lillias gasped and raised her head to stare into Mary's eyes. "D'ye know what ye're telling me?" she demanded softly.

"Aye, I do," Mary said. " 'Tis na fair to think of ye here like a bird in a cage, unable to know the pleasure of a man's embrace. I'll never tell should ye choose to ignore ye're vows, Lilli. I'll help ye all I can."

" 'Tis wickedness we're contemplating, Mary," Lillias cried. "I kinna do this thing." She paused, lowering her flushed face to her upthrust knees. "And yet when I remember the feelings he awakened in me, I dinna think I can turn away from him again."

"Shh!" Mary held up her hand in warning. Lillias raised her head and looked around fearfully. A shadow moved stealthily along the path. Lillias and Mary exchanged knowing glances.

"Beitris," Lillias called, and after some hesitation the older girl stepped out of her hiding place and climbed up to them. Her pretty face was twisted into a spiteful smile, her eyes flickered with mischief. Had she overheard their conversation? Lillias wondered.

"Did ye wish to join us?" she asked politely, although Beitris's presence was the last thing she wanted. She felt Mary's pinch through her shift. Beitris smiled serenely, unbothered by the fact she'd been caught snooping.

"I have na wish to sit on a hillside and titter over some wayfarers who wander through our land. They're little more than gypsies," she declared loftily.

"Ye don't know they're gypsies, Beitris," Lillias spoke up, loath to have the dark-haired stranger considered a ragged, lawless vagabond.

"Why, one of them knew ye when ye were but a girl," Mary reminded her. "Are ye a gypsy, Beitris?"

"So he claims," Beitris answered impatiently, and glanced at Lillias. "Yer watchdog, Aggie, has sent a servant. Ye're wanted back at the castle, at once."

"Now?" Lillias inquired, glancing at Mary in consternation. " 'Tis nearly darktime."

"She says ye must come now. She says it's imperative." Beitris's smirk was even more irksome, and Lillias longed to order her begone from them, but another thought had come to her and she leapt to her feet.

"Mayhap Aggie is ill. I'd better go," she cried, and ran down to the camp where the women were bent over their cooking fires or gathering their children in for a supper of bannock and gruel.

Glenda had taken a seat upon a small, rough bench and joined the women in their gossip. Niall, one of the stable hands, stood at the edge of the path, looking sheepish and uncomfortable in the company of so many women without their husbands present. When Lillias approached, the women fell silent, casting uneasy glances toward her. Lillias's heart constricted. The news must be very bad.

"Why ha' ye come, Glenda?" she demanded. "Has Aggie fallen ill?"

"Nay!" Glenda shook her head.

"Then why has she sent ye?"

"I dinna know," Glenda muttered. "She simply told me to hike into the hills to the shieling camp and fetch ye back to the castle, at once."

"Ye kinna go now," Mary cried. " 'Tis turned dark. The little people will be about."

"If Aggie has ordered me to come at once, I must," Lillias replied. "Besides, she's sent Niall, and he carries a stout pole."

"Aye, but he's such a great lout, he won't know how to use it. Ye'll have to protect him as well as Glenda and yerself."

"We'll be all right, my friend," Lillias said, warmed by Mary's concern.

"Am I to travel back all that way wi'out a rest?" Glenda whined behind them. "My knees are aching me now and I'll be hard put to do my chores tomorrow." She rubbed at her knees and grimaced. Glenda was well known at Cullayne for shirking her duties, but Lillias had no time to deal with her now.

"Stay here for the night, then," she ordered. "I'll go with Niall and ye can return tomorrow alone."

"Nay." Glenda sprang up from her stool without any sign of the infirmity of which she'd complained. "I kinna let ye return without me," she cried. "Aggie would have m'head."

"And rightly so." Helen spoke up from her place around the campfire.

"We'll leave immediately," Lillias decided, and hurried toward the hut to gather her belongings. Mary followed close behind.

"Dinna leave the camp tonight," she pleaded. She'd been reared on the tales of devilish forest elves who lived in the glens and set upon unsuspecting travelers caught out in the darkness.

"I must go, Mary," Lillias said, hastily stuffing her extra linen shift into a bundle. "Aggie needs me. Besides"—she paused—"this way, I' na' be faced wi' temptation again should the one with green eyes appear."

"I'll come wi' ye, then," Mary said stoutly, although brave as she was during the day, her courage fled after nightfall. Still, she'd failed Lillias once today. She meant to make it up to her.

"Nay," Lillias said. "Stay here at the shieling. If nothing is amiss, I'll return." She smiled at Mary and was unaware that her face reflected her own unease at traveling after dark.

"Take my shawl against the night chill," Mary cried, and fetched the woolen cloth.

"But 'tis ye'r new shawl, Mary," she cried.

"It does na' matter," she said, and hugged Lillias good-bye.

With a final farewell, Lillias led the way down the mountain path, back to the village and Cullayne Castle. Niall and Glenda followed close on her heels, casting fearful glances over their shoulders as night fell around them.

They reached Cullayne Castle late, when the moon rode high in the black sky, its light partially obscured by drifting clouds. The castle lay before them, dark and menacing against the black waters of the loch. When Lillias rushed forward to the causeway bridge that led into the castle, Niall, who had remained silent throughout their journey, now clasped her sleeve and turned toward the outer edge of the moat.

"Where are we going?" Lillias demanded crossly. She was exhausted from her journey.

"Shh! Aggie said to use the water gate," Glenda explained in a low voice. "It's nearest the tower. We must na be seen entering the castle walls. Niall will care for the horses in the village till morning."

What calamity had befallen them, Lillias wondered, that she could not enter her own home openly? Silently she followed as Glenda led the way around the castle, nearly to the loch itself. There a small boat had been hidden along the shore among the balsam. The red flowers, so newly opened, lay like droplets of blood against the broad leaves, a chilling omen. Lillias shivered.

Glenda clamored in and picked up the oar, so there was nothing for Lillias to do but follow. With surprising ease, Glenda rowed them across to the shallow sand and pebble shelf below the castle. There a door opened into the nether regions of the curtain wall. As a child, Lillias had sometimes defied Aggie and Red Rafe's orders and played here, but she'd never been here after dark. The place was dank and smelly, and she was loath to enter. A narrow stairway led them upward to the bailey, near the tower.

At the top of the stairs, Glenda silently waved a farewell and disappeared into the shadows. Lillias knew she was headed to the servants' quarters in the castle chambers. Reminding herself that she was not afraid to be alone in the dark bailey, Lillias pulled the woolen shawl around her head and shoulders, grateful for its dark color. She would be less conspicuous.

Silently she made her way to the entrance of the tower and breathed a sigh of relief when she was safely inside and the heavy oaken door was closed behind her. Candles had been left burning for her return. Anxious to see Aggie, Lillias turned toward the spiral stairs. Was it only that morning that she'd so blithely left her nursemaid? Her heart quelled at the memory of how she'd sassed Aggie. What dreadful event had occurred since then? She bounded up the steps, heart pounding, her worst fears crowding in on her now that she was so close to finding the answers to her problems.

"Aggie!" she cried, and threw open the door to the room they shared.

The nursemaid sat on a stool before the fire much as her mother had done on that fateful night so many years before. Like her mother, Aggie's face bore a stamp of fear and anxiety. Nearby sat an oaken tub already filled with bathwater, while a final kettle of water heated on the fire. Obviously Aggie had anticipated her return tonight. Still, she made no move to rise and greet Lillias. Her voice was harsh when she finally spoke.

"Go back to the kitchen, ye ungrateful cur," she growled in a manner Lillias had never heard before. "I told ye the mistress would na return before morning. Be about yer business."

Nonplussed, Lillias could only stare at her. "Aggie, are ye ill?" she whispered, thinking Aggie had gone out of her head. Swiftly she moved across the room to throw her arms about the older woman, but a shadow loomed, making her draw back. For a heart-stopping moment, she feared Red Rafe had returned from the dead and had come to make all her nightmares real. She blinked and the image disappeared. She saw the man before her was a stranger, dressed in a manner far more elegant than Red Rafe had ever done.

"Who are ye?" she demanded sharply. "Why are ye here in my chambers? I demand that ye leave at once."

"I'm sorry to have startled ye, milady," the man said mildly, moving forward, so the fire cast a light on him. Despite her alarm, Lillias could not help but notice his tunic was of a rich fabric such as she'd never seen before.

"Who are ye?" she demanded again.

"I am Everard Lachlan, at yer service." He bowed so elegantly that Lillias was caught tongue-tied by such a gesture.

"That—that tells me nothing, sir," she stammered.

"Aye, I quite agree, milady. But 'tis not my place to answer yer questions. 'Tis left to me only to bring ye to the castle hall where yer husband awaits yer presence, even now."

"My husband?" Lillias cried, looking from him to Aggie.

"Aye, milady. He has returned to Cullayne this day and is most anxious to greet his wife."

"I—I cannot greet him as I am," Lillias stammered. "I have traveled far this night and I am weary. I wish to bathe and rest before presenting myself to m-my husband."

Everard Lachlan shook his head. "I'm sorry, my lady," he said—so smoothly that Lillias did not at first hear the implacable authority in his words. "Yer husband has bade me bring ye to him immediately upon yer return to the castle. I must insist ye follow me."

"Ye must insist?" she snapped, her chin coming up in defiance. "Sir, I have awaited my husband's return these nine years. I vow he can wait for me until the morning. I bid ye good night." She tossed away the dark shawl that had shadowed her face and placed her hands upon her hips. On her stool, Aggie cringed and shook her head at her charge, trying frantically to instill caution in her, although she knew it was impossible at this late hour.

Everard stared at the young woman in the travel-stained clothes of a peasant. When she'd first entered, he'd truly thought her a servant as the old woman pretended, but the very tenseness of her shoulders had told him this was the woman he sought. At first, he'd felt consternation and pity for Iain MacLeod to be saddled with this piece of coarse baggage, for he'd long since heard the story of Iain's marriage to a mere child nine years before. Now, that pity disappeared as he stared at the comeliest face he'd seen on either side of the ocean—and eyes of such clear blue color they blazed with passion and fire. Ah, this was a good match for Iain MacLeod, he thought gleefully. She would defy him at every turn. And well his arrogant friend deserved such a wench. Everard felt a moment of regret that she was not a free woman, for he would have claimed her for himself in an instant.

All thought of forcing her to accompany him fled from his mind as he observed the delicate jutting jaw, the compressed lips, the flashing eyes, and a hair so fine and fair a man's fingers fairly itched to twine themselves in its spun gold. Iain was in for a surprise, and suddenly Everard wanted to be there to see the meeting between these two. He'd give her the time she demanded to rest from her travels and dress more appropriately. She deserved that courtesy, something Iain obviously hadn't considered.

"I'll inform yer husband, milady," he said, with another elegant bow, and, taking hold of her hand—the same one that had milked goats but hours before and was stained with soot from the campfire and mud from her travels—he placed a kiss upon it. Wide-eyed, Lillias could but stare at him. With a final nod at Aggie, he left the chamber.

"Lillias!" Aggie cried the minute he disappeared, but Lillias shushed her and hurried to close and bar the door behind their visitor.

"I would na' have sent for ye, child, but he arrived demanding to see ye at once. I told him ye'd gone to the village to nurse a sick child. He was in a terrible fit of temper, worse than Red Rafe ever displayed."

"Worse than Red Rafe?"

"Aye. They call him the Black Beast of Cullayne."

Now that her anger was gone, Lillias's heart quaked at the thought of facing a man more terrible than Red Rafe had been. Automatically she rechecked the wooden bar on the door. At last, sure she was safe for the night, she slid out of her clothes and into the tepid bath, feeling her tired muscles unwind. Aggie had scattered wild herbs in the water, so the perfume rose to her nostrils, further relaxing her. She undid her braid and washed her hair, then lay back with it trailing over the edge of the tub to dry while she soaked and contemplated the events of the day. She thought of the green-eyed stranger who had mesmerized her so on the hillside that she'd nearly forgotten her honor. Obviously he was one of Iain MacLeod's men returned from France.

She should have guessed, but then how could she have anticipated her husband's return when she'd not heard one word from him all these years?

Lillias lay trying to remember the young man she'd married so long ago. He'd been gentle and kind to her then. She remembered that, but he was Red Rafe's son and she wondered how nine years of warfare might have tempered him. How had that kind young man turned into a raging monster that scared even Aggie? She tried to dredge up a face to go with her memory of Iain MacLeod, but none came. She'd been a small, frightened girl and the events of the wedding supper had blessedly driven many of those memories from her head.

Once she'd been grateful for that, now she struggled to push aside the dark fears and open the mirror to her past. Iain was her husband. Surely she had some memory of him. Finally weary of the futile attempt, she stepped from the tub and accepted the towel Aggie held for her.

Suddenly there was a rap at the door. Lillias whirled to stare at it in open fear. Aggie drew in her breath and pressed a hand against her heart. Someone was trying to open the door, but the bar held it closed. The women were silent, waiting. A mighty thud sounded against the door panel and a voice like the roar of a great beast sounded.

"Open this door, immediately."

Lillias clasped the towel about her and slowly crept to the door. "Who is it?" she whispered, and had to repeat herself to be heard.

" 'Tis yer husband, madam, and I demand that ye open this door at once." Iain MacLeod! He sounded like Red Rafe in his worst rage. Lillias shuddered and backed away. Swallowing several times, she found the courage to answer.

"I am tired, my lord. I beg ye let me present myself to ye on the morrow."

"Now, madam!" came the implacable reply. The great oaken plank shivered under the assault of his fist.

A single blow, but how mightily it struck terror within her heart. She tasted the old familiar fear on her tongue and her own fury rose within her. How dare he treat her in this shameful manner? Was she not deserving of some courtesy?

"Tomorrow, my lord!" she cried, her voice equally implacable. "Ye have waited this long to make yer presence known to me, ye can wait until the morrow." There was a dreadful silence on the other side of the door.

Lillias let out her breath. "I think he's gone." A sense of triumph pervaded her. She'd defied her enemy and won. She'd never enjoyed such success with Red Rafe. In the end, he'd always bested her and humiliated her in the process. Obviously his son was not made of the same iron. Rather smugly, she brushed her hands together.

"That's the end of that," she pronounced, and pressed her hand against a yawn. "I'm weary, Aggie. Let's go to bed."

"Aye, my lady," Aggie said warily. Lillias glanced at her old servant. Never had she addressed her with such deference before.

"What's the matter wi' ye, Aggie?" she demanded in a thick Highland brogue. "D'ye na' remember who I am?"

"Aye, child. I remember well," Aggie said. "And I fear for ye. 'Tis better if ye don't test the mettle of Iain MacLeod. 'Tis not for naught the old servants remember him as the Black Beast of Cullayne."

"I'm not afraid of him, Aggie."

"Nay, lass. For yer own safety, I beg ye na' to set yerself to defy and anger Iain MacLeod. He's the whelp of the deevil himself. Sweetness gains a woman more of her heart's desire than ever an angry word."

"Enough, Aggie. I am weary," Lillias admonished. She tumbled into bed and pulled the woolen coverlet around her.

Unbidden came the remembrance of the long, cold ride to Cullayne Castle that terrible night so long ago and of a warm woolen plaid being wrapped around her and strong arms holding her secure. He'd not seemed like a Black Beast then. She'd drawn comfort from Iain MacLeod then, but the memory of him battering at her door drove away all hope that she might again. Sleep claimed her, but not before she felt the green flash of fire and the searing touch of a man's kisses on a windy hillside.

She was startled awake by the sound of pounding outside her door. The whole chamber echoed with the dull thud. Aggie leapt from her bed, crying out. Both women stared with horror at the wooden portal, their only hope of protection from whatever danger threatened them.

The wooden door shuddered beneath the battering. The sound of splintering wood came to them from the darkness. Aggie screamed and threw herself across Lillias, her arms outspread in an effort to protect her beloved charge. The door gave way and men tumbled into the room, still clutching the battering ram they'd used. Lillias pushed Aggie aside and sat up in bed, glaring at the intruders. Now that the door hung in splinters, they stood back, somewhat abashed.

"She is alone save for her serving woman," said a voice that Lillias recognized as Everard Lachlan's. The implication of his words caused her to flush with anger. She strained to see to whom he spoke. Torches had been lit in the corridor. A tall, dark figure moved out of the shadows. Light glinted on blue-black hair and broad shoulders; his face was a dark specter in the poor light.

Impatiently he motioned to the other men. Instantly they gathered up the fragments of the door and made their way back down the dark stairs. Everard Lachlan followed, carrying the torch with him. The dark figure loomed in the doorway. Light from her dying fire cast tortured shadows over his face. She caught here a glimpse of dark eyebrow, there a lean cheek, but nothing more. She had no doubt of the intruder's identity or of his fury, for he stood with legs planted apart, shoulders square, hands on his hips. She felt his rage cross the room like a burning brand.

She would not show fear, she vowed. "What is the meaning of this, my lord?" she demanded. "Have ye na conscience but to batter at my door in the middle of the night?"

"Dinna speak of conscience, my lady, for it seems ye have none." His voice was harsh, intimidating her when she wished not to be. His words were bitter and she wondered at their source. "This is my castle," he continued in a stern tone. There was no kindness, no gentleness, only anger. "I will have no door of this castle barred against me."

"I have no wish to deny ye, my lord," she said sweetly,

for she remembered Aggie's words. "I was but tired and wished to wait until morning . . . when I might present myself to my husband in the best possible light. I would have ye find me pleasing."

Her words should have tamed his fury, but seemed only to infuriate him more.

"And would ye seek to please the devil himself?" he demanded.

"It seems I must," she replied evenly. She sensed she'd bested him. He muttered beneath his breath.

"Did ye say something, my lord?" she asked sweetly.

"I will see ye on the morrow, madam, at first light," he snapped.

"But 'tis my habit to sleep late." She sighed languidly. "I will wait upon ye at the noon meal."

She heard a growl deep in his throat and thought he meant to cross the room and tear at her like some enraged beast. Aggie whimpered, and once again threw herself between Lillias and the dark shadow.

"When the cock first crows, my lady, ye will wait upon me or, by God, my claymore will taste yer flesh." He was gone, stalking down the stairs with barely a glow of light to show the way.

Long after he'd gone, Lillias's heart thundered in her chest like a team of runaway horses. At last, she drew a breath and looked at Aggie.

"So now ye've met the Beast of Cullayne," the frightened old woman whispered.

"Aye, Aggie, I've met him," Lillias replied softly. She was still shaken by the stormy encounter. Aggie had been right. Iain MacLeod was far worse than Red Rafe had ever been. She lay back on her pillow and tried to sleep, but the old terrifying nightmares had returned and she tossed upon her bed and cried out like a wounded child—only this time, it was not Red Rafe and his bloody claymore that brought her terror, but the dark, shadowy countenance of the Black Beast himself.

Chapter 5

A T THE ROOSTER'S first crow, Glenda scurried up the spiral stairs to the tower room, her normally laggard step lent speed by the scowling countenance of the new *Ceann Mor* of Cullayne.

In the kitchens below, the servants had filled the dark hours with tales of Black Iain MacLeod as a youth, each more extravagant than the last. They claimed he'd whelped more bastards on the country wenches than any man alive; his capacity to outdrink and outfight any other man had been established by the time the down on his cheek had turned to a full beard; his knowledge of horseflesh was superseded only by his knowledge of woman flesh; and he'd a temper that bowed to no man, not even his father, Red Rafe MacLeod. The two had often clashed, and many were the times, or so the old-timers claimed, when Red Rafe was forced to back down to his son in an argument.

So the castle wenches had listened with rounded eyes— and later giggled on their pallets as they speculated on the manly attributes of the new chief. More than one vowed to sample the Black Beast of Cullayne's prowess between the sheets and shivered in delicious anticipation, for they'd witnessed his towering rage upon arrival and imagined the fire of his passion. None gave any real thought to his wife who slept in the tower, for such were the ways of men that they sought their pleasures where they were offered.

Listening to the excited young serving maids, Glenda

76

had felt some regret that she was no longer young enough or comely enough to hope to attract the new lord's attention, for she was captivated by his smoldering eyes—like the devil's himself—and broad shoulders, and thought him the handsomest man she'd ever laid eyes on. However, with the advent of dawn and the sound of his furious roar echoing in her ear, she'd forgotten such yearnings and scurried to do his bidding. Now she took in the shattered frame and hinges that had once held a door and hastened to do as she'd been ordered.

"Aggie, get up at once," she cried. "The new laird demands Lillias come to the great hall."

Lillias opened her eyes and regarded the servant. She'd never seen Glenda so agitated, although the silly woman was given to hysterics over the slightest thing. Aggie rose from her stool by the fire. Her face was haggard, her shoulders sagging.

"Have ye not slept, Aggie?" Lillias asked faintly. She knew the nightmares that haunted her made her cry out and Aggie always stayed nearby to comfort her. Her own cheeks were pale with exhaustion. "I'm sorry I've wearied ye so."

"Ye could not help the night terrors that come upon ye, lass. Come now, I'll help ye dress."

"I'm not going down, Aggie. I have a need for more sleep—and I insist that ye go abed once more so we may rest together."

"Nay, child. Do not anger His Lordship further," Aggie chided. While she'd guarded over Lillias in the dark of night, she'd pondered the turn of events, and, finally, near dawn she'd consulted the rune stones. With growing dread, she'd seen the message of death and betrayal and knew such destruction would be wrought by Black Iain of Cullayne.

"Go down and greet him as a proper wife should," she advised. What was predicted could not be changed, but she hoped to soften the heart of the Black Beast and mayhap save Lillias from calamity.

"A proper wife?" Lillias cried, sitting upright in the bed

and glaring at the two women in indignation. "His Lordship has not treated me as a proper wife."

"Aye," Aggie said, nodding. "He *has* been harsh with ye, but 'tis the way with men. They come and go when they please and they expect ye to be waitin' for them when they crook a finger. He was vexed nearly beyond breath when ye were na here upon his arrival. Dinna anger him further."

" 'Tis too bad he was angered," Lillias cried, but with a lilt to her voice that made Aggie suspect she was secretly thrilled at the prospect of having angered Iain MacLeod. "Since he did not see fit to let me know of his coming, how could he be upset that I wasn't here?"

"Still, he was."

"Aye," Glenda confirmed. "We could hear his bellowing all over the bailey. Some said it sounded as if Red Rafe, himself, had returned. Some said it was worse."

Lillias shivered and cast an apprehensive glance at Aggie. Her own fear was reflected in Aggie's eyes, which further unnerved her. For a moment it seemed all her nightmares had returned to haunt her days as well, then she shook them away. Whatever terror the night held for her, the sun shone without; she would never succumb to her fears. She clenched her teeth in resolution.

Aggie saw the jutting chin and knew the belligerent defiance behind such a look. Her own fear for Lillias increased. "God save this wee bairn," she mumbled under her breath.

"What did ye say, Aggie?" Lillias asked.

But the old women shook her head and rose from her stool. "Come, child. We'll dress and go down together."

"Oh, Aggie. Will ye go with me, then?"

"Aye, only hurry, Lillias, hurry. Glenda, go tell His Lordship his lady will attend him soon. She has but to dress."

"Aye!" Glenda cried, and took off with some alacrity— until she remembered she was returning to face the dark fury of the handsome young laird.

In her tower chamber, Lillias sat in the middle of the

bed, her honey-colored hair shimmering around her shoulders and down her back.

"I shall defy him to my last breath, Aggie," she said, her gaze fixed on some distant point Aggie couldn't fathom. For a moment she thought the girl gone daft, then Lillias turned and fixed her with a fierce glare. "He's a hated MacLeod who killed my faither, and one day, I vow, I'll avenge that treachery."

Aggie stared at her in consternation. "Nay, lass. Dinna say such words. We've enough blood spilled over feuds and the like. Would ye have more spilled?"

"I would have my faither's death avenged," Lillias answered.

" 'Twas Red Rafe who caused yer faither's death, na' the son. He was kind t'ye and gave ye his name to protect ye. Ye've enjoyed safety and peace in yer life because of him."

"Not peace, Aggie. Not while I live at Cullayne Castle. I'll know no peace until I am, at last, back at Dunbeath among my own clansmen and with my faither's death avenged, if not on Red Rafe, then on his son." The words hung between them. Both women were surprised at them and the passion that prompted them.

Lillias had never guessed how deeply ran her hatred of the MacLeod chief. Having spoken of her feelings made them more real—and now they'd been voiced, she could no longer deny them. And having acknowledged her need for revenge, she could no longer ignore that the hot blood of Robert McGinnis ran through her veins. She could never be passive as her mother had been, pining to death in a convent, hiding away from the turmoil and passion and fury of life itself. Her breath quickened and her body grew warm from the blood flowing so swiftly through her veins. Impatiently she threw aside her covers.

"Come, Aggie. I must dress, for on this day, I meet my husband and become the mistress of Cullayne Castle."

She stalked across the chamber to the window with such a regal air that Aggie felt her heart lift. Aye, this was the bonny wee lass of Robert McGinnis, Earl of Mamore, and no man could put her down, not even Black Iain MacLeod. Lillias gazed out the window at the loch.

"I shall never see it from this direction again, Aggie," she said in a faraway voice. "For I shall never return to this chamber again." There was an air of prophecy about the words and Aggie shivered, remembering her own fevered superstitions in the middle of the night. Lillias turned and met her gaze. "Dinna fear, Aggie," she said lightly. "Come. Help me dress."

Numbly Aggie nodded and hurried to the clothespress to pull out Lillias's best gown. "Ye'll be looking little more than a servant," she grumbled, shaking out an undergown of plain linen that had been dyed grayish blue from the roots of the yellow flag. It was a simple gown, cut close to the body before flaring into a full skirt below the hips. The only adornment was a simple braid sewn around the square neckline.

The gown had once fit Lillias perfectly; now the tight bodice pushed her young breasts upward, so the neckline was no longer modest. She tugged at the bodice, then caught up Mary's fine woolen shawl and pinned it around her with a plain metal brooch. Impatiently she waited while Aggie braided her hair and coiled it around each ear. Although she was now anxious to meet her husband, she would look her best when she stood before him.

"I'll not need ye to go with me, after all, Aggie," she said. Pride was in every line of her figure, as with head high she made her way from the tower and across the bailey.

Strange men and hounds mingled in one corner of the courtyard, reclining on a low wall as if they'd just been rousted and were not yet awake. They cast Lillias a baleful glare as she passed, and she perceived they'd been made to rise from their pallets in the main hall in order to give privacy for the laird's meeting with his wife.

None of them looked happy, and she guessed Iain MacLeod's high-handed methods didn't sit well with them, either. Then she spied a familiar face and her smile died away. Peadair McDermott had just poured a bucket of well water over himself and stood shaking his head from side to side. He halted when he spied her, then, unable to meet her gaze, looked away.

So the green-eyed stranger and Peadair McDermott were part of Iain MacLeod's coterie. She glanced along the line of men, wondering if the soldier who called himself Hunter was among them. She caught no glimpse of a raven-haired head towering over the other men. Quickly she turned away. She must forget him. Iain MacLeod was home to claim his wife, and although she intended she would never share his bed, nonetheless she must remain forever virginal and circumspect. So be it. She'd tasted a man's kisses once on a sunlit hillside. She'd carry the memory with her for the rest of her days, and a bittersweet memory it would be. For she would be forever reminded of what she might have had if not for the MacLeods, blast their black hearts!

She climbed the steps and made her way to the great hall, pausing in the doorway to study the room that had been the scene of her humiliation on more than one occasion. The echo of ribald laughter mocked her even now. The hall was a cold, drafty place in winter and lacking in nearly all creature comforts year-round. Though large enough to host a banquet of considerable size, the chamber boasted no rich tapestries on the rough stone walls, no cushions on its benches, and no fresh-smelling rushes on the heavy plank floors. During Red Rafe's day, such refinements were spurned. Drinking and carousing had been the order of the day, and servants seldom had time to clear away the remnants of one meal before time to commence serving the next. Red Rafe's hounds snarled and snapped over the scraps of food that had been dumped onto the floor from wooden trenches seldom washed. Aggie had shuddered with revulsion and prepared meals for Lillias and herself in the tower.

Only the fireplace was adequate, tall enough for a man to stand upright and wide enough to hold a full tree trunk, so it gave off a cheery warmth if and when the slatternly servants bestirred themselves to bring wood. Even in Red

Rafe's day, such slovenliness went unpunished as long as they kept his cup filled to the brim.

A trestle table had been set up before the hearth; Red Rafe's carved high-backed chair had been placed at its head. Despite the early hour, the hall seemed empty, except for a servant who carried a pitcher and a goblet to the table. The goblet was filled and a hand reached from the shadows and lifted it. Now that her eyes had adjusted to the dim light, Lillias saw that someone was seated before the fire in Red Rafe's chair. The flames reflected on a dagger's handle and a man's leather leggings. Lillias started, imagining for a moment that it might be Red Rafe himself seated there—and that she was a child again, summoned to stand before him and endure his taunts. She shook herself free of the image. Red Rafe was dead and she was no longer a child. Her jaw jutted in rebellion.

"At last, ye've decided to make yerself known to me, wife," a voice called. Since it was far different from the rough growl of the man who'd bombarded her chamber door, she thought Everard Lachlan had spoken. Then a hand was raised and she was motioned forward, much like a reluctant child. "Come, come. Don't be coy. I've no time for a woman's games."

"Nor have I time for a man's games, my lord," Lillias replied, striding forward until she stood at the other end of the long trestle table.

Iain MacLeod, the Black Beast of Cullayne, known to his men and half the fighting force of the French king as the Black Hunter, watched her approach. Though her clothes were homespun linen, the same as the peasants wore, and the style was outdated, she carried herself with such regal bearing that she might have been a queen.

Her face was a pale oval with smudges beneath the wide blue eyes, testifying to a sleepless night. He had little pity. Had he not spent the same night pacing his chamber floor, cursing her to hell and gone? She looked innocent and serene, but he knew her innocence to be a sham—and hadn't he experienced her defiant, wayward nature last night when she locked her door against him and failed to appear when summoned? He clenched his fists and waited.

Lillias tried to peer into the shadows, so she might study the Black Beast of Cullayne more thoroughly. "I bid ye welcome to Cullayne Castle," she said pleasantly enough, for she meant to use her wiles and put him off-guard. " 'Tis many years since last ye were here. If ye'd but sent word ahead, we would have prepared for yer homecoming."

"I preferred to surprise all, especially my wife. I have learned much in so doing," he answered. Now, he leaned forward, so the firelight played on lean, tanned cheeks and reflected green fire in his eyes.

Lillias stared at him, at first uncomprehending. Then she started with recognition. Her knees trembled as if they might collapse beneath her.

"Ye!" she gasped, taking a step backward. Her eyes were wide with shock.

"Aye. 'Tis me." Iain MacLeod leapt to his feet. Now that his face was revealed, she saw the fury that drew his handsome features into a snarling grimace. "Come, wife. Ha' ye no kiss for me now, or d'ye save them for any wayfarer ye come upon in the high meadow?"

"How dare ye!" Lillias cried, aghast at his accusing tone. " 'Tis trickery ye've used, and ye judge me by that. I knew not that it was ye."

"That, my lady, is abundantly clear. God's teeth, woman, how many men have claimed ye in my absence?"

"None, my lord. Ye do me wrong to suggest such a thing." Lillias was shaken at this revelation. To have her wayward behavior caught out in such a manner was far more humiliating than anything Red Rafe might have devised. "Nor have I ever kissed a man before."

"Woman, ye are a liar!" He jabbed an accusing finger in the air and stalked around the table. Lillias retreated, keeping the table between them.

"Nay, my lord. I speak the truth. Never have I allowed a man's lips to touch mine. I am a virtuous woman."

"Hah!" he cried. "I ha' witnessed yer innocent virtue.

D'ye na know I can take yer life for this? D'ye na give it a thought?"

"My—my life?" Lillias faltered. "Ye mean ye could kill me?"

"Aye, and none would say me wrong once it was known ye dallied with a wayfarer along the path."

"But I did not. Ye know that well. I ran away."

"Only after ye let me take liberties wi' ye no man should take wi' a married woman."

"Should not, but often do," Lillias cried, smarting at the fury of his harangue. " 'Tis a mockery between men and women. Ye may do as ye wish wi' other maidens and never answer for it, but I must stand accused of wrongdoing even when I am innocent. 'Tis too much!"

For a moment he was speechless in the face of her passionate denial. "I've done no wrong. I'm innocent, for ye were my husband."

"Aye, but ye dinna ken that when ye let me hold ye and caress ye like ye were a common maid," he stormed. "How long have ye taken up this peasant disguise to sport with the common folk and their men?"

His outraged tone had angered her beyond endurance. She put her hands on her hips and squared off at him. "I have never done so before ye came upon me in the meadow. Ye swept me off my feet . . . as well ye meant to do."

"I felt no resistance, my lady," he jeered.

"I—I tried," she faltered. "Ye are a man of the world and I but an untried country maid—and ye sought to seduce me, sir. That ye did not does me credit." Anger uncurled within her. "Ye have not come home or sent me a word about yer health for nine years, and, when at last ye return to yer homeland, ye dally along the way with milkmaids and the like. What right have ye to reprimand me?"

"The right of a husband, *baille*." He hurled the insulting epithet at her.

"I am not—nor have I ever been—any man's whore," she cried. "As for yer rights as a husband, ye never acted as one. Never a word from ye."

"D'ye miss me then?" he asked of a sudden, his manner changed. If the sparkle in his eyes was not amusement, then it must surely have been cynicism. "Ye sound like a wife who's jealous," he taunted. "D'ye long for my return?" For a moment she glimpsed the handsome stranger from the Highland meadow.

"Rid yerself of that notion, my lord," she answered, her cheeks stained with color, her eyes flashing. "I had no desire of yer return. I had no knowledge of ye to wish ye well or ill, other than that ye were Red Rafe's son."

Iain studied the girl before him. He remembered well the frightened, dirty-faced child he married so long ago. He'd wondered about her over the years, whether she was alive or had been taken by a fever or in a raid, but he'd never been curious enough to try to find out. Anger toward his father had driven him away; pride had kept him from ever coming back.

He'd never guessed the pitiful child had grown into such a beautiful woman. Her glorious honey-gold hair was tamed beneath a cloth cowl, revealing the perfection of her delicate brow and chin. Her pale skin seemed translucent in the gloomy hall. He remembered her on the high hill; the alpine glow had seemed to warm her skin until she tasted of sun and wind. Even now, his blood quickened at the remembered scent and taste of her.

Last night, when his men had battered down her door, he'd seen her in her bed, swathed in a virginal white nightshift with her golden hair spilling around her in wanton disarray. Even in his anger, the thought had crossed his mind to throw out his men and the old crone who served her and claim his husbandly rights.

But outrage at her indiscretion had fired him then and did so now, so his lips tightened and his eyes blazed with fury. How dare she stand there before him, defiant and unrepentant? He'd strike her down to her knees. He raised his hand to do so, but the look in her eyes was such that he swung away from her and pounded his fist against the wooden table.

"Is a man wrong to have some expectations concerning

his wife, madam? That she remain faithful to him when he's away at war?''

"And is a wife wrong to have certain expectations regarding her husband, my lord? Ye have no cause to doubt my virtue. But I have entertained no such expectations of ye. Ye are but the whelp of Red Rafe, and like him in every way.'' She spun to leave the room, but he was there, his large hand gripping her arm painfully. He spun her around, his green eyes like emeralds that burned to the very depths of hell itself.

"Were ye a man, I'd strike ye down for that remark," he growled.

"Were I a man, I'd strike ye dead in revenge for my faither's death," she retorted. Her own eyes blazed with hatred for Red Rafe's son. His grip on her loosened, and in that instant she wrenched away from him, stalking across the hall to the great door.

Outside, in the sunlight, she blinked. Now that she'd made her dramatic exit, she knew not where to go, for she'd vowed never to return to the tower chamber, and so she would not. Deliberately she set off across the bailey, left the front gate of the castle, and blindly made her way through the village. She hadn't been aware of where her steps had automatically directed her until she was well away from the village and its surrounding fields and climbing high into the hills.

The memory of Iain MacLeod's threat hung over her head like a black cloud. She knew full well that death was often the result of a woman's infidelity, either at the hands of a maddened husband or by her own. Yet, she'd done nothing. She was innocent. Even if she had given in to Iain's blandishments on the hillside, she would not have been an unfaithful wife.

For one brief moment, she wished she had done so. She imagined the fire and splendor of a coupling with the man who'd called himself Hunter and became breathless from her imaginings. But Hunter and Iain MacLeod were one and the same—and her maiden's fantasies were but that. The dashing, attentive man on the hillside was an illusion.

Still, she felt regret that she'd run away. Ha! 'Twould have served the Black Beast right to lie with her like some common wench and then find she was his wife. The sheer idiocy of it drove her along the path.

She didn't hear the thunder of hooves until the rider was nearly upon her. Seeing Iain MacLeod's scowling face, she lifted her skirts high above her ankles and sprinted up the path. His black charger was much swifter than she. Effortlessly he overtook her. A strong arm closed around her waist and she was lifted off her feet, kicking and crying out in protest. Roughly he clamped her against his side, so she felt the heat and muscle of him.

"Put me down," she cried, flailing at him with her fists. He seemed unaffected by her blows.

In her struggles, the stitching of her too tight bodice gave way, revealing smooth white breasts. The cloth cowl fell from her head and her hair tumbled around them, fanning over the padded shoulder of his leather vest. A wind blew honeyed strands over his face, blinding him. He cursed and tossed his head, trying to free himself from the silken web. The sleek black stallion reared, then trotted off the path.

"Let me go, ye beast!" she demanded, and screamed when his thick-muscled arm released her, so she dropped to the ground. Soft grass cushioned her fall. She leapt to her feet and tried to dart away, but he'd dismounted; now his long arm reached out and caught her around the waist.

"Release me at once!" she commanded.

"Nay, wife," he answered, setting her on her feet, so she faced him. His green eyes were dark and stormy and warned of danger. "Listen to me and listen well," he ordered. "There's na place for ye to run."

"I'll return to my own clan," she answered.

"Ye're my wife and ye'll do nothing of the sort. Ye've carried the MacLeod name for nine years and ye'll take it to yer grave." His warning did not go unnoticed. Fear and rage mingled in her breast.

"Kill me then and be done with it!" she cried. "Ye've killed my faither. Be done with me, but know this, Iain MacLeod, Black Beast of Cullayne, I'll come back to haunt ye. Ye'll never know a day of certainty, no, nor a night of rest upon yer bed. I'll haunt yer every step until ye hang yerself from the tower window to be done with me."

He couldn't help but admire her. She stood with her head thrown back, seeming not to know that the rounded tops of her breasts were revealed to his gaze. Or else she felt no shame, he thought cynically. The wind molded her skirts to her long, slim legs and blew her hair from her like golden wings on an angel. But the glint in her eyes was not angelic. It hinted of a proud defiance that could only have come from the devil. Iain thought of the frightened little girl who'd turned to him so trustingly nine years before. She'd grown to a magnificent woman. Admiration turned to vexation and he turned away from her.

"Aye, lass, ye bring my blood up. I could lay ye back on the grass and take my pleasure with ye."

"Nay, my lord. I'll lay in the grass with no man until I'm ready!" she snapped.

"Ye were ready enough at the shieling." He was satisfied to see her blush. "Have na fear I'll touch ye now. I'll not be pleasuring myself after others." He swung away from her; her shoulders sagged.

Her laugh was bitter. "Ye'll na be pleasuring yerself after others," she mocked, in a thick brogue. "It's a virgin yer wantin' then, yet how can there be any virgins in the land when ye and yer men tarried all along the way to seduce each maiden ye saw? Ye dinna make sense, Iain MacLeod."

"Sense enough," he cried. "I have no particular preference for an unbroken virgin to give me my manly pleasures, but a wife is another matter."

"Indeed, my lord?" One golden eyebrow arched as she faced him, bold and unrepentant. She was elated to see how his imaginings had troubled him. Let him think her a wanton. She knew the truth of it.

"Aye, lass. Ye possess na sense of honor and fidelity. Wi' ye raised here at Red Rafe's castle, I should have expected little else." He swung around to meet her gaze and Lillias saw something of the kind young man she'd wed years before; her heart softened despite herself.

" 'Tis truth. I barely gave ye a thought all these years—
not until I stepped aboard the sailing ship to return to
Scotland. I thought of ye then and I dreamed of siring a
houseful of strong sons and of improving the MacLeod
lands, so all prospered, laird and peasant alike. Standing on
that hillside yesterday, watching ye run away from yer
shame and hearing yer name, I saw that dream dashed. By
God I'll beget no sons on loins soiled by the seed of other
men."

"Then set me aside," she flared, unmoved by his words.
He deserved to suffer a thousand hells for believing as he
did of her. She'd not be the one to enlighten him. "Send me
back to Dunbeath Castle. I'll find a husband among my
own clansmen."

Iain's eyes narrowed at her defiant words. She no longer
denied his accusations. "And rear spawns to set upon us
when they're half grown?" he growled, and the troubled
man who'd spoken so tenderly of his dream of sons and
prosperity was gone. In his place stood the ruthless Black
Iain MacLeod. "Nay, lady." He spat out the word. His
rough hands reached for her, snatching at the torn bodice of
her gown. He did not rip it away as she feared, but he held
her thus, thrusting his face forward, so it was mere inches
from her. She could feel the heat and roughness of his
hands against her breasts.

"I would na set ye aside for yer misdeeds, nor will I yet
plunge my dagger into yer soft breast, although I'd be jus-
tified to do so. I ha' a use for ye, Lilli, and ye can buy yer
life and mayhap yer freedom to return to yer kinsmen, if ye
do my bidding."

She stared into his dark green eyes. They were like moss
on the dark side of a mountain pine. They gave no reflec-
tion of light, only of shadow, and she feared in that instant
as she had not before. "What d'ye wish of me?" she asked,
looking away from him.

He released her then, so abruptly that she fell back in the
grass, her legs sprawled out before her. He towered over
her. "I would have ye continue as my wife."

"What are ye saying? Are ye daft?" she cried, sitting up.

"Ye dinna want me as yer wife, ye do want me as yer wife. Which is it to be?"

"I ha' not tarried only with the maidens on my way home," he said. "I ha' put my ear to the ground and found that my enemies are more numerous than I feared. My faither raided the lands and villages of the surrounding clans until they're chompin' at the bit t'seek their revenge upon us. The McCulloughs to the south of us, the MacDonalds to the north. I traveled through the MacBain land and I spoke wi' Douglas MacBain himself. He's promised his support, but I dinna trust him."

"I've heard ye've captured Angus McCullough?" Lillias asked curiously.

"Aye. He's t'answer to King James himself for his crimes."

"Well ye've made yer presence felt since yer return. Ye seem t'ha' na need of my help."

"Nay, Lilli, 'tis not true. I need all the help ye can spare. I have no allies, save the McGinnises to the east."

"What makes ye think the McGinnises would ally themselves with the MacLeods," she sneered. "My clan's been enemies wi' yers for more years than I was born."

"Aye, but wi' ye as my wife, I ha' a better chance to win their support than if ye're na."

"Ye dinna ken the half of it, Iain MacLeod. After ye left, the McGinnis council met to elect a new chief to replace my faither. At that time they decided to end the feud with Red Rafe. They exchanged me for a piece of land, so ye see, ye've na made such a bargain after all." She got to her feet and bent to brush at her skirts. He suspected she did it to hide the tears in her eyes, for he'd heard the break in her voice. Aye, she was a bonny lass with a strong disposition. He felt regret that she hadn't remained constant. She would have made a bonny wife.

"Ye're all I ha' as a tie to the McGinnises," he said bleakly. "Whether ye've a mind to or na, ye'll stay here and be my wife."

"I'd sooner rot in hell!" she snapped, straightening, and he saw her eyes were dark and stormy as a summer sky in a rain squall. "I'll na bed wi' the son of the man who killed my faither."

"I'll na ask ye to," he thundered. "I ha' na desire for used flesh. But by God's passion, I ha' need of ye and ye'll stay. I'll make peace wi' my neighbors and see Cullayne prosper at its own hand, na by cattle reivin' from those round about. Cullayne Castle's been a bachelor's lair far too long. I need ye t' give it a woman's touch and make it a proud place to ha' visitors, the King of Scotland, even, should he choose t'come."

She stared at him, listening to his words. Once again he'd spoken of peace and prosperity on MacLeod land and she was compelled to believe him sincere. "Ye have a mighty ambition, Iain MacLeod."

"Aye, that I have. I lived among the French for these many years and I saw some things I have a mind to use at Cullayne. The English nobility call us barbaric and uncivilized savages, and well they might—if they see the likes of my faither and chiefs like Angus McCullough."

"Would ye be like the French, then?" she asked. "I've heard they dress like women and wear makeup—and take little boys to their beds."

"Never like the French," he snapped. "I've na' forgotten I'm a Scotsman, a Highlander at that, and I won't be tryin' t'be better than my blood, nor will I be less than a loyal Scotsman. But if Scotland is ever to be important in world events, we must learn to temper our ways a bit." He met her gaze and laughter flashed behind his eyes. Gone was the black visage of his rage; in its place was the handsome rogue who'd wooed her in the braes. Still, she thought of her father's head upon the platter, a barbaric act, indeed, and all thought of passion died.

"The McGinnises hate all the MacLeods," she reminded him, settling back on the grass. He joined her there, sprawling his long legs before him. "They always have. I kinna change that."

" 'Tis na so, Lilli," he said roughly. "I've heard the story many a time. The feud between our clans began when Red Rafe asked for Margaret McCullough's hand in marriage.

She was promised to him, but she had no wish to marry Red Rafe, although he was already chief of all the Mac-Leod clan and his holdings were vast. My mither had died of a fever and I was a wee lad at the time. Yet still I remember going to McCullough Castle and sitting beside Lady Margaret. She was a gentle girl; I think my faither scared her. She always looked sad."

Long-dead feelings stirred in Lillias as she heard him speak of her mother as a frightened young girl. "Aye," she said softly. "That was forever the way with her."

"My faither did not trust old James McCullough to keep his promise," Iain went on, "so he left a spy at McCullough Castle. Word came that Margaret wished to marry Robert McGinnis. Red Rafe rode all night to reach McCullough Castle, but Margaret had already left. She eloped wi' yer faither."

"She must have been very brave," Lillias said, and fell silent remembering the tense words between her mother and Hannah during Red Rafe's raid on Dunbeath Castle.

"So ye see. The feud dinna start until yer mither abandoned her promise to my faither and chose another man. After that, Red Rafe raided McGinnis and McCullough land every chance he got. I remember him swearing he'd exact revenge by taking their firstborn. He was hoping for a son."

"So was my faither," Lillias said softly.

"Red Rafe waited for years for a son to be born to Margaret and Robert McGinnis, but there were no more children. By now ye were a wee girl and Red Rafe was in need of allies. He decided that if the offspring of the two clans were united, the alliance would be solidified. No doubt, that was the reason the king decided to let the marriage stand."

Lillias looked away from him, her lips compressed in anger. "The marriage would not have stood if my mither had appealed to the king herself."

Hearing the pain in her voice, Iain was silent. Then he reached forward and took her hand in his. "Poor lass. Ye've had a hard time of it," he said, "and none of it of yer making."

She turned to him then, caught by the gentleness in his voice. This was the man who'd protected her years before. She looked into the green eyes and marveled at the tenderness there. Tentatively she smiled, though her lashes shimmered with unshed tears.

"We've both been hurt by these feuds, Lilli. Let's end them if we can and bring peace for our children."

"Our children?" she asked. He dropped her hand.

"Aye, for I'll ha' my sons. God blast ye, lass!" He got to his feet and paced. "Why could ye na ha' been a proper wife, waitin' for yer man t'come home t'ye? I find ye comely, lass. I've made no bones about that, but I'll na' be cuckold and be the laughingstock of my clan. How many men ha' ye lain wi'?"

She thought to tell him the truth, for his words echoed her heart's own longings, but she'd vowed to revenge her father's death, and so she would. She smiled at him sweetly. "I have lost count, my lord."

"The deevil take ye then." He stalked to his mount, gathered his reins—but before springing into the saddle he turned back to her. "Ye'll be my wife in name only."

"Will na' yer friends laugh to think ye're married to a strumpet?"

"Aye, where did ye hear that word, lass?" he asked, surprised at her sophistry when she'd never left Cullayne Castle.

" 'Twas whispered in my ear by a passing wayfarer," she replied.

His face grew dark with fury. "No man will laugh at Iain MacLeod!" he snapped. "For I'll kill any man who does. So, too, will I kill any man who boasts of having been wi' ye. Have a care, lass, that ye dinna bring a man to his death unjustly."

Lillias blanched before his fierce gaze. "I tell ye once again, I have known no man. Believe me or not, as ye wish. But ye've made yerself a bigger fool in my eyes, Black Iain." For a minute she thought he might strike her, so fierce was his expression. Then one black eyebrow raised and he threw back his head and laughed.

" 'Tis but one way we can determine the truth of yer claim, lass." At first, she did not understand his meaning, then her face flamed. "Aye, the thought of it has stilled yer tongue. Come, wife," he called. "There is much between us to settle, but I have spent enough time at debating the matter. I have business at the castle."

He leapt into the saddle and leaned down to offer his hand. For a moment Lillias thought of rejecting his truce, but the dancing lights in his green eyes made her clasp his hand and place her foot in the stirrup. He pulled her up into the saddle, settling her in front of him, and turned the charger back toward Cullayne. Thus, she entered the castle a second time, cradled in the strong embrace of Iain MacLeod.

Chapter 6

"T HE VIEW IS not as good as the tower room," Aggie
said, staring out the window, "but the rest of it is
grand."

Several days had passed since Iain's return to Cullayne
and he'd been busy strengthening his position as clan chief.
One of the things he'd insisted upon was that Lillias leave
the tower and move into the living quarters of the castle. Despite her resolve to just that end, she contrarily protested, for
she was determined to remain defiant. However, she had to
concede to his argument that her presence in the main castle
would present a unified front to the rest of the clan members
and to their neighbors.

Furthermore, he wished to move Angus McCullough
from the castle dungeon to more humane quarters in the
tower. She had no choice but to agree. Iain went away with
a smirk of triumph on his face—and she took solace in the
fact that she had at last taken her rightful place as mistress
of Cullayne Castle.

Aggie was beside herself with glee. At last, Lillias was
being accorded the respect her title deserved. The loyal
serving woman never tired of comparing their new circumstances with what they'd once endured.

Considering the condition of the rest of the castle, the
private chamber allotted Lillias was surprisingly elegant,
with fine old tapestries hanging from the walls, thick cushions on the window seats, and quilted throw covers of

faded silk upon the bed. Mullioned windows of rare leaded glass opened onto the inner court, although stout wooden shutters reminded her that Cullayne Castle was the seat of the MacLeod clan and therefore nearly impregnable.

"D'ye suppose Red Rafe slept here?" Aggie asked, fingering the silk coverlet.

Lillias looked around the spacious chamber. There was a melancholy air of a place untouched by passion and human warmth. The room seemed more a sanctuary, and she sensed it had never been the setting of the debauchery and lechery of Red Rafe and his cohorts.

"Nay," she answered. "This was the room Red Rafe prepared for my mither."

"Lady Margaret? Why, she'd have nothing to do wi' the likes of Red Rafe MacLeod."

" 'Tis true," Lillias said, "but he never knew that. Iain told me the story the day he returned. Red Rafe wanted my mither for a bride, but she'd have naught to do with him. 'Tis why he feuded so long and hard with the McCulloughs and the McGinnises."

"Poor fool," Aggie said, shaking her head. "Did he love her then?"

"As much as he was able to love," Lillias replied, thinking of the passions of the coarse chief, then she remembered her father's severed head and the stirrings of pity left her. She'd have no compassion for anyone of the MacLeod clan, she told herself fiercely—until she thought of Mary McFerris and Helen MacEwan. She could never turn her back on their friendship.

Sighing, she sank down on a tufted-cushioned window seat and stared out the open window. Aggie was right. The loch could not be seen from here. Rather the window looked down on the nether bailey, where Iain's men wrestled one another in the grass.

"Did ye hear Lord MacLeod and his men return late last night?" she murmured, watching the men below.

"Aye, and a terrible racket they made, my lady."

"I'm afraid I slept right through it," Lillias said, though they both knew what she spoke was an untruth. She had lain in her bed, tense and anxious, long after horse and men had been bedded for the night. Would Iain MacLeod make demands on her? she'd wondered, and finally, when no knock sounded at her door, she'd fallen asleep again. She leaned out the window, so she might search for Iain MacLeod among the men.

One brute, taller and wider than the others, pinned every man who confronted him. From her window, Lillias could hear the men's shouts of laughter and challenge as they flung themselves at the giant.

"Ho, Leith. Ye've not been t'see the bonny Wida Fergus, of late," they cried. "Elsewise, ye'd na ha' the strength and fury of a maddened boar."

"An' ye've been too much among the village lasses, Tavis." The giant grunted, tossing another man aside as if he were a child. "Ye've sapped ye're strength between their milky thighs. Should the McCulloughs raid us naow, ye'd ha' t'run wi' yer tail between yer legs like a hound dog what's been soundly beaten."

"I'll neever run from the McCulloughs, by God's blood," Tavis declared hotheadedly. "I kin beat a McCullough wi' my hand tied behind my back and my claymore dull as a goat's arse."

"But, ye've neever been able ta take me down," Leith hooted.

Tavis made a lunge, and Leith, head lowered like an enraged bull, stood solid and absorbed the blow. Tavis staggered as if the wind had gone out of his sails and fell to the ground. Leith picked him up and tossed him over his shoulder. Tavis lay unmoving, and Leith stood over him, his great belly shaking with laughter.

"Is there na man among ye who kin provide a challenge ta me?" he demanded, arms akimbo, great fists planted on his broad hips.

"Aye, Leith. I'll fight ye," Iain called, stepping into the grassy circle. His men cheered.

Lillias drew a sharp breath. She'd not seen him for nearly a fortnight, not since their discussion on the hillside his first day back. He'd spent the time in between coming and going, visiting his border lords and acquainting himself with his holdings. She'd kept out of his way, not certain of what was expected of her. Now she sat staring down at him, struck anew by his handsome features.

He'd thrown aside his plaid and was garbed only in a quilted tunic, belted at the waist, and hose that revealed powerful, muscular thighs. His head was bare and the sun struck blue-black lights in his dark hair. His teeth were bared in a feral grin, and Lillias imagined that even from her distance she could see the dangerous green lights in his eyes.

"It's not seemly for a chief to be put down in front of his men," Leith crowed, but he brought up his hands in a defensive gesture, obviously ready to do battle.

"Aye, and I like a man who's cocky," Iain declared, stripping off his tunic.

Lillias drew in her breath as she observed his broad shoulders and the rippling muscles beneath his smooth skin. Involuntarily her breasts tingled at the remembered contact of that hard chest. Without the long tunic, his neat buttocks, flat stomach, and muscular thighs were more obviously revealed. A flush stained her cheeks as her gaze darted to the bulge between his powerful thighs.

Though as tall as Leith and broad of shoulder, Iain was no match for the giant in bulk. Lillias watched as the men began to circle, their powerful arms raised shoulder height, their hands opened, ready to grab hold of their opponent or fend him off as the chance provided itself. Warily they circled, and Lillias noticed that Iain did not waste energy in boasts. His expression was serious, his darting gaze wary.

Unnerved, Leith made the first attack, rushing at Iain. Even from where she sat, Lillias saw the folly of his action, for Iain danced out of his reach, grabbing hold of the big man's shoulder as he passed, propelling him forward with so great a force that he lost his balance and sprawled face downward in the grass. With a bellow, Leith sprang to his feet and shook his head. A crafty look came over his face as he lumbered toward Iain on cat's feet—as dainty as a dancer, despite his size. Iain dodged away, Leith feinted, and his long arms came out to curl around Iain, wrapping him in a bear hug. Lillias imagined she could hear Iain's ribs cracking.

"D'ye give, O mighty laird?" Leith cried.

Iain made no answer. Lillias jumped up in alarm and leaned out the window, her long golden braid spilling over the sill.

"Let him go, ye brute!" she cried. "Ye'll crush him."

Startled at this turn of events, Leith's attention was drawn away from his opponent. In that instant, Iain struck him on either side of his head with his fists. Bellowing with pain, Leith released Iain and put a hand over his ears. Iain flipped him over his head. Leith landed in a puddle, sending the geese honking as they hurriedly waddled away. The men's laughter mingled with the cacophony of sound.

The defeated man lay still for a moment, drawing air back into his lungs, then slowly he sat up. " 'Tis na' fair!" he cried. "Yer lady called from the window."

"She's afeared for ye, Iain," someone heckled, and the other men laughed even harder.

"My lady?" Iain echoed, and turned to stare up at the sight of Lillias leaning out the window, her braid dangling like a golden cord, her cheeks flushed, and her eyes flashing.

"Good morning t'ye, my lady," he called, bowing with an exaggerated courtly gesture that drew a smile from Lillias, despite her annoyance at his teasing. " 'Tis good t'return t'my home for such a sight as greets me from yer window."

"Good morning, my lord," she answered. "And welcome home t'ye. Did all go well?"

"Aye, though we ride soon for Glengarry. My chieftains come to the castle in three days' time t'sup wi' us. Can ye arrange a banquet on such short notice?"

"Of course, my lord," she answered, and drew back inside and closed the leaded window with a snap. What was she to do? she wondered. She'd never arranged such a thing in her life.

" 'Tis fitting we're here in these fine quarters, my lady,"

Aggie said, unaware of the byplay outside the window. Her round face glowed with satisfaction to see Lillias in her rightful place, at last. She seemed never to tire of discussing it.

" 'Tis only temporary, Aggie," Lillias snapped, "for I've struck a bargain wi' the devil himself. When he's well seated as the new chief and has allied himself wi' his neighbors, he'll return us to our own clan."

"My lady!" Aggie cried. "Oh, t'visit my mither's grave site would ease my heart after these long years."

"It's been hard to live here away from yer family, hasn't it, Aggie?" Lillias asked absently.

The old servant nodded. "But I've never regretted the coming, my lady. My mither loved ye fiercely. She's resting well in her grave to know I came and took care of ye. Aye, the Black Beast of Cullayne he may well be, but 'twas a good, kind thing Iain McLeod did when he kidnapped me to be with ye."

"A good, kind thing would have been if he'd returned me to my home," Lillias wailed, wringing her hands. Nervously she paced the floor, wondering what was required of her. She'd taken her meals here in her room since moving into the castle. Feeling ineffectual and uncertain of her new role, she'd languished, not tackling the problems head-on as she should have.

"Child, what troubles ye?" Aggie demanded, finally noticing her agitation.

"He demands too much of me," Lillias cried. "He has no right to expect me to be his wife and live here and make this great old pile of stones into a home as fine as Dunbeath. It can't be done."

"Aye, he wants a home to be proud of and 'tis yer job as mistress of Cullayne to give him what he wants."

"D'ye care for him then, Aggie?" Lillias asked in amazement. "D'ye forget the taking of my faither's life?"

"Nay, but Iain McLeod dinna do it. Ye kinna blame the boy for the faither's sins—or for him wantin' a better way now."

"Ye sound fairly smitten wi' the man, Aggie. Ha' ye forgotten how he harassed us in the night upon his first arrival? And now he has returned. Am I to suffer such treatment again?"

" 'Twas na so bad, my lady. The Beast seems not nearly so fearsome as I thought at first."

"Bah, so much for yer loyalty, Aggie," Lillias commented wryly. "Ye've become a MacLeod as surely as I stand. Still, I need yer help, for he wants a banquet served for his chieftains in three days' time."

"Then ye've forgotten about seeking yer revenge on him?"

"Nay, I've not forgotten," Lillias replied. "But I've taken yer advice, Aggie. Sweet words draw better than angry ones. I would have Iain MacLeod trust me—and when I go back to my own people, I will take with me the knowledge that I have brought shame and disgrace and even death to Cullayne Castle for all time."

"Ye'll bring it down on yer head, too, if ye're not careful."

"I have known little pride in my life, Aggie. I've been humiliated time and again at the hands of the MacLeods. Shame at my own hands will mean naught to me."

Aggie shook her head and grumbled under her breath. "In the meantime, my lady, ye must learn to run a castle— aye, and supervise the servants if ye're to have a suitable table for his guests."

"Aye." Lillias shook her head. "I have no knowledge of these things, Aggie. What am I to do? I fear I may not please my Lord Black Beast."

"Humph! He will be pleased, my lady, if ye begin wi' the kitchen. Glenda says his curses foul the air when his meal is brought. He would be shamed to have such swill served to his guests."

"Aye, ye're right," Lillias cried. "And I'm of a mind to tackle the kitchen help now. Will ye come with me, Aggie?"

"Wi' pleasure," Aggie answered, and arm in arm the two women went off to wrought their changes on Cullayne Castle and create a miracle in three days.

Though she knew with a child's thoroughness all parts of the castle outside this building, the stables, tower, and so forth, the private chambers and kitchens had been strange to her, for this had been Red Rafe's lair and she'd stayed away from it. In the days since she'd moved into the private quarters, she'd done much to acquaint herself with the castle's workings.

She had no need of guidance to find the vaulted kitchens in the basement, for the heat, sound, and stench greeted her at the top of the stairs. The room was crowded with people who all seemed to be talking at once. Three stone fireplaces—big enough to hold a whole spitted cow in each—had been built for the cook's convenience, but the coals had been allowed to die out in two of them. A rack of lamb hung over cold ashes in one, while a caldron of watery soup bubbled desultorily over dwindling coals of the third fireplace.

The tables and benches were cluttered with unwashed pots and a staved bucket in the corner sported the rotting entrails of the poor animal, which, Lillias presumed, had been gutted in preparation for their supper. Black smoke billowed from the iron door of the brick oven, signifying the day's ration of bread was burning, but no one made any move to rescue it. Now and then the master cook stirred the contents of the caldron with a large wooden spoon, tasted the broth, and spat the contents back into the cooking pot. With the same utensil he swatted a passing helper on the backside.

Servants lolled drunkenly on low benches and pallets near the stone fireplaces, even though the sun was still high. They called ribald remarks to one another and laughed uproariously at their own wit. A woman stood kneading bread dough, while a man, still bearing the dirt and stench of the stables, stood kneading her breasts. In one corner a young serving girl struggled with a brute who bore her down on the rough stone floor and fumbled with his trews. Her screams went unnoticed by the rest of the servants.

Lillias looked upon this scene with growing horror. The

debauchery that had ruled Red Rafe's castle during his lifetime was still in full force below stairs. She'd witnessed
many such scenes in the castle's great hall, and the rage
she'd felt during those long years of endurance ran through
her now, so she caught up a large wooden spoon and beat
against an iron pot. At first, her clanging was ignored, so
she continued until the idlers fell silent and glared at her
with arrogance. Even the man intent upon deflowering the
young serving wench had ceased his fumbling and stared at
the two women.

"Here now, ye can't be doing that," ordered the rotund
man who'd stirred the soup, coming to position himself before her. His long hair was greasy and unkempt, his clothes
filthy with dried blood and cooking sauce still clinging to
them. He brandished the spoon before him like a weapon.
Aggie jumped and took a step backward, which brought the
man's attention to her.

"Aye, 'tis ye, is it?" he growled. "Come for the meal for
my lady, herself. Ye can't take a space in my kitchen naow.
I've my own meal t'cook for the laird, naow that he's
home."

"I've na' come to make a meal, I'll thank ye," Aggie
sassed from behind Lillias. " 'Tis the mistress herself, and
she has a few things t'be telling ye for the laird's supper."

The cook turned to fix Lillias with a baleful glare. "Ye
dinna look like the mistress of the castle t'me," he stated
emphatically.

"And ye dinna look like the master cook of such a fine
castle as Cullayne, yet well I ken ye are," Lillias snapped.
"Ye're Beathen, are ye na'?"

"Aye, Beathen MacLeod. My fither was the third cousin
of Red Rafe himself," he said proudly.

"And ye know me as well."

"Aye, I do." He nodded his shaggy head. "I suppose
ye'll be telling me how to make my meals?" he inquired in
a deceptively gentle tone that sent the rest of the servants
edging away from him. For a moment, Lillias blanched
under his hostile stare, then she gathered her courage and

raised the wooden spoon that she still clutched in her hand. She'd not fail here and have Iain MacLeod hear of it.

"Aye, Beathen, that I will be," she said firmly. Without waiting for his reply, she moved around him and circled the kitchen, pausing to stare at each servant as she passed. "Black Iain has returned home and he's invited guests to a banquet three days' hence," she said in a loud, ringing voice. "He has na fondness for rancid meat and burned bread. His palate is used to French cooking. Remind me, Aggie, to inquire about a master cook from France." She turned and stared at the burly cook. "As mistress of Cullayne Castle, I must see to my husband's wishes." She glanced around. No gaze met her own. Those who'd lazed their daylight hours away in the kitchen glanced now at the master cook, awaiting a cue from him.

"I'll na' be threatened by a woman!" he roared. "I've been master cook at Cullayne Castle my whole life, serving under my faither t'learn my craft. God's blood, no fancy Frenchman will waltz into my kitchen and take over."

"Ye've na been listenin' ta me, Beathen," Lillias answered, raising her voice, and although she could not match his in volume, she commanded his attention. "My husband has no love for foul meat and stale bread, nor t'be shamed in front of his guests for a meager table. If ye've a mind to keep yer position, ye'll cook a better meal than ye have heretofore."

Beathen's face turned red. His cheeks puffed in and out as he struggled to answer her. " 'Tis my kitchen—and I'll not be takin' orders from a woman," he finally got out. He turned his back on her, stalking to the pot of stew, where he once again dipped his wooden spoon and tasted. "Aye, and it's a bonny stew," he declared, and deliberately turned his back on her.

"Right ye air, Beathen. The best pottage t'be found on Scottish soil," the other servants declared loyally, although they'd taken of late to avoiding some of his dishes. Still, they cast triumphant grins her way.

Lillias felt the mantle of failure fall over her. If she could not establish herself as mistress here in the castle kitchens, how could she hope to command respect from anyone, least of all Iain MacLeod? Furious at the master cook's high-handed manner, she gave no thought to her actions, but stalked across the room after him and *thwacked* him across his bottom, much as he'd done to his helper.

Voices died away. The kitchen went deathly quiet, save for the bubbling caldron. Beathen whirled, his wooden spoon raised for swift retaliation. Lillias stood her ground, waiting for the blow. She saw the flecks of red in his eyes and the furious twist of his mouth beneath the dirty beard, but she did not flinch.

He could not hit her. She was the chief's wife, and he'd already heard enough of Black Iain to know if he struck this defiant wench before him, he would answer with his life. She was no ordinary kitchen slut, but a woman of nobility. He gazed into the clear blue eyes and saw not one flicker of hesitation or doubt. She'd never back down from him. Beathen had never backed down from any man, but now he was at an impasse. Since she would not give, he knew he must—or life as he'd known it from birth would cease. His wooden spoon, the badge of his authority, wavered and slowly lowered.

Lillias was not unaware of what she'd done, of how she'd made him lose face. She cast about in her mind for some way to give him back some of the stature she'd stripped away with her blow. Yet, she couldn't back down now. Stepping away from him, she raised her chin and addressed Beathen.

"The job of master cook is a grave responsibility," she said firmly. "Not everyone is able to hold such a position. Ye've trained at yer faither's knee. Did ye na learn the principles of cooking?"

"Aye, and I'm able to cook a feast to please a king." He'd recovered his pride enough to boast.

"Then prove it to me and to Lord MacLeod by providing a feast for him and his guests such as Cullayne has never seen. It will be his true homecoming."

"Aye, I can do that," Beathen exclaimed. "I've not forgotten the things my faither taught me."

"Good." Lillias whirled and looked at the clearly amused servants. "I ken there are servants here who have duties elsewhere," she said, looking at the barreled ceiling and tapping her foot against the stone floor. "I dinna know who they are yet, but when I learn, I will send them packing elsewhere. Though 'tis spring, the nights are chilled and winter comes early to the Highlands."

At first there was no sound, then a scurry of footsteps. When Lillias glanced down, the majority of people who'd crowded the kitchen were gone. Those who were left looked apprehensive. The young serving wench who'd nearly been ravished was among them. She looked thin and undernourished, Lillias noted.

"What is yer name?" she asked.

The girl raised her bowed head. She looked even more scared than before. "I am Grace, my lady," she said, curtsying with coltish grace.

"I've never seen ye before," Lillias said. "Are ye new at the castle?"

"Aye, my lady. My faither offered my services last year, but my mum was living still and she said she'd have no decent daughter workin' at Red Rafe's castle. Mum died this spring and my faither brought me here." She stopped speaking abruptly, as if fearful she'd said too much. She hadn't much of a chance of surviving in the castle kitchen, Lillias thought. She looked far too thin to lift the heavy pots Lillias knew she must.

"How old are ye, Grace?" she asked kindly.

"I turned fourteen years my last birth date, my lady," the slender girl answered. Her smile was timid, but it transformed her thin face to a thing of rare beauty. Fine dark lashes lay against pale cheeks. She would be very pretty, Lillias realized, if she fleshed out a little.

"Have ye been ill as well?" she asked kindly.

Startled by this rare attention, the girl glanced up, then quickly lowered her gaze. "Only a little, my lady," she replied. "Oh, I may look a bit delicate, but like my faither says, I'm as strong as a sapling. I did nearly all the work at our croft, tending the crops and animals and my ailing mither."

"I'm surprised yer faither let ye go," Lillias replied.

The pale brow furrowed in a frown. "He says he dinna ha' a need for me naow. He's marrying the Wida Frasier—and she has a son with twelve summers behind him. He's stronger than me." She clamped her lips together and stared at Lillias with stricken eyes. "I'm strong and I'm a hard worker, my lady. I give my word I'll na lollygag on ye."

"Would ye like to be my maid, Grace?" Lillias asked gently, touched by the young girl's vulnerability and her willingness to work.

"Yer maid?" Aggie huffed behind Lillias.

"Aye, Aggie. Ye've a need for an assistant to climb the stairs on errands and save yer rheumy knees."

"Humph!" Aggie replied

"Will ye part with yer helper, Beathen?" Lillias asked the master cook. They both knew she was but extending him a courtesy by asking.

"Aye, take her. She's too frail t'be much use down here."

"Thank ye," Lillias said, then glanced around at the other servants. "Will that leave ye enough helpers to clean the pots and empty the pails before I inspect the kitchen again?"

Beathen's face grew very red; for a moment she thought their battle might begin again, but he took a few deep breaths and gritted his teeth in a facsimile of a smile.

"Aye, I've enough helpers left." He glared around the room. "What air ye standin' about for? D'ye want the lady of the castle t'think I kinna command my own kitchen?" When no one moved, he raised his voice to a bellow. "Get yer lazy arses moving!"

Everyone jumped and began running about, even bumping into one another in their haste to do his bidding. Only the woman who'd been kneading the bread stood still. Lillias glanced at the rising dough.

"I trust we'll have unburned bread for supper," she said sternly.

"Aye, my lady," the woman cried, and ran to the oven to rescue what she could of the burned bread.

"I have several more inspections to make before the day has ended," Lillias told Beathen. "But tomorrow, I will go over the daily rations with ye to ensure we have enough. When my husband has appointed a steward, I will handle such matters through him."

"Aye, my lady," Beathen replied, thoroughly subdued at her air of authority and knowledge over the running of the castle. Secretly he vowed to urge the clan chief to hurry in his appointment of a bailie. Receiving orders from another man would be far less fatal to a man's pride than taking them from a mere slip of a girl he'd watch grow up from a bairn.

Sensing the tenuous advantage she now held over the volatile master cook, Lillias made a regal—albeit hasty—retreat, calling over her shoulder to Grace, who followed like an eager young pup.

In the next three days, Lillias, trailed by Aggie and Grace, inspected the hall, which was in an atrociously filthy state. Immediately she set servants to cleaning it. They set to work with surprising diligence, for word of her confrontation with Beathen had spread to the rest of the castle servants and they had no wish to be dismissed. She set other servants to cleaning the sleeping apartments their guests would occupy, spreading fresh rushes on the floor and airing the linen. With the immediate problem in hand, she set about seeing to the rest of the castle's needs. She avoided the private chambers used by Iain, but set to work inspecting the storerooms, which were woefully short on flour, honey, preserved fruit, ale, wine, candles, and medicines. There were no bolts of wool or linen for clothes for the servants and retinue of troops who attended the *Ceann Mor.*

Lillias inspected every nook and cranny of the castle that had been her home and prison for nine long years. As a curious child, she'd often wondered what lay beyond these sturdy stone walls, but her rare and painful audiences with Red Rafe in the great hall had snuffed out any curiosity that would have led her to explore here. No, the tower had been her domain, her haven, cold and lonely as it had been. Now she sought every dust-laden corner of her new home, chasing away old demons and making mental notes to herself as to what must be done to make the castle more inhabitable.

She even inspected the cisterns where rainwater was collected and piped down to the kitchen to a great stone sink, and even the guardrooms, of which there were two, with their small arrow-loop windows, slab stone seats, and their stench of long uncleaned cesspits below. She descended into the basement storerooms to count musty forgotten bags of grain and would have ventured down the trapdoor into the dungeon if not for the cries of protest from Aggie and Grace. When she was finished with her inspection, they followed her up the stairs to the great hall with an ill-concealed sigh of relief.

Wearily Lillias pushed her hair back from her heated brow. Even to her inexperienced eye, her inspection had revealed a disappointing, albeit not surprising, state of neglect. The job of restoring the castle would be much larger than she'd anticipated and she wondered if she would be up to the task. Still, she'd promised Iain to try, and so she would. But no more today. She'd done the best she could. By late afternoon, guests would begin arriving and she must attend to herself if she were not to appear as drab before Iain's friends.

As if summoned by her thoughts, the outer door was flung open and Iain and his men entered the dim hall, bringing with them the smells of leather, horseflesh, sunshine, and hearty males. She hadn't expected this early arrival. Aware of her untidy appearance, she hurriedly turned toward the stairs leading to her chamber, but she was too late to escape Iain's notice.

"My lady Lillias," he called to her. Reluctantly she turned to greet him. His men milled about, openly watching them, their faces merry with the jest they'd shared.

"Welcome home, my lord," she said, forcing a smile. "Ye wished something of me?" she asked.

His eager step brought him to her; his laughter died away as he took in every detail of her disheveled appearance.

"Are ye well, lass? Have ye taken a tumble down the stairs?" He held his hands out in an eloquent gesture of entreaty. Then slowly the smile returned and he plucked a bit of cobweb from her hair.

Tendrils of gold had escaped her neat braid and curled over her ears and temple. Her cheeks were flushed like the down on a ripening peach, her forehead and chin smudged with dirt. His gaze moved down to the plain servant's garment she wore and she saw the displeasure return to his eyes.

"I—I've been busy, my lord, in going over the castle and seeing that all is ready for our guests when they arrive."

"Aye, I see that," he answered. "Is that why ye dress as a servant?"

"Partly." She raised her chin. She refused to be intimidated by him.

"And the other reason?"

"I have no other dresses suitable to a lady of the castle, save the one ye saw the morning of yer return. So I have donned these things to save my best clothes while I work. It's far more sensible, dinna ye think?"

He frowned at her words. " 'Tis not necessary for a lady of the castle to do such menial tasks. Even here in Scotland, we are not such barbarians as to not possess servants."

"Aye, my lord. 'Tis true," she said primly. "But when such things are left to the care of servants without supervision, much is left undone. Below stairs, I've found little in the way of provisions. Should the enemy lay siege to Cullayne Castle, we should have to surrender at once, for there is no food or fresh water to sustain us for even a fortnight."

His dark brows drew down into a scowl. "Are ye sure? Mayhap ye've overlooked provisions."

"I think not, my lord." She grinned, unaware of how attractive it made her. "Ye'd best be mending yer fences with yer neighbors, indeed, or ye'll be losing Cullayne Castle."

He cursed under his breath, his countenance dark and dangerous-looking. Lillias could clearly see where he'd gotten his nickname.

"We've need of a steward, when ye've the time to appoint one, my lord," she continued. "He can help with the supervision of the cleaning and repairing of the castle—and the restocking of the storerooms. There is much to be put right."

Her earnestness brought a smile to his scowling features, and, just that quickly, he was transformed into the teasing gallant on the hillside. "Ye seem almost happy, lass, at the deplorable condition of my home."

"Mayhap I am," she replied lightly. " 'Tis the wish of every woman to leave her mark on a place. I have a wish to do that at Cullayne Castle, for it's left its mark on me."

He nodded while a smile played at the corners of his mouth. Their gazes tangled and held. His eyes were the color of new grass on a spring day, when the wind blows across its top revealing the dark, silvery shadows of the underblade. Lillias felt her chest tighten and her heart go still. For a full minute they did not speak, but only looked their fill, as if lovers who had, at last, met again. Finally Lillias took a deep breath and looked away.

"Is all in ready for tonight?"

"Aye. I've so informed Beathen, and he promises a veritable feast."

"I've had my feast," Iain said in a strange, tight voice. "A feast for the eyes."

She glanced up quickly to see if his words were meant as they sounded. His gaze was dark and heated. She read the lust in his eyes—and for a moment felt the Highland wind against her hot cheeks—as she had the afternoon he first came. She blushed and looked away.

"I would ha' ye come to my chamber, Lillias," he said huskily.

The blood pounded in her ears at his words. She struggled to hold her old resolves to her. "My—my lord!" she stammered, staring at him with wide, troubled eyes. "I will not. Ha' ye forgotten our agreement so readily?"

"Nay, I've na forgotten," he replied. "But such an agreement deserves t'be broken. 'Tis the devil's spawn."

"Mayhap, but it was an agreement of honor between us."

"Ye've a ready tongue in yer head, Lillias," he declared. "Have ye not heard a woman must obey her husband?"

"Have ye not heard a man must honor his word?" she snapped back. "Or are ye too much Red Rafe's son to remember honor?"

A dark scowl came to his face. "If ye've so little faith in my honor, then why have ye made the bargain with me?" he demanded, then didn't wait for her to answer, for his chattering men had fallen silent to listen to their war of words. "Nay, Lillias. Ye'll learn to obey my commands as yer husband or feel the weight of my wrath."

"D'ye threaten me, my lord?" she retorted.

"I've no need for that, make no mistake, Lillias MacLeod. I bid ye now t'come t'my chamber at once." Without waiting to see if she followed, he whirled and climbed the stairs, his sheathed sword clanging rhythmically against each stone step.

"Aye, and that'll show her who's chief," one of his men called, and the others guffawed lustily.

Lillias remained standing where she was, heart racing, chin dimpling in her defiant thrust of it. Aggie stepped forward and took her elbow, urging her toward the stairs.

"Go on, child. Ye must do as he tells ye. He's yer lord and husband and ye would not have him lose face among his clansmen."

"I won't—" Lillias began stubbornly.

"Shh! Do as I say," Aggie commanded. "It will be better for ye in the end, child."

Shoulders slumping in defeat, Lillias made her way to the chambers above. Her heart hammered in her chest, so she could scarcely swallow. She had little doubt what Iain MacLeod wanted of her, for she'd read the lust in his glance. She'd felt it, too, until she reminded herself he was Red Rafe's son. Well, she would go to his chamber as he had bid her, but she would not submit to him. That was not in their bargain. Still, as she walked along the corridor to his room, she had to wonder if the pounding of her heart was from trepidation or anticipation.

Chapter 7

"AYE, COME IN," he called gruffly when she knocked on the heavy plank door.

He'd left it ajar, and now she entered and looked around, unsurprised by what she saw. This was much the way she would have imagined Red Rafe's room, if she'd cared to give it a thought. The room was barren of any comforts. No fire offered its warmth against the damp chill of a spring night; no tapestries graced the walls offering protection from the cold walls or beauty to the gaze; no rugs padded the footfall against the stone floor; and no padded cushions eased the back on stool or bench. The bed pad was thin and lumpy and the bedcovers smelled musty, as if they'd not been aired in a year or more. Lillias suspected there might even be fleas. The only thing that showed a new laird had taken residence was an abundant number of richly appointed carved chests, which sat about the perimeter of the room. Some were inlaid with white pearls and others were trimmed with precious gold or silver.

Lillias left off her perusal of the room and whirled to face Iain MacLeod. "Ye wished my presence, my lord?" she asked haughtily.

Iain studied her regal stance and frowned slightly. "Ye've na need to stick yer little nose into the air," he declared. "I've asked ye to come here for a special reason."

"And I can guess at that reason, my lord. 'Tis not so special, after all?" she demanded.

113

"Blast ye!" he snapped. "Will ye only think the worst of me?" They glared at each other for a moment, then turned away. "I had a hope we could be friends tonight," he growled over his shoulder, "so my chiefs and their wives could see we are indeed united as man and wife. But ye act so skittish around me, they'll soon ken something's amiss."

"Aye," she answered. "And something is. I am willing to stick t'my part of the bargain, but I canna help what yer men and their wives think."

"Aye, then 'tis a mockery, what we do," he declared. "For the servants and my men will soon see the farce of the whole thing and word will go out to the other clans that Iain MacLeod is trying to trick them. They'll trust me less than before."

"Because I do na' jump to obey ye?" Lillias asked derisively.

"Because ye make plain yer dislike of me."

She whirled to face him, her eyes flashing, and was disconcerted to see him watching her closely.

"I—I dinna dislike ye," she said grudgingly.

"Are ye sure? I've a mind ye might slip a dagger blade between my ribs when I'm not looking."

"If I were intent on doing that, my lord, I would ha' done it by now," she declared. "Or better yet, I would ha' left ye to Beathen's devises. He would soon ha' poisoned ye with his swill." Her smile was impish, but her eyes crackled with defiance.

"Then why d'ye jut yer chin at me like that?" he demanded. "If it goes any higher, I fear ye'll fall backward."

"And did ye invite me here, my lord, t'insult me with yer words?" she demanded, her hands on her hips, her shoulders high and stiff.

He took a few deep breaths, as if trying to still his anger. "Nay, lass. I've a gift for ye."

"A gift?"

"Aye!" He glanced at her dirty linen shift. "Ye canna go about looking like a servant. 'Tis na seemly."

"Ah, then ye're ashamed of me, my lord?" She shot him a withering glance.

"Nay, I—I just thought t' have ye dress like a laird's lady."

"So, ye have not brought me a gift so much as ye've thought to further the— What was the word ye used? . . . The *farce* we play?"

He looked uncomfortable and impatient at her words. "Take my offer as ye will," he rumbled. "I've brought some ladies' garments wi' me from France. I thought they might fit ye."

"Gowns from France?" She opened and closed her mouth several times, seeking some further retort to add to his discomfort, but the prospect of French gowns quite dazzled her, so she fell speechless. When she said nothing more, he stalked across the room to a chest and threw back the lid. Lillias drew in her breath at the brightly colored satins revealed therein.

Iain glanced at her over his shoulder, noting the blush on her cheeks and the sparkle in her eyes. She was no different than any Frenchwoman he'd taken as his mistress over the past nine years. Like all women, she had a love of pretty things. Carelessly he grabbed a fistful of satin and pulled it from the chest.

"Oh, have a care, my lord, ye'll muss it," she cried, running across the room to retrieve the beautiful gown. Once she'd touched the soft fabric, she seemed incapable of letting it go. Her hands slid across the full skirt and jewel-encrusted bodice. With a cry of delight, she shook out the garment and held it to herself, glancing around for a mirror to see the effect. Since there was none, she contented herself with twirling around and watching the effect of movement on the rich satin.

"There are more," he called. "Three chests full."

She paid no heed, her delight in the garment she held occupying her. Iain stood back and watched her, captivated by her sparkle and naive joy. She was a rare beauty, even among Scottish women, and though she possessed none of the coquettish manners of the Frenchwomen, he found her all the more desirable for her innocence. He flushed and turned away, remembering what he'd heard among his clansmen and villagers.

"Ye've been a proper wife while I was gone," he said gruffly over his shoulder. She stopped her twirling, staggering slightly, and stared at him.

"Is that why ye've given me this gown, Iain MacLeod?" she demanded, ever ready to take offense and do battle. "Because I do as ye command me?"

"Nay." He nodded to add emphasis to his single admission. "I wish t'see ye dressed in beautiful gowns and seated at my side tonight." He took a step toward her. "The villagers have returned from the shieling and they've been invited t'the castle as well. I want them t'see ye as I do—a fine, beautiful lady."

Her eyes widened. "Pretty words, my lord," she said, trying not to be flattered by them. "I must tell Beathen of the extra guests." She put aside the gown, preparing to rush down to the kitchen.

"Nay, I've sent word to him. All is in readiness, save for my lady. Will ye wear my gown and sit by my side, Lilli?"

She paused, struck by the simple splendor of his request. He was showing them all tonight that she was his wife, Lady Lillias, the wife of a chieftain of a mighty clan. But she sensed there was more that he asked of her, something she had no wish to give. He held out his hand to her, his dark green eyes holding her gaze.

"Will ye be my wife, Lillias?" he asked. "Ye please me well and I would ha' us put aside this farce and be truly united."

She swayed as she had on the hillside, her heart and body bending to his will while her head took a different path. "Was it only a fortnight ago that ye declared ye would not sire a son on soiled flesh? Harsh words, indeed, my lord. Yet, here ye are, after a few servants ha' whispered my praise in yer ear, wanting to consummate our marriage. Mayhap ye should wait awhile to make yer decision. There will be others who will tell ye a different story."

"Ye lie," he cried, snatching up her hand. "Ye declared yerself ye were innocent of my accusations."

"Aye. I lied, but which is the lie?" she demanded.

"Ye're a witch!" he said hoarsely. "And yer words are like a stream of water that kinna be held between the fingers long enough to determine their truth." He threw her hand away from him.

She struggled to compose herself, fighting back a sudden need to cry. "I will wear yer beautiful gowns, my lord," she said quietly, "and I will sit by yer side tonight at the banquet, but I will not share yer bed. That was the bargain we made between us and I will follow no other."

He drew a breath from somewhere deep in his chest and shrugged. "Aye. I see yer point, lass. Ye've not changed our agreement. 'Twas only me wanting something I've never yet found."

"D'ye wish me to take this gown, my lord?" she asked softly, her fingers trailing wistfully over the silken fabric.

He saw her longing and was heartened by it. "Aye, lass. I bought them with ye in mind."

"Did ye, truly?" she inquired, watching him carefully.

"Aye. I'd not forgotten I had a wife here at Cullayne."

"Yet, ye never sent a word to me." The words were said matter-of-factly, without censure. He felt all the more ashamed for her stoic acceptance of his neglect.

"Aye. What can a man say t'a captive bride who may hate him with all her heart?"

"I can think of na words that would be appropriate, my lord."

"Nor could I," he said. He turned toward the door. "I'll call a servant to carry the chests to yer room."

"Thank ye, my lord," Lillias answered.

Long after his footsteps disappeared down the hall, she stood thinking of the man who was her husband. Slowly she folded the lovely gown and put it back into the chest, closing the lid before she went to her own room. She had no taste for beautiful gowns now.

Not so Aggie and Grace, who opened the trunks immediately upon their transport to Lillias's room. Amid gasps of awe and delight, they took out every gown and exclaimed over its richness and beauty. There were headpieces and gossamer veils of the sheerest gauze, embroidered leather gloves embellished with ribbons, and brocaded cuffs and slippers of the softest leathers, branched velvet, and embroidered satin. Iain had even thoughtfully purchased pattens of inlaid wood with decorated leather straps to keep her fine new slippers free of the mud should she decide to walk in the courtyard. A small embroidered silk almoner, to be hung from a girdle beneath the gown, brought a wry chuckle from Aggie.

"Ye've never possessed a coin in yer life," she said. "Why would Lord Iain bring ye such a bag?"

"Perhaps he intends me to have coins as well," Lillias said thoughtfully. "He's been most generous so far."

"Aye, that he has, and though he may not have sent ye word during his years away, it's clear he thought of ye."

"Aye, he thought of me," Lillias said gently. She couldn't repress a shiver at the image of herself seated beside Iain that night in all her finery. She could study at leisure his fine profile and changing green eyes.

"Which gown will ye wear tonight, my lady?" Aggie asked. She and Grace had spread the gowns over every inch of available space—bed, stools, and chests—for her perusal. Brilliant fabrics of lustrous taffetas, cut velvet, velvet brocades, and sheer, rich Sendal and sarcenet silks in colors of the rainbow had been made into the latest French fashion with low, square-cut necklines, fitted waists, and full skirts that had been slashed in the front to allow contrasting underskirts to show through. A contraption of wicker hoops covered with taffeta had been supplied as well, and Lillias couldn't help but wonder what woman had helped Iain make his choices. His purchases indicated a thoroughly intimate knowledge of women's needs.

Lillias sighed. It was best not to wonder about such things, but some part of her rebelled at the thought that Iain had not remained celibate during his nine-year sojourn and had returned home suspecting her virtue.

Still, it was of no concern to her, really, for with his suspicions had come a reprieve for her and for Aggie. When Iain had finished with her services, he'd promised to return her to her own clan. She must not forget her objective and become muddled with unwanted emotions.

Still, she paced about the room, envisioning herself in each gown and wondering which Iain would find most attractive on her. All through her bath, she agonized over her decision. To have such fine gowns after a lifetime of simple garments was overwhelming. Finally she chose a satin of such a rich blue she was reminded of the sky over the loch on a bright spring day. The full skirt had been slashed, so an underskirt of striped silk and velvet in yellow and brown showed through. A gold braid trimmed the wide, square neckline, and the ruffled chemise worn beneath it did little to relieve the décolleté. Lillias's smooth, pale shoulders and the swelling tops of her breasts were amply revealed.

"It's terribly low," Lillias said, tugging at the neckline.

"The French have no shame." Aggie fussed, arranging the lace, so it might better cover Lillias's breasts.

"My lady, I've found a mirror in one of the chests," Grace said, stepping forward with a framed piece of silver. She held it so Lillias might view herself.

Lillias gasped at the regal young woman she saw. Aggie had plaited her hair into a coronet around her head and pinned a sheer veil over it that trailed down her back. Her eyes reflected the rich blue of her gown and her cheeks were tinged pink by the excitement of dressing in such fine clothes.

"Am I not very fine, Aggie?" she cried, pirouetting on the toes of her blue satin slippers.

"Aye, my lady, very fine, indeed," Aggie affirmed. "But ye must stand still so I can sew up this hem. 'Tis much too long."

"Leave it," a voice said from the door of her chamber.

Lillias whirled and flushed scarlet at seeing Iain standing there, knowing he'd caught her out in her moment of vanity. He was resplendent in an undercoat of green and gold brocade and a *chamarre* of dark brown velvet. His strong legs were encased in *chausses* of the same color. He looked incredibly handsome and virile. She could well imagine him at the court of King James himself, or even the English

king, Henry VIII, of whom rumors had come to them even
here in the Highlands.

"May I come in?" he asked, gesturing with one hand,
and Lillias nodded mutely.

"Pray do, my lord," she said, finding her voice at last
and sweeping her full skirts wide in a curtsy. Upon rising,
she caught her foot in the fabric and stumbled slightly. He
didn't laugh, for which she was inordinately grateful, although his eyes gleamed with good humor.

"Ye look very beautiful, my lady," he said approvingly.
His warm gaze lingered on her face. "Ye're as elegant as a
lady of the finest courts."

"Thank ye, my lord," she answered. "The gowns fit
quite well, except that they're a bit long. Aggie will shorten
them when she has the time."

"But ye haven't worn the *vertugale*," he cried.

"The *vertugale*?"

"Aye, lass. 'Tis why yer skirts are too long." He crossed
the room and gathered up the wicker hoop that lay in a flat
puddle of taffeta on one chest. With ease he shook it out
into its cone shape and looked at her. "It goes beneath yer
skirts t'hold them out, like so." He stepped into the frame
and pulled it up about his waist. Grace giggled, and even
Aggie hid her smile behind her hand.

"We were na sure how it was meant to be worn," Lillias
answered. "We've never seen such a thing before."

"Nor have many women here in Scotland or even En-
gland," he explained, stepping out of the hoop. "The Span-
ish call it a *farthingale*, and the French ladies have only
now adopted it. Soon it will be all the rage at the English
and Scottish courts."

"Humph! It looks like a bird cage," Aggie declared.
"How can a woman walk about with a thing like that
strapped to her body? I'd na wear such a contraption."

Iain looked at Lillias. She smiled, intrigued by the hoop.
"It does seem rather silly," she said. "And how does one
put it on?"

"I'll show ye," Iain said, kneeling before her and placing

the hoop on the floor. "Step into the center of it, lass, and I'll draw it up for ye."

Distracted by his solid presence at her feet, Lillias stood silent and unresponsive on the surface, while within a battle was waged. The green brocade of his undercoat made his eyes appear even more brilliant. She was too aware of him, of the breadth of his shoulders, the hard leanness of his hips, the smooth, clean-shaven jaw. Unbidden came the memory of him bare-waisted in the courtyard when he fought the giant Leith. Beneath the fine brocade and velvet were sleek muscles and smooth brown skin that would be warm to the touch. Her breasts tingled at the thought of being pressed against the hard wall of his chest. The sheen of his raven dark locks invited her to bury her fingertips in the lustrous strands. Licking her lower lip with her small pink tongue, Lillias clamped her hands into fists to keep from giving in to the temptation of touching him.

"Will ye not try it, lass?" Iain asked, and she started and blushed, fearful her lust for him might have been too evident.

"Aye, I will," she said, and stepped into the circle of wicker hoops. His green eyes gleamed wickedly.

"I hope ye won't take offense at what I'm about t'do, my lady," he said huskily, and before she gave thought to what must surely come next, he'd reached beneath her skirts and pulled the wicker hoops upward and over her hips.

She felt the brush of his hands against her heated skin, then his touch at her waist. He was standing aright now, his gaze capturing hers, his own face flushed and dark, his breath hot against her cheek, while his hands fumbled at the ties of the *farthingale*.

"Ach, the skirts are in the way," he mumbled, a red blush creeping up his neck.

Lillias saw it and was entranced. That he had experienced such intimate arrangements as this with other women seemed obvious by his expertise in handling women's clothing, yet he stood before her, blushing as if he were unaccustomedly moved by her presence, as she was by his.

"Aggie, Grace, lift up my skirts," she ordered, and they

moved on either side of her and held up her skirts, so he might knot the ribbon that held the *farthingale* in place. When he was done, he stepped back, and Aggie and Grace smoothed her skirts over the wicker frame.

"Aye, and it's grand." Grace sighed.

"It looks like ye're wearin' a barrel beneath yer skirts." Aggie scoffed. "It hides yer figure."

"Aye, and I like it," Iain declared so vehemently that Lillias and the other women looked at him in delight.

"Are ye jealous, then, Laird MacLeod, that ye'd not be wanting another man to see yer wife?" Aggie dared to ask the question that Lillias wondered.

"Would ye blame me if I was, Aggie?" he declared. His glance was dark and compelling, his husky voice sending shivers through Lillias. "For the first time, I understand my faither's disappointment upon having yer mither stolen from him." His words swept away all emotions save the anger she'd carried through the years. She tossed her head and glared at him with an icy stare.

"Am I to suppose, my lord, that ye'll behead the first man who tries to whisk me away from ye?"

He flushed at the remainder of the barbaric act of his father. "Aye, lass, and ye're a hard one. Ye'll na let me forget that, will ye?"

"Nay, my lord," she answered firmly. "For I've yet to forget the sight of my faither's head lying on that platter at our wedding feast. Have ye a similar surprise awaiting me at yer banquet?"

"Lillias!" Aggie reprimanded in a shocked tone. "Mind yer words." But of course, such harsh words could never be called back; Lillias bit her tongue, suddenly sorry she'd uttered them. Hadn't he been inordinately generous with his chests of gowns and fripperies?

She straightened her shoulders and raised her chin defiantly. Was she to forget her father's ignominious murder for the sake of a few silk gowns? Never! She was glad she'd spoken out. When the great chief of the MacLeod clan escorted his unclaimed bride down to the hall to show her off to his clansmen, he would do so with the absolute knowledge of how she'd been attained—through bloodshed and an inhumane act toward her own clan.

She saw the flush of anger stain his face. His eyes darkened until they were nearly black; his lips clamped together in a thin line that was not unlike Red Rafe's expression. He raised his arm and she flinched, expecting him to strike her, but he merely drew a velvet box from beneath his surcoat and held it out.

"I brought these for ye, my lady," he said, with cold formality and no trace of the thick Highland brogue with which he usually spoke.

By his stern bearing, elegant dress, and clipped English, she was reminded that Iain MacLeod was no ordinary Scotsman. He'd spent the last nine years in a country considered far more civilized than their own. What must he think of his rough, brawling countrymen? Did he find them, herself included, coarse and backward? For the first time, she considered the shame and rage he must feel that no matter what he did as the new clan chief, he could never undo the savage acts of his father. She bit her lips and looked down at the box he held. She noted first the strong brown hands holding it. These hands had never been raised to her in anger or punishment. From the beginning, he'd sought to give her comfort of sorts.

"Take it, my lady," he said sternly, throwing open the lid and displaying a pendant necklace of stunningly wrought filigree gold. From its center hung a baguette sapphire stone. A ring of the same workmanship and stone was there as well.

Lillias gasped with appreciation. " 'Tis beautiful."

"Go on. Take it," he ordered. "They were purchased with ye in mind. They came from a French countess whose husband had gambled away his fortune; she was forced to sell her jewelry to pay their bills."

"And ye bought them from her as an act of kindness," Lillias murmured. Her lashes were lowered, so she did not see the softening of his expression.

"I bought them because I remembered a little girl with eyes of that same midnight blue color and I hoped . . ."

Lillias waited for him to go on, but he merely shrugged. "I thought ye might like a bauble or two to forget the strange beginning we had." The brogue was back. She preferred it to the cold, proper English he'd used moments before.

"I thank ye kindly, my lord, but I'm not certain I can wear something bought under such sad circumstances."

"Turn round," he ordered, and took the necklace from the satin-lined box. "Women seldom hold to such sentiments for long when it comes to jewelry," he observed dryly, fastening the pendant about her slender throat. The stone fell just above the shadow of her décolletage. "The countess claimed it would give her great pleasure to think of her jewels being worn by a woman of great beauty and charged me thusly."

Lillias turned to face him, eyes shining. "And ye think me that woman of great beauty?" she asked coyly, immensely pleased at his words.

Iain's dark eyebrow arched slightly. "Aye, lass. Ye're pleasing to look upon, but ye've the tongue of a dagger."

Lillias stared into his green eyes, then dropped her gaze. Words of repentance pushed at her tongue, but she could not utter them. "Mayhap it would be better if ye save this bauble for yer true wife when ye've sent me back to my clan." She reached up to unfasten the chain, but his hands caught hers.

"For now, ye're my true wife," he said, staring into her eyes with such a compelling gaze, her knees grew weak beneath the willow hoop. "And ye'll wear the gowns and jewels I brought ye, so all may think this union is secure."

Lillias's heart stilled with regret. "In that spirit, I'll wear it then."

"Thank ye, lass." He drew the ring from the box and placed it on her hand, but it was too large by far and she was forced to wear it on her thumb. Iain laid aside the box and held out his arm. "Come, my lady. Our guests await us."

"Aye, my lord," she answered, with a pretty little curtsy that was far more graceful than the first had been, and took hold of his sleeve.

He led her from the chamber and down the stone stairs
to the great hall. Laughter and music greeted them long before they reached the hall. When they entered, all fell silent.
Peadair McDermott rose with his cup in hand.

"To the new laird of Cullayne Castle, *Ceann Mor* of the
Clan MacLeod, and to his beautiful lady," he called, and
with a cheer all cups were raised in a salute given to them.

Iain and Lillias paused until the toast was completed,
then made their way down the hall to their seats at the
head of the table. Extra trestle tables had been set up the
length of the hall and every seat was filled. All along
the way, they paused to speak to friends and clan members.
One and all wished Iain well.

"Lilli!" A voice called out, and Lillias looked around to
see Mary McFerris seated between her father and Peadair
McDermott. Lillias rushed to embrace her.

"I worried about ye so, Lilli," Mary whispered, hugging
her. "I was that surprised and relieved when I learned the
man ye met at the shieling was none other than Iain Mac-
Leod himself. No harm was done."

"Oh, Mary! If ye only knew the harm that was done,"
Lillias whispered back. "I need to talk to ye, Mary. Will ye
be at the cottage?"

"Aye, but . . ."

"What is it, Mary? Don't ye want me to come there anymore?" Lillias gazed at her in consternation.

" 'Tis not that, Lilli," Mary replied. "But ye're a lady
now and ye shouldn't be coming to the village to visit the
likes of me."

"And who would I visit if not my best friend?" Lillias
exclaimed.

"Ye're lookin' grand tonight," Helen MacEwan called
from across the table.

Beitris was seated next to her, her eyes filled with spite
and envy, her mouth twisted into a pout. When Iain passed
by she caught hold of his hand and pulled him down, so
she might whisper into his ear. Iain listened, then straightened stiffly. His gaze turned to Lillias and she could see the

cold suspicion in his eyes. Beitris smiled at her trium-
phantly.

Lillias turned away and concentrated on greeting all her
friends. They were proud of her, she realized with some
surprise.

They'd known her since she was a child, and she was the
same as one of their own, never mind that she came from
a different clan. She was the wife of the new chief of the
MacLeod clan and they swelled with pride at her new finery. She was the symbol of the new prosperity they hoped
to see under the new chief.

The wives of the chieftains were friendly but reserved.
They'd heard many tales of debauchery about Cullayne
Castle and they'd eagerly accepted the invitation, so they
might see for themselves. Now, they noted the plain, un-
adorned hall, nodding with approval that it was freshly
cleaned, but disappointed that it was not grander. They
were not disappointed in their new chief's wife, finding her
beautiful and elegant. Each one studied the new French
gown she wore, vowing to set their seamstresses to work
the minute they returned home.

Though she'd been well aware, for several days, of the
change in her status as the new chief's wife and of the privilege and authority such a position gave her, she'd never
considered the impact that would have on her relationship
with old friends. Although the villagers greeted her with
wholehearted approval and good wishes, still she sensed the
slight reticence, a deference in their manner that hadn't
been there before. Standing before them, enjoying their
laughter and well-wishing, she felt the loneliness of her position as Lady Lillias MacLeod.

One face only was turned to her in spite and envy.
Beitris MacDougall sat with her eyes downcast, save for
those times she cast Lillias a resentful glare. Her fingers
twirled her cup in irritation. Lillias thought to say something conciliatory to her, but Iain was at her side, gripping
her elbow and turning her toward the head of the table. No
sooner were they seated than the servant brought the first
course. Wooden platters and tankards had been laid at each

place, except at the head of the table, where platters of thin beaten silver and thin horn cups had been placed for the laird and his lady.

In the center of the long table sat a tall gilt saltcellar, and those who sat above the salt obviously held some high position with the clan chief. Some of them were strange faces, but some she'd come to know already. She nodded and smiled at Everard Lachlan and Peadair McDermott. She recognized the burly giant, Leith, who grinned at her cheerfully and drained his cup in one breath.

"Come, wife," Iain said, filling the fine horn cup with wine. "Let us drink a toast to our guests." He took hold of her elbow and helped her to her feet before pressing the cup into her hands. The chatter died away and smiling faces were turned toward them expectantly. Iain cleared his throat and picked up his own cup.

"I would raise a cup to my clansmen," he said, "and to their wives and children, MacLeods one and all."

"Hurrah!" The cry went up the length of the hall and cups were raised and drained with gusto. Servants hurried to refill the tankards. When the tumult had died away, Iain raised his cup again.

"We're looking forward to a new era, a time of peace and prosperity, a time when we'll keep the honor of our clan, but look to make friends wi' our neighboring clans as well. I've been in France for nine years of war and I've come home so the sweet smell of the Highland heather can blow away the stench of blood and death. I've come home to raise strong sons and bonny daughters for the good of the clan and Scotland."

Again the cheer went up and cups were drained. Lillias was becoming quite giddy from the unaccustomed wine. Her eyes sparkled and she looked at Iain expectantly. Helen MacEwan saw her smile and misinterpreted it.

"Aye, Laird Iain, ye've a fine lass t'get yer sons and daughters by," she called, and everyone laughed in agreement. Lillias's cheeks blushed even brighter.

"Give her a kiss," Leith cried out, and everyone took up the cry.

"Aye," Helen cried. "Is this na the laird's wedding supper?"

"Nay," Lillias cried at the exuberance of the company, but Iain pulled her to his chest. His green eyes gleamed with pleasure.

" 'Tis only a kiss they're wantin', lass," he murmured, and before she could protest further, his head lowered and his lips claimed hers. His mouth was firm and compelling against hers. She gasped and held herself still, enduring his touch, refusing to feel or respond, but Iain was not a man simply to be endured. She'd sensed that about him.

His arms wrapped around her, crushing her to him. Her nipples ached with a sweet longing from the contact with his hard chest. His tongue, hot and rasping, swept across her lips, parting them as if she had no will to deny him. In truth, she had not. Her knees trembled as he plundered her mouth and a core of heat began to unwind from someplace deep inside her. She felt it rising like a great bonfire on the eve of All Saint's Day, and she feared it might consume her. She put up her hand to push him away, but her arms had no strength except to slide over his shoulders, so her fingers tangled in the dark curly locks at his nape. Dimly she heard a wild cheering, but she was lost in a world of heat and lightning and breathless wonder—and in the center of that world stood Iain MacLeod.

"Aye, and there'll be a son made this night," someone called, and everyone else joined in the earthy laughter.

Iain drew back, so he could peer down into her eyes, although his arms still held her tightly against him. She was certain she would fall if he did not hold her thus.

"What think ye, lass?" he asked huskily. "Will we make a son this night?"

"Nay, my lord," she said gravely, taking care to keep her words low, so only he might hear. "For I remember well yer words that ye'd na beget a son with an unfaithful wife."

"I've talked to others about the village, lass," he said, "and I can find none who would say a word against yer virtue."

"Ye've asked about me among the villagers?" she cried, raising her voice.

"Aye," he answered. "I was discreet in my inquiries."

"Discreet?" She pushed away from him. "How discreet can such inquiries be, my lord?"

"As discreet as I care t'make them, my lady," he snapped. "Have a care ye dinna spoil the image we've tried to create." He bent and dropped a light kiss on her lips. He'd answered her in a low voice, but his tone was furious. He grinned and raised one of her hands to his lips, so it looked for all the world as if the two of them were enjoying an intimate conversation.

Anger brought color to her cheeks, and even that occasioned a jest, for their guests were certain their new laird was plying his bride with wickedly pretty words. One of Iain's eyebrows arched mockingly, as if he were anticipating the moment alone with his bride. He played the part so well. Even his kiss had been convincing. She'd believed he desired her, and her own body had trembled in response. Aye, fool that she was, to forget so quickly her own resolves.

"Don't smirk so, ye dolt," she said under her breath, and pulled away from him. When she would have fled, he held her captive with a biting grip upon her arm. Half turning so as to shield her from the rest of the room, he glared down at her.

"I but play the part of a loving bridegroom," he answered calmly, "as you would wish."

"I would wish ye to return me to my own clan as soon as possible," she whispered furiously.

"Nay, Lillias. We made a bargain—and ye'll keep it or else." His fingers bit deeper into her flesh, so she barely muffled an outcry of pain. Instantly his hold softened and he urged her down on the bench beside him.

The servants were bringing platters of roasted lamb and fish and loaves of golden brown bread. Now that their guests' attention had been diverted, Iain addressed Lillias once again.

"Tonight ye will come to my chambers," he ordered.

"Nay, I will not!" she cried.

"Ye will come," he said, calmly picking a choice piece of meat from the platter and placing it on her plate. He raised his gaze to meet hers and she felt the intractable quality of the man. "Ye will come as eagerly as a blushing new bride, without protest, or else ye will never return to Dunbeath Castle."

"Ye've promised me something in our—our bargain, my lord," she stuttered, unable to tear her gaze from his uncompromising stare. "Have ye no honor on which I can rely?"

"Aye, I'll honor the agreement between us. I'll not claim ye in my bed, unless ye wish it."

"And I never shall, my lord."

"But I'll not have ye shame me before my clansmen."

She lowered her gaze. "Then I will take yer word of honor, my lord, and come t'yer room, if I must." Her meek acquiescence angered him as nothing else could.

"Ye must, damn ye," he answered, slapping his hand upon the table. A quietness fell upon the hall and all their guests turned their eyes toward the lord and lady. Iain looked around at them, then gazed at Lillias, a wicked gleam in his eyes.

"Blast ye, woman," he roared. "I've told ye I kinna go to our chambers wi' ye now. I'll not leave our guests."

A great howling went up around the hall. Cheeks flaming, Lillias leapt to her feet.

"Ye—ye beast!" she raged, stamping her foot at him.

"Come, lass. Have ye na humor?" He chuckled. "Our company thinks it a great jest."

"At my expense, my lord."

"Aye, I was unkind, my lady," he said, and wrapping his arms around her waist, tugged her down on his lap. Immediately her hoops flew up, so many of those present caught a glimpse of the new wicker cage and all the attendant petticoats. Once again laughter swept round the room.

"Let me go, ye great brute," she ordered, slapping at him. Her palm connected smartly with his smooth cheek. Iain grabbed hold of her wrists in his strong brown hands and quickly rendered her powerless. Still, she struggled, lashing out at him with her foot.

"Aye, and she's a lively wench, Laird MacLeod," Leith roared. " 'Tis a lusty romp ye'll ha' this night."

"Aye," Iain called, laughing. "And what better way to tame a wildcat than in my lair." So saying he stood and threw her over his shoulder. Her wicker hoop flew up—and would have exposed all of her backside she was sure—save that Iain wrapped his arms round her skirts, flattening the frame against her hips. "I'm sorry, my friends," he exclaimed. "I would stay and drink wi' ye, but ye see how eager my bride is."

"Oooh, ye beast! Ye devil's spawn!" she sputtered, beating against his back with her small fists.

With a final salute, Iain waved to their guests, and to an accompaniment of hoots and ribald calls strode across the great hall and up the stairs to his chambers.

Chapter 8

"**P**UT ME DOWN, ye ruffian!" Lillias cried when the great oak door had been slammed shut behind them. Iain promptly set her on her feet and stood back, watching silently as she straightened her headpiece and veil. With a final twitch at her skirts, she stuck her chin in the air and glared at him.

"How dare ye treat me that way?" she cried.

"And what way is that, my lady?" he demanded, sparks of anger glinting in his dark green eyes.

"Like a—a common trollop," she cried.

"Did I now?" he challenged. "I thought I treated ye like a wife—and one held in high regard at that. Did I not give ye gowns and jewels and finery the likes of such has never been seen in Glen Shiel?"

"Aye, ye did that all right," she answered. "But ye dinna treat me with respect."

"Respect?" He stared at her in amazement. "Did I ravish ye? Did I speak t'ye in a harsh way?"

"Nay!" she cried, blinking to hold back the tears of outrage at his high-handed manner. "But yer actions were disrespectful nonetheless."

Iain stared at her in consternation. "Woman, I have traveled considerably over my lifetime. I've been received in the finest salons in France, and I pride myself I can treat a lady with honor and respect."

"No doubt ye've been in the finest salons—and mayhap

132

the finest bedrooms—of France, my lord," she retorted. "But ye dinna treat me with respect this night. Ye treated me as Red Rafe would have treated one of his women."

Iain's shoulders sagged at her words. "Aye, lass. And well I ken. Ye looked every inch the lady tonight and I was proud of ye. But ye wounded my pride when ye showed such abhorrence t'spending the night in my chambers that I wished t'wound yer pride as well. I feared yer grand new clothes had gone to yer head."

Her anger melted away from her. "Nay, my lord. We but made a bargain and I've a wish to stick to it."

The gentle expression left his face and he stalked about the room tearing at his hair. "And if I've a mind to change the terms of our agreement?"

"Ye've given yer word," she cried. "And I trusted ye."

"Fool that ye are."

"Am I?" She stared into his eyes. "Is Iain MacLeod to be known as a liar and a cheat?"

"Ah, lass, look away from me," he muttered, and moved toward the window that opened out over the moat. The moon had risen and cast its golden light against the black water. Its reflected glow gilded him with light.

"I've a reputation as a man of courage and daring, a man of skill and strength in battle. I've faced ferocious warriors in combat and walked away to tell of it." He turned to look at her. "Yet a wee lass with eyes like the purist sapphires and hair like spun gold, and a mouth like the petal of a flower, defeats me at every turn with her tongue like an adder."

At first his words had been softly wooing, but at the end his tone was harsh, his expression furious. She backed toward the door and hated herself for showing such timidity before him. Her words were that much bolder.

"Ye have no need of pretty flattery, my lord," she declared mockingly. "There is no one to see or hear, except me, and I do not trust yer humoring. 'Tis only to gain yer own end. In private we can be ourselves and speak plainly."

For a moment he stood outlined in moonlight, shaking his great dark head until she wondered if he'd gone daft, then he turned and she saw the humor gleaming in his eyes. "I'm glad ye find me amusing, my lord," she snapped, for she'd thought her little speech enough to disconcert him at the very least. She flushed at her own naïveté. "Ye must find me a stupid, backward thing after all the court ladies ye've known."

"Obstinate, stubborn, impossible, aye, but never stupid or backward," he replied. "Ye've a quick wit about ye I find unsettling in a lady."

"Are ladies not supposed to be quick-witted, my lord?" she asked sweetly.

"Let's just say the ladies I've known have not always displayed such wit. I believe it's considered unfashionable to be too intelligent at court"—he paused—"or in bed." He ambled toward her, his fingers loosening the fastenings of his velvet *chamarre*. Warily she watched as he drew it off.

"What are ye doing, my lord?" she demanded in alarm when he went to work on the fastenings of his undercoat.

He stopped his pacing and glanced at her. "Why, I'm readying myself for bed, my lady," he explained, as if to a simpleton. Lillias flushed at his mockery.

"B-but I—" She straightened her shoulders. Her small chin went up in the air. "I'll bid ye good night then, my lord." She turned toward the door, but he was there first, his hand holding the panel, so she could not swing it open.

"Ye kinna leave," he said sternly.

"I'm tired, my lord. I wish to retire to my chamber." She kept her tone calm and her expression haughty.

"Ye'll be spending tonight here in this room, my lady," he growled. "I'm not of a mind t'let ye go along the hall. Some servant will see ye and report t'my people below."

"Is that what concerns ye most, my lord?" she flared, deliberately arching one eyebrow in a superior manner as she'd seen him do. "Must the *Ceann Mor* of all the MacLeod clan concern himself with what others think of him?" Her gibe hit a nerve. He snatched his hand away from the door, but his broad body still blocked her escape.

"Nay, blast ye. I care naught what they think of me, save those reasons outlined when we agreed t'our bargain. It suits me well at the moment t'ha' others think our marriage has been consummated this night. Will ye fight me every step of the way?"

She dropped her gaze, knowing she must acquiesce yet again. Her words were tart. "Nay, my lord. At the moment it suits my purpose to go along with our bargain."

"And when it no longer suits ye?"

She smiled up at him, unaware of how alluring was her sapphire glance from beneath gold-tipped lashes. "Then, my lord, ye will know in due time."

"In due time?" His fists clenched and he swore under his breath. "God's blood, ye tempt a man to take his hand t'ye, and respect and honor be damned!"

She drew back in alarm. "If ye strike me, I shall scream as loud as I can," she threatened. "All the castle will hear it."

"And praise me for my manly attributes," he snapped, and turned his back on her.

"Yer manly attributes," she jeered recklessly. "What manly attributes does it take to strike smaller and weaker than ye?"

His sidewise glance was derisive and superior in a way that was maddening to her. "I was not speaking of *striking* ye," he answered, and she blushed to her roots to realize that his manly attributes were indeed something else altogether. Before she could recover enough to retaliate, he took down a key and inserted it in the heavy metal lock on the door.

"No," she cried, making a grab for the key, but he'd already accomplished the deed of locking them in together and was tucking the heavy key into his shirt. His eyes glittered with determination as he glared down at her.

"Ye will spend the night in this room, my lady," he instructed. "And I do not intend t'spend the next hours worrying over whether ye've scooted out."

"I won't sleep here," she cried, stamping her foot with vexation. "I'll stand right here by this door until ye let me out."

"Suit yerself," he answered, shrugging. "As for myself, I

am weary. I'm going to rest on yon bed. If ye've a mind to sleep there as well, rest assured, my lady, ye'll na be touched by me. I'll keep t'our bargain."

So saying he moved to the fire and stripped away his doublet and shirt, so he stood, bare-chested, in only his *chausses*. She glimpsed his powerful build, the heavily muscled shoulders and flat belly—and the bulge at the juncture of his thighs. Without glancing at her, he doffed his boots and pushed his *chausses* over his slim hips. She caught a flash of pale skin and turned away, pressing her trembling hands over her eyes. A sudden heat flared within her, bringing a misty sheen to her brow and upper lip. She had a sudden desire for the cool night air and staggered to the window and threw back the shutter.

"Please, my lord. I—I beg of ye," she stuttered, not certain of what she begged him. Finally she pulled her scattered thoughts together. "Have ye no sensitivity for the presence of a lady? I've na' yet been wi' a man, nor even seen one wi'out his—his trousers."

"I'm used t'sleeping naked," he retorted, and made no move to cover himself.

A long silence stretched between them and she ventured a peek from between her fingers. He stood before the fire, sleek and naked. The bulge that had caused her such consternation was covered by shadows, but now she was aware of the very maleness of him in every hard, lean line of his body. The space between them seemed fraught with peril.

"There's na need for ye to peek at me like that," he growled. "We're wedded and ye can look yer fill if ye've a mind to."

"Oh! I was na' p-peeking at ye like some sly serving wench," she denied hotly.

"Ye were," he said imperturbably.

Deigning not to continue their argument, she gazed out at the moonlight on the distant hills, seeking to calm her fevered mind. A muscle in her leg trembled much as she'd seen on a fine steed that had been ridden too hard and fast; she was unaware she was gulping in great draughts of night air.

"Ye'll make yerself sick," a voice said from behind her, and Iain reached around her to close the shutters. Now only the light from the fire illuminated the room. It's heat filled her body until Iain touched her and she knew the heat came from him.

"I—I dinna mean to stare at ye so," she stammered. "It's just that I never knew a man's body could be such a thing of—of beauty."

Iain MacLeod smiled slightly. Desire coursed through him at her words. He felt his shaft harden. He was touched by the guileless innocence of her observation, but more he was fired by this evidence of her sensuous response to him.

More than ever he was certain of her virtue. No woman could pretend such awkward ignorance about men. He realized now that her behavior on the hillside that first afternoon had only been the frank response of a healthy and curious young woman. That she'd been indiscreet was not in question, neither was the question of her virginity. He'd gotten them off to a bad start and thwarted his own desires with his unfounded accusations.

He must go gently, if he were to woo her out of their bargain and into his bed as his wife. The thought of sending her back to her clan was intolerable to him. She was beautiful and lively, and she came from the powerful McGinnis clan. With the MacBains and McCulloughs showing hostility, he was grateful for the connections she brought. But if he were honest, his desire for her as a wife went further than the rich alliance she brought him. The MacLeods were a powerful enough clan in themselves.

Nay, his desire for Lillias was something else altogether, something akin to the passion for pleasure he'd learned as a young man in the bedrooms of too many French ladies of noble birth. Yet standing here beside her, drawing in the flowery scent of her, he recognized this primal lust he felt was different in that it was unfettered by coy manners, undiluted by the veneer of civilization he'd learned in France.

Was he like his father, after all? he wondered, and resisted the urge to strip her of her finery and throw her on his bed to relieve himself on her. As he stood watching her with her proud head in her hands, he felt a wave of tenderness for the fine innocence she displayed. He was the first naked man she'd looked upon and she found him beautiful. Bemused, he reached out to her, barely touching the satin cloth of her gown, so intent was he on not loosening the beast that dwelled in his chest and loins.

"Aye, lass, I'm glad ye find pleasure in looking at me. 'Tis naught to be ashamed of." He grasped her shoulder, pulling her back against him. She inhaled sharply and went rigid at his touch. "I would find great pleasure in looking at ye in the same way. We might yet spend an enjoyable night together."

"I beg ye, my lord, to remember yer promise." She kept her face averted from him.

"Dinna be so standoffish, lass," he said gently. " 'Tis natural for a man and woman to find pleasure in the sight of each other. It leads them to find additional pleasure in a number of ways, such as touching." His hand slid along her shoulder, his long fingers splayed over her bare skin, barely brushing the tops of her breasts. Her nipples tingled and pushed against the tightly laced satin of her gown, as if seeking his touch.

"Our bargain." She half sobbed.

"What about it?" he murmured, bending his head to place a hot kiss at the edge of her gown, near her shoulder. His breath licked against her skin like Satan—as she imagined he would be at the gates of hell. As before, her knees grew weak, so she feared she might fall, and she was ashamed of her weakness. She must be strong and uphold the honor of her own clan. Men might not understand that women could feel a need for honor and retribution as keenly as they did themselves.

"I—I have no desire for ye, Iain MacLeod," she cried, and was certain her words were not false.

He was silent for a moment. "I don't believe ye," he said huskily, and turned her, so she was facing him. She could no longer look down, else she would be gazing at that hardened, elongated part of his anatomy that had fascinated her so before. She was forced to raise her gaze to his. Her cheeks suffused with color.

"My lord, I beg ye," she whispered.

"Aye, lass. I hear yer plea." Deliberately he chose to misunderstand her. " 'Tis the same as my own." He enfolded her in his strong arms and lowered his head.

She drew her breath in sharply just before his lips claimed hers. He plundered her mouth, using no restraint in the face of her reluctance, for he was caught up in the memory of the lively young girl on the hillside who had responded to his embrace with a fervor that had matched his own. His hands came up to cup her breasts and he cursed at the rich fabric that kept her smooth, scented flesh from him.

She was caught in his heat and passion. Her hands had meant to push him away, but glided over his smooth skin, pausing when they encountered the crisp patch of hair over his chest and forearms. She opened her mouth to utter a protest and tasted his tongue, hot and bold, vanquishing her every resistance. Her wandering touch was as searching as his own.

They had a need to know more of each other. Her fingertips were sensitive to the feel of his sleek, muscled body as she traced the contours of his shoulders, the narrowing wedge of his back, and the taut lines of his buttocks. She paused, knowing she'd wandered into forbidden territory, but wasn't all of this forbidden, if she had no wish to lie with him?

"Nay, my lord," she cried, pulling away. She could not look at him for shame that she could not stop her wayward behavior.

"What manner of game is this?" he demanded huskily. "D'ye jest wi' me, lass? D'ye tease me t'madness?"

"Nay. I cannot do this, my lord. I cannot lie with ye in yer bed and rise and walk to my mirror in the morning."

"And why not?" he demanded, his bare chest rising and falling with barely leashed lust. "D'ye na' find me t'yer liking then?"

"I cannot forget ye're Red Rafe's son," she answered,

turning away from him. She did not see the fury in his face, but she heard it in the growl he emitted. He strode away from her toward the fireplace, where he rested his arm against the stones and peered into the flames.

"Aye, and that will ever be between us," he muttered low. Once again fury overtook him and he turned on her. "Am I always t'answer for my faither's deeds?" He glared at her so ferociously, she feared to answer and stood mute before him. He stood naked still, half hidden by the shadows, but her frightened gaze was held by his eyes. They were terrible to see, black and wild with rage.

"If this is how it's t'be, I'll earn my own reputation for black deeds!" He charged across the room, his intent evident on his face.

She shrank back against the stone wall, fear making her tremble. Wildly she looked about for a weapon, a dirk or claymore, but there was none. Iain had shed his armature near the fire and it rested there. She was defenseless, as she had been so many times before Red Rafe and his cruelty, but this was a much greater peril than ever she'd faced with that barbarian.

Something snapped within her and she pushed herself away from the wall and faced her tormentor, eyes blazing, head high. She was every inch the lady, and even as his steps took him across the chamber toward her, Iain felt an abhorrence for what he was contemplating. Her words stopped him cold in his tracks.

"So, this then is the Black Beast of Cullayne," she jeered. "He lives beneath that fancy veneer ye brought back from France. I kinna stop ye, Iain MacLeod, from what ye have in yer mind, but if ye ravish me this night, ye'll bear the curse of my contempt every day of yer life."

"And d'ye not feel contempt for me already?" he cried. "When I've treated ye with naught but consideration?"

"Aye, that ye have," she answered fairly. "But with yer kind acts, ye demand in return that which I must na' give if I'm to return to my clan and find a new life. I will na return to my home dishonored, else no man will have me."

He stared at her in consternation, picturing her naked and

sprawled beneath the humping body of some unnamed man. The image would bring madness to him.

"That will not happen," he growled. "No other man will have ye."

Startled, she glared at him. "But our bargain . . ."

"Our bargain be damned!" he thundered. "I renege on our bargain, for ye'll never leave Glen Shiel, save at my side as my wife. No man shall ever touch ye, save me." He reached for her, snatching her against him. His mouth claimed hers in a kiss that took her breath away. His tongue dueled with hers, subduing her, mastering her.

She could not fight him, could not resist, but she would not be a party to this outrage against her. Passively she stood until his onslaught had ended and he tore at the silk ribbons that held her gown in place. When it fell at her feet in a cloud of blue satin, she could not hold back the tears that filled her eyes and poured down her cheeks.

Iain did not notice. Impatiently he tugged at the ties of the *farthingale*, which he himself had lightheartedly tied around her waist. The wicker cage went the way of the gown. She stood only in her thin chemise. It, too, fell to the floor. Her scent filled his nostrils. Like a greedy child who's been offered a sweet, he pulled her braids free of their coronet and unplaited them, so her hair tumbled about her shoulders and down over her breasts. She was like a beautiful wildflower. With the peeling away of each petal, he seemed closer to that which he sought, wonders and delights such as no man had dreamed.

"I would see ye naked," he whispered, and shoved the linen undergarment, with its virginal ruffle, over her shoulders. It, too, fell to the floor.

In wonder, he stood staring at her perfection. The raging beast had been tamed; now he sought only to worship her with his eyes and hands. She was too fine to rush, he perceived. She was a woman to be taken with patience—and every nuance of sensuality a man possessed. He was committed to using every ounce of expertise he'd learned in the beds of France. Even as he made that vow, even as a brief image of those long forgotten conquests returned to him, he cast them aside, for he was not an expert in making love to a woman, he was but a callow boy, discovering for the first time his own passions as a man.

She touched him as no other woman had. He was prepared to spend the night teaching her the special mysteries that existed between a man and a woman and showing her the paradise only lovers can achieve. With a low groan, he swept her up in his arms. Her golden, fragrant hair draped over his arm, reaching nearly to the floor. As he turned toward his bed, the glint of moonlight fell across her face and he saw her tears.

"Nay, lass, dinna weep," he murmured. He moved to his bed. She was like featherdown in his arms. He tightened his grip, fearful suddenly that this was but a dream, that she was not there in his arms, a flesh-and-blood woman, but a fairy sprite playing a cruel jest.

She made no resistance as he placed her against the pillows, nor when he lowered himself to the mattress beside her, half covering her body with his own. He felt the smoothness of her limbs and his senses were inflamed. Silken tresses covered her breasts; he swept them aside to expose the rosebud nipples. He bent his head and laved a nipple with his tongue.

"I will not hurt ye, lass," he whispered. "Put yer arms around me and we'll travel on a journey such as ye've never seen before."

She did not answer, nor did she put her arms around him. They lay at her side. Her face was turned away from him, her hair fanning out away from her. He drew back and stared at her.

"Will ye na look at me, lass, and speak t'me?" he inquired. Only a single tear rolling down one rounded cheek was his answer.

"I'll make ye want me, too," he muttered, and claimed her mouth. He clamped one muscular leg over her thighs as if to hold her captive, but there was no need, for she did not fight him.

She lay as one in a trance. He pushed his throbbing shaft against her, his hands gripping her soft buttocks, so he might have better access to her body, but he did not enter her. He trailed a fiery kiss down her slender throat, to the swell of her breasts, his teeth nipping at the tender, swollen nipples. She stiffened.

No more! She could bear no more. He didn't notice her small white fist gripping the bedcoverings.

"Lilli," he murmured. He wanted more than her body. He wanted all of her, her fire and passion, her very soul. In despair, he gripped her chin and placed his lips against her cheek, tasting the salt of her tears. He wanted to sob as he'd seen men do when bested in battle, for surely he'd been bested this night. Slowly he drew away from her.

"Ye win, lass." He sighed wearily.

At last, she turned her head and gazed up at him, her eyes dark with some unspoken pain. "I may go t'my room?" she asked hopefully.

"Nay," he said, shaking his head like some wild beast and stepping off the bed. "I will na accept defeat that soundly." His dark eyes regarded her. "I've never had a woman say me nay," he said. "Yet my own wife does so."

"I am not truly yer wife," she said, sitting up, so her hair covered her nakedness. "I was but a pawn between yer faither and mine. Yer faither won and I was given in marriage to a man who did not want me—or think of me for nine years."

"Ye know full well, ye were but a mere child."

"Aye, a mere child," she echoed. "With no recourse but to endure the fearsome taunts of yer faither and his men, with naught to succor me but Aggie and the few friends I made in the village. When ye returned and agreed to return me to my clan, I thought my exile was nearly ended. Now, ye tell me nay. My life hangs on yer whim alone."

He turned away then and reached for a plaid, which he wrapped around his hips, leaving his furred chest bared. In bare feet he paced the cold stone floor and finally turned back to her.

"Ye shame me, lass, as none have before ye," he said huskily. "I cannot undo what was done t'ye by my faither, but I've a wish t'have ye for my wife." He pushed a large hand through the wild black tangle of hair falling across his brow. "Once I have made peace with the MacBains and the McCulloughs, so I no longer need the McGinnis support, I will return ye to yer clan as I promised, if ye wish t'go."

"I will," she cried fervently, half rising to her knees— and in the movement revealing one pearly round breast with its rose-tinted aureole. His hungry gaze swept over her, lingering where the long tresses mingled with the short silken curls at her mons. She noted his fixed stare and crossed her hands over her loins.

"Will ye?" he asked, and his voice was thick with desire. "Have ye heard of handfasting, Lillias?"

"Nay," she said, with some puzzlement.

" 'Tis a term for a practice among all clansmen."

"What is that practice, my lord?" she asked. Her pink tongue flickered nervously across her full pink lips.

" 'Tis a trial marriage. Ye will spend yer nights here in this room with me."

"Nay!" she cried, her eyes wide and dark as the midnight sky.

"If ye wish to return to yer clan, ye must," he declared roughly. "I will not take ye against yer will, but I will do all that is within my powers t'win ye for my wife."

" 'Tis a futile effort, my lord."

He stared at her, remembering the involuntary responses she'd tried so hard to hide from him at the beginning. Only when he'd tried to force himself upon her had he driven away her newly burgeoning passion. He'd not make that mistake again. He'd use gentleness, patience, guile, even treachery to win her.

" 'Tis an effort I look forward t'making," he answered softly. He whisked away the plaid and walked to the bed. Bending, he pulled the covers over her, then got into bed beside her. She scooted away, but his long arms reached out and pulled her close. She felt the heat of his body along the whole length of hers, and one tender nipple brushed against his furred chest, loosening those feelings within her that were dark and disturbing.

"Please, my lord. I beg ye to let me return to my own room."

"I wish ye here beside me," he said. "I will keep my promise t'ye, Lillias, but I'll ha' ye here in my bed."

"To give credence that our marriage has been consummated?" she asked.

"Nay, lass," he whispered wearily. "Some men wear a hairshirt t'do penance for a wrong. This is my torment—to lie beside ye and not take ye as I wish."

She'd needed reassurance that he would not dishonor his promise a second time. His words gave no such assurance, only added to her anxiety, for she could not hold him at bay again. Her body clamored with a need that was new and wonderful and terrible at the same time.

She wanted to hate him, but she was touched by his behavior. He'd wanted her and yet he'd pulled away. The contradiction confused her. Were not all men like Red Rafe, especially his son?

"Ye could end yer torment by sending me back to my chamber," she tried again.

"I've no desire to end it, lass, except in one way," he whispered. "I believe ye'll come t'me of yer own accord, for ye are not immune t'me."

"What d'ye mean?" she asked nervously.

"Ye did respond t'my kiss whether ye meant to or not. I think ye will again."

"Nay," she cried. She clenched her fists against his chest and lay trying not to reveal by one ragged breath the hot, sweet liquid that ran through her like a river.

Unknowingly, Iain was himself the catalyst that drew her mind from forbidden pleasures. "I've been thinking, lass," he murmured against her hair. "I've just appointed Everard as my steward. He'll take some of the burden off ye, but ye'll need more help wi' the making of clothes for the castle servants and whatnot. If ye've a mind to ask Mary McFerris t'come t'the castle and help, ye may."

"Mary McFerris?" Lillias cried joyously. "Ye'll not mind?"

"Nay, lass. I would have ye happy wi' yer friends about ye. I want ye t'feel this is yer home now."

Her elation died. As she'd already observed, with every gift he gave, he expected something in return. If she weren't careful, she might be committed to promising something she could never give, for she discerned Iain wanted not only her body, but her heart and mind as well. Still, she would take this unexpected gift, for she'd missed Mary and the confidences they'd shared. There was so much to tell Mary, so much to ask her about, for Mary was far more knowledgeable about men and their strange needs. Comforted by the thought she would have her friend near, Lillias closed her eyes. Her body relaxed, sagging slightly toward Iain.

He lay for a long time after she slept, breathing in the fragrance of her, allowing himself the luxury of caressing her sleek, soft body until he feared he might spill his seed into the bedcovers, as he had when a young lad and no willing serving wench was handy. He sighed and moved away from the sleeping golden-haired girl. He'd thought to eventually win her over by insisting she share his bed without fear of deflowering, but he hadn't reckoned on the effort such a promise would cost him. A hairshirt would have been a far easier thing to endure.

Chapter 9

S HE WAS IN a world of wonder, of sensation and beauty such as she'd never experienced before. There were no boundaries around her world, no beginnings, no endings, only endless possibilities. She was naked in her world and unashamed of her nakedness. Her limbs were sleek and long and liquidly graceful, her skin silken and soft to the touch, her hair like a golden skein spun by the fairy people themselves.

She was not alone in her world. She could not see the other person, but she could feel him. She knew he was a man because his limbs were hard and strong against hers and she felt his hot, pulsing rod against her belly. She moaned with anticipation.

"Lass," he whispered in a husky voice, and she turned toward him. His mouth claimed hers and she opened her lips, accepting his thrusting tongue, feeling a liquid core bubble to life inside her. He tore his mouth away from hers and trailed a hot, moist path down her throat to her breasts, cupping them, so the nipples were more readily accessible to him. She arched her back, a mewling sound escaping her. She wanted to feel his hot mouth against her flesh.

"Are ye sure, lass?" he whispered. She smiled and pulled his head down to her nipples, sighing when she felt his teeth graze the sensitive buds. He nipped then laved the pink rosebud until she felt her bones melt and her long,

147

slender legs thrashed and parted in wanton invitation. He drew back and she whimpered, reaching for him.

"Nay, lass," he said softly. "Open yer eyes and look at me, so I may know ye want this as much as I do." She whimpered and turned her head away, not wanting her beautiful world to be disturbed. "Open yer eyes, Lillias, and say my name." The stern words shattered her dreamworld. She started and opened her eyes. Finding herself entwined in Iain's arms, she pulled away.

"Ye promised!" she cried. She could just make out his features in the light from the dying fire.

"Aye, that I did, but ye've been dreaming," he informed her. His large, warm hands clasped her shoulders and the heat of his body held her captive. Remembering her erotic dream, Lillias flushed under his unwavering gaze.

"Was it only a dream, lass?" he murmured. His voice was rich and thick in the half darkness. The room seemed very close, so she could not breathe.

"I—I remember no dream," she said stiffly.

"Then yer passion was a reality?"

"No, I— Ye've confused me."

"I'm confused myself," he answered. "I desire ye, lass, and I think the feeling's mutual, but my hands are tied by a hasty promise. It's up t'ye to tell me yer desire."

"I—I dinna desire ye, my lord," she said primly.

"Then kiss me good night," he whispered. "And I'll not bother ye again."

She looked into his eyes and saw dark passion. Caught in that bold hot gaze, something inside herself was forever lost. A fire licked along the edge of her awareness and she wet her bottom lip with her tongue, and, leaning forward, deliberately placed a kiss upon his lips. He made no move to gather her close, but simply waited for the kiss to end. When she drew back, she felt the scrape of crisp chest hair against her swollen nipples and she drew a deep breath and closed her eyes.

"Lass, ye set me aflame," he whispered huskily.

She felt him shudder beside her and knew he was exercising great self-will to keep his promise. She felt the power of herself as a woman and wondered that a man as commanding as Iain MacLeod could be brought to heel by a woman's body.

His mouth claimed hers, his tongue probing relentlessly until her tongue met his challenge and she moaned low in her throat. The world of passion and wonder was back, yet she couldn't resist testing her newly discovered powers.

"Good night, my lord," she said softly, and felt his body go still.

"Lass, ye but jest wi' me," he said.

"Nay, my lord. Ye instructed me to give ye a good night kiss and so I have. I bid ye good night now."

He growled then like a great beast from the forest; she shivered and drew back from him. "My lord?" she asked fearfully, but he only turned on his side away from her and lay still as marble. She knew he did not sleep, for he made no movement, not even to breathe.

Sighing, she turned on her side, but in her movements, her soft buttocks brushed against his, so he gritted his teeth and cursed every woman that had set foot upon the earth from Eve to Lillias herself. On her side of the bed, Lillias smiled. She felt heady with triumph. Never had she had such control over a man. She went to sleep again, smiling.

"Iain, the McCulloughs have struck again!" Fists hammered against the heavy oak door. Lillias woke with a start, aware she'd slept warm and succored within Iain's strong arms, but now, as the knocking continued, he disentangled himself and leapt from the bed, cursing. Without bothering to gather up a shirt, he strolled to the door and threw it open.

"What is this racket?" he demanded, standing with fists planted on his hips. His black hair was tousled, his eyes dark and glinting with anger at being awakened so abruptly.

Peadair stood on the other side of the portal. Upon catching a glimpse of Iain's nude state, his glance automatically went to the bed where Lillias sprawled, the hastily thrown-back covers scarcely covering her own bare limbs. Quickly he looked away, thinking of the dusky beauty of Mary

McFerris. Though she drove him crazy with her kisses, she would not tumble with him in a hayrick. He envied Iain the right to claim his lady so quickly.

"What d'ye want, Peadair?" Iain demanded.

"A messenger came with word that the McCulloughs struck Glengarry."

"The bastards! When?"

"At first light. They must have ridden all night across MacBain land to reach Glengarry without a warning being raised."

"Aye, and they'll have t'go cautiously t'make their way back." Iain hurried to pull on his *chausses* and shirt.

"They've taken twelve clansmen for ransom."

Iain paused in tugging on his boots. "Twelve men?"

"Aye. They claim they'll kill one each day until we release their chief."

"No women or children were taken?"

"None. Fighting men all."

"Praise be t'God for that," Iain said, and slumped down on the stool to stare into the gray ashes of the fireplace. "I kinna be blackmailed like this, else no man will respect our boundaries."

"Aye," Peadair said somberly. He knew what was coming.

"We'll try to rescue the men, but if we don't, their lives will be forfeited."

Peadair nodded. Lillias listened to their conversation with growing horror. Wrapping the coverlet about herself she bounded out of bed.

"Surely, ye dinna mean to let yer own men die?" she exclaimed. "They fought brave and true for ye."

"I kinna back down t'the McCulloughs," Iain said quietly. His eyes were terrible to see in their pain for his captured men.

"Is yer pride worth the lives of twelve good men?"

" 'Tis more than pride," he flared, springing up from the stool to face her. "If we let the McCulloughs bamboozle us on this, we'll never know a minute's peace. I'd thought to avoid out-and-out feuding by keeping Angus McCullough alive and having him stand before a council of all the clans t'answer for my faither's death."

"Red Rafe was an evil, cruel man who pillaged and raped his neighboring clans without mercy," she stormed. "He deserved to die."

The back of his hand struck her across the cheek, driving her backward against the bed rail. He followed after her, towering over her, his chest heaving, his eyes black with rage.

"No man deserves t'die," he said quietly. "Stay out of it, Lillias, for ye know naught about this business. 'Tis for a man to determine such things, not a mewling woman."

Her cheek throbbed from his blow—and though tears rolled down her face, she would not give him the satisfaction of backing down.

"I see no man," she said, and spat on the stone floor beside his feet.

Iain's fists doubled and his teeth showed in a grimace of warning. Her every instinct was to flinch against the blow that must surely come, but she stood defiant, her chin stuck out, her eyes flashing with scorn.

Peadair stood silently watching. He'd never seen a woman defy Iain in such an open manner, and those few men who had, had died for their insolence. He had been stunned to see Iain slap his wife, for never had he been known to strike a woman. Still, her words had been unforgivable. One could hardly blame Iain if he punished her further. But Iain turned on his heel, grabbed up his weapons, and stalked from the room.

Lillias's gaze followed him all the way to the door; when he was gone, she slumped over the bed, cupping her face in her hands and weeping, unaware that Peadair still stood observing. Slowly he approached her. Lillias's name had come up often in his conversations with Mary McFerris and he knew the two were close.

"He's not himself, my lady. 'Tis a hard thing for a man t'prove his leadership t'other men." Awkwardly he offered words of commiseration.

She stood weeping and raised her head. Her eyes glinted

with unshed tears like sapphires sparkling with a splendor of their own. One pale cheek was already turning dark with a bruise.

"Ever since he's come back to Cullayne Castle," Peadair rushed on, "he's been made to prove himself."

"Ah, yes, the great MacLeod pride," Lillias cried bitterly.

"I don't think it's pride, my lady. He's told me something of his faither. Ye were right, he was a cruel man, and as a boy, Iain was often the butt of that cruelty."

Her expression grew stiff. "Only until I was kidnapped and brought here," she said. "Then Iain left and I was the butt of Red Rafe's madness." Her body, held so rigidly, seemed to quiver. Peadair saw in her the same pain and fury he'd witnessed in Iain when he first spoke of his faither. Slowly he shook his head.

"Aye, and Red Rafe's left the two of ye a terrible legacy," he said sadly, and went away to join the rest of the men who were gathering in the bailey. The chieftains who had traveled to the castle for Iain's banquet would send their wives back to their own castles under heavy guard. Word had already gone back to their own strongholds to muster more men.

"We'll ride on McCullough Castle at once," Iain was saying.

"D'ye think they'll bring their hostages there," Peadair called, "or will they take them t'some other hiding place?"

Iain shook his head. "They'll come to McCullough Castle. 'Tis on MacBain land. It's easier t'defend."

"They'll be expecting us this time, Iain," Sinclair answered. "They'll na leave the castle unprotected a second time."

"Aye, but with enough men we can overpower the castle guard. They've not had time to bring their forces back from Glengarry. Our clansmen will meet at McCullough Castle." Iain looked around the gathering of Highlanders, seeking the right one. "Adhamh."

"Aye." Sinclair's oldest son stepped forward, his cheeks puffed with pride that he'd been so singled out by his chief.

"Ye and Uilliam stay behind with the rest of yer men t'guard Cullayne Castle."

The lad's cheeks deflated and he stared at Iain with disbelieving eyes. "I've a mind t'go wi' ye, sir," he said.

Iain had already started away; now he turned and eyed the young man. "If the McCulloughs get wind of what we're about, they'll come here to rescue their faither. I need a reliable man who's not afraid t'lead his people against the McCulloughs should they attack."

Adhamh Sinclair looked impressed with his new task. "Aye, sir," he said, straightening his shoulders.

"Something else, lad," Iain said, clamping him on the shoulder. "My wife is here. I'd na have her molested by the McCulloughs."

"I'll defend her wi' my life."

"I knew I could depend on ye." Iain turned away. "All right, lads, let's ride to rescue our clansmen. *'Vincere vel mori!'* "

" 'Victory or death!' " they cried in unison.

In short order the men were mounted and ready to ride. The bailey was filled with servants and children and women come to see their husbands off to fight. Dogs ran among the horses' hooves, barking and setting the mounts to rearing. The men cursed and tightened their holds on the reins. Iain glanced around to see that all was ready and his gaze was caught by the flash of color in the castle window.

Lillias stood there, clad in a dressing gown of scarlet velvet, plaiting her long golden hair into a braid. He thought of their angry words and the look on her face when he'd slapped her. His hand burned where it had contacted with her fair skin. He clenched his fist.

There was no need to feel guilty. She was only a woman, and many a woman had been struck to still her wagging tongue. But what if he never came back from this battle? Did he want her to remember him only as the man who struck her in anger?

The men waited expectantly, their mounts snorting with impatience; still he could not give the signal to ride away.

Nudging his horse he rode beneath her window and held up his sword.

"Will ye give me a token, my lady, to take into battle wi' me?" he called up. She gazed down at him, her face somber. "Can I not carry a smile from yer pretty mouth?"

"I have no smile, my lord," she said sternly.

"A smile of forgiveness?" he asked gently.

His men waited, and he knew they heard every word. He'd not beg for more than this, but his words seemed to have been the right ones, for she picked up a pair of scissors and cut a golden curl of her hair, tied it with a blue ribbon, and, leaning forward, attached it to the point of his blade. His men cheered. She blushed and her eyes flashed with pleasure when they met his again.

"I shall wear yer token next to my heart, my lady," he called. "It will be our talisman."

"A pretty speech, my lord," she answered, "but when ye return I will offer ye another token—and I hope it will please ye as much."

"If it comes from yer fair hand, I vow I will," he declared. He saw the anger was still in her eyes. She'd not yet forgiven him his barbaric act, but she'd played a pretty game for the benefit of his men. Iain could ask no more than that for now. Nudging Lucifer, he signaled his men forward.

They rode at full tilt out of the castle gate, over the causeway, and through the village. Only at Mary McFerris's gate did Peadair pause long enough to tell her of the attack and to exchange one hasty kiss. This was the second time in a fortnight they must ride to McCullough Castle, and Iain's thoughts were not on the business at hand, as they should have been. They lay back at the castle with a golden-haired siren with eyes like the finest sapphires and skin like alabaster. Even now if he licked his lips, he could taste the sweetness of her, for after a night of holding her, she seemed to have become a part of him. Cursing, he pushed her out of his thoughts and concentrated on the fate of his twelve clansmen.

* * *

Lillias watched the men gallop out of the castle and wondered how many of them would return. The thought that Iain MacLeod might not be one of them was strangely unsettling. Then she raised her hand to her burning cheek and blinked back tears. How could she feel this need for a man who could strike her as he had done? Yet she recalled the tenderness he'd shown to her during the night and acknowledged her words had been as cruel as any Red Rafe himself might have uttered. She knew Iain was laboring to find his place here at Cullayne. He seemed torn by some strange sense of guilt over his father's death.

Many times, she'd thought he would cast aside his restraint and take her as was his right, since she was by law his wife. Still, he'd sought to woo and cajole her. He'd tried to awaken her passion and so he had, although she'd tried hard not to reveal the depth of her responses. Even now, if she thought too long of his warm, hard body lying beside her in the darkness and his strong hands molding her body, a flower began to unfold in her belly, spreading its strange elixir through her.

She got to her feet abruptly. She'd not sit here mooning over him like the calf-eyed milkmaid he'd first mistaken her for. She set about such a furor of cleaning, the servants grumbled and threatened to run away. By nightfall, she was too tired to think, and fell asleep instantly.

And so it went in the days that followed, until Aggie chided her gently for overworking and sent her down the hill to the village to visit Mary. Remembering she'd intended to ask Mary to the castle as a seamstress, Lillias agreed.

She dressed quickly, choosing once again a simple shift such as the village women wore. The women were working in their garden patches, and though they stopped to lean on their hoes, few waved or called to her as they once would have done.

"Good morning, Helen," Lillias called blithely. "Isn't it a beautiful day?"

"Aye." Helen returned her greeting, her face wreathing in a big grin. "Wait, I've got some fresh butter for ye." She hurried into her cottage and was back almost immediately with a bowl of creamy butter.

"I kinna take yer butter," Lillias cried. "Ye can sell it at market day."

"Nay, I meant this for ye and the new chief," Helen said, shoving the wooden bowl into Lillias's hands.

"Thank ye, very much. I'll save it until he comes back and put it upon his bread with my own two hands."

"That's a good wife," Helen said approvingly. Her face took on a leer. "I'm that surprised t'see ye walking so well today."

Lillias blushed. "I'd best be getting on to Mary's, else she'll be gone back into the hills to the shieling."

"I fear John McFerris's cows will suffer some this summer," Kendra said. She'd walked down the lane to join them over Helen's fence.

"Why is that?" Lillias asked, then at the women's knowing glances, she grinned.

"He's a handsome man, is Peadair McDermott," Kendra observed.

"Aye, that he is," they all agreed.

"But na so handsome as the new laird," Kendra teased, laughing when Lillias's face flushed.

"D'ye na mind that Doug has gone off wi' Iain and his men?" Lillias asked.

Kendra rested a hand on her swollen stomach and shook her head. "Nay, he dinna go off to France wi' Iain all those years ago. I kinna ask him to turn his back on his friend now that he has returned. It would kill Doug's spirit to stay behind safe while everyone else defends the clan."

"Are ye not worried?" Lillias insisted.

"Aye," Kendra answered bleakly, so Lillias knew she was indeed concerned for her husband's safety.

Lillias continued up the lane to Mary's cottage, calling out greetings as she went, for now that the ice had been broken and the women saw she was acting no differently simply because she was mistress of Cullayne Castle, they hailed her as always.

Lillias was surprised when she reached Mary's cottage,

for the door stood open and the sound of weeping came from within.

"Mary?" Lillias said from the doorway. Her friend sat on a stool by the cold fireplace, sighing. "What's wrong wi' ye, Mary?" Lillias inquired, going to kneel before Mary and hug her. She wasn't used to seeing strong, resilient Mary weep.

"I dinna ken," Mary whispered tearfully. "I was getting ready t'lay my fire and suddenly came the image of Peadair laying dead before me. I could na stop the weeping."

"Oh, Mary, 'tis only a—a—" Lillias could think of no word that would put her friend's fears at ease. Then a thought came to her. "If Peadair were t'fall in battle, then likely so would Iain. The two are so often together."

"Aye," Mary said, wiping at her eyes with her apron. "Why d'they go out to fight so? Why can't they live in peace?"

"The McCulloughs attacked the village Glengarry and captured twelve men. They have t'avenge such an act."

"Aye," Mary flared. "But they only attacked because our men had taken their chief—and so it goes, on and on. They must save their precious clan honor, and in the meantime, women sit and weep."

"Mary, I thought ye were loyal t'yer clan," Lillias chided.

"Loyal, aye," Mary snapped. "But I don't have t'like what they're doing that risks their lives."

"They'll be all right, Mary," Lillias murmured.

"Why didn't they just release Angus McCullough and be done wi' it?" Mary demanded tearfully. Fresh tears rolled down her cheeks and she sat rocking, her arms crossed over her chest. Gazing at her, Lillias felt her own alarm growing.

"Iain wants him t'go before the king himself, t'answer for the murder of Red Rafe."

"He could still make his appeal t'the king wi'out Angus McCullough being present," Mary said. "They dinna need to bring him here to Cullayne."

"I think they were afraid he'd be whisked away to safety," Lillias said in a low voice. Fear was knotting in her stomach and she wondered why she should care about Iain MacLeod. The plain fact was, she did care. She sat staring at Mary's tear-blotched face and an idea formed in her mind. Leaping to her feet, she hurried to the door, then remembering the reason for her visit, she turned back.

"Mary, if I can find a way t'save Peadair and the others, will ye come t'the castle t'be seamstress? We need ye badly."

"Aye, Lilli. If ye need me, I'll come. But what can ye do t'save our men?"

"I kinna say now. Only would ye be willing t'give up yer horse if ye knew it might mean the end of fighting wi' the McCulloughs? Iain would replace it for ye."

"My horse?" Mary repeated in puzzlement. "Aye, I'd give him up willingly, but— What is it ye intend t'do?"

"I kinna say now." Lillias hurried out of the cottage and fairly ran back up the hill to the castle.

Inside the curtain wall, she turned not to the main part of the castle, but traced a familiar path to the stone tower, where Angus McCullough was being held prisoner. Adhamh Sinclair had posted his moss-troops to guard the castle gates, but they were stationed along the ramparts. No one thought to question her or her destination.

She must have a plan, she thought, and for once, she must be patient. Angus could never make his escape in full daylight. She forced herself to retrace her steps to the castle to wait for dark.

"Ye're jittery, my lady," Aggie observed when Lillias threw down her embroidery and paced to the window to peer out at the waning day. "Are ye concerned for yer husband?"

"Aye," Lillias answered, and forced herself to settle on her stool again.

Finally evening drew near. Dark shadows lay in the hollows and glens. Lillias pleaded a fatigue that was not an untruth and went off to her room, then sneaked down the back stairs and made her way across the bailey to the tower. Unchallenged, she slipped inside the stout plank door.

A familiar gloom pervaded the lower room and she hurried toward the stairs, climbing quickly toward the light that spilled in through the arrow-hole windows. At the landing, she paused. A new door of thick planking had been hung. The hinges and key lock were of heavy iron. Now that she was here, faced with the reality of her plan, she felt helpless and uncertain; then her eyes spied a heavy iron key hanging from a peg and her resolve returned. Grabbing the key, she knocked lightly on the heavy door.

"Who's there?" a voice bellowed from the other side.

"Shh!" Lillias cried. "Please, sir. Dinna make a racket and I'll set ye free."

"Ye'll what?" The voice was suddenly toned down to a whisper. "Who the devil are ye?"

"That does na matter," she said. "But if I set ye free, ye must promise to do na more harm to any of the MacLeods and to live in peace with them."

"Wha—?" The voice was back to a bellow. "I'll never live in peace wi' the devil dog MacLeods. I'll hunt them t'my grave and drink a toast t'each one that falls beneath my sword."

"Then I'll not release ye wi'out that promise," Lillias said. She waited. There was a long silence on the other side.

"D'ye mean wha' ye say. Ye'll set me free?"

"Aye! And I've seen to a horse for ye."

"Ye're an angel of mercy, a fairy come to spirit me home," he cried.

"I'm a flesh-and-blood woman," Lillias replied tartly, "who wants to see peace between our clans. Make yer promise that ye'll never raise a broadsword against a MacLeod again."

"Aye, I promise," Angus said.

"This means ye kinna go back on yer word," Lillias insisted, for she wasn't sure whether to trust the wily old chief.

"I never will!" he cried. " 'Tis a pact between us until our deaths. Open the door, lass, so I can be on my way."

Lillias fit the iron key into the slot and turned it. Immediately the door flew back and Angus McCullough stood before her, his black eyes fierce as they glared at her. Lillias knew a moment of fear and backed away from him until her back was against the stone wall. Slowly he followed her, his gaze taking in every detail of her appearance.

"Why, yer naught but a milkmaid," he declared.

Lillias straightened and pulled her shoulders back. "I am Lady MacLeod, wife of Iain MacLeod, Earl of Shiel and *Ceann Mor*."

"Ye dinna look it," Angus said, thrusting his face close to hers. "Ye look like a serving wench, and a comely one at that." His intentions were clear.

"If ye intend t'assault me, ye'll pay a heavy price," she said calmly. "For I shall scream as loud as I can and the men my husband has posted below will come running. Ye'll be clamped back in yon cell and likely beheaded by my husband immediately upon his return."

Angus stared at her, then threw back his head and roared with laughter. "Aye, and ye're a sassy wench t'boot," he exclaimed. "I'll be on my way, but I'll be lookin' t'meet ye again someday."

"I desire nothing less," she said. "Come and I'll show ye a secret way out of the castle."

Angus's eyes grew shrewd, but he followed her down the spiral stairs. "Ye're risking much t'set me free. Why?"

"I am tired of the feuding," Lillias replied over her shoulder. "I know ye and Red Rafe have been enemies for many years, but he's dead now and Lord Iain is a different man. He wants peace between the clans." They'd come to the outer door now. She paused and gazed up at him. "I hope ye'll take this gesture as one of peace and do yer part t'end this bitter feud."

Angus stared into her clear blue eyes and was touched by the innocence he found there. He'd planned to break her neck and thus insure no outcry as he made his escape, but now he saw the sincerity in her gaze and decided to let her live.

"I'll think on yer words, wen—my lady," he said.

"And ye must remember yer pledge t'me," she insisted.

"Aye, my pledge," he mumbled, unable to meet her eyes for he knew the moment he was safely back at McCullough, he would muster his men and ride on the MacLeods with a vengeance. He couldn't admit that to her, though, for she might yet cry out a warning to the guards.

"When ye go out this door, ye must turn to the left and take the stairs. At the bottom is a water gate, which will lead ye outside the wall. Ye'll find a boat at the head of the moat, where it flows into the loch. Take that to the other side. Go into the village, to the last cottage. There is a horse tethered in the back. Take that. God speed ye."

Once again her words left him flummoxed. Not only did she free him, but she wished him God speed. He hesitated, studying her fair coloring. "Ye are na' a MacLeod born?"

"Nay," she answered. "My faither was Lord Robert McGinnis, Earl of Mamore."

Angus stared at her. "Be yer mither Margaret McCullough?"

"Aye," Lillias said. "Ye be my uncle. I've long known that. Go quickly now." She threw open the door.

Angus peered out at the guards ringing the castle walls far longer than need be, for he was studying the castle's strengths as well. "Ye dinna give me a weapon," he mumbled.

"Ye'll not need one if ye go in peace," she answered. "Please go before ye're discovered."

"Aye." He stepped out into the shadows and calmly walked toward the stairs she'd mentioned.

Once he was safely away from the glen, with the fine mare running strong and sure beneath him, he thought of the golden-haired angel who'd set him free, and, remembering the pledge he'd made, he laughed out loud. He'd keep that pledge, by God he would, but he'd never stop feuding with the MacLeods.

A few miles from the village, he came upon a Highlander walking his lame horse. Angus's wily gaze noted the fine weapons strapped to the man's saddle.

"Kin I help ye?" he asked, coming to a stop beside the man.

"Not unless ye have a spare horse," the Highlander answered tartly. "I was on my way t'join Iain of Cullayne at McCullough Castle."

Angus was startled to hear such news. His niece had not been as forthright as she might have been, he surmised, but he was not one to let such things stand in his way. He grinned at the MacLeod clansman.

"I was just on my way there, too. Mayhap we kin ride double until we reach a village where ye can find another horse. Ye kin hide yer saddle in those rocks yonder and come back for it later."

"I'd be much obliged," the Highlander said, with some relief. He hurried to gather up his weapons and hide his saddle.

"I'll help ye," Angus said, dismounting.

But when the man had carried his saddle to the clump of rocks, Angus leapt upon him from behind, bore him to the ground, and broke his back in one mighty jerk. Saddling his stolen horse with the dead man's saddle, Angus shoved the Highlander's dirk into his waistband and picked up the lochaber ax and the targe. Deliberately, he left behind the broadsword and claymore, so all would know that he intended to honor his pledge to Lady MacLeod never to raise a sword against the MacLeods again. Remounting, he set off at a gallop for the McCullough stronghold, hoping his luck would remain true this day and he might yet meet his old enemy's son and send him the way of his father.

Chapter 10

*I*AIN AND HIS men rode hard and by early afternoon had reached the outskirts of McCullough Castle. McCullough's sentinels had alerted the castle of their approach, so a force of men marched out of the gate to meet them on the flat plains beyond the walls.

"Why would they leave the safety of the castle to fight wi' us out here in the open?" Peadair asked in bewilderment.

"They're confident they can win," Iain declared. "That's the first step toward defeat."

"They outnumber us two to one," Sinclair observed grimly.

"Aye, they've brought MacBains here t'help them," Doug McFerris declared. "I recognize Duncan MacBain himself riding there beside Godfrey McCullough." He pointed to the two powerfully built men at the front of the column. Both wore chest plates of metal.

"They'll cut us t'ribbons," one of the lesser chieftains warned.

"Take heart, men," Iain cried. "Two t'one evens up the odds for the McCulloughs."

The men grinned at his jest and felt easier. But the McCullough troops were in position before the castle now and sat waiting, a formidable line with their lances and shields held before them. The dying sun glinted off their cabassets.

163

"Peadair," Iain said quickly, before the men could lose their confidence in the face of McCullough's superior numbers. "I'll take half the men and climb that hill to the east. Ye keep the other half here. Have them spread out. Stagger yer lines so ye look greater in number."

"Aye!" Peadair cried, grinning. Many a time he'd seen Iain outwit a larger—more deadly—enemy and come out victorious.

"When ye see me charge down that hill, ye take the rest of the men and engage the west end of that line."

Peadair nodded. Iain signaled Sinclair and half the men to follow him. To camouflage their numbers, he led them around and came up the hill from behind.

"All right, men," he called. "Turn yer plaids wi' the dark side out." The men looked at one another sceptically but did as he bid. "Now, I want ye to listen carefully and do as I tell ye. We must be quick about this." He outlined his plan and the men began to grin.

When they were ready, with bows fitted to their arrows, he led them in a gallop up the hill. No sooner had they topped the ridge, than they loosened their arrows, not pausing in their headlong gallop.

The MacLeod Highlanders were skilled archers. Their arrows found their marks, thinning McCullough's line considerably. When they were done, they turned and galloped down the back side of the hill, changing their plaids as they rode. Iain signaled to them and they wheeled their mounts and climbed the hill again at a dead gallop. At the top they loosened their deadly missiles and Iain could see the gaps that had widened in McCullough's defensive line.

Sounding the wild Highland cry, Iain led his men in a charge down the hillside toward the McCullough troops. He could see Peadair's men racing across the glen at the other end of the line. The McCulloughs and MacBains watched the headlong flight of the oncoming men and their faces blanched. They were certain there were more MacLeod troops just over the ridge of the hill who would soon join the others. They had been foolish to come out to face the enemy thusly, Godfrey deduced and, wheeling his horse, raced back toward the castle.

The line broke even before Iain and his men reached it. The McCulloughs and MacBains were making a mad dash to gain the safety of the castle walls, leaving their dead behind them to be trampled under the hooves of the MacLeod clan. And the MacLeods were fast on their heels, engaging in combat with those who lagged behind.

"Go after Duncan and Godfrey," Iain shouted at Sinclair, and the two men raced after the leaders.

Iain knew if they gained the castle, they'd raise the drawbridge and leave their men without to fight off the MacLeods as best they could. Godfrey's mount had no sooner disappeared through the gate than the drawbridge began lifting from the banks of the moat.

With a curse, Iain urged Lucifer on, clamping his powerful thighs and lifting himself in the saddle as the two of them sailed over the widening gap between land and drawbridge. The black stallion's hooves struck against the wood planking as he galloped down the steep incline caused by the rising drawbridge. Iain's sword was at the ready, and as he galloped past, he struck out at the gatekeeper. The man fell backward, mortally wounded. Iain wheeled Lucifer in the narrow enclosure and rode back toward the gate. He was aware that Godfrey McCullough brandished his sword as he maneuvered his own mount toward Iain.

Iain hacked at the stout ropes that held the drawbridge aloft. One rope gave beneath his onslaught, but the other held firm and he was out of time. The drawbridge was stuck halfway up—and he was alone in the castle of his enemy. He brought up his sword to ward off Godfrey's blow.

The two men skirmished, fighting to maneuver their mounts into position, so they might have a better strike. Behind him, Iain heard a thud against the stalled drawbridge and guessed that Peadair was about to gain entry to the castle. He gave his attention to his fight with Godfrey, who was not particularly skilled with the sword. He was far too clumsy. Too quickly, he became frustrated with his own ineptness, and, with a growl, rode his horse a short distance away, dismounted, and brought out his claymore, which was heavier and needed two hands to wield. "Come on, ye black dog," he snarled. "Come meet yer doom. Or air ye afraid to fight with a manly weapon?"

"Nay," Iain said calmly. "I bested ye once, Godfrey, and saw yer backside at Clunes Forest."

" 'Tis a lie. No McCullough ever ran from a MacLeod."

"If they be women and children," Iain said.

The giant lumbered at him. He'd learned nothing from their last encounter. Iain nimbly sidestepped his wild rush, and at the last moment drove his thin-bladed sword deep into Godfrey's chest. A cheer went up at the gate; and he rushed back to find that Peadair had managed to enter the castle and cut the other rope, so the drawbridge fell across the moat. Quickly his men entered and overcame the McCulloughs and MacBains.

"What do we do with them?" Peadair asked.

"Kill them," Sinclair and several other men demanded, but Iain shook his head.

"Put them in the dungeons below. We'll take no more lives than we have to." Iain looked at his friend and clamped him on the shoulder. "Ha' ye put sentries to watch for the McCulloughs who raided at Glengarry?"

"Aye, they're in place." Peadair nodded.

"The raiders had t'ride hard to reach Glengarry undetected. They'll ride through the night wi'out rest in an attempt to reach the castle before dawn. Tell the others not to attack until the McCulloughs are inside the castle. We want them to think all is as it should be so they'll bring their hostages in unharmed. Once they're inside, wi' the gates closed, they'll be easily overcome."

"I'll inform the men."

Peadair and Sinclair settled down to wait. The men were exultant at the victory they'd achieved over greater forces—and all through their new chief's wiliness. They admired such a trait almost more than they did bravery.

Near dawn the raiders rode into view just as Iain had known they would. Their horses were lathered and spent;

the men slumped in their saddles, their exhaustion making them less wary than they might have been.

From the castle ramparts, the watching MacLeods could see their own clansmen tied to their horses, their bloodied heads unbowed. Muscles bunched, tempers flared, but under Iain's whispered instructions, they held their silence and waited until the men had entered the courtyard and the bridge was raised before leaping down on the unsuspecting McCulloughs. The battle was an uneven one. McCulloughs and MacBains fell beneath the strong arms of the Mac-Leods; only Iain's shouted orders for leniency saved the clan from near extinction.

"We've got our own back," Iain shouted. "Let's quit this place."

With a roar of approval, the men fell in behind him, but on their way through Glen Garvan, they rounded up many of Angus McCullough's prize shaggy-haired cattle and fine horses and drove them back to Strathan. In Strathan, they paused beside the River Pean. Across the river lay MacBain land, so they did not tarry.

"We're grateful for yer speedy rescue," Harold Bethune of Glengarry said, clasping Iain's hand. "We pledge our support t'ye as our new chief."

"I'm happy t'hear that," Iain said. "It's my wish t'end this eternal feuding, but I'll never buckle t'anyone's demands."

"Aye, and we would ha understood, even if it meant our deaths at the hands of the thievin', murderin' McCulloughs. We need a strong chief t'follow after Red Rafe."

"Take one-third of the cattle and horses to compensate ye for yer trouble," Iain called, and men hurried to cut out the designated livestock.

The Glengarry men waved their thanks and rode off toward their home, driving the McCullough livestock and thinking of the surprise on the faces of their women when they returned so promptly. They mulled over the stories they'd have to tell when they gathered around campfires.

Iain and the rest of his men turned east, feeling jubilant and expansive. Despite their own weariness, they joked and laughed easily. As they pushed toward Cullayne, other chieftains dropped away to return to their own castles; each took a portion of the booty they'd taken from McCullough lands.

Most importantly, they carried with them a new confidence in their new leader. He was not Red Rafe, they discerned, and some were beginning to suspect he was better, for Red Rafe had brought about much of the feuding that prevailed now with his raids and cruelties. They liked the thought of a more peaceful time.

Iain was anxious to return to Cullayne Castle, but when he came to the River Mallie, he reined Lucifer to a halt.

"What's the matter?" Peadair called, riding up beside him.

"Cullayne Castle lies just over that next ridge," Iain said. "I'll na return t'my wife carrying the stench of death about me."

"Aye, it would na be pleasing to a woman's sensibilities," Peadair agreed.

Iain motioned to the rest of his men and dismounted. Throwing off their clothes, the men waded into the chilly waters and set about flailing their arms and legs to warm themselves. They splashed and frolicked and raced one another in such a lighthearted manner, an onlooker would never have guessed they were the same ferocious Highland warriors who'd overtaken McCullough Castle. When he tired of the rough play of his comrades, Iain floated on his back and stared at the dark sky. An evening star was just lighting the velvety blackness.

"It was a job well done," Peadair said, and Iain righted himself to talk to his friend.

"Aye," he replied. "We rescued our men, bested the McCulloughs in battle, and have Angus in captivity so he must stand trial for his treachery. With the McCulloughs broken, the MacBains will be more likely t'negotiate a peace."

"Aye." Peadair nodded in agreement.

The sound of a galloping horse came to them. The men

tensed and crept toward the banks where they'd left their clothes and weapons, but the horse passed on by.

" 'Tis a clansman returning home tae his shrewish wife," a man called, and they laughed, for they all had experienced their wives' razor-sharp tongues when they'd tarried overly long at the village tavern.

"Time t'go," Iain called, and they dressed and buckled on their swords.

Peadair glanced at his friend. "Ye've another battle when ye return to Cullayne," he said. "One of yer own making."

"Aye, I've thought of little else," Iain acknowledged. "I've carried the image of her face when I struck her. It was a terrible thing I did. Somehow I have to convince her I'll never commit such an act again."

"Aye, it will be hard for the lass t'trust ye again soon." Peadair glanced at Iain's drawn expression. "However, dinna blame yerself too much. Her words regarding Red Rafe were unseemly harsh."

"Remembering Red Rafe, they were probably well earned. No doubt, she suffered at his hands. I should send her back to her own clan," he said. "That's what she wants."

"And ye?" Peadair asked. "What d'ye want?"

"The thought of it is more troubling than I could ever have imagined. I've never known such a need for a woman. Peadair, if I tell ye something, promise me ye'll never laugh?"

"I never will."

"I dinna consummate my marriage the night of the banquet."

"Ye dinna?" Peadair asked in amazement. His dark gaze flashed to Iain's face to see if his friend was jesting with him. In the pale moonlight, Iain's face was serious.

"I wonder even now at my supreme restraint," Iain was saying in a humorous, self-mocking tone, but Peadair sensed he found no humor in the situation.

"Man, I saw her in yer bed with her hair let down and her clothes all about the floor."

"Aye, but nothing happened between us. I gave her a vow and she called on me to honor it."

"Still, she was there all naked and golden."

Iain gave him a hard glare. Peadair shrugged.

"I am a man," Peadair declared. "I notice such things as naked women with pretty limbs barely covered. Ye need not fear my competition, though. I've a longing for a lass with midnight-black hair and eyes as blue as the pools of the Five Sisters."

"I was not worried about yer competition," Iain declared flatly. Usually such wordplay would have elicited a boastful challenge between them. "Ye're right to wonder. Even now, I kinna believe I showed such restraint. I wish I'd used such patience in my treatment of Lillias. Since I returned to Cullayne Castle, I've done naught but bedevil her, accusing her of adultery and striking her. Little wonder she looked at me with hatred when I sat below her window begging a talisman to carry with me."

"I dinna see hatred in her face, Iain," Peadair advised. "Confusion mayhap, but not hatred for ye."

" 'Tis good then," Iain said. "For by God's teeth, I'll not let her go back t'her clan."

The rest of the ride back to the castle he spent thinking of Lillias and how he might persuade her to forget their agreement. He wanted to explore the sensuality her innocent kisses hinted at; he wanted to learn her moods and listen to her intelligent conversation: he wanted to watch her eyes darken and grow light again when he caressed her and she discovered, despite herself, some new level of pleasure. He'd never display anger toward her again, he vowed, no matter what she said or did. He was going to continue wooing her until she forgot he was Red Rafe's son and learned to desire him back.

Feeling buoyant, he nudged Lucifer's sides and brought his men into the castle bailey at a brisk gallop. Night had fallen and he was weary, but automatically his eyes went to the mullioned window where last he'd seen Lillias. A light burned bright there and he pictured her warm and silken in her bed. Peadair saw the direction of his gaze and took hold of Lucifer's bridle.

"Go on wi' ye. I'll take care of Lucifer. Ye've better things t'do."

"Dinna ye want t'see Mary McFerris?" Iain teased.

"Aye, I will, in my own time." Peadair grinned, his teeth flashing white against his weathered skin. "Ye've bridges t'mend, Iain. Get on wi' it."

Iain didn't want for any further urging. His long legs bounded up the steps and into the great hall. His gaze searched among the people seated near the fire, but Lillias was not to be found there. Aggie looked up from her sewing and pointed to the stairs. Iain gave her a grateful salute.

Now that he was home again and about to face Lillias, his mouth was dry and his mind as empty as an addlepated lad. Slowly he climbed the stairs and started along the hall toward Lillias's chamber.

Suddenly her door flew open and she stood in the open space, her glorious hair loosened about her shoulders and down her back. Candlelight from beyond cast a halo about her figure. She wore a shift of such fine linen, it was diaphanous in the candle glow. Her slender limbs were plainly outlined, the dark rose aureoles of her breasts a beckoning invitation.

Oh, Lord, Iain thought, he could not withstand another time of temptation as he had the last night they'd shared a bed.

"Ye're home," she said softly, and took a step toward him.

"Lillias," he murmured, striding toward her. "I've thought of nothing else but ye." He wanted to take her into his arms but was fearful he might push her further away from him.

Her face was glowing. "I have some wonderful news to tell ye."

"I have something I must tell ye first," he declared. "I'm sorry I struck ye. It was an unmanly thing t'have done."

She made no answer, only stared at him with her eyes wide with surprise and her lips parted in wonder.

"I should be horsewhipped, I know," Iain declared. "I hate what I did t'ye, and if ye feel the same about me, I'd understand. But before ye determine ye do, listen t'my words. I've a desire for ye, Lilli, like I've never known for any other woman. I see a lass that's witty and spirited and beautiful enough to tempt a saint from his perch. And I'm just a mortal man. I want ye as my wife, Lilli," he whispered. His outpouring of words hung between them.

"I don't hate ye," was all she could think to say. Her voice sounded strangely hollow to her ears, but she was breathless with the import of all he'd revealed, for his feelings so exactly matched what was in her own heart. How could she feel this way about a man she'd vowed to hate and destroy? she wondered. Yet, she did.

The memory of his powerful body lying naked beside her own caused the blood to pulse through her veins, thick and hot with lust for him. Iain looked into her eyes and with a low groan reached for her. She came into his arms willingly, her lips parted for him. Her body, willowy and warm beneath the shift, molded to his own. Her firm breasts crushed against his chest, her graceful arms wrapped around his waist with surprising strength, and she pressed her belly against his loins in an age-old invitation.

Iain swept her up in his arms and carried her along the corridor to his room, where he placed her on his bed. Then he knelt beside her, touching, caressing, seeking. There was a wildness, a flame that had flared to life between them the night they'd spent together, and now the conflagration threatened to overwhelm them.

Iain had to remind himself that she was a virgin still, and, despite his own needs, he must go slowly. But she was eager for him, unmaidenly so, her mouth opening to him again and again, her hands glancing across his body in a restless, feverish seeking that left them both breathless.

"Lilli," he murmured, cradling her gently and raining fiery kisses along the edge of her jaw and down into the hollow of her throat. She shivered in delicate response and he felt hot blood flood his member, so it throbbed and rose between them, nudging at her belly insistently. "I must slow down if I'm to make this night memorable for ye, too." He drew back.

"Dinna leave me," she cried, reaching for him.

"I must shed my clothes," he said, laughing softly.

Wide-eyed, she watched as he slipped off his linen shirt and then his *chausses*. Her hands reached for him greedily, sliding over his shoulders and furred chest. Before she could lock her arms around his neck, he nudged them aside and lifted her linen shift over her head. Her hair, wavy from the braid she'd worn through the day, whirled over her bare shoulders and down her body, covering as completely as her shift had done. Iain pushed the silky gold from the lithe body, his gaze drinking his fill of her womanly beauty.

"I have a need t'see ye, Lilli," he murmured, cupping the creamy fullness of her breasts in his hands. She closed her eyes and swayed toward him when he rolled the rose tips between his fingers.

"I fantasized about this while I was gone," he whispered, and bent his head to take one hard pink bud into his mouth. His teeth glazed their tender points, his tongue laved away any pain, so she felt only the pleasure.

She moaned, threading her fingers through his dark locks, and he gathered her against him, bearing her back against the pillows. Her legs instinctively parted in readiness for him.

"Nay, lass, not yet," he murmured. "There's much ye need to learn and experience before we reach that moment."

She gazed up at him in silent supplication and he grinned to think how quickly he planned to turn that innocence into wanton abandonment. His mouth claimed hers with renewed fervor, his large hands skimmed over her pliant body, tracing, molding, adoring. At last they found their way to the nest of golden curls at the juncture of her thighs. Gently he parted the warm, giving flesh until he found what he sought, the tiny bud of female pleasure. Gently he stroked her, intuitively knowing the fragile state of her virginal body. When he heard her gasp and sigh, he increased the rhythm of his strokes, each time dipping deeper into the moist core of her until she arched her back and opened to him.

"Please," she murmured, and wasn't certain for what she begged, only knowing that it would give her surcease from the burning desire that threatened to consume her.

"Not yet, my bonny lass," he murmured, although to delay further threatened to render him forever crippled in certain areas of his body.

He suckled her breasts, stroking her until she was gasping with need. Only when she whimpered and raised her head to stare into his eyes with mute supplication, her eyes dark and glazed, did he relent and trail a blaze of kisses down her smooth belly.

His tongue laved the bud his hands had stroked. She started, and her knees clamped together against his ears with such force he felt pain. He continued stroking her with his tongue; her legs fell away in languid surrender. Her back arched, her breasts coned and peaked with passion. Her fingers wound in his dark locks, tugging at him with impatience, and when she could no longer resist, she gave way to the shattering climactic response of her own body, bucking beneath him.

Only then did he raise himself above her and enter her moist passage, thrusting against her maidenhead, so it was sundered without an outcry from her. He felt her tightness and his own orgasm erupted, so he spilled his hot seed deep inside her.

She felt as if she'd been on a great journey, to a land of exquisite wonder and sensation, and now she must return. She would never be the same, she perceived. Her chest rose and fell with each breath, her sweat mingled with that of the man who'd claimed her. He lay with most of his weight to her side, so as not to crush her, but his hips and thighs still claimed her. His rod was buried deep in her. His dark head rested against her shoulder. Languidly she brought up a hand and smoothed back a tumble of raven hair.

"Are ye all right, lass?" he mumbled.

"I never knew the mating between a man and woman

could be so wonderful." She sighed. "I will never be the same again."

"It will be better next time," he said. "There will be no pain and we'll take more time."

"When will we do this again?" she asked softly.

"When ever ye want."

"Now?"

He groaned, but already his shaft, seated so deep inside her, stirred. She felt the movement and her own body pulsed in answer. Iain chuckled.

"Ah, Lilli. Ye'll be the death of me."

"Oh, I didn't know," she said, preparing to pull away from him, but he rose above her, pinning her with his hands on her shoulder, his hips holding her captive.

He moved against her with long silken strokes that made her eyes open wider. Her slender legs came up to cradle him, then timidly wrapped around him, urging him closer, deeper, faster. He moved against her and felt a roaring rush inside his head. Her muscles clamped around his rod, pulsing and gripping until he felt himself swell. He stroked harder and faster, wanting this never to end, wanting to lose himself within the perfumed silken folds of her body.

Lillias thought she might faint. She couldn't endure more, couldn't feel more, couldn't tighten anymore than she had. She felt pain, sweet and pleasurable, and wondered that it could be so. With each thrust, she was driven closer to an edge, a pinnacle that could never be reached again. With one final thrust, Iain shuddered inside her. She felt the shattering eruption of his orgasm, the hot pulsing head buried deep inside her, and her own body clenched in a series of spasms she could neither control nor halt. She wasn't aware that she screamed; then her throat constricted and she couldn't breathe. Mouth opened in a silent cry of ecstasy, she fell over the edge of the pinnacle and drifted slowly back to earth.

Only when her heartbeat had resumed and her breath returned to normal did she open her eyes and stare up at the man who hovered above her. His eyes were like dark emeralds, enchanting her, mesmerizing her. She was caught in a trance of his making and she'd never be free again. What's more, she never wanted to be.

She pushed aside all thoughts of the vows she'd made to avenge her father's death on him. She was Iain's wife, and she'd given him her heart and soul and body. She must move forward from that indisputable fact. Tomorrow, she thought sleepily as she cuddled against him, reveling in the feel of his strong arms cradling her. Tomorrow, she would work out the problems. Tonight, she would enjoy the passion of her husband.

"I've a gift for ye, wife," he said, late in the night, when they were too sated to move. He retrieved a box from a nearby chest and brought it to her, laying it on her sleek belly and opening it, so she might see the emerald jewels that gleamed within.

"They are so beautiful, like yer eyes when ye laugh," Lillias exclaimed, sitting up, so she might see them better. Her hair tumbled forward, half covering her nakedness in a manner that was innocent and seductive at once.

"Their beauty is dimmed beside ye, lass," he whispered, stealing a kiss from her. "When ye wear these, I would ha' ye think of this night, and when I see ye wearing them, I will remember the passion we've shared."

"I ha' no need of jewels to remember this night," she answered, and he drew her into his arms.

The priceless emeralds fell from their box and lay forgotten in the tangle of bedclothes as he claimed her yet again. When they'd scaled that peak of pleasure and descended, Iain folded her close against him and they slept.

Her last thought was that she hadn't told Iain about Angus McCullough and the pledge she'd extracted from him. She would tell him in the morning over breakfast—and glory in the praise he would heap on her for her uncanny wisdom.

Chapter 11

*T*HE MORNING AIR was intoxicating, the sunlight burning away the mists on Beinn Bhan and bathing the foothills with a golden alpine glow. From her window, Lillias could see the whole world. The thatch roofs of the cottages were magically gilded, the village itself turned into a fairyland. From the stables in the nether bailey came the bleat of a lamb; a goose girl crossed the drawbridge, driving her squawking gaggle before her.

Lillias sighed, wrapping her arms around her knees as she made herself more comfortable on the stone window seat. She'd never been so happy. She knew problems awaited her, problems she must resolve, but she was imbued with a rosy-hued confidence that assails all new lovers.

Iain had not wielded the ax that took her father's life. He had helped her when she was first kidnapped, given her comfort, brought her Aggie, so she would not be without one of her own clanswomen. And all this for a frightened little girl who had no power to return his kindness. He might be Red Rafe's son, but there the resemblance ended. Iain wanted peace between the clans. Hadn't he enlisted her help toward that end?

She wriggled on the cold, hard stone. She would have to make cushions to add comfort, she reminded herself. Oh, there were many things she would do to see to her husband's comfort. She glanced over her shoulders with a possessive air and was disconcerted to find he lay staring at her through half-veiled eyes. His face was flushed with passion and his eyes were dark, emerald fire, bathing her in their warmth.

Iain awakened to find himself alone in the bed. Muscles bunching in alarm, he prepared to leap from the bed and go in search of her, then he saw her sitting on the windowsill, wrapped in his tartan, the tangled, golden skein of her hair flowing nearly to the floor. Lying back against the pillow, he studied her clear profile against the morning sky. Never had he known a lass so bonny, and that she was his wife seemed an immense good fortune. She turned to look at him and he saw the look in her eyes; his heart swelled. Everything he was thinking and feeling seemed mirrored there on her beautiful face. He put out a hand to her.

"Lillias, come here," he called softly, and at once she rose and ran across the room in her bare feet.

The plaid flew out behind her like butterfly wings and her slim, pale body was revealed to him in all its glory. Her young breasts were a thing of beauty, her sleek, flat stomach, the golden tangle of curls at her mons, her slender legs and graceful feet the stuff of poets. Her face was filled with joy as she hovered over him, her golden hair making a tent around them.

"Come ride, Lilli," he whispered thickly, and pulled her down, so she must straddle him.

He was already stiff with need for her and he gasped as her hot, silken flesh enfolded him. Her eyes widened, her cheeks blushing with surprise and delight. She wriggled— and was so astounded by the effect the slightest movement had on him that she repeated the motion.

Mischievous lights danced in her sapphire eyes and she arched her back, knowing her firm young breasts were more fully revealed to his view and his touch. He cupped her breasts, rubbing the nipples between his fingers until they were rigid and pronounced and she was purring low in her throat, her hips pumping against him rhythmically.

They climaxed together, in a thundering, rushing darkness that overtook them, held them in its thrall, then slowly released them. She still straddled him, her breasts rising and falling with each labored breath she took, her skin glowing with a fine moist sheen. Her hair clung to her damp skin. Slowly she regained her breath and gathered her heavy tresses in her hands and held them atop her head, trying to cool herself. The movement brought her breasts high. Iain rested with his eyes closed, but when she moved he opened them, and, seeing her perfect breasts, moaned as his member stirred yet again.

"No more." He sighed. "I kinna fuck ye again."

His coarse words startled her, then enticed her by its very rareness. The words between a man and a woman in an intimate situation, she perceived, were quite different when used at other times. Suddenly she saw no vulgarity in the word, but recognized that it described an act, a highly erotic, beautiful act that she hoped to repeat time and again.

"Aye, my lord, ye can," she murmured boldly, "and ye will many times before we're done."

"But na all in one night," he objected, laughing.

" 'Tis morning, my lord, and ye've rested throughout the night. I am here for yer pleasure, now pleasure me."

"By God's teeth, I've a woman of insatiable appetite."

"Ye've a woman who was made to wait far too long for what is her right. Now ye have much to make up for, my lord, and I am an impatient woman." Her eyes danced with laughter.

"Aye, and ye've a wicked look about ye, wench, for one so newly initiated into the ways of men and women."

"I am quick-witted, my lord. Dinna ye say so yerself?" she said lightly.

"Ye learn faster than I can teach, ye minx," he growled, and pulled her down beside him on the bed. Still, she couldn't resist peeking at him. His rod lay depleted and flaccid against the nest of dark hair.

"Yer weapon is spent, my lord, she said impishly.

"Dinna underestimate it," he warned, pulling her head back against his shoulder. She sighed contentedly and snuggled closer to him. His hand stroked her hair languorously.

"Ye're a bonny wife," he murmured contentedly.

"Aye, I *am* a good wife," she said, sitting up suddenly as she remembered Angus McCullough.

Below, in the courtyard, a man called out sharply and someone shouted an answer.

"Ye'll be very pleased with me, when ye hear what I've done," Lillias continued, drawing out the telling, so she could prolong the pleasure of her surprise.

Boots marched across the stones of the courtyard. Men cursed and bellowed to one another. "God's blood!" Iain cried, throwing aside the cover and leaping out of bed. Striding to the window, he stuck his head out.

"What's this racket about?" he hollered down.

"The prisoner's escaped," someone answered.

"Ye dinna mean Angus McCullough?"

"Aye, my lord."

"How did ye let him get away?" Iain bellowed. "Send Peadair to me, and get mounted at once. We ha' t'go after him." Iain drew back inside the window and reached for his breeches. His face was distorted in a scowl. Seated on the bed, Lillias felt a dawning dread.

"What's wrong?" she whispered.

"The fools!" Iain was raging. "They kinna ha' let him get away, na after all I've gone through t'get my hands on him." Hastily he pulled on boots and stamped his foot on the stone floor to seat them.

"D'ye mean Angus McCullough?" she asked in a small voice. Her hands trembled as she reached for a coverlet and pulled it about her shoulders. Her face was pale, her lips quivered.

"Aye, I mean Angus McCullough. Come in!" Iain bellowed in response to a knock at the door.

Peadair entered. "There's na sign of him about the castle. I've got men scouting the village and the fields beyond. He can't have got far."

"Dinna any man see him? How could he ha' got away wi'out being seen?"

"I don't know how he could have got out of the curtain wall without being seen. I'll set the men to search the castle again. He could be hiding anyplace." He turned to Lillias.

"In the meantime, my lady, ye should stay inside yer chambers with the doors locked. He could be dangerous if he's cornered."

Lillias pressed her trembling hands over her mouth. "Iain, I must talk to ye."

"Not now, Lilli," he answered brusquely, then turned to Peadair. "Are the men ready t'ride?"

"Aye."

"Let's go then." Iain snatched up his plaid and wrapped it over his linen shirt as he strode to the door.

"Iain, I must tell ye now," Lillias cried. "It's important."

"Later," he called over his shoulder, and ran down the stairs.

Jumping off the bed, Lillias ran to the window and peered out. Men on foot were combing every inch of the bailey and the buildings, using their swords to prod the hay in the stables, startling the pigeons to flight as they examined the dovecotes, for a desperate man might wedge his body into that small space. They even searched the chapel, which brought down the priest's wrath as he indignantly shooed them out of that holy place.

Other men were already on horseback. A stable boy held Lucifer's reins. The black stallion reared impatiently as Iain came out of the castle and mounted. Without a backward glance for her, he rode out of the castle. Lillias sat back on her heels and listened to the thunder of hoofbeats against the plank drawbridge, then slowly closed the window.

Iain hadn't let her explain. She was stunned by his anger that Angus McCullough was gone. She hadn't reckoned on that when she'd made her plan. She'd thought only of how he would praise her when he found out the pledge she'd elicited from the chief. And perhaps that would appease his anger, she thought, and felt the tight bands around her chest loosen a bit. Another thought came to her: Iain might unknowingly break the truce. She had to find him and tell him.

She flew about the room, flinging on clothes. Leaving her hair unbound, she buttoned a green velvet cape over her linen shift and ran to the stable.

"Quickly, saddle me a horse," she cried to the stable boy, and he hurried away to do her bidding. Fuming at the delay, she barely waited until the saddle was cinched before she was in it and racing the horse through the bailey.

"Lillias," Aggie cried from her window. "Where're ye going, lass?"

Lillias took no time to answer but spurred the horse across the drawbridge and turned toward the village. Villagers and men alike were searching the cottages, garden patches, and hayricks. Frantically she looked for Iain.

"Lillias," Mary called, and Lillias reined to a halt before the McFerris cottage.

"Mary, have ye seen Iain?"

"Aye, he and his men went off in that direction. She pointed to the west. "It's true, then, that Angus McCullough escaped. He must have taken my mare. She's missing this morning."

"Oh, Mary!" Lillias said, sobbing. "I fear I may have made a terrible mistake."

"What d'ye mean, Lillias?" Mary inquired, her dark gaze studying the fair face. Slowly comprehension dawned. She shook her head disbelievingly. "Ye dinna ha' anything t'do wi' Angus McCullough's escape, did ye, Lilli?"

"I must go. I must talk to Iain before he does something—something terrible."

She wheeled her mount and sprinted off down the westward path. She would never catch up with them, she feared, and imagined Iain and his men riding right up to the doors of McCullough Castle and engaging in warfare. The truce would be forever broken.

She kicked her heels against the little mare's sides and rode as if her life depended upon her reaching Iain, for if not hers, then surely someone's did. Topping a ridge, she gazed down on the River Mallie and was relieved to see Iain and his Highlanders had stopped to rest their horses. They were gathered around something. Nudging her tired horse, she rode down the ridge, her approach claiming their attention long before she was close enough to hail them.

"Lilli, what are ye doing here?" Iain demanded, with some impatience.

"I have to speak with ye, Iain," she said, sliding out of the saddle and running to him.

She saw the look of dismay and anger in his gaze. "Not now, lass. I told ye, I've something far more important to concern myself wi' than yer women's concerns."

Lillias felt a flare of irritation and tried to tell herself he hadn't meant that the way it sounded. He wasn't trying to brush her aside. At any rate, it didn't matter.

"Ye have to take the time to hear me out, Iain," she insisted.

"I'll talk wi' ye when I've solved this dilemma," he snapped. "Go home, Lillias." He turned away from her to return to his men, who still clustered near a clump of stones. Lillias took a deep breath.

"It's about Angus McCullough," she called, and saw him freeze in his tracks.

Slowly he turned to face her, his green eyes nearly black, his expression stern and savage-looking.

"What about Angus McCullough?" he snapped. "Ha' they found him? Speak up, woman."

"Nay, m-my lord." She stammered in the face of his ferocity. "He won't be caught now. He's surely back at McCullough Castle by now." Emotions shifted across his face as he studied her.

"Why d'ye say that?" he asked finally, and his voice was deceptively mild. She saw the fury in his gaze.

"Because he escaped last night."

"How d'ye know?" he demanded, advancing on her. "Why didn't ye warn someone?" His anger mounted as he thought of the night just past. "Why d'ye let me lie beside ye, knowing my enemy was making his escape?"

She took a step back from him. "It was already too late when ye first came home," she said, then plunged ahead. "He escaped just at nightfall."

"And ye did na sound the alarm?"

"I—I helped him escape."

"Ye helped him escape?" He sputtered in rage. His hand

drew back and she cringed against her horse, certain he meant to strike her as he had once before, but slowly, he lowered his hand. "Why, lass? Explain it t'me t'make me understand yer treachery."

"Not treachery, Iain!" she cried, reaching out to him then. He shook her hand away. "I feared for yer life, and Mary"—she glanced at Peadair, who stood apart, but had plainly heard their conversation—"Mary was in tears with misgivings about Peadair's safety. I knew ye wanted peace between the clans. I thought if I freed Angus, it would show him our good faith. Before I freed him, I made him pledge that he would never again raise a sword against a MacLeod. Don't ye see, Iain?" She held out a hand in supplication. Her expression was elated. "He promised na t'fight anymore. A truce has been achieved."

"Ye little fool!" He gripped her shoulders, shaking her slightly. "Dinna ye ken. Angus McCullough is not a man t'be trusted. He could have killed ye."

"Aye, I knew that was a risk, but I was willing to take it, if it meant making a truce."

Iain's mouth opened and closed as if he had many things to say and wasn't sure where to begin. She perceived he was still furious with her. "Come wi' me," he growled, half dragging her across the ground to the clump of rocks. "I want ye t'see yer truce."

They rounded a boulder. The other men looked up. "Iain, she should not be here," Peadair said, stepping out in front of them.

"Stand aside, Peadair. I want her t'see what her meddling has wrought." Peadair held his ground for a moment, looking from one to the other. Finally he shrugged and moved back.

For the first time Lillias glimpsed the body of a man. She gasped and tried to step back, but Iain pushed her forward.

"Is he dead?" she cried, turning her face away.

"Aye, he is!" Iain snapped. His hand took hold of her chin, forcing her to look at the dead man. "Angus

McCullough killed him last night when he made his escape."

"He promised," she said, tears gathering in her eyes. She'd been responsible for a man's death. "He promised never again to raise a sword against a MacLeod."

"Aye, he'd promise anything to be set free," Iain jeered, releasing her, so she no longer had to look at the dead man's vacant eyes.

"Angus dinna use a sword against Lennox," Peadair said, squatting to examine the body more closely. "He broke his back."

"Nay." Lillias turned away then, bending double against the sudden nausea that assailed her.

"Then he dinna raise a sword against a MacLeod," Sinclair said glumly.

"He'll not keep that pledge once he's returned to McCullough Castle and seen what we've wrought," Peadair warned. "He'll gather as many men as he can to avenge Godfrey's death. Ye'll be his target, Iain."

"Aye." Iain nodded. "Like as not he'll enlist the Mac-Bains as well. Still, he can't muster enough men to outnumber us, unless he draws on the western clans."

"Would he do that?" Peadair asked.

"We took a lot of lives back there. Mayhap he'll figure avenging is not worth the additional lives such a move will cost."

Fighting the nausea as she was, Lillias did not at first attend their words. Slowly the portent of their conversation sank through her discomfort and she raised her head and stared at Iain.

"What are ye saying?" she demanded weakly. The two men stared at her in silence. "Did ye go to McCullough Castle and slay his son?"

"There was a battle. Men were killed," Iain snapped.

She had never seen him like this, so implacable, so deadly. She didn't recognize him as the same man who had gently cradled her in his arms and made love to her.

"Ye killed a man, my cousin by my mither's side, and

came to me with his blood on yer hands," she cried, with horror. "Ye're truly no better than Red Rafe."

He saw the old revulsion in her gaze and reached for her. "Dinna touch me," she cried, sidestepping him. Her eyes blazed with hatred. Iain saw it and feared it was for him.

"Lillias," he cried, "there was a battle. Godfrey challenged me. It was either kill or be killed."

"He was defending his property, as ye would defend Cullayne Castle if anyone came to attack it. He was defending his home, as my faither was the night he was killed."

"Lillias, it was not the same," Iain said placatingly.

He tried to take her hand, but she wrenched free of him and ran back to her horse. She hardly knew what she was about as she pulled herself into the saddle. The rich dark folds of her velvet cape flared around her as she pulled herself into the saddle. Her golden hair, tangled and vibrant, spread like a blanket over her shoulders and the mare's flanks.

Iain ran after her, for once not mesmerized by her proud beauty. His own anger flared. The full weight of her treachery was only now being felt. He was not at fault. She had done a grievous wrong in setting Angus McCullough free. That she should act in such a high-handed manner irked him beyond endurance. He grabbed the prancing mare's bridle and glared up at Lillias.

"Would ye ha' had Godfrey kill me?" he demanded.

"Nay, that was not yer only choice," she answered, almost sadly. Tears poured over her pale cheeks and her eyes held such pain he might have been touched by it—if not for the dead Highlander who lay in his final sleep a short distance away.

"What other choice has a man, when his enemy rides at him with a broadsword drawn? Ach! Ye talk woman talk and expect a man t'listen. I'll not answer t'ye for what I've done, but ye will answer t'me for yer treasonous act." He let go of the mare's bridle.

"Treason?" She forgot about riding away from him.

"Aye, ye sided wi' our enemy."

"There was no treason in my deed. There could have been a truce, if ye had na killed Godfrey."

"There could ha' been a truce with the McCulloughs if ye had not freed Angus," he shouted. "Their clan leaders were dead, except Angus, who was captured and would answer for murder. The McCulloughs defiance was broken, but now, with Angus's return to them, they'll rally again. More lives will be lost because of what ye've done." In the face of his verbal onslaught, her defiance dwindled. She looked at Peadair and saw the truth of Iain's words. Horror washed over her.

"I dinna understand," she whispered.

Iain's eyes darkened. "Ye played me for a fool, granting me the privilege of yer body t'keep me occupied—so I would not find out about yer perfidious behavior."

"Surely ye dinna believe I gave myself t'ye for that reason?" she declared. The mare pranced; she reined her under control without breaking eye contact with Iain. "I meant t'tell ye last night, but when I saw ye—"

"Go home, Lillias. Go back to Cullayne Castle and wait for my return," he ordered, and turning on his heel, stalked away.

She opened her mouth to call to him, but the rigid set of his shoulders told her he wouldn't listen to anything she had to say now. Sadly she turned the little mare and slowly rode back to Cullayne Castle.

"Lillias, did ye find Iain?" Mary called from the castle steps. Her dark eyes were filled with worry. "Was Peadair with him. Are they all right?"

"Aye, they are safe, for now," Lillias said wearily, and, sliding out of the saddle, handed the reins to the stable boy, who'd come running. Lillias looked up at Mary. "Are ye here t'stay?"

"Aye, if ye still want me." Mary grinned with confidence that her presence was, indeed, still wanted.

The sight of Mary's smile tore at Lillias's heart. Was it only weeks ago that they were carefree and happy, preparing to go to the shieling in the hills? Life had been so simple then. Lillias thought of all the changing emotions she'd endured since then. Now she was the chatelaine of the castle, but to what avail if she were hated and reviled for her deed? Tears flooded her eyes and poured down her cheeks.

"Lilli, what's wrong?" Mary cried, running down the steps to take her arm. "Are ye hurt?"

"I've done a dreadful thing, Mary." She sobbed, leaning on her friend's strong shoulder. Mary turned her toward the steps.

"It can't be that bad," Mary replied. "Ye're the kindest person I know, Lilli." She guided Lillias through the great oak doors and up the stairs to her room, ordering from a passing servant that ale and food be brought at once.

"I kinna eat," Lillias cried.

"Then I will eat it," Mary said.

She helped Lillias out of the cape and threw back the covers on her bed. Gratefully Lilli sank back on the soft pillows. Mary tucked the covers under her chin as if she were a child and smoothed the hair back from her face. Aggie had remained silent, but she hurried to the fireplace and brought back a cloth dipped in warm water and bathed Lillias's face. When their ministrations were done, Mary perched on the side of the bed. Aggie hovered at the foot.

"Tell us what horrible thing ye've done," Mary said gently, rubbing Lillias's hand.

"Oh, Mary." Lillias looked at her with stricken eyes. "I've brought about the very thing I was trying to avoid— more fighting. I helped Angus McCullough escape."

"But why did ye do that, Lilli?" Mary demanded.

"I thought if I released him, he would see that we want a truce. One of the sides had to take the first step toward ensuring that. I thought— I made him promise first that he'd not raise a sword to a MacLeod ever again." She blinked back tears at the thought of her own gullibility. "But he tricked me. He planned all along to continue the feud."

"Ye had no way of knowing he'd be so wily," Mary said. "Ye tried in good faith."

"Aye, but not Angus McCullough. On the way back to McCullough Castle he killed one of Iain's men by breaking his back. He dinna break his vow t'me, but the feud goes on. Iain says it will be worse than ever now because they killed Godfrey McCullough."

"Good riddance, I say," Mary replied.

"That man was my cousin," Lillias said wearily. Why could no one understand how she longed for peace and a surcease from the killing?

"Lilli, I'm truly sorry," Mary said contritely, kneeling beside the bed.

" 'Tis no matter," Lillias replied. "I ha' never laid eyes upon him, save when he attacked us on the way to the shieling. In all these years the McCulloughs made no move to rescue me from the MacLeods. They seem not t'feel a family tie, either." Mary regarded Lillias's somber face and exchanged a quick glance with Aggie.

"Without Angus, the McCulloughs would have had no leader t'carry on, and the feud would have been ended. 'Tis my fault it's not."

Mary enfolded her in her arms to halt the tumble of words. "Dinna let them place the guilt on ye, Lilli," she whispered. " 'Tis not women who make war and feuds."

"Aye," Aggie said fiercely. She came around the foot of the bed and sat down beside Lillias, patting her shoulders with work-roughed hands. "The MacLeods ha' feuded ever since I can remember, and the McCulloughs have been a cowardly, bloodthirsty lot from time beginning. They ha' not the guts t'fight back at Red Rafe when he was alive, but they've been harrowing us ever since. 'Tis true, Iain must break their defiance to end the feud, but 'tis not a game of yer making. Now dry yer eyes and get dressed in something fine and dignified. When he returns, he'll find the lady of the castle awaits him."

"Oh, Aggie! Fine clothes will not mend this rift between us." She wept. "Last night, when he returned, I gave myself t'him and he believes I did it to delay his discovering Angus had escaped." Mary and Aggie exchanged glances. The problem was much more serious than they'd imagined, but they didn't tell Lillias that.

"Then all the more reason ye should prepare yerself and

look as bonny as ye can," Aggie cried. "Dinna let him find
ye here in bed, weepin' yer eyes out. Let him see ye strong
and resolved in yer actions."

Lillias looked at her wise nursemaid. "Ye're right, Aggie," she cried, throwing aside the covers and leaping out of
bed.

With their help, she rummaged through the chests and
chose a rather simply cut gown of a rich golden brown brocade; it was made with a square neckline trimmed with a
braid of black-and-gold threads and a tapering waist that
ended in a point in front. The sleeves were slashed, so tufts
of the elegant silk chemise could be pulled through. Aggie
drew up one side of the full skirts to display the matching
underskirt of yellow silk and Mary dressed her hair, combing the silken strands back from a center part and securing
them under a black velvet French hood edged with pearls.
Mary's eyes widened when she stood back to view her
handiwork.

"Ye truly are beautiful, Lilli," she cried. "Ye look every
inch a lady."

"Aye, and so she is," Aggie snapped. "I've been telling
her that all along. She would not listen, but must galavant
around the country like a common peasant." She paused,
aware she might have given offense to Mary.

Lillias, ever sensitive to the responses of others, crossed
the room to an open chest and caught up a rich gown of
rose-colored velvet. "Mary, ye must wear this," she cried.
"It will look good wi' yer vivid coloring."

"I cannot wear something so fine," Mary said, crossing
to finger the rich fabric. " 'Tis a gown for a lady. I'm but
a common milkmaid."

"There's na' about ye that's common, Mary," Lillias
cried. "Come, it's my turn to help ye. Peadair will be so be-
dazzled when he sees ye, he'll na be able to turn his eyes
away."

"I kinna," Mary cried. " 'Tis too fine for me."

" 'Tis not fine enough, Mary," Lillias cried, and rummaged again for a matching chemise. She found one of
white linen and an underskirt of pale green.

"And look, Mary," she cried, holding up another French hood made of black velvet and trimmed with pearl biliments. "We will look quite elegant today."

Mary laughed and hugged her friend. "And we'll sit by the window and sew like ladies who have naught t'do with their time but stitch."

"Save we must not stitch some inconsequential thing," Lillias cautioned. "We must make cushions for the benches in the great hall and begin making garments for the castle servants, or they will ha' naught for winter."

Mary feigned a sigh. "Aye. A lady's lot is far harder than imagined."

"Aye, and I'd planned t'dance tonight wi' the King of Scotland himself," Lillias said, falling in with their playacting and practicing a curtsy as if, indeed, she was before the king.

"Was he expecting ye, then, my lady?" Mary inquired, fluttering an imaginary fan.

"*Mais oui,*" Lillias cried, as if offended. "He sent for me himself. He wants to consult with me on matters of state. The chancellor is furious; the queen is green with jealousy." The two girls dissolved into laughter. Aggie shook her head at their spritely behavior. How quickly tragedy was forgotten in the joys of youth.

A sound at the door made them whirl and stare at Iain MacLeod, who stood glowering at them. His angry gaze took in the opened trunks and scattered finery and his lips thinned. Lillias read the disapproval in his expression before he spoke.

"I see ye've recovered sufficiently from yer distress over Jaimie Lennox, my lady," he snapped. His gaze raked over her contemptuously.

"Jaimie Lennox?" she asked.

"The man Angus McCullough killed after he escaped Cullayne Castle. Ye've been able t'put him out of yer mind fast enough." Lillias blinked back a sting of tears.

"We were just— I—" She could think of no adequate excuse. "I'm sorry if I've offended ye, my lord."

"The offense is not against me," he said. "When ye've

finished wi' yer merriment, I would see ye below in the great hall."

"Yes, I'll come now." She moved toward him, but without waiting for her, he stalked away down the hall. Lillias's heart squeezed painfully in her chest at the insult before Mary and Aggie. She paused, pressing trembling hands to her mouth while she fought for some modicum of courage and composure.

"Dinna let him flummox ye, Lilli," Mary said stoutly. "We've done no wrong here."

"Aye, I know that, Mary. My wrongful deed was done when I released Angus from the tower and revealed the way to leave the castle without detection." She stared at Mary, her eyes wide.

"Mary," she cried. "I told Angus about the secret gate into the castle."

"Lilli, ye dinna!" Mary whispered.

Even Aggie looked alarmed. "Ye must tell Iain, at once."

"Aye, I will," Lillias said, and raced after him.

But he was already in the great hall. At the bottom of the steps, she paused, aware that her chance to tell him in private was past. She could hear the voices of the other chieftains and knew a council had been called. What would they do to her? she wondered. Drawing a deep breath, she squared her shoulders and walked toward the great hall.

Chapter 12

SHE WAS SURPRISED at the number of chieftains who had been so quickly assembled. Darkness was falling without, so candles had been lit to provide illumination in the great hall. The chieftains sat about the trestle table, their faces stern. Their wives sat on benches placed along the wall. They would have no say in the proceedings, but they would hear all. Their glances were accusing, so Lillias knew they'd already heard much about her deed. Even Peadair, Everard, and Kenneth Sinclair, all of whom had become her friends, wore grim expressions.

"Come in, Lillias," Iain called to her, and she slowly walked the length of the great hall, feeling the weight of the men's censorious gazes. None of them looked at her or rose from their seats as a sign of respect for a lady.

Holding her head high, she was aware of the image she must present to these rough chieftains. Despite Iain's disapproval at finding Mary and her preoccupied with clothes, she was glad she had donned a fine gown instead of the linen shift and apron she so often wore. She must appear every inch the lady, serene and above reproach.

Her thoughts went to her mother, ethereal and aloof. Had that been her defense against a world fraught with harsh realities and dangers? Lillias glanced at Iain's set face and for the first time faced her greatest fear. Would they truly believe her a traitor? If so, would their punishment of her be death? She blanched and her footstep faltered. Then she gathered herself and gracefully moved to the empty chair beside Iain.

"My lord, gentlemen." She bowed her head slightly in acknowledgment of their presence and seated herself without waiting for an invitation from Iain to do so. She would not assume a role of guilt.

"Lady MacLeod," Iain said, rising abruptly, as if he couldn't bear such close proximity to her. He paced like the restless black wolf after which he was named by his men.

"Ye requested my presence, my lord," she said, and marveled that her voice sounded so calm when inside she shook with fear.

"Aye, we have," Iain said abruptly. He glanced at the men along the table. "We would have ye repeat t'us, my lady, just what transpired last night."

Lillias took a deep breath. "Surely, my lord," she said stiffly. "Just before nightfall, I went to the tower, to the chamber where Angus McCullough was held prisoner. After exacting a promise from him that I thought would bring about a truce between our two clans, I released him with a key that hung on the rafters nearby."

She fell silent and waited. Although she had merely repeated what she'd already revealed to Iain that morning, she was aware that the other chieftains had not heard her account firsthand. She waited for them to digest the information.

Sinclair was the first chieftain to clear his throat and lean forward in his chair. Lillias looked at him, gratefully aware that his mind was open to her.

"Ye said ye exacted a promise of a truce from Angus McCullough before releasing him, my lady?" he asked, emphasizing her title. His tone was one of deep respect, a reminder to all present that she was a nobly born lady and not to be treated unkindly.

"Aye. I thought if he saw we were willing to make that first gesture, he might follow through with one of his own."

"Did ye not consider that his release was Iain's decision t'make and na yers?" Logan MacCuag, a chieftain from Glengarry, demanded.

Lillias colored under his stern gaze. "Nay, I dinna," she said softly.

"Dinna ye care that as *Ceann Mor* his word is law?" the chieftain declared.

"I—I dinna think of it that way," Lillias answered meekly. "I thought only of the danger my husband and his men were in and . . ." Her voice faded away at his scowl.

"Dinna ye have faith in his ability t'protect himself and his troops?" MacCuag asked. She saw the same question on the faces of the other men. Clearly she had not been a proper wife in their estimation if she had not believed in Iain's ability or in his power as clan chief.

"I—I . . ." She hung her head, unable to answer.

"Gentlemen." Iain interceded. "Ye must remember that my wife's faither was killed in a raid when she was but a bairn. This fact alone would explain the deep anxiety she might ha' felt."

"It was not that I doubted his ability to fight off the McCulloughs and protect the clan," she said, finding her voice again. "I knew he desired a truce with them and— and I thought I could help bring that about. I wanted to please my husband."

Her words hung in the air. The men exchanged glances. A sigh came from the wives. She could see a softening in their expressions. They understood. Then one man, red-haired and wild-looking, stood up and glared at her. Lillias recognized Hugh MacLeod. She had not seen him since Iain's return.

"I dinna believe yer reasoning, my lady," he said coldly. "Angus McCullough would not ha' agreed to such a truce."

"He did," she declared calmly.

"Have ye any proof of that?"

"Proof?" She looked at the chieftain in bewilderment.

"Did he sign a treaty?"

"Nay, there was no time and I dinna think of it."

"No paper, only yer word that he agreed to this truce never t'raise a sword against a MacLeod?"

"Ye belabor the point, Hugh," Peadair snapped. "We al-

ready know he is honoring the agreement he made wi'
Lady MacLeod."

"Do we?" Hugh declared, looking around the table.
"Consider this. She is related to the McCullough clan on
her mither's side, is she not? How d'we know her sympathies dinna lie with them?"

" 'Tis not so!" she cried, springing to her feet. "I never
saw Angus McCullough before I released him from the
tower. How could my sympathies lie with him against my
own husband?"

"A husband ye ha' not known for long, my lady," Hugh
said. "Why d'ye give him a weapon?"

"I dinna give him a weapon."

"My point exactly," Hugh exclaimed. "The fact that
he dinna raise a blade to kill Jaimie Lennox dinna mean he
keeps a pledge ye claim he made, it means only that he
dinna ha' a weapon." He pounded his fist against the table
to press his point. "He was wi'out a broadsword or any
other weapon, so he broke poor Jaimie's back. There is na
real proof of this vow he supposedly made t'this woman.
We have only her word."

"I have not lied to ye," Lillias said.

Hugh leered at her. "Dinna deny ye hated Red Rafe."

All eyes turned to her. She sensed Iain had moved to
stand behind her chair, his strong hands gripping the back.
Instinctively she knew she must tread lightly, for these men
were loyal even now to the memory of Red Rafe, yet Hugh
had neatly trapped her, for nearly every soul in the castle
knew of her animosity toward her captor.

"Aye, I hated Red Rafe," she said quietly, for she could
not lie. "He murdered my faither."

"Ha' I na told ye she's a traitor to the MacLeod cause?"
Hugh shouted, pointing a finger at her.

Iain sprang forward as if to protect her, should any man
rush forward to do her harm. "Ha' a care, Hugh MacLeod,"
he roared. His hand rested on the hilt of his dirk.

Hugh faced him, hatred and spite seething in his dark
eyes. He'd not forgotten how close he'd been to becoming
clan chief. Lillias seemed the symbol of all he'd lost.

"Many's the time I saw yer wife try to kill yer faither," he exclaimed. "Now she's sided wi' our enemy, the very man who did the murderin'. She must ha' been in on it wi' him. Would ye continue t'protect a traitor in our midst?"

Iain turned to Lillias. "Is it true, lass? Did ye try to murder my faither?"

Lillias thought of those times Red Rafe had summoned her to the hall to mock and humiliate her before his men, giving her the claymore and egging her on to try to kill him. And she *had* tried with all her might.

"Aye, I did," she answered in a low voice.

Bedlam broke out among the chieftains as they shouted their bitter recriminations. She saw the condemnation in Iain's eyes. With a wave of his arm, Iain quieted the men.

"I need hear no more," he said. "I will pass sentence."

The room fell silent. Lillias's face paled. She wanted to cry out to him that he had not heard the whole story, but his expression was closed to her.

"I will ha' our vows of marriage set aside and return ye to yer clan," he said quietly. Voices were raised in protest.

"She's a traitor!" Hugh cried, wanting blood and vengeance for the slights given him by this beautiful woman.

"Silence! I am chief and my word is final." Iain glared at them and no man dared to refute him. "I will accompany my wi—my lady back to her own clan immediately. We will leave for Dunbeath Castle within a fortnight."

"That's the stronghold of the McGinnis clan, man. Dare ye go there?" a chieftain called from the end of the table.

"Dare I not?" Iain demanded. "I will take a small troop of men. Sinclair, will ye join Peadair and me?"

"Aye, my lord." Sinclair had remained silent throughout this interchange, his expression troubled.

Hugh MacLeod stood. "Is there t'be no punishment then of Lady MacLeod?"

Iain stared back at his men, then turned to look at Lillias. "None," he answered. "We are in need of the McGinnis clan's support to overcome the army the McCulloughs and MacBains will surely raise against us. While I am at Dunbeath Castle, I will meet with Garth McGinnis to enlist his aid against Angus and his army. It will na be forthcoming if I've killed one of their clan members."

Lillias's cheeks flamed to think how callously he spoke of her death. Her heart hammered in her chest to think how close she was to death.

The chieftains nodded in agreement with all that Iain said. He looked at her. "Prepare yerself to travel, my lady."

She rose and met his gaze evenly. She looked regal and untouched by all that had occurred. No man there knew what effort her poise cost her. The inside of her lip had been cruelly bitten until she tasted blood. They saw only the serene face she presented them. Iain clenched his fist. Never had she looked more beautiful or treacherous. He turned away from her.

Lillias saw his rejection and her chin went higher. She dared not speak for fear of betraying her emotions, but she flicked her skirt in a disdainful gesture that told them all what she thought and felt. No one spoke until she'd left the hall.

The council was ended. The chieftains filed out of the hall, silent and troubled. They had no wish to discredit the laird's lady. Only Kenneth Sinclair and Peadair McDermott hung back to speak to Iain.

"My lord, I kinna countenance this charge against my lady Lillias," Sinclair spoke up. "Her heart is pure. There is no treachery in her."

"Say no more," Iain directed him. "The decision has been made," he snapped.

"Did ye not act hastily, Iain?" Peadair asked quietly.

"Nay," he said. "She has proven herself unprincipled. I'll not forgive her betrayal."

"My lord." Adhamh Sinclair stepped forward. "I must share the blame wi' my lady for all that has happened. I allowed the prisoner to escape the castle. She only released him from the tower."

Iain regarded the young clansman. "D'ye na place guards along the gate?"

"Aye, my lord," Adhamh replied. "I set my best men there—and they tell me none could ha' escaped that way."

"Then how?" Iain paused. "By God's blood, she could na ha' revealed the loch gate to him?"

The men exchanged uneasy glances. "And she said naught about it!" Iain swore, then glared at them all. "Adhamh, set a guard at the postern gate," he ordered.

"At once, my lord," Adhamh said, stunned at this new development. He'd only spoken up to protect Lady Lillias. Now it seemed she had played them false after all. Confused and angry at the perceived treachery, he hurried to do as commanded.

"D'ye need any further proof of her treachery?" Iain demanded, glaring at the two men left.

"Perhaps ye dinna listen strongly enough t'her reasons."

"I'll say na more about this, Peadair. If ye've a mind t'believe her lies, then do so, but dinna tell me about it. Christ's blood, I thought ye smitten by Mary McFerris."

"Aye, I am."

"Then what draws ye t'this woman?"

"The desire for justice," Peadair said. "If ye were not thinkin' wi' yer loins, man, ye'd be better able to determine her guilt or innocence."

"What are ye saying?" Iain snapped, glaring at the man who'd fought beside him unwaveringly. He trusted Peadair with his life, yet now he could not trust Peadair's words.

"I'm saying yer pride is hurt and ye're not thinking clearly. She did naught against ye or the clan. She made a mistake."

"She gave herself t'me t'hide the fact Angus had made his escape. What manner of woman makes that kind of sacrifice so lightly?"

"I dinna believe she did," Peadair answered quietly, and stalked from the room.

Long after he left, Iain stood before the fire, gazing into the dying flames. Servants came to refill his cup and tend the fire, but upon seeing his black countenance, scurried away again.

Lillias was numb with disbelief. She climbed the stairs to her room and stood in the door as if struck dumb. Her eyes were black and tragic in her pale face, her lips bloodless.

"My God, what has happened?" Aggie cried, running to take her cold hand and pull her into the room.

"Lilli," Mary murmured, putting an arm around her shoulders and leading her to the fire. Gently she pushed her down on a stool. Lillias seemed unmoved by their ministrations. Numbly she stared straight ahead. There was no color in her cheeks.

"Quick, Aggie," Mary cried, "make some tea."

"Aye," Aggie said, and scurried to find her bag of herbs. Sprinkling a handful into a cup, she poured boiling water from the kettle she kept on the hearth. When it had brewed, she carried it to Mary.

"Lilli, drink this," Mary ordered, and spooned some of the hot brew into her mouth.

At first, Lilli didn't swallow, then the muscles in her throat constricted. Tears streamed down her face and she raised trembling hands to her mouth. Her lips moved, but no sound came.

"I kinna hear ye, Lilli," Mary said softly. "Tell me what is wrong?"

"I'm to be sent away," she whispered. Her tear-filled eyes turned to Mary. "He does na want me for his wife."

"Oh, Lilli!" Mary cried. "Where is he sending ye?"

"Back t'my people. Back to Dunbeath." Lillias spoke as if in a trance.

"When will ye go?"

Lillias turned her head sharply and peered at Mary. "Within a fortnight," she whispered, and great sobs tore from her throat.

Mary stood beside her, cradling the fair head and listening to the torrent of weeping. When Lillias had cried herself out and was limp with exhaustion, Mary and Aggie stripped away her clothes and put her to bed, then seated themselves beside the bed to keep watch over her.

She lay with her eyes open, staring into the dark shadows, then started upright when Iain entered the chamber. Her face was stark with pain, her eyes mutely beseeching. Her hair lay around her in a tangle.

He closed his mind to her beauty as he stalked across the

room and towered over her. "Tell me, my lady," he demanded roughly. "Did ye send Angus McCullough out of the castle by way of the loch gate?"

Alarm washed over Lillias's expression. "Aye, my lord," she said simply, and offered no further explanation. Her gaze was unwavering.

"Lilli, ye dinna tell him?" Mary cried.

Iain's lips thinned and he clenched his fists until his knuckles whitened. "Nay, she failed to mention such a fact."

"I meant to," she said. "But I . . ."

"Aye, speak up," he commanded.

". . . I forgot to tell ye," she finished lamely.

With a low curse, he spun away toward the door, where he paused, gathering his control. His hands braced against the door; not one of the women doubted he longed to tear it from its hinges, so great was his rage. At last, he turned and spoke quietly to Aggie. He did not spare a glance for Lillias.

"We will leave at first light," he said roughly.

"So soon, my lord Iain? Why such haste?" Mary asked.

" 'Tis a thing better done quickly. See that her things are packed and ready."

"We have little, my lord," Aggie answered. "It will be ready."

He drew back, preparing to leave the room.

"My lord Iain," Mary spoke up, leaping to her feet. "I will accompany Lillias tomorrow."

"There is no need. She has her woman with her." He nodded toward Aggie.

"Aye, but she will also need a friend." The unspoken reprimand was clear. Lillias would have few friends on her journey home.

"D'ye plan to abandon yer own clan for hers, then?" he demanded abruptly.

"Nay." Mary shook her head slowly. "I will return to my own village, but I want to know she is happy among her own people again."

Iain stood silent and thoughtful, then turned a last long

look on Lillias. She sat like a child on the bed, her hair a
curtain hiding her face. There was innocence and sorrow in
her slumping shoulders and averted face, but he'd been
fooled once by her. He would not be again. He left the
room as swiftly as he'd come, the quiet closing of the door
like a clap of thunder to those left behind.

"He looks as sorrowful as ye feel, Lilli," Mary said
hopefully, but Lillias did not answer. She lay back and
turned her face to the wall.

"D'ye wish me t'go t'the council, Lilli?" Mary offered.
"I'll tell them it was me that first put the thought in yer
head, me wi' my mewling fears for Peadair's safety."

"It does not matter, Mary," Lillias whispered. "The deed
was mine and punishment has been made." She fell silent
and did not move again, but both women knew from the
rigidness of her body that she did not sleep.

Finally, when the hour was late and the fire had died
down to a bed of coals, they gave up their vigil and readied
themselves for bed. Aggie retired to her cot in the corner.
Mary lay down at the foot of Lillias's bed and pulled a coverlet about herself.

At dawn, they rose and dressed with few words. Lillias
spoke to no one. She plaited her hair in a single braid down
her back and pulled on the linen shift and shawl of the
common women. With her few belongings wrapped in a
plaid cloth, she waited for Iain's summons and stared out at
the hills she would never see again. In the distance the
peaks of Beinn Bhan were obscured by mist, but the sun
had topped the eastern peaks and rose, spreading its golden
light like a benediction upon the land.

She blinked away tears. Until now, she had been numb
with grief that she must leave Iain when she had come so
newly to love and passion with him; now she realized how
much she would miss Cullayne itself—the glens and bens,
the loch and rivers.

Men gathered in the bailey below, the snorting of their
mounts and jangling of bridles reminding her the time for
departure was upon them.

Iain came himself, rapping impatiently at her door.

"Madam, are yer trunks ready?" he demanded when he'd been invited to enter.

Lillias rose from the window seat and stood before him, her simple bundle ready. Aggie gathered a similar bundle. Mary stood in the common shift she'd worn from the village. Iain's gaze darkened when he saw them.

"Ye are not dressed," he said testily. "The men are ready t'go."

"Aye, we are, my lord," she answered. Her gaze was unwavering.

Her head was high, and Mary wondered if Iain had any inkling of how she had suffered through the night. Her face was as pale as the guelder rose at first blooming, save for the dark circles beneath her eyes, which testified to her restless night.

"My lady, d'ye seek t'defy me at every turn?" he demanded impatiently.

"Nay, my lord," she answered. "I but do as ye bid."

"Then why are ye dressed as a beggar? I would na send ye home in such common garments."

"I thought to leave the fine French gowns for—for yer next wife, my lord," she answered, with such an air of detachment, he longed to throttle her then and there.

He cursed her, staring at her cool demeanor, and wondered that he hadn't seen from the beginning what a heartless bitch she was.

"I order ye to dress appropriately as a lady. I will not have yer kinsmen think I've treated ye badly."

"Indeed, my lord?" she inquired. One perfectly shaped golden eyebrow rose expressively, and Mary could have applauded to see Lilli's old spirit return. He clamped his lips together in exasperation.

"When ye've changed yer clothes, send Aggie t'me and I'll have yer trunks collected and loaded on packhorses."

"As ye wish, my lord."

He paused, his assessing gaze moving over Mary. "Mary, I would ha' ye wear the gown ye wore yesterday."

"As ye wish, my lord." Mary echoed Lillias's words and barely suppressed a grin at his scowl. He slammed the door on his way out, which occasioned an outright giggle. Lillias did not join in her merriment, but Mary was happy to see color suffusing the pale cheeks. Quickly they set about donning the fine gowns they'd worn the evening before.

Over the brown brocade, Lillias drew on a velvet cape of dark green. Its sleeves were trimmed with fur and its weight would be a welcome addition against the mountain chill until the sun warmed the air. Lillias left her hair in its single braid, but drew on the French hood with its black velvet fall and nodded to Aggie, who went below to summon a man to carry down the trunks. There were six in all; three packhorses were needed to carry them.

With one last glance around, Lillias left the chamber that had briefly been her home and made her way downstairs. She did not think as Peadair came to assist her into the sidesaddle. To think was to feel pain, and she could endure no more. Like that little girl who'd survived the horrors around her by drifting into a world of shadows, so this older version of the person who was Lillias McGinnis survived by burying her need to cry out at this further injustice.

There had been no justice for her or for her murdered father. There was only survival of body and spirit in a world too ruthless and uncaring to help her. Mary cast a glance at her pale face and silently grieved, for she felt Lilli slipping away from her, away from them all. When they were mounted, Iain led them out of the bailey and across the bridge. Lillias did not look back. She rode with her gaze straight ahead. She had already left Cullayne—and so sorrow did not touch her.

Mary went to Iain. They had paused for their noonday meal. "D'ye na' see? She's becoming addled. Her spirit has left her body. I fear for her mental state."

" 'Tis but a trick, Mary," he scoffed. "She can appear anyway she so desires, looking like an innocent girl or a wanton, a loving wife or a vixen found out. I dinna blame ye for being taken in by her for I, too, was flummoxed by her, but dinna believe her."

"Ye're a fool, Iain MacLeod!" Mary cried, heedless of

the fact that he was the *Ceann Mor* and an earl. She went away and wept on Peadair's shoulder, taking small solace in the tender caresses he gave her.

Likewise, Kenneth Sinclair approached Iain, but when he would have spoken about Lillias, Iain cut him off abruptly and stomped away.

They traveled eastward, skirting Beinn Bhan, then turned southward. They forded the River Lochy, then spent the night on its banks, where the River Spean flowed into its basin. A small campfire was built and bedrolls spread around its warming glow. Aggie helped the soldiers prepare a supper meal of roasted hare and bannocks baked upon a rock. Lillias sat apart, staring into the green dark shadows of the forests. She had spoken to no one thus far, save to answer those questions put to her. Iain crossed before the fire and her gaze flickered toward him hopefully, but when he made no move toward her, her lashes lowered, and when she glanced up again, her eyes were once again blank.

"Look at her," Mary said to Peadair with a sigh. "She breaks my heart."

" 'Tis naught we can do. I have tried to speak to Iain, but he believes her capable of the vilest of manipulations."

"Ye dinna think that, d'ye, Peadair?" Mary asked softly.

"Nay. I ha' listened to the things ye've told me about her and I ha' seen for myself her character. She is impulsive and quick to act, but no more. Her gullibility comes from her lack of experience with men, not her knowledge of it. If she were a loose woman as Iain believes her, she would not ha' believed Angus's pledge, nor would she have risked her life as she did, for he could ha' killed her before leaving the castle." Mary shivered at her friend's close brush with death.

"Why did he not, d'ye think?" she inquired.

Peadair shrugged. "Angus McCullough is a cruel, bloodthirsty man who would not be stopped by the thought of killing a woman. Something she said must have turned him away from such a deed."

"The very fact that she's alive should prove to Iain and

the council that she speaks the truth about the pledge Angus made."

"Aye, or it could prove her alliance wi' the McCulloughs. She hated Red Rafe and might have acted as a spy for McCullough. Someone had to reveal his plans on that final raid on the McCulloughs."

Mary drew away from him. "I thought ye believed her innocent?"

"Aye, I do," Peadair hastily reassured her, drawing her back against his side. "I merely play the devil's advocate and voice the accusations made against her."

"But if she's guilty of treason, then so am I, for I wept for yer safety and cursed Iain for not releasing Angus. 'Tis I who started this chain of events."

"Nay, Mary. Dinna blame yerself." Peadair sighed. "Lillias was the one who acted, and her reasons were her own."

Mary thought of all he'd revealed and slowly nodded. "Aye, it looks bad against her."

"She might have been killed, hung for a treasonous act, if Iain hadn't acted so hastily."

Mary's eyes widened. "Suddenly, I'm glad she's returning t'her own clan. At least there, she'll be safe."

"Aye," Peadair said softly. "She has enemies at Cullayne."

"I can guess that Hugh MacLeod is one," Mary bitterly observed.

"Aye, he presented the strongest case against her." He cocked a head at Mary. "Why would he be so against her?"

"He desired her for himself," Mary answered tartly. "He was always after her at the castle, or if he saw her on the village road. Lillias was frightened of him."

"Were ye? Did he bother ye?" Peadair asked possessively, thinking he would take Hugh's head if he had molested Mary.

"Nay." Mary shook her head slowly. "I could wrestle him down when we were but wee bairns, and later, when he was stronger, I could outwit him." She grinned, revealing dimples, and Peadair couldn't resist kissing her. She seemed not to mind, for she wound her arms around his neck and kissed him back.

Seeing that Peadair was summarily occupied, Sinclair approached Iain and tried again to speak to him.

"If ye've come t'plead her case, dinna speak t'me," Iain snapped. He'd spread his plaid upon the ground and sprawled on it with his back against a log. Now and then, his dark gaze darted to the slim figure who lay upon her bedroll, covered by a plaid. Sinclair saw the grim lines of suffering on his chief's face.

"Ye're chief of all the clan. If ye choose to forgive her, there's none that can say ye nay."

Iain sat considering. "Nay, 'tis best she return t'her own people. 'Tis what she's wanted all along."

"Aye, she has no cause to love the MacLeods." Sinclair responded without realizing how deeply his words hurt. He rose from the log and moved to his own pallet.

Across the way, he saw Hugh MacLeod beneath his plaid. Only his head was revealed, but his black eyes glittered like a stoat about to spring on a hare and his gaze was fixed on the golden-haired girl who slept beside the fire.

In the morning, they rose and broke camp, then set out, following the River Spean eastward, passing through rich forests until they came to Glen Roy and turned north again, this time following the steep, winding river trail. Lillias's heart quickened, for she sensed they were nearing Dunbeath Castle and wondered if she would recognize her childhood home. For the first time, she roused herself from the stupor that had claimed her.

Her senses were flooded with the beauty and scents of the countryside. Towering pine trees gave off their pungent fragrance and filtered the sunlight in slanting rays above their heads. A quietness prevailed in the forest, for pine needles cushioned each footfall. Clumps of bracken fern grew along the banks and the high wind rattled the branches in a stand of birch trees.

She began to recognize the forest paths where she and her father rode and the narrow river gorge where they'd fished. Then they rounded a bend and there, bathed in the midday light, stood Dunbeath Castle. It rose amid a tangle of saplings and trees on the banks of a bounding, rock-strewn stream. The village nestled against a foothill some distance to the west.

Lillias reined in her mount and sat staring at the pale stone walls and corbeled towers. After the fortresslike air of Cullayne Castle, Dunbeath seemed strangely vulnerable with its low curtain wall and open courtyard. No wonder Red Rafe had found it so easy to raid Dunbeath. She had no defenses. Yet even as Lillias made these notes, she saw that the east curtain wall had, indeed, been reinforced and raised. Likewise the west wall. Only the front portion of the wall remained as she remembered it.

"So ye're home," Iain said at her elbow. "Is it as ye remember it?"

"I suppose it is," she answered, still entranced by this, the first glimpse in nine years of her ancestral home.

"Shall we go, then?" he said brusquely, and led the way across the swiftly flowing creek to the opposite bank.

She should feel joy at her return, she reflected, following after him, but her jubilation was tempered by all that had gone before. Cullayne, its wild lochs and valleys, its people—and yes, even its Black Beast—were forever lost to her. Suddenly apprehensive as to the welcome she might find in her new home, she fell back behind Mary and Aggie.

A messenger had been sent ahead to warn Dunbeath of their arrival, and now, as they approached, the castle bridge was lowered and the gate thrown open. They rode into the inner bailey and halted before the steps leading to the first floor of the castle. A cluster of people were gathered before the entrance, a welcoming committee, she perceived, and searched among them for a familiar face. There were none, although Aggie drew a sharp breath, her face wreathing in a smile.

A man with fiery red hair stepped forward to greet them. He was rather finely dressed in *chausses* and velvet boots and a fine coat of scarlet velvet trimmed in heavy braids of gold and purple. Heavy gold chains bore pendants of

carved gold and silver, and his fingers were heavily en-
crusted with gold rings bearing precious gemstones of emerald and sapphire. So richly was he dressed that, for a
moment, Lillias thought the King of Scotland himself might
stand before them.

Behind him stood a woman in equally regal dress, her
gown so ornately adorned that she dazzled the eye. Her
French hood was of black velvet, but was heavily embellished with gold-jeweled biliments separated by white satin.
In contrast, the other women were rather plainly dressed
and stood behind the woman in deference, so Lillias
guessed they were attendants. The woman might have been
the man's wife, except that she appeared too old.

Below the elegant hood, her face was puffy and pale, her
dark eyes nearly hidden by folds of fat. Her mouth was
pinched, giving her a sour expression, and her gaze was
speculative and somehow furtive. Suddenly a memory
tugged at Lillias, a memory she prayed was false.

The man stepped forward, drawing attention from the
woman. "Welcome, Lord MacLeod," he called. "I am Lord
Garth McGinnis, Earl of Mamore, and this is my mither,
Lady Catriona. We welcome ye to Dunbeath Castle."

"Thank ye, Lord McGinnis, for yer hospitality," Iain responded smoothly. "I pray our hasty descent upon ye has
caused no inconvenience."

"None at all," Garth McGinnis answered magnanimously. "We are honored to have the Earl of Shiel attend
us." He glanced along the line of mounted guests. His gaze
flickered to Mary, who sat with graceful ease in the unfamiliar sidesaddle, her rose velvet skirts draping over her
mount's flanks.

"I am delighted to welcome back my niece," Garth continued, his glance saying plainly he found her quite beautiful. So bold and inappropriate was his gaze that Mary
looked away. Peadair felt a growl of protest start low in his
throat.

"Ye are mistaken, sir," Iain said. "This is yer niece." He
motioned to Lillias, so there was nothing for her to do but
nudge her mare forward and raise her head to meet her

kinsman's gaze. His startled black gaze darted toward her and froze. He was visibly stunned.

"By God's teeth, 'tis Lord Robert come back t'haunt me!" he cried.

Catriona McGinnis seemed flustered as well. From behind her attendants came an outcry, and a figure pushed forward. She was dressed in the simple garments of a nun, even to the draping hood that shadowed her face; then she raised her head and the hood fell away, revealing her identity. Lillias felt her breath catch. There was no serenity in the woman's pale blue eyes, no ethereal reserve. Her eyes widened in shock, her mouth opened and closed but no sound came. Lillias stared down at the face she'd last seen that night so long ago.

"Greetings, Mither," she said bitterly. "I thought ye were dead."

"Lillias!" Lady Margaret McGinnis whispered, and slid to the stones in a dead faint.

Chapter 13

"God's blood, take that woman away," Garth McGinnis ordered, his nostrils flaring with distaste.

Catriona fluttered about like a plump bird while her women attendants gathered up Margaret's slight body and bore it inside. Seeing the mother she'd thought was dead, alive and helpless, tore at Lillias's heart.

"*Mither!*" she cried out, and, dismounting, ran up the steps.

"Ye must forgive this little display," Garth was saying to Iain. "We'd heard Lady Margaret was dead some years ago. Then this woman showed up on our doorstep claiming to be her ladyship and demanding to see her daughter. We've tried to humor her, for she's rather given to the vapors."

"Of course, we dinna believe her story," Catriona commented unkindly. "Can ye imagine Lady Margaret hiding out all these years right under our noses, pretending to be dead? 'Tis na possible."

"Lillias seemed to recognize her at once," Iain commented, "so there can be little doubt as to her identity."

"Naturally, we're pleased at this turn of events," Garth said, casting his mother a warning glance. "Lady Margaret's only just arrived at Dunbeath this morning and we've had little time to hear her story. It seems that she's been cloistered in a nearby monastery for some years now."

Lillias heard no more. Gone was her bitterness for the

years of silence between her mother and herself. Anxiously she followed the women who carried Margaret's prostrate form up the stairs to a back chamber, once used for the servants in the days of Robert McGinnis. She paid scant attention to the sparse surroundings but knelt beside her mother's cot.

The face was unchanged, and yet it was not the same. The delicate bones were the same, covered by a translucent skin that seemed ageless. Her eyelids bore spidery blue veins, and the hands that rested at her waist seemed so thin Lillias imagined one might see right through them. Gone was the gloss of youth. The beauty of the woman was lost in the widow's grief that tugged at the corners of her eyes and mouth.

Lillias whisked away the gabled hood. Thin gray hair tumbled over the pillow—and thereby spoke of the sad torment Lady Margaret had endured over the loss of her beloved Robert and her daughter. Lillias's heart went out to her; she took hold of one of the pitifully thin hands and pressed it to her lips. Tears flowed down her cheeks.

"Mither, I dinna know," she whispered.

"How is she?" Aggie said from behind her.

"She looks so fragile, Aggie," Lillias said. "She hardly seems to be breathing."

"I'll brew her some Mayweed tea," Aggie said, and rummaged in her bag.

A serving woman brought a basin of water and a cloth. Impatiently Lillias took it from her and sponged her mother's forehead. Aggie found a small corked bottle in her medical supplies and held it beneath Margaret's nose. Lady Margaret coughed and rolled her head away.

"Mither," Lillias cried softly. "Open yer eyes and look at me. I'm here, Mither. It's me, Lillias, yer daughter."

Slowly Margaret moved her head toward the sound of Lillias's voice. Finally her lashes fluttered and she opened her eyes. Gazing into the violet eyes that once had poets and singers tell of their tranquil beauty, Lillias felt like weeping. Their color had faded, their beauty forever dimmed. Lady Margaret blinked and studied the young face so close to hers.

"Lillias, my child," she said wondrously. She reached out and touched a golden curl that had escaped her daughter's hood. If Lillias had doubted her mother's love, she had only to look into those sad pale eyes to know the truth of Margaret's feelings.

"Ye've grown so beautiful," Margaret whispered. "Like Robert—with his fine features and his blue eyes. Ye have his eyes, daughter."

"Aggie told me so," Lillias said, "though I could not remember." She frowned and looked away. She'd blocked the memory of her father's face from her mind. "They told me ye were dead."

"Nay, though I prayed for such a release." Margaret's tender smile died away and her face held such a look of fear that Lillias started and glanced over her shoulder. "Ye're in danger here, Lillias," her mother cried, half sitting up and gripping Lillias's shoulders. " 'Tis why I've come back. To tell ye this. Ye must leave Dunbeath, now."

"Calm yerself, Mither." Lillias spoke gently, as if to a child. "There is na danger." She looked around at the curious serving women. "Leave us," she ordered. "I would speak to my mither in privacy."

When they had gone and only Aggie remained, Margaret made as if to rise from the bed, but Lillias pushed her back against the pillows. "Ye must rest."

"Lillias, listen to me," Margaret said urgently. "There is danger for ye here. Tell Lord MacLeod ye must leave at once."

"I cannot, Mither. Iain has brought me back to Dunbeath to stay."

"What d'ye mean?" Margaret's pale eyes searched her daughter's face. "Ye are his wife. Red Rafe swore yer vows were blessed by the church."

"Aye, they were," Lillias replied. "But Iain is displeased with me." She paused to bite her bottom lip and gain control of her wavery voice. "He is setting aside our vows."

Margaret lay back, despair in her voice when next she

spoke. "Then all is lost," she whimpered. "I tried so hard to protect ye, my child. That is the only reason I agreed to have ye remain with the MacLeods. I knew as the wife of a MacLeod, ye'd be safe."

"Safe from whom, Mither? What danger is there for me here?"

Margaret opened her mouth to speak, then her eyes grew wide and she placed a finger against her pale lips. Lillias glanced over her shoulder, and, seeing what Margaret had, crossed to the half-opened door and flung it open. Catriona stood in the doorway, a sly, petulant look upon her face.

"Did ye want something, Aunt Catriona?" Lillias demanded.

"I've come to see if yer mither is recovered," the woman said arrogantly, and swept into the small, comfortless room. The contrast of her rich attire in the plain surroundings was not lost on Lillias, who wondered why her mother had been given such a mean compartment.

"Are ye na well, Lady Margaret?" Catriona asked solicitously, but her tone sounded false to Lillias.

"Aye, my lady," Margaret's lips twisted at uttering the title. "I've quite recovered for now." She struggled to sit up. Her thin gray hair trailed around her shoulders in wisps.

With a bright glance at Lillias, Catriona reached out a hand and brushed Margaret's forehead as if she were loath to touch the other woman. "Why, Lady Margaret. Ye have a fever. I've ordered a servant to bring hot broth for ye. I noticed ye ate little at noon meal."

"That's kind of ye, but I'm na hungry—and I have na wish for yer medicine," Margaret said, without any of the old graciousness for which she'd been known. She put her head in her hands and Lillias rushed forward.

"Lie back against the pillows, Mither," she urged gently. She pulled the rough woolen blanket over her mother. A servant appeared at the door with the broth. Despite the distance from the kitchen, the soup was still steaming hot.

Catriona inspected the tray, her back turned to them as she stirred the broth for chunks of meat and vegetables. "Good, 'tis still hot." She brought the tray to the bedside.

"I kinna eat now," Margaret said. She was wracked with chills.

"Ye must try, Mither," Lillias said, taking the tray from Catriona and spooning the contents for her mother. "Please try, for me."

Margaret's face softened. "Aye, for ye," she said, and opened her mouth. With Catriona hovering nearby, Lillias fed her mother most of the broth, but Margaret balked at the meat and vegetables.

" 'Tis enough for now. I am weary." Margaret closed her eyes. Her chest barely rose and fell with her breathing.

"I'll let ye sleep, Mither." Lillias glanced at Aggie.

"Aye, I'll stay with her," Aggie said.

"Come, Lillias. I'll show ye to yer room," Catriona said, and the words were more a command. Silently Lillias followed her from her mother's room and down the corridor, which seemed at once familiar and alien to her.

Catriona paused before a door. "This is yer room, Lady MacLeod. I hope ye'll be comfortable here."

"I'm sure I will be," Lillias replied stiffly, and immediately entered the room and closed the door behind her, although her hostess still stood in the corridor. At the sound of the door closing, a figure rose from the window seat.

"Lillias," Mary cried. "I wondered where ye'd gone. I tried to follow ye, but that old witch would na' let me. She brought me here and told me not to wander around the castle unaccompanied. She said there were ghosts, but if ye ask me the only monster here is her." Mary shivered in revulsion, then, seeing Lillias's face, she rushed over and took hold of Lillias's hand.

"How is yer mither?" she cried. "Is she all right?"

"Aye, for now," Lillias said. "Although she's so fragile, I fear for her. . . . And sometimes she has about her a look of—of madness, as if the years have been more unkind than any soul can endure."

"Ye're here, Lilli," Mary reminded her. "Ye can take care of her and see she gets proper attention."

"There's something else," Lillias exclaimed. "She

warned me to leave Dunbeath at once. She said there was danger for me here."

"What danger?" Mary asked.

"She had na time to tell me, but she did say that the reason she'd left me with the MacLeod clan is because she knew I'd be safer there."

"Safer with Red Rafe?" Mary asked wonderingly, for she'd heard some of the stories of the old chief's treatment of Lillias—and she'd believed every word of them.

"What else did she say?"

"There was nothing more than that. When I told her Iain was setting aside our marriage vows and had brought me back here for good, she was in such despair."

"What can it all mean?" Mary said worriedly. "I fear for ye, Lilli. I don't like it here at Dunbeath."

"Nor do I," said Lillias, glancing around the grand room. Here, tapestries had been hung and cushions were placed on the stone seats. Every effort had been made to provide comfort. If rooms like this had been available, why then had her mother, a noblewoman by birthright, been placed in the servants' quarters? "There are many questions that need answering," she said softly.

"Will ye tell Iain of yer mither's words?"

Lillias sat for a long time considering. How she longed to find Iain and plead with him to take her back to Cullayne, but she would not. His decision had been made. Slowly she shook her head. "Nay. 'Tis not his concern now." She rose and paced the room. "He will leave in a few days to return to Cullayne and I shall never see him again. I must take care of myself and my mither."

Mary watched her proud chin set and determined that if Lillias was too stubborn to tell Iain, then she would tell Peadair—with instructions that he relay the information to his chief. Something was terribly wrong in this castle, and Mary did not want to abandon her friend.

A banquet had been planned for that evening. Lillias and Mary stripped off their outer garments and lay down to nap in their chemises.

"D'ye remember yer aunt Catriona or yer cousin Garth?" Mary asked.

"Only a little," Lillias said, staring overhead at the rich drapery round their bed. "Aunt Catriona was not well liked by my mither and faither. Mither said she was a mischief maker."

"Yer mither was kind, I suspect," Mary said.

"Aye, I do not trust Catriona, either," Lillias said.

"What about yer cousin? Would he make life easier for ye here and protect ye from any mischief that old witch might devise?"

"I don't know." Lillias sighed. "Garth came to live at Dunbeath when he was still a boy in his teens. He was rather strange and the servants crossed themselves whenever he walked by. No one seemed to like him. My faither called him a coward and said he was lazy because he never practiced his archery or broadsword, and he whined when the other boys beat him at those skills. He would do things to them behind their backs."

"What things?" Mary asked avidly. She was enjoying hearing the stories of life in a castle. Her simple life in the village seemed tame by comparison.

"Once I saw him place a burr beneath the saddle of one of Faither's favorite mounts. Faither let one of the stable boys ride the stallion about the bailey that day. When the boy put his weight against the saddle, the horse reared so the stable boy fell off and cracked his head against the stones. He never recovered. Faither had the horse put down."

"That's dreadful! And ye never told?"

"Aye, I did, but Garth claimed I was wrong. I was quite young when it happened and Faither tried hard to be a fair man, so he gave Garth the benefit of a doubt. The worst part was that Garth showed no remorse."

"None?"

Lillias shook her head. "I remember coming upon him when he had captured a puppy and taken it down to the riverbank, where he was torturing it."

"What did ye do?"

"I warned him I would tell if he didn't let the puppy go. He threatened he would do the same to me, so I ran back to the castle and told my faither. He hurried out to the riverbank, but he was too late. The puppy was dead. That was the first time I ever saw my faither so fearsomely angry. He struck Garth down to the ground."

"He deserved it," Mary said.

"Aye." Lillias nodded. "The next day, Garth was sent back to his parents."

"I dinna like the way he looked at me when he thought I was ye," Mary said, shivering delicately. "Beware of him, Lilli."

"I will," she answered.

They dozed and woke late, so they had to hurry to dress for the banquet. When Mary reached for the rose-colored velvet, Lillias opened one of her trunks.

"We'll wear something new and very fine, tonight," she said. "I want to outshine even Aunt Catriona." She didn't say she wanted Iain to find her irresistibly beautiful, but Mary knew.

"I dinna think we can," Mary replied, "or should." Still, they dived into the chests and chose gowns that were elegant enough for King James's court.

Mary wore a gown of green brocade with jewel-encrusted braid trim and a gold underskirt. Lillias chose a gown of pale yellow cut velvet with a ruffled neckline of the finest lace and an underskirt of pale green silk. Her wide sleeves were puffed and slashed with tufts of ivory silk pulled through. Her square-toed slippers were of the same pale yellow velvet that had been slashed and embroidered. She left off the fall from her French hood, using only the graceful curving cap of gold satin with its jeweled biliments, and let her unbound hair fall down her back like a veil spun of the finest gold.

From the chest she pulled a small box that housed the necklace of gold and emeralds Iain had given her the night they consummated their marriage. She must remember to return it to him before he left, she thought, then on a whim pulled the jewels from their velvet cushion and clasped

them about her neck. They blazed against her pale skin like
the fire in Iain's eyes as he hovered over her. She reached
for the clasp, meaning to take them off, but Mary's hand
stayed her.

"Wear them," she urged.

"I kinna. 'Tis too painful," Lillias cried. "They remind
me of the love that was building between us."

"If the jewels remind ye of that love, might they na remind Iain, as well?"

Lillias looked into Mary's dark eyes. "Ye're a sly one,
Mary McFerris."

"Aye, and I'm not afraid to fight for what I want." They
were silent for a moment while Lillias drew strength from
her friend.

"Nor will I be," she answered. She squared her shoulders. "Shall we go down?"

"My lady." Mary curtsied lightly. Arm in arm they left
the chamber.

"I must go see my mither before I go down to the banquet," Lillias said. "Knowing she's resting will ease my
mind somewhat."

"Aye, and I'll come wi' ye," Mary said.

Together they moved down the corridor, entranced by the
silken swish of their skirts and petticoats. But as they
neared the narrow corridor leading to her mother's room, a
servant woman stepped forward, blocking the way. Lillias
halted, her eyes widening with anger.

"Out of my way. I'm going to see my mither."

"Lady Margaret is sleeping, my lady," the woman said,
"and has left instructions na t'be disturbed."

"I'm her daughter. She will na mind me."

"She said no one, my lady," the woman answered im-
placably. She folded her arms over her bosom and glared at
Lillias.

Lillias's ire rose. "Where is my servant?" she demanded.

The woman was unintimidated. "She's gone to the
kitchen for a bite of supper. She said she will return soon."

Mary took hold of Lillias's arm. "Mayhap yer mither or
Aggie did leave instructions," she suggested.

"Mayhap." Lillias glared back at the servant. "I'll come again after the banquet, and at that time I will see her— regardless of yer instructions."

The woman made no answer, so Lillias turned on her heel and marched back to the stone stairs that led down to the great hall. She could hear the sounds of merriment long before they reached the great doors.

"Ah, here is our guest of honor," Garth called, jumping to his feet when she entered. "Come, Lillias, and be seated here at my side." Lillias glanced at Mary, who gave her a small wave and went to claim her seat at Peadair's side.

Lillias saw that Iain was already seated beside Catriona McGinnis. He looked somber, but elegantly handsome in a dark velvet tunic with slashed sleeves of burgundy and gold. His raven black hair had been combed back, but re- bellious locks curled forward onto his brow. He wore a heavy chain of gold that held a medallion of carved gold, set with a large topaz stone worth a king's ransom. Lillias saw Garth's greedy gaze dart time and again to the price- less medallion.

Iain kept his gaze lowered until Lillias paused beside his chair, then he looked up, his glance halting on the emerald necklace. His gaze met hers for one brief moment, then darted away. Lillias passed on and was seated on the other side of her cousin and his mother. Iain was too far away for her to speak to him, and he seemed determined once again not to look at her.

He could not look at her. After that first dazzling glance, he'd looked away, his memory forever branded with the image as she stood before him, like a fairy queen with her hair all down her back and her little golden hat like a crown upon her head.

Her beauty seemed to grow each time he saw her, mock- ing him, punishing him with the thought that he could never possess her. Bravely she'd faced him, with her eyes like midnight, all full of sadness and wisdom and beckon- ing yearning. She was here in her home again, where she wanted to be. He shifted in his seat, so he might glimpse her again.

At that moment, she raised her head and gazed at him with unwavering concentration. Iain looked away. Beside him, Garth spoke and Iain nodded, but he knew not one whit of what the man said. Finally he remembered the pressing need he had for help from the McGinnis clan and cleared his throat and leaned toward his host.

"Our clans are united by marriage," he began, "and I've come to call upon that kinship."

Garth cocked one eyebrow, a sly smile upon his lips. "And how may I be of service t'ye, kinsman?"

Iain's eyes narrowed as he studied the other man. He didn't like Garth McGinnis. Something about him rang false. Mayhap it was a McGinnis trait. His thoughts automatically went back to Lillias's betrayal. He could see her now, standing in the doorway with the light spilling behind her, her face luminous. I have something wonderful to tell ye, she'd declared happily. Iain blinked, running his mind over the scene once more. Yes, those had been her words. But he'd insisted on speaking of his own feelings first— and then he'd taken her into his arms and their communication had been of a different sort.

"Lord MacLeod?" Garth said expectantly, and Iain looked at him blankly. His thoughts seemed to come back from a great distance. "Ye wished to ask me something," Garth prodded.

"Aye." Iain nodded, bringing his thoughts to the problem at hand. "When my faither was chief, he raided among our neighboring clans wi'out mercy. Feuds ha' been a way of life wi' us. Since my faither's death, the McCulloughs ha' marched against us time and again. It's been my hope that we can affect a truce wi' the McCulloughs and MacBains, but they will na listen. If the McGinnis clan would ally themselves wi' us, we could raise a big enough army to put down the insurrections of the McCulloughs and their allies. Mayhap then they'll agree to a truce."

"Peace by force," Garth said thoughtfully. He stroked his beard with long, pale fingers. His dark eyes glittered with speculation. To ally himself for the time being with the powerful MacLeod chief would be an effective step in his own plan. Long had he turned his eye to the fertile glens and fish-laden lochs to the west of his own boundaries. That they were held by another clan bothered him not one whit. Now, Iain's request had opened that door to him.

"It pleases me that my new kinsmen has asked for my help," he said, smiling benignly. "I will order my chieftains to muster two hundred men and accompany ye back to Cullayne. Will that be enough?"

"Aye, quite enough," Iain said. "I speak on behalf of my whole clan when I say we are grateful t'ye for this alliance."

"As ye have pointed out, we are kinsmen, are we not?" replied Garth, shrugging negligently. "When d'ye return to Cullayne?"

"I'd planned to go in a few days, but as long as we've reached an agreement, I will go tomorrow at first light. I wish to inform my council of yer response and ready myself for whatever plans the McCulloughs have against us."

"I see. Ye think there will be war between ye, then?"

"Aye." Iain nodded grimly. "It can't be helped. It is for that reason that I've brought Lady Lillias back to Dunbeath."

"Ye wish to leave her here in safety?"

"Aye. She's sorely missed her kinsmen these many years," Iain said, without revealing that he had no intentions of claiming her again. There was no reason to alienate this new alliance before it had begun. But there was another reason not to declare he was setting aside his marriage vows. He glanced down the length of the table at Lillias. Her beauty and poise won his admiration despite what she had done.

"Then I will ha' a hundred men mustered for ye by dawn with a hundred more to follow in two days' time," Garth declared.

"I'm most grateful t'ye," Iain said, surprised at Garth's swift and generous loan of men. Immediately, his host summoned a guard and issued his orders.

Now that he'd been assured of the reinforcements he needed, Iain fiddled with his drinking cup, wishing the feast were done, so he might make his excuses and retire, but the great doors were thrown open and acrobats and jugglers ran into the room. Iain sighed. He could not escape. He must stay and be entertained.

Lillias, too, sighed with exasperation. She was impatient with the conspicuous show of wealth in food and drink and costly cloth—and the rude comments of her hostess. The more she was with Catriona, the more she distrusted the woman. Concern for her mother filled her every thought, so she could not eat, but crumbled the bread on her plate. Finally she could bear no more and half rose from her seat, but Catriona's hand on her arm stayed her.

"Ye canna go until ye've seen the entertainment," Catriona said. "Gypsies are encamped nearby and my son has hired them to perform for us. He has spared no expense to offer ye Dunbeath's best."

"I am most grateful," Lillias murmured, and sat down again.

Impatiently she watched as the brightly garbed gypsies filed into the room and began their show. Musicians walked among the tables, playing their violins and concertinas and accepting coins whenever they were offered. One old gypsy woman, wrapped in a splendid multicolored plaid, made her way along the line of diners, offering to read their palms. Laughing, Mary held out her hand. As the gypsy spoke, Mary's face paled, then she forced a smile.

"Lillias," she called. "Ye must have yer palm read. 'Tis enlightening."

"Nay," Lillias said as the gypsy shuffled nearer.

"Then perhaps I can read my lady's palm," the woman said in a deep voice as she reached for Catriona's hand.

"Get away from me, ye dirty creature," Catriona cried, and jerked her hand away, wiping it against her skirts as if she had been contaminated. The gypsy turned away, her shoulders slumping.

"Wait, ye can read my palm," Lillias called, feeling pity for the hapless woman.

"Aye, my lady," the gypsy mumbled hoarsely, and leaned over Lillias's hand, her back turned to the offensive

Catriona. "Beware, my lady," she intoned in her deep, rough voice. "A great misdeed is about to take place. Ye will lose someone ye love, if ye dinna act quickly."

Lillias bit her lip. The gypsy must be referring to Iain.

"What poppycock," Catriona declared, and turned away in disdain to reprimand a servant. The noise in the hall had increased in volume as the onlookers called encouragement to the performers.

"What can I do?" Lillias asked, bending closer to the gypsy woman, so she could be heard.

"Go to yer mither's room, at once," the woman said, and the voice was Aggie's. Lillias drew back, staring at the woman with wide eyes. The gypsy let her shawl slip, so her face was revealed. Aggie's bright eyes looked back at her. "Hurry, my lady," she whispered. "Something is afoot. They ha' locked me out of her room and will na let me enter."

Lillias leapt to her feet, heart pounding. Aggie pulled the shawl about her face and moved on.

"I must see my mither," Lillias cried loudly.

The people seated at the head table turned to look at her with puzzled eyes. The musicians, seeing something was amiss, stopped playing, and the acrobats and jugglers ceased their gyrations. All eyes turned to the two women.

Catriona's face blanched. "My lady, are ye ill?"

"Nay," Lillias said, glancing about until her glance collided with Iain's. "Nay, I am quite well," she said, "but I fear for my mither's well-being. I wish to go to her now."

"But ye kinna," Catriona cried. "She's—she's resting."

"How do you know that?" Lillias's eyes blazed.

Catriona's jowls quivered as she darted a glance at her son and Iain. "I—I, too, have been concerned about yer mither's health and I sent a maid along to check on her. She's just returned and told me yer mither was sleeping quietly. She seems much recovered."

Lillias sensed Iain frowning at her for the scene she was creating. She bit her lips and drew a breath, seeking the words that would help her through this difficult moment and gain that which she sought.

"I am grateful for yer solicitude for my mither's care—however, I should like to see for myself that she is resting well."

"I assure ye, my lady, ye can trust the word of my servant; she is quite reliable," Catriona said in an aggrieved tone.

"I'm sure she is, Lady Catriona. However—"

"Come, Lillias. Rest yer concerns," Iain spoke up. "I'm sure yer mither is in good hands."

"I dinna question that, my lord," Lillias answered, with a nod. "However, I hope ye will indulge me, since I have not seen my mither for some years and I am not yet used to having her near. I should like to go to her now—unless, of course, there is some reason I may not see her."

Catriona's pale cheeks bore two round smudges of color and her lips pinched together in anger. "Of course not, my lady," she conceded, with ill grace. "We are sorry ye dinna find our company of sufficient quality to make ye stay with us this evening."

Lillias made no effort to reply to this, but curtsied prettily before her cousin. "I thank ye for yer hospitality," she said graciously, "and I bid ye good night"—her gaze went to Iain—"and farewell." She turned and left the hall without a backward glance.

The musicians looked to the laird for a signal, and, receiving none, resumed playing on their own. The performers commenced their acts once more and slowly attention was reverted back to them.

Mary watched Lillias leave the hall and gripped Peadair's hand. "She will need our help," she said. "Come with me."

"She only goes to her mither's side," Peadair protested.

"Aye, but when we tried to see her mither before supper, we were stopped. Lillias will not be stopped so easily this time. I dinna want her to be hurt."

Peadair rose at once, and hand in hand the two of them slipped along the edge of the hall and out the door. When they reached the stairs, they fairly flew up them. Mary led the way down the narrow corridor toward Lady Margaret's

cell-like room. She could see Lillias ahead. The same servant stood with her arms crossed, her mouth grimly determined to carry out her mistress's orders.

"I order ye to let me pass," Lillias was saying.

"I kinna. I have my orders," the woman said smugly.
Seldom was she given the opportunity to defy her betters.

Lillias glared at her in frustration. The woman was far
larger than she, so she could not be pushed aside—and her
bulk neatly blocked the door to Lady Margaret's room. She
would have to be outwitted.

Lillias feinted to one side; when the woman moved to
block her, Lillias darted to the other side. Her hand was on
the door latch, but the woman pushed her away.

"I said ye kinna enter," she said, her elbows akimbo, her
meaty hands on her ample hips. "I have my orders."

"I have new orders for ye," Lillias cried, and doubling
her fist, struck the woman on the nose.

Blood gushed over the woman's face and down onto her
apron. With a loud wail, she clasped her injured nose and
drew back her hand to strike Lillias.

"I would na do that, were I ye," Peadair said sternly.
"Lady Lillias is a noblewoman."

"She struck me," the woman said belligerently, clasping
the end of her apron to her bleeding nose. Her eyes glared
at Lillias malevolently.

"Ye should have stepped aside as she requested," Peadair
replied. "Now, if ye will be so kind . . ." The woman stood
her ground, glaring at Peadair now. Peadair was
unintimidated. "Would ye rather I removed ye from this
portal, woman?" he demanded. The defiance went out of
the servant and she moved aside. Peadair reached for the
door latch and found it locked.

"The key," he demanded sternly, holding out his hand.
The woman opened her mouth as if to utter a protest, but
he glared at her so ferociously that she reached into her
apron pocket and drew out the key. With a last baleful
glance at them all, she stalked away down the corridor.

"We have na seen the last of her," Mary said.

"I fear not," Lillias said.

Peadair opened the door and stood aside. Lillias rushed inside. The room was dark and ominously still, without even the sound of breathing.

"Bring the candle from the corridor," she ordered, and Mary did as she bid. The weak light revealed Margaret was still in the room, but her face was so pale, Lillias feared she was no longer alive. She rushed to kneel beside her bed.

"Mither," she cried anxiously. The pale lashes fluttered upon the thin cheeks and Margaret looked at her daughter.

"Are ye an angel come to show me the passage to heaven?" she whispered. Her skin gleamed cold and damp with a sheen of perspiration.

"Nay, Mither. 'Tis yer daughter. I've come t'help ye."

"Save yerself, Lillias," Margaret whispered desperately. " 'Tis too late for me." She fell back against the pillows and closed her eyes. Her breath rattled in her chest. "They have poisoned me!"

Chapter 14

"MITHER," LILLIAS CRIED, and buried her face against her mother's shoulder.

Mary looked at Peadair beseechingly. Troubled, he felt for a pulse.

"She's still alive," he said.

Lillias raised her head, hope flaring on her face. "We must get her away from here," she whispered.

"'Tis na safe t'move her," Peadair said. "Besides, ye dinna know what she says is true. Why would anyone want to poison her? This may only be a fever. I've seen men go out of their heads wi' it and say strange things."

"If it were yer mither, Peadair, would ye be willing to take that chance?" Lillias demanded. He saw the fear in her eyes and he had no answer for her.

"Where will ye take her?" he asked heavily, for he knew Mary would expect him to help.

"I dinna know," Lillias whispered. Her face brightened. "But Aggie might. She has family here. Mary, find Aggie."

"Aye." Mary hurried from the room. Lillias turned back to her mother. "Peadair, what can I do?" she cried. "I kinna lose my mither so soon after regaining her."

"I dinna ken," Peadair replied helplessly. "I can but offer my sword, my lady, for yer protection and for yer mither."

Lillias smiled at him through her tears. "I am grateful, Peadair, for I know yer loyalties lie with Lord Iain."

"Aye, but he is sorely wrong, my lady. I dinna believe the lies told against ye by Hugh MacLeod."

"Thank ye." She gave him her hand and he placed a fervent kiss upon it, then drew away as she turned back to her mother.

He watched her with a heavy heart—thinking if his gaze had not had the good fortune of falling first upon Mary McFerris, he might have loved this woman, for she was strong and brave. He cursed Iain's pigheadedness for not seeing her goodness and believing in her.

The door opened and Mary entered, followed by a hooded figure. When they were within the chamber with the door closed, the shawl was thrown back.

"Aggie," Lillias cried, pulling her to the bed where Margaret lay. "She says she's been poisoned."

Aggie bent over the prostrate form and checked for a pulse. Carefully she pulled back one of the translucent lids and examined the eye, then bent to listen to the labored breathing.

"Aye, 'tis poisoning. I've seen it before," Aggie replied.

"Kinna ye do something?" Lillias pleaded.

"Mayhap." Aggie nodded. "There is a woman among my family who knows the proper theriac to draw the poison out. We must hurry and take her there. She has little time."

"What if my cousin won't let us leave the castle?" Lillias whispered.

"By God's teeth, he'll answer t'my sword," Peadair declared, "and t'Iain's. He'll na look kindly on a man who would poison his mither-in-law." He scooped Margaret's slight form up in his arms.

"Quickly, cover her. We must keep her warm," Aggie ordered, and they wrapped Margaret in several woolen blankets.

"Look to see if the corridor is clear," Peadair ordered, and Mary opened the door and peered out.

"Aye, it's safe."

He carried Margaret out and turned toward the front stairs. From below came the querulous voice of Catriona and the high-pitched, impatient snarl of Garth McGinnis. They ducked back into the room.

"They will never let us pass," Lillias muttered.

"They kinna keep me, by God!"

"Ah, Peadair. Ye kinna fight off the Dunbeath men if ye had to. And what of the men Garth has promised? D'we na need the McGinnis men despite this treachery?"

"Aye," he acknowledged in defeat. What treacherous waters they tread. He wished Iain were nearby with all his wile.

"There is a way," Lillias cried. Her eyes were bright with excitement. "There's a secret passageway. Ye can take her out that way. Aggie knows the way."

"Aye, I do," Aggie said, and took up her shawl and wrapped it about her head and shoulders.

"Aren't ye coming?" Mary cried.

"Nay." Lillias shook her head. "If I stay here, I may be able to delay them long enough for ye to get my mither to safety."

"There may be danger for ye," Mary warned.

"They dare na harm me while Iain is here," Lillias replied, far more bravely than she felt. "Tomorrow, we'll talk to Iain and tell him the way of things. He'll na make me stay where there's danger. Go now and hurry."

"We'll return for ye as soon as we can," Mary promised, and turned down the corridor after Peadair and Aggie.

The voices were closer now on the stairs. Lillias quickly turned back to her mother's room and slid the bolt behind her. Frantically she looked at the empty bed and hurried to plump the cushions and roll a thick plaid to place beneath the coverlet, so it seemed Margaret was still there. No sooner was she finished than came a knock at the door. On trembling knees she walked to the door and pressed her ear against the panel.

"Who is it?" she called softly.

There was a silence, then Catriona's careful voice came to her. "My lady, we are concerned about Lady Margaret."

"Ye were right, Aunt. She is resting."

"May we see her?" Lillias had feared this.

"Mayhap in the morning," she called.

"Margaret may need more care than ye can give her," Catriona coaxed, but Lillias heard an edge of impatience.

"She is better," she called. "She's sleeping, and I dinna wish to disturb her."

Another rap sounded loudly on the panel, causing Lillias to jump. "Then I insist ye open this door immediately," Garth ordered. "Like ye, I wish t'see for myself that she is well."

"Aye, Cousin," Lillias answered. "I must find the key." She stood back from the door, her gaze fixed on the slender bolt. An impatient knock sounded again.

"Lillias, if ye dinna open this door, I shall order my men t'come and open it." Lillias's breath caught in her throat as she thought of another man who'd made such a warning. Slowly she picked up the candle, and, walking to the door, slid back the bolt.

"I— Forgive me, Cousin. In my excitement, I dinna remember I had used the bolt instead of the key." She stood in front of the door, the candle held before her. Such a ploy lit her plainly, but left the rest of the room in darkness.

"Stand aside," Garth said coldly, "so I may see yer mither."

"Please, Cousin. I beg yer indulgence. She's resting easier now. I've bathed her forehead and given her a sip of wine. I think she'll sleep through the night."

"Nevertheless . . ." He pushed past her and entered the small room, glancing around disdainfully. Catriona contented herself with blocking the doorway, as if Lillias might try to bolt.

Purposefully he moved toward the bed, his hand reaching for the coverlet. When he pulled it aside, her deception would be revealed. Had Peadair had time to carry Margaret from the castle? She was certain he had not. Desperately she took a step toward the bed.

"As ye can see, Cousin, my mither sleeps—and I plan to sit beside her bed throughout the night." A cold wind blew against the shutters. They protested with a shrill creak.

Garth cocked his head as if listening, his gaze roaming about the room.

"D'ye hear that?" he whispered.

"Aye," Lillias answered. "The wind rattled the shutters."

"Nay, the voices," he said. His eyes were dark and wild-looking in the flickering candlelight. " 'Tis Sir Robert. He walks the castle at night in search of his head." Lillias shivered.

Catriona stepped into the room, alarm evident in her darting gaze and pale cheeks. "We'll leave ye, Lillias," she said, taking hold of her son's arm. "Come, Garth. We must let Lady Margaret rest."

"Aye, she must rest," he said, moving with his mother as if sleepwalking. Catriona guided him out of the room and into the corridor, then turned back to face Lillias.

"I would lock my door, Niece," she said rather portentously, and moved down the narrow passage with her son.

Lillias watched them go, then felt the dark shadows close around her. Shivering, she hurried back into her mother's room and slid the bolt home. Wrapping a plaid about herself, she sat on her mother's bed and waited for the long night to end. Tomorrow, she must find Iain and tell him of the danger for her here.

Before dawn, Iain rose and prepared for the journey home. Rather than explain his need for a separate room, he'd only pretended to go to the chamber provided for Lillias and himself, but instead had gone to bivouac with his men in the bailey. Now, with his troops mounted and ready to depart, he cast a last glance at the castle and thought of Lillias sleeping there, warm and serene in her ancestral home. Perhaps when the feud with McCullough was behind him, he might come again to Dunbeath Castle and resolve the anger between them. Then he remembered the innocence of her face the night she gave herself to him and knew he could never forgive her that final lie. Worse, she'd had the audacity to fling her treachery in his face by wearing the emeralds he gave her to mark that night. He clenched his fists.

Springing into his saddle, he signaled to his men. Besides the small troop he'd brought with him, a hundred McGinnis Highlanders mounted their horses and sat waiting his command. Garth McGinnis had been as good as his word, mustering a hundred men from his nearest neighbors. They'd arrived throughout the night. A hundred more would follow within days.

Kenneth Sinclair rode up. "My lord, Peadair and Mary McFerris are na wi' us."

Iain smiled. "Like as not they found something to occupy them at first light. They will soon catch up."

He led the way out of the courtyard and across the rushing creek. He had said his farewells to Garth and his mother the night before, so he resisted the urge to look back. He would not acknowledge the dull pain in his chest whenever he thought of the golden-haired woman he left behind.

They followed the trail they'd traveled to Dunbeath. The sun climbed high, unimpeded by clouds.

"My lord, ye've set a brisk pace and Peadair has na yet caught up wi' us," Sinclair reminded him.

"He'll have t'push himself some, won't he?" Iain said, not a little nettled by Peadair's dalliance. He had seen his friend and Mary whispering together before they left the hall and he had little doubt as to how they'd spent the night. His own thoughts had gone to Lillias—and he thought how it would be to go upstairs and strip away her finery until she stood before him with naught to hide her nakedness save her golden hair. He thought of her breasts and creamy thighs and cursed himself.

"Traveling with a woman will slow him down," Sinclair said, and Iain jerked his thoughts back to the problems at hand.

"Mary's a sturdy girl. She can keep up," he snapped. "And the McGinnises are our allies now. Peadair and Mary will come to na harm."

"Aye, if she's in a condition to sit a saddle after the night," Sinclair replied wryly, and Iain looked at him in surprise. The stern lips moved in the barest hint of a grin.

"All right, Kenneth, ye win," he said. "We'll rest along the riverbank and wait for them to catch up t'us."

"Aye, I'm immensely happy for yer decision, my lord," Sinclair said, and waved the men to halt for a rest. They dismounted, tied their horses, so they could crop the sweet grasses, and settled down to wait.

"I dinna like this delay," Sinclair said, coming to hunker down beside Iain. " 'Tis not like Peadair."

"Peadair is not himself since he met Mary McFerris," Iain said, skimming a flat stone over the glassy, sun-spangled surface of the river.

"Aye, I guessed as much," Sinclair said. "She's a bonny lass."

"Aye."

"A levelheaded lass who would not be taken in by someone who was false."

"Nay."

"An intelligent young wench who would see right through—"

"Aye, Sinclair. I see yer point. No need t'belabor it."

"Aye," Sinclair looked smug. "Then why did ye leave yer lady back there? I dinna like the feel of the place."

"Nor did I," Iain said. "But 'tis where she wants t'be, with her people."

"Mayhap when she was nine, but not now, my lord."

"She would not ha' left her mither," Iain snapped. "Now speak no more of her."

"I will speak of yer faither, then," Sinclair said stubbornly. He waited to see if Iain made a protest against that subject; when none was made, he went on in his measured way. "For some reason yer faither relied on me to act as his conscience."

"That's because he had none," Iain said bitterly.

"Aye, I often thought that." Sinclair drew up his knees and rested his thick wrists against them; his mind went back over the years, recalling the memories. "Red Rafe was a rough man, full of temper and malicious glee. For those who were caught in his power, life was often hell. Ye either joined him or ye were against him." He paused for a long time. "I did neither, but I was there as an observer and Red Rafe seemed intent upon shocking me with his stunts."

"Ye were the antipathy of his own indecencies," Iain observed.

"I believe ye're right. He seemed obsessed with the struggle between good and evil. Often he would set his chiefs against one another and laugh as they fought to the death. Sometimes he would bring one of his captives in and torment them for his chief's amusements. I saw strong, courageous men shamed and brought to tears before Red Rafe's cruel hand. I remember one captive in particular who never cried—and so was brought back time and again to endure the taunts and ridicule. No matter how courageous the captive, Red Rafe would not let up, but would spend his time devising new ways to torment and humiliate. He never laid a hand upon the captive, but the battery of the human spirit was a fearsome thing to see. Still, that captive survived."

"Why d'ye tell me these things?" Iain snapped. "I know my faither was a cruel man."

"Aye, ye know about yer faither, but ye dinna know about the captive. She is yer wife."

Iain breathed a curse and sat up. "I dinna ken it was so bad for her."

"She spoke the truth in the council meeting. She hated Red Rafe, and well she had reason to. And aye, she tried to kill him. It was his favorite game to give her a claymore, not a broadsword, which she could wield, but a claymore, which her childish arms could barely raise from the stone floor, and with his own claymore, he would jab at her and taunt her. She tried with all her might to wield the claymore—and if she could have, there was not a man there, including Red Rafe himself, who dinna believe she would have run him through."

Iain remained silent, thinking, then he sighed. "What ye've told me makes no difference," he said. "She released Angus McCullough against my wishes and failed to tell us she'd revealed the secret gate into the castle."

"Mayhap she had no time to tell ye," Kenneth observed,

"for she was brought to the great hall and set upon by the MacLeods in a manner not unlike Red Rafe's cruel tauntings."

"Enough!" Iain cried.

He turned away from his chieftain feeling beleaguered. The things Sinclair had told him made him see Lillias in a new light. She had mentioned only a little of the ill treatment she'd received at Red Rafe's hands and he had guessed the rest, but what Sinclair had revealed had gone far beyond what he could have imagined. He could see her now, a slim, young girl, all delicate golden beauty as she'd been last night—surrounded by men she could only consider her enemies—and made to face Red Rafe's cruelty with no one to offer her help. His mind balked at the thought of his father—so eaten with hatred and need for revenge he could show no mercy. And what of himself? Had he shown her mercy?

The sound of hoofbeats came to them.

"Peadair has arrived," Iain said, with some relief, and got to his feet.

But the galloping horse was coming from the other direction, and Iain signaled to his men to have their weapons at the ready. Logan MacCuag came into view, his horse all lathered and spent. Sinclair whistled; immediately MacCuag reined in his mount and looked around.

"Iain," he called. "I've ridden all night t'reach ye."

"What is it that ye must waste good horseflesh?" Iain demanded.

" 'Tis the McCulloughs. They've marched on Glean Fionnlighe, killing every man, woman, and child in their path."

"The bastards!" Iain cried, clenching a fist.

"My lord, no one was slain with a sword," MacCuag continued.

"What are ye saying, man?" Iain cried, reaching up to grasp his shirtfront.

"No broad swords or claymores were used, only the lochaber and bows and arrows." MacCuag looked away.

"Yer lady dinna lie, my lord. She claimed a pledge from Angus McCullough and he's holding to the letter of it."

Iain could not look at his chieftains. He'd listened to their council and branded Lillias a liar—and lost her forever. He had no time to sort out what to do. His clan was in peril. He glanced back along the path they'd traveled that morning. Still, Peadair had not come, and Iain felt a chilling premonition.

"Are our men gathered?"

"Aye," MacCuag answered. "They march to meet Angus before he reaches Glean Suileag. We're five hundred strong, my lord, but Angus has mustered the MacBains for his side as we knew he would."

"Sinclair," Iain called, and squatted and picked up a stick. "Take the McGinnis men and cross the River Lochy here." He drew a map upon the ground. "March southwest and come upon Glean Suileag from the east. Ye can trap the McCulloughs between ye. I'll ride back to Dunbeath to see about Peadair and lead the rest of the McGinnis men and join ye."

"Aye," Sinclair gathered up his reins and vaulted into the saddle. Signaling to his men, he galloped off to the north.

When they were out of sight, Iain turned back toward Dunbeath, his heart heavy with apprehension. Something was terribly amiss, else Peadair would have joined him by now. He pushed Lucifer as hard as MacCuag had his mount—and was nearing the final miles to Dunbeath— when a horseman appeared on the trail before him.

"Peadair," Iain hailed him. The rider drew to a halt. Mary clung to his back.

"Iain," she cried, leaping off the horse and running to him. "Praise be to God ye've come back." Her hair was wild, her cheeks wet with tears.

Iain's heart hammered in his chest. "What is it?" he demanded.

" 'Tis Lillias. She's in danger. I fear for her life," Mary cried, gripping his stirrup.

" 'Tis true, Iain," Peadair said. "We've just spent the

night whisking Lady Margaret to safety, but when we returned to the castle, they would not let us see Lillias."

"We fear she's being held prisoner. Lady Dragon Catriona claimed Lillias dinna want to see us. She would not refuse t'see ye, Iain."

"Nay, she would not," he agreed. "Which room is hers?"

"I believe she's still in Lady Margaret's room. There were no windows save arrow loops with the shutters closed fast."

Iain glanced behind him. "We kinna storm the castle and demand her release," he said. "I've sent ma men ahead wi' Sinclair. The McCulloughs have gathered their army and begun their march." He glanced at Peadair. "She dinna lie to us. She affected a pledge from Angus not to raise a blade against us."

Peadair's eyes gleamed. "Aye, I knew she ha' not told us false. She's a bonny lass."

Iain looked at him crossly. " 'Tis well ye've pledged yerself t'Mary," he snapped. "I would not like to raise my sword to a man I call my friend."

"And ye'll never have to," Peadair said stoutly, glancing at Mary with such affection, she had no doubts as to his feelings.

"If ye two have decided whether or not ye're enemies, mayhap we can figure out a way to rescue Lilli." She grinned at them impudently, then rushed on. "We know a secret way into the castle. Aggie showed it to us."

"Ye say ye took Aggie wi' ye when ye whisked Lady Margaret away?" Iain demanded.

"Aye."

"Then Lillias is alone in there?"

"Aye."

"God's pox on Garth McGinnis," he swore.

"And that witch that mithered him," Mary said, unoffended by a good round of swearing.

"We'll wait for nightfall," Iain said, "and slip into the castle through the secret passage. If Garth McGinnis tries to stop me, he'll answer to my sword, for I'll not be held back by a claim of kinship."

They left the path and made their way through the forest, taking refuge beneath the creek bank until dark. By that time, Iain's teeth seemed permanently fused, so tightly had he clenched them to keep from springing up and riding into Dunbeath with his broadsword drawn.

" 'Tis time," Peadair whispered, and Iain nodded.

"Mary, ye'll stay with the horses."

"But I want t'go."

"The less there are of us to move about, the better. I'd go alone, except that I don't know the way in."

"Ye'll need horses," Mary said. "I'll fetch some."

"Nay." Iain and Peadair spoke at the same time.

"Dinna move from this spot," Peadair warned, "or I'll beat ye."

"Aye," Mary answered meekly.

The two men moved off through the wild grass—and it was only when they were about to enter the castle through the secret passage that Peadair remembered that she'd answered far too meekly. He cursed.

Lillias stood at the door, listening to the sounds of the castle. Smells of roasted meat and boiled vegetables wafted up to her, causing her stomach to cramp. She hadn't eaten all day, despite the thin pottage that had been brought at her request on the pretense of feeding her mother. The pottage might be poisoned. She'd been afraid to leave the room at mealtime and take nourishment at the common table, afraid someone would discover her deception during her absence; so she'd waited throughout the day.

Now, as the last rays of light disappeared between the cracks in the shutters, she wrapped a plaid around her shoulders and wished for sturdier clothes than the delicate gown she'd worn to the banquet the night before. During her long hours in her mother's room, she'd devised a plan, and now she waited only for darkness to put it into effect.

When she was sure darkness had fallen, she pressed an ear against the door, listening for any whisper of sound that might suggest someone lurked beyond. When she was satisfied, she opened the door and stepped into the corridor, locking the door behind her. Wrapping the dark plaid over her pale gown, she moved toward the kitchen passage, keeping well in the shadows. It had been a long time since she'd walked here; she hoped she remembered the labyrinth of turns to the rear door.

She missed the turn and stepped out onto the landing leading down into the kitchen. Servants rushed about preparing a meal and did not notice her at first. When they did, they ceased working and stared up at her as if she were a vision. Lillias drew in her breath and edged backward until she was once again in the shadowed corridor. Retracing her steps, she searched frantically for the side passage and discovered it only by accident when she tripped and stumbled, headlong, into the yawning black cavity.

She pressed herself against the stone walls and gasped, flattening a hand against her chest to ease the thundering of her heart. When she was calm again, she moved deeper into the bowels of the castle. She should have saved the candle in her mother's room, rather than burn it through the night like a frightened child. She thought of Garth McGinnis and his claim that her father's ghost walked the castle. She would not be afraid, she reminded herself, for if her father's ghost truly haunted these halls, he would not hurt her. Mayhap he would even help her find her way out of these passages.

She began to fear she was to remain forever lost and would die here, when she heard a noise and pressed herself against a wall. She peered into the dark shadows with such concentration, her eyes refused to focus anymore and she felt light-headed. Suddenly something brushed the back of her hand. She screamed and drew back.

Something or someone was there in the darkness. She could sense it breathing like a living thing. She thought of her father's ghost and pressed a hand against her lips. A whimper escaped, and, once she'd made a sound, she could not hold back her cries of terror. Someone cursed. Ghosts didn't curse, she thought dimly, but couldn't stop her stumbling backward flight.

Arms wrapped around her; a hand closed over her mouth.

"Be quiet!" a voice ordered sternly, and she nodded and went still in the rough clasp. Whoever held her captive was not a ghost. "I'm going t'remove my hand. Ye must not scream," the voice said again, and Lillias threw her arms around the tall figure and pressed her lips to his.

"Lillias!" Iain exclaimed when she released his mouth.
"Peadair, 'tis Lilli."

"Peadair's here, too?" she exclaimed joyously.

"Aye, we came t'rescue ye." Peadair lit a small torch. Its wavering light revealed their relieved faces.

"Ye kinna rescue me," she cried. "I'm rescuing myself."

They stopped talking and wrapped their arms around each other.

"I was so scared," she said in a small voice.

"I was, too, when Peadair told me all that had happened."

"Peadair, how is my mither?"

"Aggie's kinswoman may well be a witch, for she had the proper theriac to counteract the poison. Lady Margaret rallied, but she's woefully weak."

"Thank ye, dear friend," Lillias cried, hugging him gratefully. She didn't see Iain's frown. "And what of Aggie?"

"She stayed to help nurse Lady Margaret. She'll see yer mither's kept safe among her people. They ha' no love for yer kinsmen. There are whispers of betrayal and treason. He uses his clansmen hard and they hate him for it—"

"Let's get out of here," Iain interrupted. "I ha' no love of these close places."

Quickly they made their way back along the path the two men had taken. When they reached the open, they crouched and followed the creek, taking care to stay in shadows.

"Mary, we ha' her," Peadair whispered when they reached the bank where they'd left her. "Mary?" Peadair slid down the bank and felt around in the darkness. He could hear the horses snort and move in the darkness, but there was no sign of a beautiful, dark-haired Highland lass. "She's gone," he whispered furiously.

"I'll beat her myself," Iain vowed, looking back at the castle. "We'd best go look for her." He pushed Lillias down in the long grass. "Stay here until we come back."

"Nay," she protested.

"Stay by the horses. We may need to make a quick run for it and we kinna look for each of ye over and over."

"Aye," she said, acquiescing.

The two men moved off through the grass and she waited, straining to see which way they'd gone, but the moon had gone behind a cloud and the shadows were dense. She sat back in the grass and thought of all that had occurred—and of the way Iain had responded to her kiss . . . with a hunger that told her he still felt a need for her.

Footsteps thudded along the ground and she sat up. At that moment, the moon slid from behind its covering. The clearing was well lit. Iain was running toward her, while behind came Peadair and Mary, astride some of Garth's finest horses.

"Lillias, get to the horses," Iain shouted. His strong, muscular legs flashed beneath his plaid, his arms pumped.

"Lilli, hurry," Mary called, coming abreast of Iain.

Lilli leapt up and ran to the horses. Lucifer whinnied a warning and she feared he'd not let her mount him, so she led the other stallion to a nearby log and fought with her full skirts to sit astride in the saddle. She heard running footsteps and Iain ran past, giving her mount a slap across the flanks, so he bolted away. Almost at once, Iain was beside her, astride Lucifer, with Mary and Peadair riding close behind.

They rode through the dark forest, bent low over their saddles, pursued by the castle guards. They rode with all the daring and verve for which the Highlanders had gained their reputation, and, eventually, they drew ahead. When they were certain they were no longer pursued, they slowed their mounts to a canter.

"Why did ye na stay wi' the horses like I told ye?" Peadair demanded of Mary.

"I knew we would need two more horses," Mary replied

calmly. "We could na ride double all the way back to Cullayne. They would have overtaken us in no time."

Peadair had no rebuttal for her logic. He sighed hugely to convey his dissatisfaction with her behavior and spent some time reflecting upon the quality of his future life with a woman of such impetuosity. They rode in silence, their way lit by moonlight, their steps dogged by urgency. Lillias slumped in her saddle, the toll of the past sleepless nights all too evident, but she was determined not to cause them delay. Finally Iain, glancing over his shoulder, became aware of her valiant effort and halted the horses.

"We must rest," he said.

"Nay, I can make it," Lillias protested.

"We are all tired, lass. 'Tis not for ye alone we pause." He glanced around. " 'Tis growing cloudy. The moonlight will soon be lost to us and the river is some distance yet. We'll not be able to ford her in the dark. We'll rest a few hours and resume our journey at daybreak."

"Till the morrow, then," Peadair said, and, signaling to Mary, turned off the trail, seeking a place where they might have privacy.

Iain watched them go, and, taking hold of the bridle of Lillias's mount, led them off the path—in the opposite direction—until he found a place beneath a ridge.

Gratefully she slid off her horse and stood watching as he gathered leaves and spread his plaid for her. He looked up and caught his breath. The moonlight shone on her, so she shimmered.

"Ye look like a fairy queen herself," he said softly, and held out his hand. "Will ye share a pallet wi' me, Lilli?"

For answer she ignored his proffered hand and walked away from him a little ways, unaware of how the moonlight spangled across her hair and gown with every movement. Mesmerized by her exquisite beauty, Iain followed her until they came to a small rill that made a chuckling sound as the water moved over dark pebbles. Iain stood listening, but his thoughts were on the girl who stood beside him.

"A great wrong has been done t'ye, Lilli," he said. "First by my faither and then by me. I've denied ye twice over, listening to others who spoke against ye and believing their words over yers."

"And ye believe me now?" she asked, the tight bands around her heart giving way at this evidence that he cared for her and trusted her.

"Aye. I should have from the beginning. I dinna expect ye to forgive me." He paused and knew more was needed, much more. "I'm not a man of a suspicious nature that I should turn on ye like this," he went on. "I can but think that since returning home, I am haunted by the old ways of my life at Cullayne, times of harshness and cruelty and ugliness. There was no kindness or beauty or hope, no trust." He glanced at her. "I need na tell ye of Red Rafe's legacy. Ye've lived it as well. We were not taught to believe in the goodness of others, ye and I, so how can we ha' trust?" He turned to her then and gripped her shoulders, pulling her close.

"I ha' a need for ye, lass, that goes beyond the desires of the flesh. I need yer gentleness and yer innocence and yer love. I need something t'believe in besides the baseness of men. Ye must understand these things I say, for ye've lived them, too. We are sore spirits who need to be made whole again, to see the sunlight and feel it in the darkness we've borne inside our souls." She made a strangled sound of denial.

"Dinna turn yer back on me, Lillias," he whispered roughly, and went down on his knees there, beside the gurgling brook. His arms wrapped around her hips and he buried his face against her waist. "I love ye, Lilli," he murmured, and the anger in her heart thawed like spring snow on a sunlit hillside.

"I love ye, too, Iain," she whispered. "I've tried to hate ye for being the son of Red Rafe, but I saw the fairness in ye. I saw a man who would never stoop to cruelty and brutality. I dinna give myself to ye the night Angus escaped to cover my deed, as well intentioned as it was meant. Ye came to me with yer face all earnest and caring and I remembered the handsome young man who covered me with his plaid and gave me comfort the night I was kidnapped.

I knew ye were different from Red Rafe, but it served my need for revenge to brand ye so. Dinna kneel at my feet, for I need yer strength and pride. I need yer love."

Iain rose and gazed into her eyes. "Ye ha' that, lass, and ye will until the day I draw my last breath. I so pledge it."

Lillias blinked back the tears and raised her mouth to his. His arms were strong around her, protecting her, strengthening her. His kiss was filled with adoration. She felt him tremble and knew he was holding himself in check. Drawing back, she glanced up at him saucily from beneath gold-tipped lashes.

"These pretty declarations of love may win a maiden's heart"—she sighed—"but I'm a flesh-and-blood woman, Iain, and ye've awakened things within me that kinna be forgotten. Now that ye've become a proper suitor, have ye forgotten how to be a lusty man?"

He stood as if stunned, then threw his head back and laughed heartily. The sound rang through the woods, startling Peadair and Mary from their embrace.

"All is well," Mary whispered.

"Aye." Peadair chuckled and closed his teeth over a rosy nipple in a lover's kiss that made her whimper and arch her back.

Iain's laughter died away and he gazed down at Lillias, his eyes going dark and heated. "I have na forgotten ye're a flesh-and-blood woman," he said huskily. "I've thought of little else these past days." Bending, he swooped her up in his arms and carried her through the woods.

Her gown trailed down about them and her unbound hair flowed over his arm like a golden veil. He carried her to the pallet he'd made and lowered her onto the leaf-cushioned plaid, then hovered over her, gazing at the pale beauty of the woman he could never stop loving. Slowly he unfastened her gown, raining kisses on each part of her body revealed, her creamy shoulders, her smooth breasts, and the puckering bud of her nipples, her curving waist. He buried his face against the soft flesh of her belly.

"My sons will grow there," he vowed, and swept away the rest of the skirts that hampered him.

When she lay pale and naked in the moonlight, he rose and threw off his clothes; she could see the hardness of his erection. She reached for him as he knelt beside her, her soft palms sliding over his hardened shaft, cradling, kneading, urging him to claim her.

"Nay, I would take my time wi' ye," he protested, but she moved her hands against his rod, so his need rose within him like a rushing torrent. He parted her thighs and poised himself, plunging against her hot, welcoming flesh, impaling her, so she cried out with ecstasy. And now her moist woman's flesh caressed him as her hand had done, throbbing against him until he was helplessly lost. His buttocks tightened, thrusting deep and true to that hidden core that brought pleasure and release. She cried out and held him, while she soared as light and unconquerable as the Highland mist.

Chapter 15

DAWN WAS JUST BREAKING when Iain gently nudged Lillias to wakefulness. She yawned and stretched beneath the warmth of his plaid and wound her arms around his neck.

"Ye must rise and dress," he said huskily, though he would have preferred nothing else than to stay here with her in their warm cocoon and make love until they were both spent. But the needs of his clan called to him, so he disengaged himself and drew back.

She made a pretty moue with her lips and let him go, watching with unabashed pleasure as he shoved his long, muscular legs into trews and drew on his shirt. The sun had not yet risen to burn away the gray mist that shrouded the trees and muffled sound. They were alone, untouched by the weighty concerns that awaited them beyond the parameters of that misty world. Yet, she, too, felt the wild Highland cry that was a call from their clan.

Lillias sighed and rolled out of bed to reach for her chemise and petticoats. Would the MacLeod clan truly accept her again as their own—given their deep suspicions? If not, where was she to go? For she could not return to Dunbeath with Catriona and Garth there. What was she to do about her mother? Would Margaret return to the convent? The questions buzzed in her head, and always she returned to the most important one.

"Will the council let me return to Cullayne?" she asked.

Iain grinned at her attempts to fasten her muddied, bedraggled gown. Her glorious hair was a tangle down her back, her face fresh and renewed-looking, despite the short hours of rest.

"Aye," Iain said, going to help her. Brushing aside her hands, he deftly laced the back of the gown. "A messenger came yesterday with the news that the McCulloughs are not using swords against our clan. The council knows now that ye told the truth about the pledge and yer reasons for releasing Angus McCullough."

Lillias turned to stare up at him. "And ye? Did ye have to hear the words from someone else before ye could believe me?" she whispered. "Was that yer reason for the change of heart and for rescuing me from Dunbeath?"

Iain flushed; she read the answer in his eyes. "Nay, lass. I would ha' rescued ye, regardless, after Peadair told me of yer welcome there." He paused, shifting his broad shoulders uncomfortably. "It's as I told ye last night, lass," he said softly. "Ye'll have to be patient wi' me while I learn to trust myself and ye. I've not had a faither t'show me that."

"Nor have I," she answered, with a steady gaze he found hard to meet. "But I've trusted ye."

"I will not fail ye again, Lilli," he said humbly.

She blinked against the tears that blinded her, and, despite herself, was moved by his humility. Gone was the old arrogance. His gaze was beseeching, and though his large hands curved possessively at her waist, he held himself in restraint, giving her the right to deny or accept him and his words. Caught in a maelstrom of emotions, she turned from him and reached for the reins of her mount.

Iain's shoulders slumped in defeat. Silently he held a hand for her slim foot and helped her mount. Astride Lucifer, he led the way to the place where Peadair and Mary had rested. They, too, were mounted and ready to ride.

"D'ye think McGinnis will pursue us?" Peadair asked, studying the forest behind them.

Iain glanced back toward Dunbeath. "They dinna track us with any great enthusiasm last night," he answered, shifting in his saddle to peer back the way they'd come. "Mayhap they mistook us for raiders come t'steal their cattle and believe they've driven us off."

"Aye, could be," Peadair agreed. "Dare we ride back and demand the men he promised?"

"I think not. If all is well, he'll send the men as soon as they're mustered. We'll take the ladies back t'Cullayne and ride for Suileag."

"Aye." Peadair nodded and spurred his horse forward.

They regained the trail and galloped at full speed until they reached the River Lochy, just as the sun was staining the distant rim of the horizon. When they came to the road that would lead them north to Cullayne or south and west to Suileag, Mary reined in her mount.

"Ye dinna need to take us home," she called. "Lillias and I can find our way."

"I will not have ye traveling alone," Iain answered, and Peadair nodded in agreement.

"Who will harm us?" she demanded. "Every man of the McCullough clan will be engaged at Suileag and na MacBain could penetrate this far into our land wi'out being recognized and driven back."

"God's teeth, she's right again," Peadair grumbled. Mary flashed him an impudent grin.

"I've no need for ye t'protect me, Peadair," she asserted. "'Tis not yer mighty sword arm that draws me t'ye."

"Be quiet, ye brazen wench. I see I shall have t'beat ye when ye're my wife."

"And who says I'll be yer wife?" she answered, eyes flashing. Before he could utter a reply, she rushed on. "Go off wi' ye now. They need ye in Suileag." The laughter left her. "And go with care, for ye carry my heart, Peadair McDermott."

"And ye mine, Mary McFerris."

Lillias knew their words were a pledge, a commitment as final and binding as marriage vows spoken before a clergy. She looked at Iain and saw his somber gaze was fixed on her. She swallowed hard.

"Have a care, Iain," she said tentatively.

At her words, his gaze lightened. "Then ye do love me, Lillias?" he cried. "Tell me so."

"Nay, I kinna," she cried, but his green gaze was so compelling she caught her breath and pounded her heels against her mount's sides, so he started away. "I love ye, Iain MacLeod," she cried to the wind, which carried her words back to him.

"I love ye, too, Lilli," he shouted, but feared she was already too far away to hear. Sheepishly he glanced at Peadair and turned his horse toward Suileag.

Without the women, they were able to travel faster, setting their sturdy mounts at a pace that soon had horse and rider covered with lather. They heard the sounds of battle long before they reached Glean Suileag.

When he rode into camp, Iain was greeted by the sight of wounded men lying in rows on the ground while a physician worked over them feverishly. Their death cries were less painful to hear than the stony silence of those who refused to acknowledge their severed limps or fatal wounds. As Iain rode by, Duncan Phipps looked up from his task of applying a tourniquet.

" 'Tis bad, sir," he cried. "The McCulloughs are not using blades, but their expertness with the lochaber is without peer."

"Where's Sinclair?"

Duncan pointed ahead; Iain and Peadair followed his direction toward the sound of battle. Sinclair rode back to meet him.

"We've managed to hold them back from the village, but the cost in men has been great," Sinclair said, and did not reveal that his oldest son, Adhamh, was one of the wounded back in camp. "They're even more formidable wi' their axes."

"Surely our broadswords give us the advantage?" Iain snapped. "The axes are more unwielding."

"Aye, but they're making use of their sword breakers," Sinclair answered, referring to a daggerlike weapon with a toothed blade. Held in the left hand, the weapon was used to parry a sword thrust and trap the blade between its teeth, causing it to break, virtually disarming a man.

Iain cursed beneath his breath. He'd seen such weapons used on the battlefields in Italy, but hadn't believed the McCulloughs would have access to them.

"Withdraw the men," he shouted.

"Retreat?" Sinclair cried in disbelief.

"We kinna go on losing our good men," Iain said curtly. "We'll retrench and find another way."

"Aye, sir." For a moment, Iain saw doubt in the old warrior's eyes, then Sinclair nodded and signaled to one of his men to sound the Highland cry, which would become a retreat—something a Highlander never dreamed himself of doing.

The MacLeods fell back and the McCulloughs, weary and heavily wounded themselves, did not pursue them. Iain retreated his men up a low incline and whirled to face the McCullough forces.

"I dinna think turning our plaids will fool them now," Sinclair shouted.

"D'ye think Dunbeath will send the men he promised?" Peadair asked, riding up.

"We dinna need more men," Iain declared, studying the terrain. "If I remember rightly, Suileag Bog lies off there t'the south.

"Aye." Sinclair nodded. "We've been cut off from our camp at times by it."

"It's time to use it t'our advantage," Iain declared. "Divide yer men. Put half of them mounted on that ridge, strung out in a solid line."

"Man, we cannot fool the McCulloughs wi' the same trick. Even they are keener minded than that."

"Aye," Iain agreed. "We have t'teach an old dog new tricks. Peadair, take the other half of the men on foot into the bog."

"Afoot into the bog?" Sinclair cried incredulously. His face was red with fury to think of the disadvantage of his men against the mounted McCulloughs. "They'll be cut to pieces."

"Think on it, man," Iain cried, too angry to argue. He turned back to Peadair. "Have yer men find the firmest stand they can."

"Aye," Peadair said, and turned to do as bid when Iain called him back.

"Pikes and daggers, Peadair," he ordered. "Tell them t'leave their targes behind."

"Man, ye kinna," Sinclair cried, nearly in tears. His stern old face was distorted with grief and fatigue. Iain's heart softened toward the stubborn old man.

"Have faith in me, Kenneth. Ha' I led us wrong yet? Am I na' yer *Ceann Mor*?" The words spoke of pride and history of the clan, and after a moment Sinclair nodded.

"Ha' yer men break out their pikes. They may use their targes, for they're to charge the enemy." The old commander had to bite his tongue not to utter another protest. Iain ignored his obvious reluctance and went on. "When ye've engaged the enemy, retreat to the bog."

"I kinna lead my men to a death trap," Sinclair said, unbuckling his sword and handing it over. His frosty blue eyes met Iain's.

"I ha' no time t'convince ye otherwise," Iain said flatly. "I dinna wish ye to resign."

"I dinna wish to." His gaze wavered. Slowly he rebuckled his sword at his waist. "If I lead my men to death, I will die wi' them."

"And I," said Iain. "If God be wi' us this day, we'll drive back the McCullough forces and break their aggression."

With lips pinched together in a thin line, Sinclair signaled to the line of cavalry and led them in a charge down the ridge. The McCulloughs had thought themselves granted a reprieve, but at the sound of the wild MacLeod cry, they grabbed their weapons and hurried to meet the charge.

Sinclair watched with a heavy heart as his outnumbered men fought valiantly. Finally, when it was clear to all that the fury of the battle was against them, he sounded the cry of retreat and led his men toward the bog as Iain had instructed. Their horses floundered in the quaking, giving mud, and the riders struggled to lead them to higher ground. Behind them came the McCulloughs, full tilt into the bog.

Sinclair turned his horse and brought up his sword, prepared to fight as best he could. His eyes widened when he saw that the McCulloughs were already engaged in battle with Peadair's footmen, who had hidden themselves and now rose up out of the mud to use their dirks and pikes to rip out the bellies of the horses and dispatch the riders.

Sinclair's seamed old face broke into a grin—and he himself sounded a Highland cry that rallied his horsemen, who turned and set upon those McCulloughs who had escaped the pikes. The battle was short-lived after that. Angus McCullough fought valiantly, his mighty arm swinging the lochaber ax above his head, his flaming red hair flowing about his head like a wild man, but in the end, a MacLeod dagger found its way to his heart and he fell in the mud of Suileag Bog. Iain was nearby and saw the chief fall. He rode over, and, dismounting, knelt beside the wounded chief.

Angus's breathing was labored, his eyes dimmed with approaching death. He gazed up at Iain without rancor. "So ye've won, lad." He gasped. "Aye, and it was a worthy battle ye fought."

"I had no wish for it to end like this," Iain said. "I'd hoped we could have peace between us."

"Nay." Angus shook his head. "Na wi' the son of Red Rafe." He paused and coughed. "Mayhap now, when I'm gone. My youngest son speaks of peace even wi' ye who slay his brother."

"It was in a fair battle," Iain replied.

"Aye, so I've heard. Mayhap yer way is right. Red Rafe and me, we're from another time. We knew no other way." He paused for a long moment, struggling to breathe. " 'Twas Hugh MacLeod who betrayed yer faither t'me," he said finally.

"Hugh MacLeod?"

"Aye. He wanted Red Rafe dead so he could become

Ceann Mor of the MacLeods. He was riding at Red Rafe's side that day and led him away from the rest of his men to a place we'd agreed on. After we killed Red Rafe, he begged us to wound him slightly to make it seem he'd fought, but we would not. He was a traitor and deserved t'be found out. He slashed himself wi' his own dagger and threw himself over Red Rafe's body. We thought t'kill him, but we knew he was a coward. He'd never come against us as Red Rafe had." He turned his head and stared at Iain with flat opaque eyes. "We hadn't reckoned on ye comin' home. No one thought ye would."

Iain remained silent. Angus grinned. "Ye've a bonny lass for a wife," he said. "I meant t'kill her when she set me free, but I could not. She was that grand a lady. Tell her— tell her I kept my pledge t'her."

"She knows it," Iain said. The old warrior's eyes closed and he slumped in the mud.

Iain stood over him for a moment—thinking of all the bloodshed over the years between the two clans and of the men who'd given their lives in a mad pursuit for victory. Even today, the battlefield was littered with bodies of good men, so Iain felt like weeping. It had always been so at the end of a battle. Even the victors were defeated. In his deep melancholia, he did not see a wounded McCullough rise from the mud and throw his dagger. With unerring accuracy, it sailed through the air and buried itself deep in Iain's back. Without a cry, he fell forward, facedown in the bog.

Lillias and Mary made a mad dash back to Cullayne Castle. Despite their brave, confident assertions to Iain and Peadair, they were uncomfortable traveling without an escort of clansmen. The countryside was fraught with the war between the clans. Common sense and reason seemed put aside for the moment. Neither girl could blame the MacLeod clansmen for their ferocious need for revenge. Their villages and crofts had endured many ruthless raids by the McCulloughs. Still, women like Lillias wondered if any of them had considered the possibility they might be killed and their wives turned to widows. She was relieved when they reached the familiar hills surrounding Cullayne.

Her relief was short-lived, for nearly a week had passed since she and Iain had parted at Glen Loy, endless days in which no word had come from the battlefield and her fear had grown to alarming proportions, endless days of wondering if he were dead or alive.

Upon their arrival back at Cullayne, life had seemed impossibly dull to Lillias and Mary after their dangerous adventure, then worry had overcome them and they thought only of Iain and Peadair. How many men would not come home from this battle? they wondered. Lillias set herself to tasks that seemed meaningless in the face of her greater concern for Iain, and Mary haunted the castle ramparts like a hollow-eyed wraith searching for the first sign of Peadair's return.

Lillias joined Everard to go over the lists of supplies needed to restore the castle's storehouses. He was surprised by her thoroughness and her attention to detail. Every servant to the lowest one was thought of and provided for. He nodded approvingly, for the hospitality offered at Cullayne in the future would be far different from that which greeted them upon their first arrival.

He grinned when he thought of her subtlety as well. One by one the lazy or insolent castle servants had been weeded out and replaced by more accommodating village people. Those servants who'd survived her test of wills had turned in quite tolerable services since her intervention. Everard grinned as he thought of Beathen, the master cook. Though Beathen's dishes were often prepared with a heavy hand, they'd begun to display a surprising delicacy. With a palate better accustomed to the finer efforts of French chefs, Everard truly appreciated this improvement.

Now, with their lists complete, Everard gratefully accepted the cup of ale left at his elbow by one of the new servants. She was a spritely young woman with bold glances and seemed to find him amazingly interesting. Everard was flattered by her attention, for he was a reserved man, not given to seeking immediate and indiscreet dalliances as the other men were wont to do. His tastes were a little more discerning—and he was surprised to find himself admiring the wench's trim waist and voluptuous breasts. Lillias spoke to him and he flushed, turning his eyes from the sleek young serving girl.

Lillias hid a smile and pretended not to notice, for Everard, she perceived, was a man of such great dignity and such rigid moral nature that the lithesome Isabal had her work cut out for her. Still, Lillias had been surprised to see the flare of passion in his gray eyes when he'd gazed at the comely maiden. Her thoughts of matchmaking were interrupted when Mary ran into the hall. Her face seemed abnormally pale beneath the cloud of raven dark locks that swirled around her shoulders.

"Men are approaching Cullayne," she cried.

"Iain!" Lillias whispered, leaping to her feet. Her face was alight with anticipation. She threw aside the tiresome needlework with which she'd sought to occupy herself and ran to take Mary's hand.

"They're back," she said, smiling, then seeing Mary's face, her elation died.

"Is it not Iain and his men?"

"The lookouts say nay. The riders wear the green plaid of yer kinsmen."

"McGinnis men? What d'they want?"

"Mayhap 'tis the rest of the men yer cousin promised Iain."

Lillias looked at Mary sharply. "Would he send those men after all that has occurred?"

"I dinna ken," Mary said, shrugging. Impatiently she rubbed at her brow. "Mayhap Garth dinna believe Iain had anything t'do with yer leaving Dunbeath."

"Aye. Iain had left early that morning with half the promised men. What reason would he have to return?"

"And yer cousin wishes to please the powerful Earl of Shiel," Mary pointed out.

"That is true. He wouldn't want to anger him by not honoring his promise." Lillias paced, considering all the ramifications of the arrival of McGinnis men. "So 'tis best to assume they are here to help Iain and they must be sent on to Glean Suileag immediately."

"Aye." Mary nodded. "So it seems t'me, Lilli."

"Let us go down and greet them. I'll dispatch one of the castle guards to guide them to Iain."

"Mayhap this is the answer to our prayers," Mary said, with such fervor that Lillias recognized the depth of her fears.

They hurried to the front steps of the castle just as the riders appeared at the drawbridge. Catching sight of the lady of the castle, a guard came running.

"They're from the McGinnis clan, my lady. D'ye wish me to let them enter?"

"Aye, open the gate," Lillias ordered, and the guard ran off to deliver her message.

Wood rattled against stone grooves as the portcullis was raised and the heavy wooden doors thrown open. She heard the thunder of hooves against the drawbridge, then the courtyard was filled with men and horses. Garth had promised Iain one hundred more men and it seemed he had kept his word, but even as she stood counting the new recruitments, a rider came forth and dismounted. Only when he'd thrown aside his hood did she see that her cousin stood before her.

"I dinna think we would see each other again so soon, Cousin," he said, throwing aside his tartan cape, so his rich doublet was revealed. His gray eyes were icy as they stared at her, belying the smile on his lips. Lillias drew back, despite herself. Mary bristled beside her.

"Why ha' ye come, Cousin?" Lillias asked, forcing a calm tone, though she trembled inside.

"Why, Lilli, where is the hospitality for which we Highlanders pride ourselves? Ye would keep me here in the courtyard like an unwelcome guest?"

"I'm sorry, Cousin," Lillias answered, digging her fingernails into the palms of her hands to remain calm. "My lack of attention to yer needs is only because there is a greater need I must attend first."

"And that is?" He smiled pleasantly, slapping his leather

gloves against his thigh as he climbed the steps to stand beside her. With a mutter of dislike below her breath, Mary retreated inside the castle.

"My husband and his forces fight at Glean Suileag to repel the McCulloughs. I have not heard from him for two days and have much concern for his safety. I see that ye've brought the extra men ye promised him. I'll arrange for escort to Glean Suileag, at once."

Garth McGinnis looked about the courtyard, his brows lowering over his eyes in a way she remembered from his youth. "My men will need to rest before they resume their journey." He turned back to her and forced a smile.

"Surely, in the face of our need, ye would na delay t'rest yerselves," she cried, looking around the gathering of men.

Garth's chieftains could not meet her gaze. She had the look of Lord Robert McGinnis about her and many of them remembered their old chief with pride. Only their loyalty to the ways of their clans made them accept Garth McGinnis as their chief. Save for the slender girl standing on the castle steps, he was the old earl's only heir and so entitled to be called *Ceann Mor*. Furthermore, he'd been able to produce documents showing Sir Robert had indeed appointed him Tanist and heir to the title. They would follow him, though their hearts were not in it.

"Aye, Cousin," Garth replied. "Elsewise, my men will not be able to fight when they arrive in Glean Suileag."

Lillias recognized Garth's maneuvers as a delaying tactic and felt afraid. "Of course, I—I hadn't meant to overlook the needs of yer men," she faltered. For the first time she noticed that Garth and his mounted troops far outnumbered the castle guards. She had unwittingly given them access to Cullayne Castle. "It's just that I'm so worried about m-my husband. I'll have my servants see to food and ale for yer men. There's a meadow there beyond the wall where they can camp."

Garth turned to one of his men and nodded. The officer gathered the majority of the men and cantered out of the bailey. Still, there were more than a dozen McGinnis clansmen left within the castle walls, enough to overcome the guards if they so desired.

Lillias tried to dismiss her fears. Garth was here to honor his commitment to Iain, a powerful clan chief and the Earl of Shiel. Still, she was uneasy, for she remembered her mother's warnings.

"Won't ye come inside, Cousin, and partake of food and wine? The ride must have been wearying."

"That it was, Cousin," Garth replied, following her inside the hall. His bright gaze went over everything, measuring, gauging. "But then ye must be well aware of the rigors of such a trip, for ye've recently made it yerself. I was sorry ye dinna choose to stay at Dunbeath as yer husband had informed me ye would be."

"I'm sorry t'leave ye so abruptly, Cousin," Lillias replied lightly. "I was homesick, as was my mither. She wished to return to the convent where she'd lived these many years and I wished to return to Cullayne, which seems more my home now."

"Understandable, Cousin," Garth said agreeably, choosing the cushioned master chair where Iain normally sat. He stretched his legs toward the fire and smiled up at her. It was the same smile he'd worn as a youth when he held something helpless and weak within his power. She suppressed a shiver, reminding herself that castle guards were just beyond the door and she had only to call. "And pray, Lillias, how d'ye affect yer flight from Dunbeath, a woman all alone?"

"Actually, I was na alone," she replied lightly. "I had my servant, Aggie, and when I saw Mary and Peadair preparing to leave, I hurried to join them. I know I should have sent word to ye of my intent, but there was no time if I was to have an escort back to Cullayne. Fortunately for me, I saw them return to Dunbeath."

"Fortunate, indeed," Garth said quietly. A servitor brought a cup of ale and he quaffed the contents eagerly. "Ye say Lord Iain himself is away at Glean Suileag?"

"Aye, he's intent upon repelling the McCullough invasion once and for all. That's why he'll be most grateful to see additional men."

"I'm sure," Garth said, but displayed no urgency for sending his men on their way.

"D'ye think yer troops could travel yet today?" she asked tentatively.

"We shall see, Lillias," Garth said, snapping his fingers at a servant who had brought wood to replenish the fire. Imperiously he pointed to his boots.

The man scowled and glanced at Lillias, then at her nod, knelt to pull off Garth's boots. With a disgusted look, he tossed them on the hearth and strode away toward the kitchen stairs.

"A most insolent servant," Garth observed. "If he were mine, I should beat him with my sword blade."

"We dinna treat our servants in that manner here," she replied stiffly. "Now, Cousin, if ye will excuse me. I'll see that meat and bread are brought to ye and see ye on yer way to Glean Suileag. Ye must be anxious to be off and join the others in battle."

"Come now, Lillias. Surely ye remember I had no taste for bloodletting?"

His languid air angered her, so her tongue was sharper than she intended. "Well I remember yer penchant for violence, Cousin, if there was no danger to yerself."

He shrugged. "I have not changed. I see no reason to risk my life for any cause."

"Then send yer men on to Glean Suileag. I beg of ye, Cousin," she cried, kneeling on the footstool before him. He studied her with amusement, holding her impaled with his serpentine gaze.

"Ye truly love this barbaric clan chief, dinna ye?"

"Aye, I love Iain MacLeod," she said fervently. "And he's na barbaric. He's kind and fair."

"Yet, ye bear him no progeny?" Garth's gaze had darkened and fixed on her intently. She blushed and looked away.

"He has only just returned from years of fighting for the French king. There's na been time."

"Time enough to beget his seed in yer belly. Are ye barren, Lillias?"

She blushed and looked away, not deigning to answer his coarse inquiry. Garth frowned at her stubborn silence and turned his taunts in another direction.

"Laird MacLeod is a hired soldier, is he not?" He sneered. "An adventurer, a man with few allegiances except for his own good."

"Nay, 'tis not like that," she said. "He and his faither dinna get along. He stayed in France during all those years to avoid seeing his faither."

"An unsatisfactory solution," Garth observed. "When he might have overthrown his faither and taken the title for himself."

" 'Tis not the way of the clans," Lillias answered, wondering that he had not that clan loyalty, which was so much a part of every Highlander's nature.

"And now he's returned to a boiling caldron of intrigue and feuds."

"Aye." Lillias looked away. "He wishes to make peace with the McCulloughs and the MacBains and end the feuds—and he thought such a peace might come when he captured Angus McCullough."

"But ye let him go, did ye not, Lillias?"

Her head jerked up; her gazed searched his face. "I see Iain has told ye everything." She felt a sick disappointment that Iain had revealed so much of their problems to her cousin. Somehow she'd thought he would protect her from the shame of being labeled traitor.

Garth smiled like a cat who finds himself trapped overnight in the creamery. "Aye, I know everything of yer disgrace," he said. "That is why I was so surprised that ye left Dunbeath to return to Cullayne. They dinna want ye here."

"They've learned the truth of my actions," she cried. "I released Angus only after securing a promise of peace."

"Ah, and he has broken his pledge?"

"Nay, he misled me." She looked into the fire, feeling deflated. "Now he leads his men against the MacLeods again." She looked back at Garth beseechingly. "That is why it is imperative that ye ride to help him."

"I have given one hundred of my men already," Garth replied sharply. "Why should I give one hundred more?"

"Because ye've promised."

He leaned forward, so his face was close to hers and she could smell his rancid breath. "Like Angus McCullough, I dinna feel duty-bound t'honor my promises," he snarled.

Lillias drew back. "Then why have ye come?" she demanded. "If ye are not here to help Iain, I demand that ye leave Cullayne, at once."

"Ye demand, Cousin?" His voice was very quiet, and far too reasonable. "D'ye forget yourself? D'ye forget to whom ye speak? Ye dinna have Sir Robert here to protect ye now or to mete out punishment against me."

Lillias drew a sharp breath and rose from the footstool. Her movements were jerky as she moved to put the table between them. Her heart hammered with fear.

"I dinna mean to offend ye, Cousin," she said placatingly. "I simply dinna see the reason for yer presence here."

"I have come to reclaim something that is by rights mine," he answered pleasantly. He rose from the chair, once more smiling and affable. He stumbled slightly, signifying he'd partaken too readily of the proffered ale. Lillias looked at him with some puzzlement.

"I—I dinna understand what ye mean," she stuttered, but before Garth could reply, the doors were thrown back and Hugh MacLeod strode in.

"The deed is done," he exclaimed. "Iain MacLeod is dead."

"Nay!" Lillias cried. " 'Tis na true." Her knees trembled and she feared she might swoon. She gripped the trestle table, fighting for air to return to her lungs, life to her body, but there would be no life for her if Iain were dead. " 'Tis a trick," she repeated piteously.

"Nay, my fine lady, 'tis truth I speak," Hugh said ruthlessly. "I myself saw him felled by a dirk in the back."

"And tell me, my dear friend," Garth McGinnis said. "D'ye throw that dirk yerself?"

With wide-eyed horror, Lillias watched the two men exchange gloating looks.

"Nay," Hugh said. "Though, in truth, I was prepared to. A half-dead McCullough rose up out of the bog and hurled the deadly blade. Iain was too busy congratulating himself over the death of Angus McCullough."

"So the McCullough clan is broken. Congratulations are in order, Hugh." Garth crossed to the table and poured him a cup of ale.

Lillias raised her tear-ravaged face and stared at them disbelievingly. There were pieces of a puzzle that did not fit together. "Ye know each other," she said dully. "How is that?"

Garth glanced at Hugh, grinned, and turned to Lillias. "D'ye na remember the incident wi' the puppy?" he asked. "Yer faither beat me, then exiled me from Dunbeath. My mither was furious, but Catriona has always been a resourceful woman. She was distantly related t'the MacLeod clan and begged Red Rafe to take me in. I spent three years here at Cullayne Castle." He grinned. "D'ye not know that, Lillias?"

"Nay, no one told me," she whispered. Secrets seemed to swirl around her, overwhelming her. Dimly she remembered Hugh's face the night of Red Rafe's raid on Dunbeath. He and Garth had stood talking.

"That's why—" She paused, fighting the shadows of the past. "I called to ye, Garth, there in the kitchen at Dunbeath the night Red Rafe came. I called for ye to help me and ye turned away."

"Ye ha' a good memory, Cousin," Garth answered. "I could na stay and be recognized by the McGinnises. They would know I was the traitor who led Rafe into the castle through the secret passageway."

"Ye betrayed us," Lillias cried.

"Aye, I enlisted Red Rafe's aid to take Dunbeath Castle from Sir Robert. He was to kill his old enemy, take Lady Margaret for himself, and leave ye t'be my wife, but he dinna play true wi' me. He took ye instead and married ye to his son, thereby establishing a possible claim against

Dunbeath and McGinnis lands." He paced restlessly. "I had to agree to let the marriage stand in order to retain McGinnis land."

"Yer the one who traded me away for land?"

"Aye." He nodded. "Wi'out ye as my wife, my claim as head chief was weakened, but Lady Margaret agreed na to oppose me if I left ye wi' the MacLeods."

"Ye fiend!" Lillias cried.

"As my wife ye'll think differently of me, Cousin," he replied easily.

"Yer wife?"

"Aye. I would ha' what is mine," Garth said coldly. "My clansmen are restive. With our marriage, my position as *Ceann Mor* will be strengthened. None would dare oppose me then."

"Never! I hate ye. I won't be yer wife. I—I'll enlist the help of the MacLeods to throw ye out of Dunbeath and reclaim my home."

Garth laughed, a sick, dry sound. Hugh strode across the room and gripped her wrist cruelly.

"I am the MacLeod clan leader now"—he sneered—"and I say ye'll get no help from me." He flung her hand away. "Ye had yer chance, my lady, but ye chose t'turn yer back on me."

Garth's smirk wavered. "What say ye, Hugh? 'Tis agreed I will take her back t'Dunbeath." He stumbled around the table, his eyes suddenly wild. "Ye know I must have her t'appease Lord Robert. I kinna return t'Dunbeath wi'out her. Ye know that, Hughie. Ye know." His voice lowered to a whisper of madness and his shoulders hunched. He seemed to shrivel in front of Lillias's very eyes, so great was his terror. Flecks of spittle wet his pale lips. "Ye know I kinna go back wi'out Lord Robert's daughter."

"Aye, I know that," Hugh said placatingly. "I meant naught by my words." He patted Garth's shoulders and straightened his doublet. "Come, my old friend. Ha' some more ale."

"Aye, I will," Garth said, somewhat mollified. The madness left his eyes and he straightened his shoulders. With a shaky hand he raised the cup to his mouth.

Filled with horror at all she'd heard, Lillias backed away from them, hardly knowing what she was about, but Hugh raised his head and stared at her.

"Ye kinna get away from us, Lillias," he cried, and nodded.

Strong hands clasped her from behind. Two men in McGinnis plaids held her in their grip. She struggled, trying to free herself, but they were far too strong for her. Where was Mary? Lillias wondered dimly. Why didn't Mary bring help? She opened her mouth to scream and felt a hand clamped across her mouth, so she couldn't breathe. She struggled wildly, trying to draw air into her straining lungs, but a roaring darkness closed over her. Iain's face rose up before her and she saw no more before she sank to the cold stones.

Chapter 16

SHE HAD TO find Peadair. Peadair would know what to do. If he were alive! The thought tore at Mary's heart. She'd stood in the shadows below the stairs, listening while the two men stood over Lillias's prostrate body, arguing as to who had won her. In the end, Garth McGinnis had persevered, for he had a force of one hundred men camped in the meadows beyond the castle. At the moment, his might was greater than Hugh MacLeod's, but Mary had seen the look of cunning on Hugh's face and knew it would be but a matter of time before Hugh mustered the MacLeod clan to march on Dunbeath and reclaim Lillias as his own. Hugh's lust for her had grown to a madness in the weeks since Iain's return. Lillias had been right to feel alarm in his presence.

All these thoughts raced through her mind as she made her way from the castle and to the village.

"Mary, where's yer fine dresses," Helen called from her garden. Her broad amiable face was wreathed in a smile. She obviously felt no petty jealousy for Mary's good position as castle seamstress.

Gratefully Mary hurried to Helen, leaning over the stone fence to talk to her urgently. "Helen, kin I ride yer Blue Lochy to Glean Suileag? 'Tis urgent I reach Peadair."

"*Tsk, tsk*, child. Show some restraint. The man'll be back in na time as soon as they set down those McCulloughs. Can't ye wait till then?"

266

"Nay, Helen. 'Tis na me longin' for Peadair that prompts my request."

"Why d'ye na take a mount from the castle, Mary?" Helen asked reluctantly. She was loath to refuse the girl's request, but she set great store in her stallion. He'd belonged to her late husband and carried him to many a raid and back again safely. "They ha' many more horses than I."

"Aye, they have, but I feared someone would stop my leaving," Mary said earnestly. "Something's amiss at the castle and I must reach Peadair." She didn't tell Helen of Iain's death. That must come later, along with the lamentations and grief. Now she must save her friend. "Lillias is in danger."

"Aye?" Helen studied Mary's distraught expression. "Take Blue Lochy. He's a bit on the lazy side, but take a switch t'him and he'll move right enough."

She led the way to the small pasture at the back of her cottage where the horse in question was contentedly munching the green summer grass. His normally emaciated ribs were covered with a layer of flesh and his coat was almost sleek. He rolled his eyes at his mistress when she placed the bridle over his head, and, when she laid the saddle over his back, he whickered his disapproval. When he was saddled, Mary climbed up and prodded the old stallion, who laid back his ears in warning and refused to budge. Helen handed Mary a switch broken from a juniper bush. Mary applied it rather sparingly, but still the old horse set his heels. Helen slapped at him in frustration.

"Come on, ye stubborn old pot," Helen muttered. "Ye were willing to go fast enough when Jaimie climbed aboard yer back." She paused and looked at Mary, a wicked gleam in her eye. "Hold on, Mary, lass." She put a hand to her mouth and let out a Highland cry that would have curdled the blood of a McCullough on his best day.

Blue Lochy's ears shot forward—and before Mary had time to do Helen's bidding and tighten her grip on the reins, the horse leapt forward, skimmed the low stone fence with plenty to spare, and sped down the road. Nearly unseated by his sudden bolt, Mary was far too good a horse-woman to give in to fear. She pulled at the reins and assumed control of the mount. When she was certain he was attending her commands, she bent low over his neck and let him run himself out. Like as not, such a wild gallop would end his days as a runner, but there was a desperate need to summon help.

Blue Lochy had far more stamina than she'd suspected; she was grateful that he was able to maintain his pace for the next few hours. Still, he began to limp long before they reached Glean Suileag. He'd been valiant in this, his last hurrah, but he would never make the rest of the journey. Mary felt frustration—and a desire to sit on the side of the road and give way to weeping—but she'd never been one to be defeated by anything, so she climbed off Blue Lochy, unsaddled him, and left him to graze near a running brook. With his limp, he wouldn't wander far; she would pick him up on her way back.

The last orange glow of sunset spilled over the long, narrow ridge of Druim Glean Laiogh. Soon darkness would fall in the valleys, and there were no welcoming lights from a lone croft where she might stay. She shivered, thinking of the mischievous fairy folk who preyed on travelers caught in the forests at night. She trudged on, wondering what had happened to Lillias after she'd fled. Should she have stayed and tried to fight off Garth and Hugh? Nay, they were far more powerful than she—and should they need to, they had only to call out for other men to rush in and help subdue her. She was but a lone woman. She'd acted properly, she consoled herself, but fear for Lillias drove her on to place one foot before the other.

She was startled to see a light ahead in the woods. Was this a campfire of the fairies that lived here? Had they started the fire to lure her closer, so they might more easily capture her? She darted behind a tree, and, holding her breath, peered around it at the glow of light.

Blinking, she looked and looked again to be sure, for it was a favorite trick of the fairies to display that which the unwary traveler desired the most—and the thing Mary wanted most was to see Peadair. There he stood in the woodland clearing, the campfire casting a light over his dark head and broad shoulders. While she held her breath and watched, he knelt and added a log to the fire. That single act broke her spell of indecision, for if the blaze was a fairy fire, it would not need someone to feed it common wood.

"Peadair," she cried, and ran toward the fire. A hand rose up out of the darkness and grabbed her, clamping her in an ironlike grasp. She was betrayed after all. "Peadair!" she screamed, and the dark-haired image at the fire whirled to peer through the dark shadows. Mary felt herself being propelled toward the fire and fought to free herself, calling out the one name that meant anything to her.

"Mary," Peadair cried, leaping forward and pushing at the brute who held her.

"I found her skulking in the woods," a rough voice said.

"It's all right. She's one of our clanswomen," Peadair said stoutly.

"Sorry, sir," the man said, and stepped back. Mary did not recognize his face and so assumed he was one of the McGinnis men who'd been set to patrol the perimeters of the camp.

"Come to the fire, Mary. Ye're trembling," Peadair said, leading her toward the warmth and light. Gratefully she leaned against his strong body.

"Ah, Peadair. I feared ye were dead," she cried, impeding their progress with her need to stop and press kisses upon his mouth and jaw. He clasped her to him for a moment. "When I heard Iain had been killed, I thought I would never see ye again."

Peadair drew back and gazed down at her. "Iain is not dead," he said softly. "Who has told ye this?"

"He's not dead?" she echoed faintly, then repeated it joyously. "Hugh came to the castle and said he saw Iain fall dead with his own eyes."

"Hugh MacLeod?"

"Aye!"

"Damn him!" Peadair cried, swinging away from her as

if the news were more than he could bear. "We figured he'd run to the MacBain stronghold, not back to Cullayne."

"He's claiming to be the next *Ceann Mor* of Cullayne."

"That will be hard t'do, since Iain still wants the title," Peadair said dryly. With a hand at her back, he propelled her toward the fire until she was standing beside a pallet of leaves. Iain MacLeod lay there, looking wan and weak, but he smiled up at her, his green eyes sparkling.

"Hello, Mary," he said cheerfully, then he caught a look at her expression and struggled to sit up. "What is it?" he demanded. "What's wrong?" The effort cost him, so he fell back against his pallet, a sheen of sweat breaking out on brow and cheeks.

"Ha' a care, Iain," Peadair said, hurrying to kneel beside him and wipe his brow with the edge of his plaid. "Ye're in no condition to be trying to get up yet."

"Damn me! I'm weak as a bairn," Iain exclaimed. "Dinna pamper me, Peadair." His gaze went back to Mary. "Is Lillias safe?"

Mary longed more than anything to tell him she was, but looking into the green, pain-racked depths of his gaze, she could not. Briefly she told the two men what had occurred between Garth McGinnis and Hugh MacLeod.

Iain swore and sat up, ignoring the flow of blood that stained his back.

"Iain, be sensible," Peadair exclaimed. "Ye'll be no good t'her dead."

"I'm no good t'her lying here while that bastard takes her off to Dunbeath again. He must be mad to try t'kill her mither and now t'kidnap Lillias. Dinna he ken the Mac-Leods will not let her go? We ha' to ride immediately for Cullayne." He forced himself to rise from the pallet. Peadair rushed to help, lending the strength of his shoulder for Iain to anchor himself on his feet.

"Ye'll na be able t'ride," Peadair observed.

"I'll ride farther than ye," Iain roared, and let go of Peadair.

At first his steps were wobbly, his shirt was soaked with sweat and blood as the wound opened and began seeping, but sheer willpower drove him toward Lucifer, who was staked nearby. Once there, he leaned against the stallion's sleek back and glanced back at Peadair.

"Of course, I'll need ye to saddle my horse."

"Iain," Mary cried, running to him. "Peadair's right. Ye kinna ride in yer condition. Lillias will not want ye to."

"Though she's my wife and I honor and respect her, I dinna do what Lillias wants," he replied stoically.

Mary glanced at Peadair, who shrugged and picked up Lucifer's saddle. Lucifer stood still, curbing his usual impatient prancing, seeming to know Iain was dependent on him. In no time Iain was in the saddle, the stallion's reins clasped surely in his grasp.

A force of men had been ordered to mount and join them and a horse provided for Mary. Without regard to the wee people that might be abroad at night, they set out for Cullayne. When they reached the site where Mary had left Blue Lochy, a man was left behind to bring the horse at a more leisurely pace. They rode through the night and arrived at Cullayne at the hour before dawn when all is still and the moonlight has waned. The castle, no more than a sprawling shadow against the black waters of the loch, was silent. Exhausted and sorrowing, all within slept, secure in the news that the McCullough aggression had been forever repelled, but at the cost of the chief's life. Only an occasional torch burned along the castle wall.

Iain led his men down the trail and to the drawbridge. The guard didn't wake and challenge them until they were nearly across. When Iain gave his identity, there was a moment of stunned silence, than a guard ran out, a torch held high.

"Praise be to God," he said fervently when he saw his chief was alive and had returned. He threw open the gates and they rode into the bailey. The sounds of men and horses roused the dogs, who began to run about and bark, which further roused the castle servants, who rose from their beds to see who had arrived.

Hugh MacLeod, having availed himself of Beitris's voluptuous pleasures for several hours before finally drinking himself into a stupor, was the last to be roused from sleep by Iain's arrival. He staggered down the stairs and out onto the castle steps, blinking in the torch light. As his bleary gaze took in the man seated on the black stallion, he gasped and drew backward.

The Black Beast of Cullayne stared back at him, his black eyes spitting green fire, his brows pulled low, his teeth bared in a ferocious snarl.

"What have ye done wi' Lillias?" Iain demanded.

"I—I've done naught wi' her, Iain," Hugh said, backing away toward the safety of the castle door.

Two Highlanders stepped forward to block his way. Hugh whirled round, his darting gaze looking for support, but there was none. No one wanted to return to the days when Hugh had declared himself chief and lazed in the castle while the McCulloughs overran them. Their pride had been restored and they meant to keep it. Now they watched with disgust mirrored on their faces as Hugh sniveled before them. Fear was naked on his face.

"I dinna ken ye were alive," he cried, turning back to Iain. "When—when her kinsman came for her, I—I thought it best she return to her own people. Ye remember how she betrayed us once. She might do so again."

"She dinna betray us!" Iain roared. "Every man here knows that now. She but tried to make a truce wi' the McCulloughs."

"I—I dinna know that," Hugh stammered. "What else was I to think when she had betrayed yer faither and had him killed by the McCulloughs?"

"Yer lies no longer work, Hugh," Iain replied sternly. "We know who the traitor was. It was ye who betrayed my faither and led him to his death. Angus McCullough told me himself."

"A-Angus lie—he lied." Hugh looked around the circle of men, his tongue darting out to wet his lips. He smelled of sweat and ale and fear.

Above his head, the window from Lillias's room swung open and a blond head poked out. Iain's heart leapt with hope, then hardened when he saw Beitris MacDougall lean out. When she saw all that was transpiring, she quickly withdrew and ran to hide herself in the servants' quarters, wondering if a distant Glengarry cousin might take her in.

In the courtyard, Iain dismounted, his movements slow and deliberate to hide his weakness. With great effort he turned to face his cousin, his sword at the ready.

"Arm yerself," he growled. Hugh's eyes widened and he drew in his breath sharply.

"I will not fight ye, Cousin," he replied.

"Arm yerself while ye can, Cousin, for this night ye die."

"I have pledged to myself that I will not fight a kinsman," Hugh cried. "Would ye have me break my vow?"

"What matter this one when ye've broken so many?" Iain said angrily. "Peadair, a sword for my cousin."

"Nay," Hugh cried, but had no choice but catch the blade that was tossed to him.

"I will not fight ye, Cousin."

"Aye, so ye said the last time I confronted ye, but this time, by God's teeth, I'll run ye through as ye stand there. Put up yer sword and fight me. At least die like a man rather than the craven viper ye've been so far."

Hugh looked at Iain's fury-darkened face and wet himself. Men looked away in disgust at this sign of weakness. Tears poured over Hugh's cheeks.

"I dinna mean t'betray yer faither," he blubbered. "I was everything t'him, everything a son should be. When ye ran off to the wars in France, I became his son, but he—he laughed when I asked him t'name me his Tanist, t'make me his successor as head of the clan. I deserved it. I was the one who remained here and did his every bidding." Hugh wiped a hand across his leaking nose and raised his head to stare at Iain with hatred. "I was his son, not ye, but he taunted me. He said I wasna as brave as ye. I couldna carry yer armor. He said I wasn't fit t'wear the MacLeod plaid. After all I'd done for him." Hugh curled forward, as if he might fall forward onto the ground. Peadair's sword dangled in his hand, forgotten.

Iain watched him for a moment and shook his head. "My

faither was right," he said. "Ye're na fit to wear the plaid." Sheathing his sword, he turned back to Lucifer, pausing to gain strength to pull himself into the saddle.

"Iain, look out!" Peadair cried. There was a flurry of motion behind him.

Iain spun in time to see Hugh charge toward him, his sword raised. His face was twisted with hatred. There was no time for Iain to draw his sword. Pinned against Lucifer's side, he was helpless before Hugh's onslaught. Suddenly Hugh threw up his arms, his eyes widening in surprise and pain, Peadair's knife buried in his back. The sword fell from his nerveless fingers. His stumbling charge carried him forward into Iain's arms. His fingers clawed at Iain's doublet. His pupils were distended, his gaze fixed and staring.

"I was a better son," he whispered hoarsely. His knees buckled beneath him and he slid to the ground, his clasp on Iain's sleeve carrying him down with him until Peadair stepped forward and lent his shoulder.

" 'Tis over," Peadair said softly.

"Aye, save for Lillias," Iain said wearily. "We must find her. Garth has taken her back to Dunbeath." He turned toward his horse.

"Are ye able to ride, man?" Peadair cried. "Let me go alone. I vow I'll return wi' her."

Iain shook his head. "That is my vow, my friend," he said softly, and pulled himself into his saddle. At a full gallop, he led the way out of Cullayne and on the road to Dunbeath.

She was too tired to fight anymore. She had resisted every step of the way, until Garth had ordered her tied to her mount and had taken charge of the reins himself.

"No more," he'd warned. "I'll not ha' others witness yer defiance."

"Why not?" she'd demanded, her glance contemptuous. "Are ye afraid of what they might do if they knew ye've kidnapped me, risking a feud with the powerful MacLeods? Would they rebel against ye if they knew ye force me to a marriage I dinna want? And what would the king say if he knew ye broke the truce between our two clans?"

"Be silent!" he'd ordered, and slapped her viciously across the face. She'd swayed in the saddle but had still held her head high and proud.

One pale cheek bore the ugly bruise of that proud defiance. He'd not loosened her ties even when they'd paused to rest, nor had she been given water to drink or food to eat. She was weak and dizzy from fatigue by the time they rode into the courtyard at Dunbeath, yet she sat her horse with a straight back. Garth dismounted at once and ran up the steps to greet his mother. Catriona was dressed in a brilliant gown of black and scarlet velvet with a green brocade underskirt and puffs of yellow silk showing between the fur-trimmed slashes of her sleeves. She turned an adoring gaze upon her son.

"Ye're home sooner than I expected," she called, holding out one pudgy hand for him to raise to his lips.

" 'Tis good news, Catriona," he fairly crooned. "Iain is dead and Hugh is once again at the head of the MacLeod clan."

Catriona smiled. "Good news, indeed. He hasn't the backbone to fight back when we start claiming the land north of the River Lochy."

"I fear that's true of my old friend," Garth said complacently. He glanced at Lillias. "Though he wanted Lillias, he quickly relented when I laid my claim."

"What will ye do wi' her now?" Catriona inquired.

Garth sent his mother a smirking glance. "I shall marry her at once," he stated. "With Lady MacLeod as my wife, dinna I have a right to lay claim to the MacLeod lands?"

"I'll never marry ye," Lillias raged. She sat astride her horse, still bound. "Even wi' Iain dead, I will not. I carry his child." It was news she'd hugged to her heart, waiting for Iain's return from the battle at Suileag. Now he was dead; it didn't matter who knew. If not for the knowledge she carried his child, she would have thrown herself into the raging river waters rather than return to Dunbeath under such circumstances.

Garth and his mother exchanged gleeful glances. "More's the better," he chortled. "I'll claim the MacLeod for the chief's son."

"Ye monster!" Lillias cried.

"Enough! Free her!" Garth commanded, and a trooper stepped forward with a small dirk. Tears streamed down Lillias's cheeks, but her head was still high—and all who saw her knew her tears were not from fear or pain.

Only when they'd cut the ropes that bound her and blood flowed freely again through her veins did she whimper, then bite her bottom lip to keep from crying out further. They helped her from the horse and she stumbled, her legs unable to support her. Garth signaled to a servant, who ran down the stairs and lent her shoulder for support. Painfully Lillias climbed the steps and paused before Catriona, tossing her head proudly and meeting the older woman's glare with one of her own.

"As ye can see, Niece, to run away from my son is useless," Catriona purred, glancing at Garth with rapt adoration.

"I will do so again, Aunt," Lillias said. "And the next time he will not find me so helpless and trusting."

Catriona studied her with narrowed eyes. "Take her upstairs and lock her in her mither's old room. There will be no more pampering until ye've learned yer place here at Dunbeath."

"Is that to be as mistress of Dunbeath, Catriona?" Lillias asked. "For so I will be if Garth takes me as his wife."

The older woman's face mottled with red. "Ye were always an arrogant, troublesome little girl," she spat out, "and yer mither and faither doted on ye far too much. They are not here now, and ye must answer to me at all times." She drew back her hand and slapped Lillias first on one cheek and then the other. The unexpectedness of the attack left Lillias speechless. She clamped her hands over her smarting cheeks and stared at her aunt.

"Enough, Catriona," Garth snapped. "I'll na have her bruised and marred for the wedding. I want the clan chieftains to see a happy, willing bride."

"Never!" Lillias spat out, dropping her hands and glaring back at him. "I will tell them that ye've kidnapped me against my will and they'll help me."

"They'll do nothing, my dear cousin," Garth said, with amusement. "Ha' ye not forgotten ye were kidnapped by the MacLeods. Ye've simply come home to live wi' yer own clan again. No man will raise his hand to return ye to the MacLeods." He grinned.

She stared at him with waning hope, for what he said was true. They would believe she'd finally been rescued from the clan that had taken her when she was a child. She looked from Garth to Catriona and saw the evil purpose behind their smug gazes. She was truly powerless now. Iain was dead. There was no one to help her, no place to turn.

Gathering her skirts and her tattered courage in trembling hands, Lillias swept into the castle—and without waiting for the servant to lead the way, ran up the stairs and down the familiar narrow corridor to her mother's room. Once inside she slammed the door and threw herself on the bed to weep with anguish. Iain was dead and she was alone—and in the power of Garth and Catriona, who hated her. She was but a pawn in their schemes. She barely noticed the scrape of a key turning in the lock of her door.

When they brought her a tray of food, Lillias pushed it away without eating. She remembered too well her mother's claims of poisoning and of the terrifying night when they'd spirited her away to safety. There was no one to do the same for Lillias. She was on her own.

Huddled on the bed, she thought of all the bloodshed and betrayal in her life and of the people she'd loved and lost— her father and even her mother, who was forced to flee to a monastery and give up any hope of seeing her child again. Lillias thought of her mother's face, pale and translucent as always, yet lit with some inner light, shining with love for the daughter she hadn't seen in nine years. Why had Lillias ever believed her mother didn't love her?

She wept now for the loss of those years with her mother. They were never likely to meet again. But perhaps the loss that was the hardest to bear was the dark-haired

Black Beast of Cullayne, for he'd taught her the most about forgiving and loving. She had blossomed under his touch, had opened her heart and soul and reached for a dream of life and love she'd never thought existed. Now to have that love stripped from her seemed all the more cruel for the years of loneliness and deprivation that stretched ahead of her. Those passionate hours locked in his arms would stay in her heart forever. She curved her arms around her stomach, cradling her unborn son. She would protect him with her very life, and one day he would know what a proud Highland chief his father had been.

"Have ye a plan?" Peadair looked at his chief and bit back a curse. Iain's face was gray with fatigue and he held himself stiffly, signifying the pain he was in. As soon as they had arrived at this hiding place near Dunbeath, Peadair had examined the knife wound, which had been opened by Iain's riding. It seeped an ominous discharge. Though he'd packed the wound with mud from the riverbank and tightly bound it, he feared it was not enough to offstay infections.

"Ye'll set our Highlanders to attack the main gate," Iain said. "I'll take a handful of men and enter the castle through the secret passage."

"Nay, ye're in na shape for it," Peadair protested. "I'll lead the men through the secret passage."

"Nay." Iain shook his head stubbornly. "Remember, he believes me dead. If he sees ye leading the men against the main gate, he'll na suspect we attack him from behind."

Peadair fell silent. It was a good plan, typical of the checkmates Iain devised for his enemies. Peadair knew his presence at the front gate was necessary to lull Garth's suspicions. He also knew that Iain must lead the men into the castle. No one else knew the way. Sighing, he nodded his head in agreement.

"Aye, ye're right. But take Uilliam Sinclair wi' ye."

"I will," Iain said.

Peadair turned away to hide his worry from Iain. He was thankful Mary was not here. She'd be like a wildcat trying

to keep Iain from fighting in his condition. Woe to Peadair
if he let Iain be killed now. Mary'd never marry him. The
grimness of his thoughts lessened a little as he considered
the fiery country lass. She was like no other woman he'd
ever known, with her magnificent sturdy figure and flaming
nature. Again he wondered what his life would be like with
such a woman. He would have to battle every day to maintain his manhood, yet at night, she would surrender to him
like a whelping pup, all soft and sweet.

"It's time," Iain said, and Peadair pushed Mary's disturbing memory from his thoughts and glanced at his chief.
Rivulets of sweat rolled down Iain's cheeks; Peadair knew
the effort this attack was costing him.

"God go wi' ye," Iain said, with a thin smile.

"I pray God will be too busy watching out for ye, my
friend," Peadair answered softly, and with a final slap on
Iain's shoulder, he rose and signaled to his men. They
mounted and regained the path to Dunbeath, no longer
keeping their presence a secret.

Iain looked at the handful of men who were left behind
and signaled to Uilliam Sinclair. "Ye'll all follow me, and
when we get inside the castle, spread out to the apartments
until ye find my wife."

"Aye, sir," they said.

A thought occurred to him. "Her mither was kept in one
of the servant's chambers. Try there as well." The men nodded. "When ye've found her, take her back out the secret
passage. We won't fight our way out unless we must. I
dinna want her injured." He glanced around the circle of
grim faces and nodded. Peadair had left him the best of the
best, but he saw the doubt in their eyes. They weren't certain he was strong enough to lead them.

" 'Virescit vulnere virtus,' " he said, meeting their gaze
unflinchingly. Courage grows strong at a wound! It was an
old saying and seemed to reassure them, for their morose
expressions lightened. Iain leapt to his feet, feigning an energy he did not feel.

" 'Vincere vel mori!' " He cried the MacLeod motto and
the men stood and raised their arms.

" 'Victory or death.' " They echoed his Gaelic cry.

Swiftly Iain turned toward the castle, running through the woods until they came to that place beside the brook where they must turn and make their way around the back of the curtain wall. His greatest fear was that somehow the secret passage had been blocked and they could no longer enter, but the opening was there, hidden by strategically planted bushes and a mound of dirt.

A torch was lit and showed the way down the narrow stone tunnel. They moved, swift and silent as wraiths on a misty night. When they caught a glimpse of light ahead, they extinguished the torch and crept forward. Iain peered around the edge of the tunnel, along the long, silent corridor. No one was about. Even the servants seemed occupied in some other part of the castle, obviously distracted by Peadair's attack at the main gate.

Iain moved back into the tunnel to converse with his men. "It appears clear, but go cautiously," he warned. "Uilliam, ye take half the men and follow the corridor to the left. It will take ye to the kitchens and servants' quarters. Search every room. I'll go to the main apartments."

They split apart as he'd indicated and made their way along the corridors of Dunbeath, keeping to the shadows as much as possible. They would engage the enemy only if they had to. Rescuing Lillias was their primary concern.

He'd gained the main corridor and moved quickly to the door of the room that had been Lillias's when first they came as guests. Nodding to his men to spread out on either side of the door and wait, he slowly lifted the latch and pushed the wooden door inward, praying it wouldn't squeak and reveal his presence, but the iron hinges had been well oiled. A single candle burned on a small table and a warm flame danced in the fireplace. Lillias's trunks sat about the room, the lid of one thrown open to reveal the gleaming brocades within. But he had no interest in any of these things. His gaze went to the bed, where a woman lay with her face turned to the wall, her long pale hair flowing over the pillow.

"Lillias! Praise be t'God, I've found ye!" he whispered, and, pushing the door wide, stepped into the room.

The woman sat up and looked at him, a triumphant smirk on her face. In the flickering candlelight, Iain could see her features were far too coarse to belong to Lillias. His brain signaled a warning, but too late. The wooden door was slammed shut behind him. He'd walked into a trap. Iain whirled, his arm bringing up his broadsword, but the point of a blade was already at his throat.

"So, we've caught a rat in our little trap," a voice said smoothly, and a man stepped out of the deep shadows. Garth McGinnis stopped in front of Iain, his face registering shock as he recognized his prisoner. "I'd heard ye were dead."

"I'm na easy t'kill, McGinnis," Iain spat out. "Ye're henchman, Hugh MacLeod, found that out well enough, but at the cost of his life. I've come for my wife."

Garth stood silent, assimilating this new turn of events. The blond woman slid off the bed and came to him, placing a hand on his arm and pressing herself against him. Viciously Garth flung her away.

"Get out," he ordered.

The woman gathered her loose garment about her, and, with a resentful gaze, crept out of the room. When the door opened for her exit, Iain glimpsed his men slumped on the corridor floor in a pool of their own blood. His fists tightened with rage. He whirled to face Garth.

"Ye'll pay for this," he vowed.

"Nay, my lord. Ye've attacked Dunbeath, and after I gave ye help with the McCulloughs. *Tsk! Tsk!* What a way to repay me. What treachery!" Garth shook his head. "Ye'll hang for this, Iain, and none will say me nay for it."

"Ye bastard," Iain snapped. "Peadair will tell the truth of what ye've done in kidnapping my wife. 'Tis ye who've been treacherous."

"I dinna care to debate it wi' ye, my lord," Garth said airily. "Take him away. Tomorrow we hang him at Mamore."

Iain struggled, but Garth's men overpowered him. One

landed a blow with the hasp of his sword and Iain slumped in their grasp. "Take him to the dungeons," Garth cried, and they dragged him away. Garth wrinkled his nose at the pools of blood from the slain MacLeod clansmen. "Clean this up at once," he ordered, and hurried down the corridor to his mother's chambers.

She was seated by the fire, her dark hair unfurled and hanging down her back. She rose at once and raised her face to him for a kiss.

"Yer trap worked, Mither," he exclaimed. "But ye'll never guess who we've caught."

"That arrogant man who helped whisk Lady Margaret away?" she said, her eyes gleaming with anger for Peadair McDermott.

"Nay, Mither. He's led the attack on the main gate. Our superior numbers have already driven them back to the woods. We'll have them routed in no time."

"Then of whom d'ye speak?" Catriona asked impatiently.

Garth's eyes gleamed. "Iain MacLeod himself."

"But he was killed in battle."

"Nay, Hugh told us wrong." Garth drove a fist into his palm. "I would kill him m'self if he were not already dead."

"Hugh, dead?" Catriona asked, a smile curving her thin lips.

"Aye. We can thank the Earl of Shiel for that favor." Garth paced the room in gleeful agitation, his eyes feverish-looking. "We must act swiftly, before the MacLeod clan can name another chief."

Catriona's small bright eyes studied him. "Where is Iain MacLeod now? Have ye killed him?"

"Nay, na yet," Garth said, chuckling and wringing his hands in his excitement.

"Are ye mad? Run him through with a sword now."

Garth stopped his pacing and stared at his mother, his nostrils quivering with unleashed anger. At once she saw the error of her words.

"I dinna mean to imply ye're mad, my dearest boy," she cooed, coming to run a soft hand along his cheek. "Ye are so clever, but he is the devil's spawn, seeming always to evade death's scythe. Would it na be wiser for ye to kill him at once?"

"Nay, he'll not escape this time," Garth said, somewhat mollified by her words. "He's completely at my mercy— and so is Lady MacLeod, as well."

"Ye kinna marry her with him alive."

"We'll have the marriage set aside. It was made against her will when she was but a child."

"She has to be the one to petition for the annulment. She'll never agree, not when she's with child. Why not kill Iain and make her a widow once and for all?"

"Aye, I've thought of that," Garth said smugly. "But with Iain dead, she cares naught about anything. She believes her mither is safe, so she had nothing more to lose. I kinna stand her before an assemblage of my chieftains and force her at dagger point to say the wedding vows. It would defeat the purpose of my marrying her. My chieftains would object. Nay, Mither. They must think she comes to our marriage a willing participant. With Iain MacLeod in my hands, she'll be far more malleable."

"Ah, ye're clever," Catriona said, with a dulcet tone. She took hold of his hand and pulled him toward the fire. "Will ye stay wi' me for a while?"

"Nay, not now," he answered. He didn't mention that he had a serving girl waiting in his bed, but Catriona knew. She suppressed her anger that he should spend himself on some insignificant snippet. Hiding her true feelings, she smiled lovingly.

"I'll bid ye good night, then," She raised her cheek for a kiss.

When the door had closed behind him, she sat before the fire, plaiting her long hair. Her lips tightened into a thin, cruel line as she considered how on the morrow she would find the identity of the girl who filled his bed tonight and banish her from Dunbeath.

In the narrow stone hall, Garth's good humor quickly vanished as he looked at the dark shadows stretching from his mother's door to his own. Nervously he took a step and paused. A white mist seemed to gather at the end of the corridor. Garth swallowed and gasped for breath as the mist took form and slowly moved toward him.

"My Lord Robert," he whispered, and licked lips gone dry. "I dinna do it," he cried. "I dinna."

The mist came closer, moving and shifting, so first an arm was exposed, then a thigh. But no matter how hard he strained, Garth could not see that which he sought, a head. Lord Robert's ghost was headless. The mist was closer to him now, surrounding him, choking him, so he backed against his mother's door and clawed at the wooden panel.

"Mither!" he cried in a high, thin voice. He was suffocating. The mist was taking his breath from him. Suddenly the door was flung open. His mother took hold of his arm and dragged him inside, slamming the door behind them.

"Mither!" he sobbed. "Lord Robert is there in the corridor. He'll na leave me be. I dinna know what t'do."

"Shh, my son," Catriona said, leading him to the stool by the fire. She shoved him down on his knees on the stone floor and seated herself, so she could wrap her arms around his shoulders. He buried his head against her breasts, sobbing out his fears. She rocked him back and forth until the sobs had dwindled to an occasional whimper.

"That's a good boy," she whispered against his ear. "Stay here, my son. Mither will na let anyone harm ye. Ye are safe wi' me."

"Mither?" he asked hopefully. His hand fumbled at her nightdress and she did not deny him. He was her son.

Catriona smiled and continued rocking as his hand found her full, heavy breast and his mouth settled on her nipple. Smoothing her hand through his dark hair, she suckled him as she had from his birth.

Chapter 17

T HEY WERE DRIVEN back into the woods, fighting every
step of the way, but the McGinnis numbers were too
great for them and Peadair's men were weary from fighting
at Glean Suileag. There had been no rest since that battle
and their forced ride to Cullayne and then to Dunbeath.
One by one the brave MacLeods were being cut down.

"We have to retreat," Sinclair cried.

"We can't abandon Iain and the others."

"My son is with Iain," Sinclair answered stoically. "I've
given one against the McCulloughs. D'ye think I wish to
abandon another? For all we know they're all dead. We
can't let more good men die."

Peadair swore. He knew Kenneth Sinclair was right. Iain
wouldn't want his men sacrificed like this. Despite his own
wishes, he agreed to retreat. The McGinnis forces pursued
them, but darkness had fallen, and in that time, when black
shadows claim the land and the moon has not yet risen
above the rim of the earth, the MacLeods slipped away
through the thick trees and headed for the fording place on
the River Lochy. Here, at last, they were safe from McGinnis blades.

"Retrench on the other side," Sinclair cried to the struggling wounded men. "Hold fast, lads. They may come after
us in the morning."

The Highlanders took up positions on the opposite shore

and settled down to wait. Morale was low, but being back on their own soil gave them new heart.

"Ye must rest," Sinclair cried. "We'll ride again on the morrow. Reinforcements will have arrived by then."

"Aye, but tomorrow may be too late." Peadair sighed and settled against a boulder to stare across the river. He had failed his friend and commander. Never had he let Iain down in all the years they'd fought side by side.

Near midnight, a watchful guard called out a warning. A lone horseman was seen crossing the river. They set arrow to bow and waited. The horse stumbled out of the river and stood shivering, while its rider slumped in the saddle, then slid to the ground. Men surrounded the unknown rider and hauled him behind the surrounding boulders, where a small campfire had been set. When the light of the fire fell on his face, the men looked at Kenneth Sinclair.

" 'Tis Uilliam himself," they exclaimed.

The newcomer coughed and opened his eyes. They widened when he saw he was surrounded and he swung an arm.

"Whoa, Uilliam," Logan MacCuag called. "Ye're among friends."

"Praise be t'God," the young man said, and collapsed back against the pallet. "I must talk t' Peadair," he exclaimed.

The men shuffled and Peadair leaned over Uilliam Sinclair's prostrate form. "Where is Iain?" he cried, gripping the young man's shirt. "Damn ye, where is he? Why d'ye leave him?"

"He was captured and the others killed." Uilliam gasped. "It was a trap. McGinnis was expecting someone to come inside the castle."

"Why would he? He thought Iain was dead."

"I dinna ken." Uilliam gasped again. "But the minute Iain entered the chamber, they fell upon him. He had no chance to escape."

Peadair swore.

"They're going t'hang him tomorrow," Uilliam said. "I heard Garth tell him so. They've got him in the dungeon tonight." He looked at Peadair. "I dinna abandon him," he gasped. "I came out to get more help to rescue him, but ye were routed and it was all I could do to avoid the McGinnis men."

"Aye, I ken ye did yer best," Peadair said. "We were just outnumbered. We should have waited for the other troops t'catch up wi' us before attacking the McGinnis clan." He looked about him. The faces of his troops were dark and uneasy. He stood and raised his voice. "Iain has named me Tanist, and so I have taken that title. I am his successor, should he die. But he is not dead, nor will he be if I can help it. I pledge my life to rescuing our *Ceann Mor* and his lady."

The men perked up and cheered. "Rest now, for when our reinforcements come, we will ride to Dunbeath and rescue our chief and fair Lillias."

The Highlanders split up, half to guard for a few hours while the other half slept. Peadair was too restless to sleep, so he paced until Sinclair called to him sharply. Both men knew that to do well in battle the next day, they must rest now. They were disciplined soldiers, so Peadair settled beside a boulder and willed his thoughts from Iain. Finally he slept.

Garth came early to Lillias's bedchamber, barely knocking before he threw open the door and strolled in. Servants followed, bringing her trunks. Garth waited until they'd set the trunks down in the tiny chamber and departed. He was dressed in a most resplendent manner—in black velvet embellished with silver braid over green *chausses*, as if for a celebration. His eyes were bloodshot, his face haggard, as if he'd not rested well, but his glance held a fiendish glee when he looked at her.

"Ye slept well, I trust, Cousin?"

"No better than ye, Cousin," she retorted.

For a moment his face twisted. The pleasant urbane expression was gone; in its place the youth who tortured small animals and defied all authority.

"Ye've a glib tongue this morning," he replied, forcing a smile. "I'm glad t'see yer humor has improved."

"Not one whit," she answered, and would no longer look at him, but stared into the flames on the hearth.

"Come now, Lillias. Surely ye kinna blame me for Lord MacLeod's death. Ye heard Hugh's account of how he was killed by a McCullough."

"Aye, I heard," she answered, and swung to face him. "I heard much of what he said yesterday—and the fact that neither ye nor Hugh wielded the dagger that took my husband's life is of little import t'me, for yer intentions were to do so. Now ye've kidnapped me and plot to take over Cullayne Castle."

"Not just the castle, but all of the MacLeod lands," Garth replied. "But I fear Hugh won't be a part of that. Ye see, he's met a most untimely end."

"Ye killed him?" Lillias accused.

"Nay, although that task would eventually have fallen to me, for I'm a most ambitious man."

"Ye're a madman," Lillias exclaimed.

Garth's face darkened and he crossed the room and slapped her full across the face. Lillias staggered backward from the force of the blow. "Ye will ha' t'mind yer tongue, Cousin, for I'll na have a shrew for a wife."

"I'll never be yer wife," she cried, straightening to face him defiantly. "No matter what ye do t'me, ye kinna force me to utter those vows that would bind us."

"Ah, dinna say never, dear Cousin. I think ye'll be most anxious to become my wife."

She stared at him with dread, thinking of her mother. "Wh-what do ye mean?" she stammered.

Garth smiled, pleased at this sign that he was breaking her defiance so quickly. As eager as he was to tell her of his capture of Iain MacLeod, he decided not to enlighten her just yet, but leave her in suspense.

"I wish ye t'go for a ride wi' me," he said. "I want t'show ye something."

"I dinna feel like a ride," she said, drawing that haughty air about herself again.

"Ye won't want t'miss this, Lillias," he said in so soft and silken a tone that shivers of fear ran down her spine.

"Ye've found my mither," she cried. "What have ye done with her?"

Garth grinned again, enjoying the power he had over her. "I ha' had yer trunks brought, my lady," he said in a conversational tone. "I thought ye might like to bathe yerself and change yer clothes before we begin our ride."

"I dinna want—" she began.

"Nevertheless, I wish ye to make an effort t'look yer most elegant, my lady, for ye'll be traveling through the countryside and I wish all t'see my beautiful cousin and bride-to-be." The affable smile left his face. "I shall return for ye, my lady, on the half hour. I trust ye will na keep me waiting." He strode from the room. The men who had brought the trunks followed him out.

Lillias sank down on the stool and wondered what to do. Garth must have found her mother, otherwise, why would he be so certain he could force her into marriage? She had no choice but to go with him. Her mother would need her. Eagerly she rose from the stool when servants brought hot bathwater and filled the wooden tub. She did not tarry at her bath, but quickly dried herself and chose a dress from the trunk. Garth expected her to garb herself as richly and ornately as Catriona did, but she chose a simple brown velvet with a black silk underskirt and white ruffles and puffings at her bodice and the elbows of her slashed sleeves. She hid her shining tresses under a French hood of plain black velvet without any ornamentation, not realizing the stark contrast set off her shimmering beauty more surely than gems would have.

She was ready and waiting when Garth entered. He frowned upon seeing her attire.

"Ye've dressed as somberly as a nun," he complained.

"Ye forget, Cousin, I'm in mourning for the death of my husband," she answered.

Garth smiled grimly. "Nevertheless, I would have ye wear something more festive."

"I dinna feel festive," she said stubbornly.

"In that case, Cousin . . ." He turned toward the door.

"Nay, I will do as ye bid," she said quickly, fearful he would leave without her and she would not see her mother.

Garth grinned. She was not so difficult to control. "I'll await yer presence in the courtyard."

He left the room and Lillias hastened to change into a more elegant gown, choosing a deep hunter's green velvet. She added a girdle of embroidered gold with a pomander of painted enamel to hang from her waist and a neckpiece of gold filigree. When she drew back to examine herself in the silver mirror Iain had given her, she saw the deep shadows beneath her eyes, which spoke eloquently of her suffering.

The nights of fear and danger had taken their toll on her, robbing her of appetite and rest, so she'd lost weight. Her cheekbones and delicate jaw stood out more prominently beneath pale, smooth skin. No matter now, the man she chose to please was dead. She turned to the door and was surprised to find it left unlocked.

A servant woman lurked in the hall, but other than that, no one guarded her. Garth seemed to know she was helpless. She thought of the secret passage she'd taken before and considered flinging herself against the watchful servant to throw her off and racing down the corridor. Surely she could lose the woman in the maze of passageways. But the servant crossed her arms over her chest and glared at Lillias warningly.

Sighing in defeat, Lillias turned toward the main staircase. Perhaps she should go along with Garth and make him trust her, before trying to escape again.

A horse was saddled and waiting for her. A small group of moss-troops were mounted at the ready. A stable hand sprang forward to help her into the saddle and Garth rode along beside. "Come, Cousin. I think ye'll find this outing amusing."

"I am not easily amused," she retorted.

"Ah, but I promise ye, this will impress ye."

"Ye fiend," she cried, suddenly unable to bear this baiting a moment longer. "Ye have my mither. What have ye done with her? She's naught but a helpless old woman."

"Aye, she's an old woman, but na helpless by any means," Garth replied pleasantly. He spurred his horse toward the gate; she had no choice but to follow. "Yer mither is the widow of Lord Robert MacLeod, and as such still asserts far more influence with the chieftains than I'm willing for her t'have," he continued when she rode beside him again.

"So ye sought to poison her," Lillias snapped, regretting that she had not believed her mother from the beginning.

"I dinna do that," Garth answered. "Catriona has always had, shall we say, a disliking for Lady Margaret."

"A deadly hatred for her, ye mean," Lillias said. "My mither is sick and wants only to live out her days in peace. She would never have left the convent if ye hadn't used me as a ploy."

"Ah, ye've a sharp mind, Cousin," Garth replied. "Ye've come to understand what we're about."

"I understand ye and yer greed and ambition all too well, Cousin," she answered bitterly.

"Then be aware that I am serious in my intentions today, Lillias. And only ye can change the outcome by agreeing to marry me."

"Ye dinna need my agreement," she answered.

"If the chieftains believe ye are being forced into this marriage they will not uphold it. They may even take their complaints to the king."

"King James?" Lillias stared at him—and could not hide the flare of jubilation.

Garth laughed. "Ye naïve fool. D'ye believe I will let that happen?" He spurred his horse and rode ahead.

They had left the castle behind them now. Ominous clouds gathered overhead and soon a chilling rain began to fall. The forest was silent, save for the drip of water against the leaves.

"Where are we bound?" Lillias called after they'd ridden some time in silence.

"We go to Mamore," Garth answered. "D'ye remember the place, Cousin?"

Lillias's heart leapt in her chest, for though she'd never

been there, she knew well the meaning of Mamore. Set deep in the Mamore Forest, it was the hanging place.

"Ye willna hang my mither," she cried desperately. "The chieftains would rise up against ye for such an act."

"Aye, they might," he conceded, and rode on with that maddening smirk on his thin lips.

Lillias hated him with all her heart. All the words with which he'd taunted her churned in her head, and in her despair, a small hope came aborning.

When they'd ridden an hour more, he slowed his mount and rode beside her again. "Have ye reconsidered, Cousin? Will ye agree t'be my wife?"

"I will not," she answered sullenly, and wiped at the raindrops that fell against her cheeks. Her velvet skirts were damp and heavy against her legs.

"Even if it means the life of a loved one?"

She bowed over her saddlehorn, her courage deserting her for a moment, then she raised her head and met his gaze defiantly.

"Ye dinna find my mither!" she cried, praying she was right. "Even if ye had, ye couldna hang her, for such an act would cause a rebellion within the clan, as ye've said. Ye have nothing t'show me. Ye're bluffing!"

"Am I?" He stared at her with such intensity, her heart quelled within her. "Just over that hill, Lillias, is the scaffold of Mamore. Are ye prepared to risk the life of the one who waits there? I ask ye again, will ye marry me?"

Lillias regarded him for a long moment, afraid to call his bluff, afraid not to. Who was there over that hill? If not her mother, then who? Aggie, mayhap. Nay, not Aggie, for she was too wily to be caught—and she had too large a family here in Dunbeath. If she were taken and was about to be hanged, there would be such an outcry, Garth would have to free her. Who then? Who else mattered so much to her?

She raised her head and peered through the drizzle, trying to see beyond the rain-soaked branches and earth. Mary or Peadair! It had to be one of them. They'd come to rescue her and been captured. Her chest rose and fell rapidly as she thought of her friends and the risk they'd taken for her.

She must do all she could to save them. She was about to speak, when Garth nudged her horse.

"Come, Lillias. I will make yer decision easier for ye. I will show ye who is beyond that hill."

They rode on, topping the rise and riding down into a small cleared valley where a scaffolding had been erected with a heavy crossbar above. The hanging place! During her father's time, only the most unredeemable of sinners had met their fate here, traitors and murderers. Now a solitary man stood on the platform, his hands bound behind his back, a heavy rope draping from the crossbar and looped about his neck.

Highlanders were clustered about the clearing, their expressions troubled, their faces grim. They had no liking for this particular hanging. Sullenly they moved aside when Garth and Lillias approached. Garth sensed their mood and turned his head sharply from left to right.

"This is far enough, Cousin," he ordered, reining his mount to a halt and motioning his personal troopers to surround him on three sides. "Observe yonder on the platform."

He had no need to order her thus, for she strained to see the identity of the man. "Peadair?" she whispered. His back was to her, but she saw the raven dark hair, the broad shoulders beneath the blood-soaked shirt, the long, powerful legs; her heart began a slow, heavy thud in her chest. A clansman stepped forward and tied a blindfold over the man's eyes, then turned him, so Lillias could see the molded lips and strong jaw.

"Iain!" she cried out, and the man's head came up. Her pulse pounded in her ears and she feared she might faint.

"Lillias!" he called, but she could not answer him, for Garth had clamped his hand over her mouth.

"Little fool. D'ye wish him to know ye're here watching him die?" She shook her head and Garth released her.

"Ye said he was dead!" She stared at him but could not conceal her elation.

"And so I was told," he answered. "Hugh was a bungler to the end. Yer husband was but wounded."

"And he came t'rescue me," she said.

"Aye, I knew someone would come for ye, so I set a trap, expecting to capture Peadair McDermott. Imagine my surprise."

"Ye're a monster," she railed.

"Enough! This is the moment of decision, Lillias," he said sternly. "Tell me, d'ye wish to see yer lover die or will ye marry me?"

"He is my husband. I kinna marry ye," she cried. Tears filled her eyes and wet her cheeks, but her beautiful lips trembled in a triumphant smile.

"The vows can be set aside. Ye made them under duress. Ye ha' only to request they be put aside and ye'll be free t'marry me."

"Is this not duress?" she asked bitterly. "Are ye na fearful I'll have our wedding vows set aside at first chance?"

"I ha' no more patience for sparring, Lillias. Tell me now—or see Iain MacLeod's feet dance on air. I will ha' his eyes unbound so ye may see them bulge from their sockets while he fights for air, so his last sight on earth will be the one of ye watching his death wi'out lifting a finger to help him."

"Nay," she cried, turning her head away at the image he'd painted. She looked back at him, her eyes filled with hatred, her lip curling with loathing. "I will marry ye, Cousin," she said, "but ye must let him go free and return him to his own clan."

"Aye, that is the bargain," he agreed. His face took on a look of cunning, so she did not trust him.

"I will not ride away from this place until I see ye free him and give him a horse so he may return to Cullayne."

Anger crossed Garth's face, then he smoothed his features and smiled. "As ye wish, Cousin," he replied. "I can be magnanimous in the face of yer surrender. Of course, I, too, have my requirements. Ye will tell no one yer true reasons for marrying me. Everyone must think ye've come willingly to this marriage."

She turned to gaze at him with the same cold blue eyes he remembered from Lord Robert. For a moment he was taken aback, then drew a breath. "I require this promise from ye, Cousin," he warned, "or I'll have the hangman do his work this moment." He raised his hand.

"I so promise," she cried, whirling to stare at the figure on the platform. She did not see Garth motion some of his men away. Quietly they moved back along the trail and hid themselves.

"Release him," Lillias demanded, and with an indulgent smile, Garth nodded to the hangman, who stepped forward and cut the ropes that bound Iain. He looked startled when the blindfold and noose were removed.

"Go, my lord," Garth called, riding forward, so Iain might see him. "Ye're free to return t' yer homeland."

Iain peered across the clearing at the man on horseback. "To what do I owe yer clemency?" he demanded.

"I ha' no wish to war wi' ye, MacLeod," Garth called. "Our feud was settled by the king himself some years ago. I dinna wish to break that truce, although ye've done so with impunity by attacking my castle."

"I merely come for my wife, whom ye've taken against her will," Iain shouted. "Return her to me and there will be peace between us."

The McGinnises who'd ridden with him against the McCulloughs shifted in their saddles and turned to stare at Garth. None of them seemed to grasp the incongruity of a lone MacLeod so close to death now making his own demands to the head of the McGinnis clan. Such was his daring that they were persuaded by him and silently championed his cause. More than a few had witnessed Lady Lillias arriving bound to her horse; the truth of her return had spread among the Highlanders. They had no liking for such lowly deeds against the daughter of their beloved old laird. Garth sensed their disapproval and clenched his teeth.

"She dinna wish t'go wi' ye, my lord. She sent word I must come and rescue her."

"Liar!" Iain leapt to the edge of the platform, his strong legs braced as if he meant to launch himself toward Garth.

Garth seemed unperturbed by his predatory stance. "Ask

the lady, yerself," he said calmly, and nodded toward
Lillias. The men parted, so she might ride forward. Iain
stared at her as if at a holy revelation.

"Lilli, are ye well? Has he used ye badly?"

She swallowed. Her gaze couldn't seem to move from
him. "Nay," she said slowly, shaking her head. "I am
treated well."

"So well, in fact, my lord, that she does not wish t'return
to Cullayne. She has decided to stay and become my wife."

"She kinna. She's my wife," Iain declared, pounding his
chest with his fist. His eyes were dark and furious.

"Tell him, Lillias," Garth commanded.

She couldn't meet his gaze. She couldn't bare to see the
pain she knew she must inflict to save his life. "I dinna
wish to return to Cullayne," she said. "I'm petitioning the
king to set aside our marriage vows so I may wed my
cousin."

"Ye dinna mean this," Iain said disbelievingly. "Look at
me, Lilli. Meet my gaze and tell me this lie. Then I'll believe it's true."

She gripped her hands until her knuckles were white
upon her pummel and forced her gaze to his. If she failed
to convince him, she knew he would take on the whole of
the McGinnis clan to rescue her. He would be killed, and
now that she'd felt the joy of having him alive again, she
couldn't throw it away.

"I dinna love ye, Iain," she said quietly. "I kinna forget
the cruelty of yer faither. It will be between us for all time.
I wish to remain with my own people."

"Then why did ye run away when ye were last here at
Dunbeath?" he demanded.

"I—I was confused," she stammered, not meeting his
gaze. "It was a hard decision to make, but now I have—
and I will not change my mind again."

Iain's eyes were dark with disbelief as his gaze captured
hers. His face registered astonishment. "What of yer
mither? Ye feared she was poisoned by this man." A murmur went up among the onlookers. Garth looked apprehensive.

"My mither is safe. I was wrongly informed about the poisoning. Garth had no hand in it." At least she spoke a partial truth, she thought bitterly, since it was his mother's hand set against Lady Margaret.

"I beg ye now to return to Cullayne and let there be no more bloodshed between our clans," she pleaded.

Iain recoiled as if facing a viper. She saw the light die out in his eyes and knew she'd killed something for all time. He searched her face for the truth, but she schooled herself and remained impassive before him. Finally his shoulders slumped in defeat.

"Aye. 'Tis what ye've always wanted," he said wearily. "I'll leave ye be, then."

"My men have a horse for ye," Garth said. "Ye'll be safe until ye reach the borders between our two lands, but if ye ever return, they will have orders to kill ye."

Iain ignored them. Silently he mounted the horse brought to him and rode through the crowd of men without looking at Lillias again.

"Iain," she whispered, and bit her lips to keep from crying his name out loud. He was free, with a promise of safety back to his land. She could not jeopardize that now. Through a veil of tears she watched him ride away. She could not stop the tears that slid down her cheeks. If he but turned his head and saw them, all would be lost. She turned her head away.

"Well done, Cousin," Garth said when Iain had disappeared around the bend. "Shall we go back to Dunbeath?" A rider entered the clearing and came directly to Garth. The two whispered hurriedly, then Garth turned back to Lillias.

"It seems that I'm never t'be done with this business," he complained. "Even now, Peadair McDermott approaches Dunbeath with a full army at his back. It seems ye must convince him as ye have Iain MacLeod that ye're na' being held against yer will."

"Peadair McDermott is here with an army?" Lillias whispered.

"Aye, but make no mistake, Cousin. Iain rides alone on

a different path. If Peadair tries to take Dunbeath again, I shall send my men after Iain with instructions to run him through with a sword."

"Nay. I will do as ye say, Cousin." White-faced, she followed Garth back to Dunbeath.

Peadair and his army had surrounded the castle. Garth cursed with rage when he saw his mother standing on the ramparts, her red velvet dress a beacon to him.

"Ye'll pay for this, Peadair McDermott," he swore, and ordered his men to rig a flag of truce. When it was ready, he looked at Lillias.

"Dinna fail me now, Cousin," he warned. "If my mither is harmed in any way, Iain MacLeod willna see the light of another day. If ye dinna convince yon MacLeod wolfhound that ye stay of yer own accord and that Iain has been released, yers is the first head that will roll beneath the swords of my men."

"I will tell them as I did Iain," she cried, and taking hold of the sword that held the white banner, she rode forward to meet Peadair McDermott. The look of worry on his face lightened when he saw her.

"Praise be, ye're safe," he called long before she'd reached him. Her lack of greeting and somber expression brought him up. He glanced at the white flag. "What is this, Lilli?"

" 'Tis a flag of truce, so I might have time to tell ye that ye've come in vain, Peadair," she replied, keeping her gaze steadfast. "Iain has been released and is even now on the road back to Cullayne."

"We dinna see him."

"He was released within the hour. If ye take yer men and turn round, ye'll soon catch up with him."

Peadair studied her expression. "Is this true, lass, or does yer cousin force ye to say this?" He nodded toward Garth McGinnis and his small entourage, who had followed at a slower pace and now approached.

Her lashes flickered for one brief moment, then she set her chin again. "I tell ye true, Peadair," she said. "I have myself seen Iain set free and given a horse to return to his homeland."

"I dinna ken how ye brought this about, but I praise ye for yer efforts. We've lost men enough over this excursion."

"Aye, men enough," she said sadly.

"Then come and we'll be on our way back to join Iain." His word brought such a wellspring of longing that she feared she might cry out as a child does who's been mortally thwarted. But Garth had pressed his horse close to hers and his dark eyes burned into hers.

"I will na be returning with ye, Peadair," she said stoically. "I choose to remain at Dunbeath."

"The devil, ye do," he exclaimed. "Does Iain know of this?"

"Aye." Her gaze did not waver.

"And he agreed to it?"

"Aye. He had no choice—unless it was to take me back against my will. He dinna try to do that, and ye must not, either."

"Why would ye stay now, lass, when ye fled the castle before? Mary and I were there. We helped ye. We took yer mither to safety."

"Say no more," she warned, drawing up her shoulders. "I stay by choice, Peadair. That is all ye need to learn of this. Please, take yer men and go back to Cullayne. Let us be done with this bloodshed. Iain desires a peace among the clans. Let it begin here, today."

Slowly Peadair accepted her words. She saw the change in him, the easing of the fearsome expression, the slacking of shoulders. His hand no longer played upon his sword hilt, but rested on his pommel.

"I must do as ye say," he said finally. He glanced at Garth and frustration was plain on his face. "D'ye swear these words are na coerced upon ye, Lilli? Ye ha' only t'say they are and my sword will end the charade. My men and I will take ye back to Cullayne."

"Nay, these are my words, freely given," she said, and there was nothing left for him to do but accept them as Iain had done.

He nodded to Sinclair, who signaled to his men to withdraw. Those men who had surrounded the castle rode back to join the other troops. Peadair sat looking at Lillias.

"Why would ye stay?" he asked thoughtfully. For the first time Garth spoke up.

"She's to become my wife," he revealed. "She's petitioning the king to set aside the marriage vows forced upon her when she was a child."

Peadair's face reflected his outrage. His eyes flashed with derision. "Ye're a treacherous, two-faced bitch," he sneered.

"Iain did not insult me so, why should ye?" she asked, and turning her horse, rode toward the gates of Dunbeath.

Peadair watched her go and wondered what he would tell Mary about this day. Anger filled him and he stood up in his stirrups.

"Ye were not worthy of him, after all," he cried. "Ye've returned to yer kind and good riddance." She did not look back, but rode with her shoulders stiff and proud, her veil fluttering behind her.

"Get off McGinnis land, Peadair McDermott," Garth ordered, "or I'll have my men cut ye to ribbons."

"I'm going. I have no wish to stand on ground so tainted by treachery and betrayal," Peadair said, and spurred his horse away.

At the main gate, Lillias looked back to see the familiar plaids of the MacLeod clan disappear through the thick forests. She was home again, and she was more frightened than she had ever been as a child, when first she was taken by the MacLeods. Would she ever know surcease from this pain in her chest? She rode into the courtyard and dismounted. The walls seemed to close about her.

Lifting her eyes to the sky, she caught a glimpse of Catriona's vivid gown. The woman stood glaring down at her; Lillias shivered with fear and exhaustion, for she knew the other woman hated her and would never stop plotting to rid Dunbeath of her, even if it meant by poisoning. She must guard herself, at least until Iain's son was born, and somehow she must see it to safety. But there was no one to help her. No Iain, no Peadair, and no Mary. She was on her own.

Chapter 18

THE WEEKS PASSED slowly. Garth prepared for a quick trip to Edinburgh to carry Lillias's petition to King James personally. The petition beseeched an annulment of her marriage to Iain MacLeod, since it was made when she was a mere child and newly kidnapped by the MacLeods. If Iain did not object, and there was no reason he should, then it seemed likely that King James would grant the petition, for he held little patience for the old acts of feuds between warring clans.

Garth had not revealed to Lillias his own petition, which would grant most of the MacLeod land between Loch Eil and Loch Arkaig to the McGinnis clan as recompense for the attacks made upon Dunbeath and the breaking of the nine-year-old treaty between the McGinnis and MacLeod clans. That she carried a MacLeod heir in her belly only added strength to Garth's petition for MacLeod lands.

In the meantime, Lillias tried to exist in a world that was filled with suspicion and hatred. She'd elected to go to the great hall to take her meals, for food from the common dish was less apt to be poisoned than that sent on a tray to her room. Yet, these meals, taken with Catriona, were fraught with tension. She must endure the older woman's baiting and insults much as she had done with Red Rafe years before. Catriona was every bit the tyrant Red Rafe had been.

Lillias kept to herself as much as possible, remaining in the small cell-like room that had been her mother's, and she wooed the servants with gifts of colorful underskirts, bits of ribbon, and some of her finest chemises. She carefully guarded her jewelry, for she knew one day she would need that to bribe someone to take her son to safety once he was born. She plotted and planned her own escape many times, but when she was driven to execute a plan, she found her way blocked. She was being watched every moment. All she could do was wait and pray Iain would not believe the things she'd said at Mamore and would devise a plan to rescue her. She dreamed of him, strong and well again, riding up to the gates of Dunbeath with a full army behind him. But with each day that passed, she began to lose hope. Her despair could be no greater, she was certain, until one day when she answered Catriona's summons to the great hall.

"Come in, Niece," Catriona said in the tone that made Lillias shiver with dread, for it usually boded no good for anyone. "Ye have a visitor." She nodded toward the high-backed chair that had been turned toward the fire.

Curious despite herself, Lillias moved across the room, straining to see the figure seated there. She gasped when the woman's hood fell back and her mother's face was revealed.

"Mither," Lillias cried, running to throw herself on her knees before the frail figure. "Why are ye here? Why did ye come back?"

Lady Margaret's frail hand smoothed the golden hair from the smooth cheek. "Ye look so much like yer faither," she said softly. " 'Tis like seeing his beautiful face on our wedding day." Her face lit with an inner beauty at the memory. "But ye've lost weight, child. Ye must take better care of yerself."

"Mither, how were ye captured?" Lillias cried.

"Nay, child. I was not brought here against my will. I heard that ye'd returned to Dunbeath and were but awaiting the king's annulment of marriage to Iain MacLeod to wed Garth."

"Aye, 'tis true," Lillias said, bowing her head, so her mother could not see the distress this fact cost her.

"Ah, 'tis true!" Lady Margaret repeated, glancing at Catriona. "Then I've come for my daughter's wedding."

"Nay, leave while ye still may," Lillias urged. "I will not have ye stay here."

"Would ye turn me out, then?" Margaret asked. "I will stay here with ye for the time I have left." A cough rattled her chest.

"Mither," Lillias said in such despair it broke Margaret's heart. "I kinna bear to lose another that I love."

"Shh, dearest," Margaret said lovingly. "I've come back to be with my daughter. Naught will drive me away." Lillias looked at her mother's proud face and drew courage from it. She served no purpose sitting on the cold stone floor sniveling in front of her hated aunt.

"Then, come. I will get ye hot broth and wine so ye may eat and regain yer strength." Fiercely she glared at her aunt. "My mither will stay with me," she said regally.

Catriona smiled, unmoved by Lillias's haughty air. Lady Margaret had walked back into their trap. Garth would be pleased when he returned from the king.

"There is a servant in the kitchen," Margaret whispered as she leaned on Lillias's arm all the way up the stairs. "She is a cousin to Aggie and looks very much like her. She will help ye. Her name is Moire."

"Moire. I will remember, Mither," Lillias whispered, and felt better. She was not alone after all.

In the days that followed, Lillias contented herself with caring for her mother, paying scant attention to the people who came and went from the castle. Moire, who was dark-haired, stout, and bore an amazing resemblance to Aggie, made herself known to Lillias, then discreetly stayed in the kitchen, so no one would suspect her. Lillias was unaware Garth had returned until she heard him shouting on the stairs below. Creeping out onto the landing she listened.

"Calm yerself, my son," Catriona soothed. "Ye've achieved part of what ye went for, and with that ye'll accomplish the rest. The king did agree to annul the marriage."

"Aye," Garth snapped, pausing to glare down at his

mother. "But he would not award me MacLeod lands beyond the River Lochy. He claimed they were natural borders and the land beyond would be too hard to defend against the MacLeods, who would surely fight such a grant."

"But that was his only reason for denying ye? If ye take the lands and hold them, he'll have to see ye're capable of defending them, then he'll grant them."

"I dinna mention that, Mither," Garth said impatiently. "The MacLeods enjoy far more of the king's sympathy than they've a right to. I will take the land, and when I've beaten the MacLeods, he must gi' me title. I'll be too powerful then for him t'deny me."

He took a step up the stairs.

"Will ye na come into the great hall and join me in a private supper?" Catriona inquired. "I would hear the news of court and the latest fashions."

"I am tired, Mither," he said impatiently. "I'll tell ye tomorrow."

He ran up the stairs and attained the landing before Lillias had time to withdraw. She stood in the shadows praying he wouldn't see her, but he sensed her presence and drew his sword.

"Who's there?" he cried out, his voice suddenly thin. "Step forward!"

Though clad only in her white shift, she moved out of the deep shadows toward the light. The effect on Garth was startling.

"Lord Robert." His voice broke on a high, hysterical note and he scuttled backward, brandishing the sword before him. His expression was stark with fear. "Why d'ye torture me thus?" he sobbed. "I dinna do it. I swear on my mither's life, I dinna take yer head."

Lillias stepped forward into the light, so her face was revealed; his eyes widened. "Lillias," he snarled, and the glazed look left his eyes. "Why d'ye skulk around these corridors? D'ye na know they're haunted?"

"By the ghost of my faither?" she asked. "Why?"

"I dinna ken." His gaze shifted. His manner was evasive. He shoved his sword back into its sheath.

"Yer petition for annulment has been granted. Tomorrow we wed."

"Is this not hasty, Cousin?" she asked, assuming a mocking tone. "Would it not sit better with yer chieftains if ye give a great banquet and have our vows said before all assembled?"

"Aye, 'tis so," he answered. "I spoke in haste. I am weary from my journey. Ellie, where are ye?" He turned away to his room, shouting for the serving wench he'd favored when last he needed a woman.

Grateful he was so easily deterred and did not press such needs upon her, Lillias scooted back to the room she shared with Margaret. She'd won a short reprieve for herself, but the significance of the annulment was sobering. Iain had not protested her petition. Well, why would he? Hadn't she told him this was her wish? Still, she wished just once he'd had faith in her love.

"Is all well, Lillias?" Margaret asked from the bed. She had remained there for several days now, too weak to rise again.

Lillias gripped her mother's frail hand and forced a smile. "All is well, Mither," she whispered, pressing the frail hand to her cheek. "Soon, Iain will come to rescue us." Never had she felt so helpless and alone. She prayed someone would come.

Despite Margaret's presence—or perhaps because of it—Lillias had continued to take her meals in the great hall. When she had finished, she always prepared a tray for her mother and carried it up herself. Margaret's health was so fragile, Lillias knew she would never be able to recover, as she had before, should someone try to poison her.

After Garth's return, Lillias was loath to share a meal with him and his mother, yet she knew she must do all she could to keep up her strength for the sake of her baby and to bring nourishment to her mother.

"Aye, my bride-to-be joins us," Garth jeered when she entered the hall and took her place at the table. "See how wraithlike she's become. Is it she who haunts the halls of this castle or is it truly the headless ghost of Lord Robert?"

"Neither," Lillias said.

"Please, Garth. Let's not speak of such things before the servants," Catriona said nervously.

She cast a glance about the hall to see who might have heard his ranting, but the servitors kept their faces stiff, as if they'd heard nothing. Lillias guessed it was quite a different matter when they were below stairs in the kitchens. There they must regale the others with tales of headless Lord Robert, who stalked the dark halls seeking revenge, and of a master who was so frightened he went no place within the castle without two guards beside him. The men even stood guard outside his chambers while he slept. The servants would flee if Garth kept on. Yet he seemed disinclined to stop.

"Ye seem certain, Cousin," he said, his eyes dark and unfathomable.

"I am certain that I dinna walk the halls," she snapped. "And why should my faither haunt Dunbeath seeking revenge? Though ye betrayed him, 'twas Red Rafe who took his head. Would my faither na wish to seek his revenge at Cullayne Castle? Yet I never heard a word of his presence when I was there."

She'd thought her words of logic might ease his obsession, though she wondered why she tried, but Garth and his mother exchanged uneasy glances and seemed more morose than ever. Lillias got to her feet, her food barely touched.

"I will make a tray for my mither and take my leave of ye," she said, spooning mutton and broth into a bowl. Catriona watched as she gathered a flagon of wine and a cup, spoon, and bread.

"Why dinna ye let me send a servant with Lady Margaret's food?" Catriona inquired brusquely. Her small dark eyes snapped with frustration.

"I have not been with my mither these many years. I enjoy waiting on her," Lillias said sweetly, knowing even Catriona could find no argument against that. Lillias left the hall, relieved to be out of their presence.

From the darkness beneath the stairs, a shadow moved. Rough hands grasped her, startling her, so she dropped the silver tray. She was dragged into the dark shadows before the flagon and wooden bowl crashed against the stone floor. A hand clamped across her mouth, so she could make no sound. They waited, she and her captors, barely breathing, while voices sounded from the great hall. The doors were thrown open. Garth stood in the doorway, surrounded by his personal bodyguards.

"Make no outcry or we'll kill ye," a voice warned in her ear. Lillias nodded.

Broth and wine ran in rivulets among the uneven slabs of stone. One of Garth's wolfhounds ran out and began to lap it up.

"Who's there?" he called fearfully. He'd drawn his sword. "Lord Robert? Is it ye?" His voice had taken on a hysterical edge of madness. "Who's there, I say?"

"Answer him, but dinna give us away," the man holding her whispered. She nodded and was immediately released. She stepped forward into the light.

"Lillias. What are ye doing there?" Garth demanded.

"Ye scared me when ye threw open the doors. I—I dropped my tray." She took a deep breath and rushed on, trying to allay his fears. "Could ye have a servant clear it and bring another up to my mither?"

"How d'ye drop yer tray?" he asked, stalking across the dimly lit stones toward her.

Lillias drew back, then realized she would lead him to discover the men who lurked beneath the stairs. She knew not who they were, save that they were enemies of Garth's and therefore her friends. She walked toward him, as if grateful for his presence.

"I—I was so frightened," she said, making her voice high and reedy, as if afraid. "I saw something there at the top of the stairs, something pale and misty." Garth drew back into the hall, his head twisting from side to side like some great beast who's been surrounded and brought to heel.

" 'Tis na there now," Lillias said. "Surely it was but my

imagination. Good night, Cousin." She put her foot on the bottom step and began to climb.

She'd nearly reached the top before she heard the doors close below. The entry was once again in shadows. Quickly she ran downstairs and paused before stepping into the darkness.

"Whoever ye be," she whispered. "If ye're an enemy to my cousin, ye're a friend to me. I beg ye follow me. 'Tis not safe here."

She led them upstairs and through the back corridor to her own room. Only then, when they were safe within and the door bolted behind them, did she turn to peer through the shadows at the intruders. "I knew my friends would come for me," she cried jubilantly.

Hands grasped her and jerked her into the glow of firelight. "Ye be na friend of ours, witch of Dunbeath," Peadair McDermott growled.

"Peadair." Lillias launched herself at the sound of his voice, winding her arms around his thick waist. "Mither, 'tis Peadair. He's come back for us."

"Peadair," Margaret said from her bed. "Praise be to God."

"Where's Iain? Iain?" Lillias cried, looking at the other men. There was young Uilliam Sinclair and Doug McFerris and Logan MacCuag. Iain was not among them. "Does he wait for us below?"

"What is this jest?" Peadair growled, taking hold of her arm and shaking her roughly. "Iain is not among us and well ye know it. If he's dead, then ye breathe yer last this night."

"Iain dead? What are ye saying, Peadair? He's alive. I saw him set free myself. He rode toward Cullayne."

"He dinna arrive," Peadair whispered harshly.

" 'Tis not true. Garth promised." She fell silent.

"Garth's promises mean naught, save to a fool," Peadair said.

"I have been tricked yet again." She moaned. "I pledged to marry my cousin if he set Iain free. I saw Iain ride away myself."

"D'ye think she speaks the truth?" Uilliam Sinclair asked.

"Aye, she's proved true before when we thought she lied," Logan MacCuag reminded them.

"D'ye know if he's locked in the dungeons below?"

"Nay, I would not know that. Garth led me to believe Iain was alive at Cullayne. He's tricked me in every way."

Peadair slumped. "Then he's likely dead," he said.

"Nay, he's na dead," Lillias cried. "Elsewise, why would Garth need my marriage annulled? He must have Iain locked below."

Peadair grabbed her shoulders in a hurtful grip. She didn't mind, for his face reflected the hope she felt. "Can we find out?"

"Aye, I think we can," Lillias replied. "There are some servants here who will help me, others are amenable to bribes. I have my gowns and jewels." She hastened to the trunks and began digging through them. Desperately she made up packets of her belongings, and, slipping on a long robe, secured her booty beneath its loose folds.

"Follow me, but keep some distance back. I will signal ye when it's safe to come forward."

"D'ye trust she's not leading us into a trap?" Uilliam Sinclair asked.

"Mary says she's no traitor, and I trust my sister's judgment," Doug McFerris cried. Lillias sent a silent prayer of gratitude for her steadfast friend.

"We must move swiftly," she said, and, opening the door, peered out.

The corridor was empty. Not even the ghost of Lord Robert was present. Quickly she made her way down the corridor to the kitchen, where she signaled to Moire. Moire left her tasks and sidled around the wall to join them. Without speaking, they moved into one of the dark, narrow corridors seldom used. Lillias waved to Peadair and the others to join them.

"Moire, we think Iain MacLeod may be held prisoner here in the castle. Have ye heard anything of it?"

"Aye, the servants speak of a mystery prisoner kept below in the dungeons. They're uneasy about him, especially with all this talk of ghosts about the castle."

"D'ye think we can get to him?"

Moire glanced over her shoulder. "Aye," she whispered. "Some servants are here from Lord Robert's time. They don't like Garth McGinnis and feel no allegiance to him, but they keep their thoughts to themselves. They've seen the way Catriona eliminates her enemies. If I tell them ye're Lord Robert's daughter and are being held against yer will, they'll help."

"Could ye ask them?" Lillias gasped, scarcely believing her good fortune. She'd thought she was all alone here at Dunbeath. She was heartened by the news she was not.

"Aye, I'll get their help," Moire declared, "but I must be careful, for Catriona's spies are everywhere. Wait here." She disappeared.

Peadair and his men waited, growing more edgy by the minute. In a short time Moire was back, bringing a tall, well-muscled man clad in a leather shirt and McGinnis plaid. Lillias recognized the soldier who'd helped her from her horse upon her arrival at Dunbeath.

"Moire!" she cried in alarm. Peadair and his men reached for their swords.

"Nay," Moire hissed. "Put away yer weapons. 'Tis Lucais Galbraith. He'll help us. He knows the way to the dungeons and which guards can be bribed." She saw the mistrust in Peadair's eyes. "He'll not betray ye. I stake my life on that." She gave the soldier a warm, trusting glance that spoke plainly of what lay between them. "Ha' a care, love." With a final smile, she hurried away.

"Follow me. I'll take ye where ye want t'go," Lucais said. "Ye're in luck that I know the guard on duty now. He's one of us."

"Who are ye?" Peadair asked. "Are ye not McGinnis?"

"Aye, once and always," Lucais answered. "But we've no stomach for the rule of a man like Garth McGinnis. He's evil and cowardly and he seeks more power and land, regardless of the suffering his ambition brings to the clan. I kinna blindly follow a man like him." He paused, nodding toward a black yawning hole and steep narrow stairs. "We go doon there."

"Wait here for us, Lillias," Peadair whispered. " 'Tis no place for ye."

"I'm coming," she replied. "I kinna bear not to see Iain."

"Ye'll see him soon enough, when we bring him up."

" 'Tis best to take him through the drainpipes to the moat," Lucais suggested.

"Then come. We must be quick." Peadair followed Lucais.

They descended several flights of stairs, going deep beneath the castle. The air was dank and damp from the stones. At the top of one flight of stairs, Lucais motioned them back out of sight. " 'Tis here we'll need the bribe," he whispered.

"Aye." With trembling fingers, Lillias fumbled beneath her cloak and brought out the sapphire pendant Iain had given her the night of their wedding banquet. Lucais's eyes lit up.

"Nay, my lady. 'Tis far too fine for the favor we ask." His black-rimmed nail poked at a matching earring. "That will do."

"Take it, then," she whispered. "And take the other for yerself for the trouble ye've taken."

Lucais cast her a shy glance. "I kinna—" he began.

"It will help ye when ye and Moire are wed," she insisted.

Without further argument, Lucais took both gems, leaving the larger pendant behind. Lillias stored it beneath her cloak again. They waited for what seemed an eternity before they were summoned down to the cells below. Lillias was trembling now that she was so close to Iain again. She braced herself for what they might find on the other side of the stout door the jailer unlocked.

"Iain," Peadair cried, and rushed inside the cell.

Lillias followed close behind, while Logan MacCuag and Uilliam Sinclair took up watch outside the door, swords drawn and ready. They had no wish to be trapped inside the cell should the jailer remember he owned his allegiance to

Garth McGinnis. So fiercely did they glower at the poor man, any thought he might have entertained of springing a trap on them was quickly forgotten.

"Iain," Lillias whispered as she moved toward the huddled form in the straw. The cell was foul with dampness and decay. A furry creature skittered across her shoe top and she bit back a scream. Mindless of the filthy straw, she knelt beside Iain. His face was slick with sweat, although his body trembled with chills.

"He's out of his head with fever," Peadair cried, and, taking off his cloak, wrapped it around his friend. "I must get him out of here."

"Iain, 'tis me, Lilli. Dinna ye know me?" She leaned over him, needing to touch him and hear his voice. He mumbled something low in his throat. "Oh, Iain," she whispered, and kissed his cheeks and mouth.

"Lilli," he moaned. "Dinna betray me like this. Dinna—"

"I dinna willingly betray ye, my love," she whispered, placing her mouth against his cheek. "I love ye, Iain. Dinna forget me."

"We must go," Peadair urged. "Ye can talk later."

Lillias got to her feet, while Peadair scooped Iain up in his arms. He staggered under the weight of him, then shifted him over his shoulder and left the cell.

"Lead the way to the drain," Peadair ordered, and Lucais obligingly climbed the stairs and led them through a labyrinth of dark tunnels, their way lit only by the wavering light of a torch.

Breathless with fear and dread, Lillias followed Peadair, her gaze pinned on the limp figure that gave no sign he was aware of their presence. At last, Lucais halted. Three steps led down to a foul-smelling rivulet of water.

"This will take ye out of the castle. 'Tis not deep. Ye can wade through it until ye get to the moat," Lucais assured him. "Then ye'll ha' t'swim."

"Logan, Doug, carry Lilli," Peadair ordered, but she drew back.

"I kinna go wi' ye," she said.

"Are ye daft? Ye'll not let a little sewage stop ye?"

"I kinna leave my mither here in the hands of Catriona and Garth. Take Iain to safety."

"Ye'll be at his mercy when he discovers Iain is gone."

"I'm learning to handle him. For some reason, he has a great fear of my faither's ghost," she answered. "God speed, Peadair."

"Ye're a brave lass, Lilli. Mary will ha' my head for not bringing ye back wi' me."

"Tell her my mither has returned to Dunbeath and is too ill to travel. She'll understand my decision."

"Aye. Dinna think we will forget about ye. We'll come back for ye—aye, and yer mither, too. I'll carry her out as I did the last time."

Lillias smiled at his words. She had little trust such a miracle would come about. They'd tested their luck too much already.

"Go, Peadair, and God speed," she said sadly.

Peadair looked at Lucais.

"I'll try t'watch out for her," the soldier promised.

Peadair nodded grimly and climbed down the stairs. He shifted Iain's weight, then stepped into the sewage. Very quickly, they disappeared into the darkness.

"Come, my lady. I'll lead ye back to yer room," Lucais said kindly, and there was nothing for her to do but follow him.

"Lilli, what has happened? Were they caught?" Margaret sat up in her bed and stared at her daughter.

"Nay, Mither. They've rescued Iain and escaped from the castle." Lillias threw aside her cloak and went to warm her hands near the fire. Though it was summer without, in the damp cellars of the castle, the chill had seeped through to her bones.

"In God's holy name, why dinna ye leave when ye had the chance?" Margaret chided wearily.

"Shh, Mither. I kinna leave ye." Lillias hurried to the bed and knelt beside it to hug her mother close.

"Ye're courageous and steadfast like yer faither," Margaret whispered. "I'm proud ye're my daughter." Lillias forced a cheerful smile, knowing it would hearten her mother a little, and held a sip of wine to Margaret's pale lips.

"I've had a fine example to follow," she said lightly. "I'm sorry, Mither, for all the anger I carried in my heart for ye these past years. I never understood before, and now, at last, when I ha' ye near again, I can do naught to help ye, but rub yer cold hands in a vain attempt to put a little warmth back into them."

"Ye've done so much more than that," Margaret said. Her smile died away and she rolled her head in frustration. "I've been a millstone about yer neck. If I had not returned to Dunbeath, ye'd be free now, free to ride back to Cullayne."

"Nay, dinna blame yerself." Lillias brushed the wispy hair back from sunken pale cheeks. Her mother's strength had failed even in the days since she'd returned to Dunbeath.

"It was selfish of me to return." Margaret looked around the barren room. "So many memories of this place. I was a bride when Robert brought me here. We loved each other so. I came back to Dunbeath to be wi' ye for a while and to die in the place where I'd known the greatest happiness."

"I'm glad ye came. These past few days have meant much to me, Mither. No matter what my future may hold, I'll always remember that I had a mither who loved me better than her own life. I'll love my bairn that way."

Margaret studied Lillias's luminous face. "Ye're with child?" she whispered wondrously.

Lillias's smile grew until it filled her eyes and curved her sweet mouth. "Aye, Mither, I carry Iain MacLeod's bairn."

Margaret gripped her hand, chortling weakly with glee. Slowly the laughter died away and she lay back against her pillows. "Ye should not be here. Ye should ha' gone with the MacLeods back to Cullayne."

"When ye're stronger, we'll both return to Cullayne," Lillias whispered. She lay down on the bed and placed her head on the pillow beside her mother's, then wove a magic tale to ease Margaret's fears. "Ah, Mither. The castle needs such a strong hand. We'll take Aggie back with us, and her cousin Moire, and we'll turn Cullayne into a showplace the way Dunbeath once was."

Margaret's smile died away. "I'll never leave Dunbeath," she said weakly.

"Shh, Mither, rest." Lillias sighed. Her mother's breath grew shallow and the fragile, blue-veined lids closed. Without rising to undress, Lillias dozed, her arm wrapped around her mother's waist. Sometime during the night, she felt a chill and started awake. Margaret was restless, moaning in her sleep.

"Mither, wake up," Lillias cried gently, shaking her shoulder, but Margaret's eyes remained closed.

Lillias rushed to the hearth where a kettle of water was kept warming and knelt to wet a cloth. She heard her mother moan and glanced over her shoulder. Lady Margaret sat up in bed, moving easily, as she had when a girl. Her arms reached out, her gaze fixed on something near the door.

"Robert!" Margaret cried, her eyes blazing with joy.

Dumbfounded, Lillias glanced at the door. A mist seemed to have gathered there. There was a sound of rushing wind, which grew to a roar that filled the room. Lillias fell back against the hearth, frightened. She was in the presence of a force beyond the world she knew. Lady Margaret seemed to feel no such fear. Her cry was filled with joyous ecstasy. Her face grew young again, her eyes as clear as a summer pool. Her laughter mingled with the roar of the wind, then the wind died away and Margaret fell across the bed, her eyes opened and fixed.

"Mither?" Lillias rushed to her mother's side, taking one of the lifeless hands into her own. "Mither?" There was no movement. Even the pulse that beat in the delicate throat was stilled.

"Nay," Lillias cried, backing away in disbelief. Whirling, she rummaged through a trunk until she found the polished silver mirror and ran to hold it before Margaret's mouth. There was no fog of breath, no promise of life. Slowly Lillias drew the mirror away. "Mither, dinna leave me now," she cried softly, then fell across the bed and cradled her mother. Sobs tore from her throat. She was alone again. The unfairness of life overwhelmed her, so for one moment of madness she thought of taking her own life. Then a voice so thin and sweet she thought she'd dreamed it, spoke to her.

"Remember yer bairn," the sighing voice whispered. "All will be well." She felt a warmth about her shoulders, as if her mother had hugged her—or was it her father? Lillias raised her tear-stained face and stared into the shadows.

"Mither? Faither?" There was no answer to mortal ears, only to her heart. Renewed strength flooded her heart and she rose and prepared her mother's body for burial, then sat beside the fire to wait for the dawn of a new day.

Chapter 19

"YE BITCH, YE'VE betrayed me!" Garth McGinnis cried, entering her chamber without knocking. His bodyguards took up station on either side of her door. Lillias turned from her contemplation of her mother's dead body and faced him.

"I dinna ken of what ye speak," she said calmly.

"Ye've freed that son of a whorehound." His face was livid.

"Of whom d'ye speak, Cousin?" Lillias kept her face expressionless, but her heart leapt with joy. Peadair had gotten Iain away safely. By now, they'd be across the border and riding for Cullayne.

"Ye know of whom I speak!" Garth raged. "Dinna act the innocent wi' me, Lillias. 'Tis Iain MacLeod."

"But he was set free some weeks ago in the forest of Mamore, was he not? Surely, he would not ha' returned to Dunbeath."

Garth's cheek muscles twitched and his eyes bore a madness that became more noticeable with each day's passing. "He dinna leave Mamore Forest," he raged. "My men recaptured him and put him in the Dunbeath dungeons, as well ye know. There's no need to lie t'me."

" 'Tis not I who lie, Cousin," she declared, staring at him with wide, accusing eyes. "Ye promised to let Iain return to his clan. Ye dinna keep yer word."

"Nay, nor did I ever intend him to return to Cullayne,

where he might gather his men and ride against us. I am not that big a fool, Cousin. I locked him away for good and all. Now he is gone."

Lillias smiled then. "I am elated to hear that news, Cousin. Iain MacLeod is not a man to be easily held against his will."

In his vexation, Garth drew back his hand and slapped her. She staggered and fell against her bedpost. Garth's eye was drawn to the still figure resting there.

"What is wrong wi' yer mither? Why does she not waken?"

Slowly Lillias straightened and stared at him. "She can never waken again, save with her Lord. She is dead. So ye see, Cousin, with Iain escaped and Mither dead, ye no longer have a hold over me. I will not marry ye."

Garth, who had recoiled upon hearing of Margaret's death, whirled on Lillias, his eyes blazing with evil fury. "Be quiet, wench!" he cried. "Ye'll do as I tell ye, or I'll cut off yer head as I did Lord Robert's!"

Lillias gasped, her eyes going wide with horror. "Ye killed my faither and cut off his head?"

"Aye, I did—and sent the head to Red Rafe to show him I was a better man than he, for I'd succeeded where he'd failed," Garth said, with some satisfaction. His eyes gleamed maniacally. Spittle flecked his lips as he spoke. "I did not kill him first. He was wounded and weak, so I had two men hold him and used my claymore. A claymore is not as efficient as an ax. I hacked and hacked at his neck before I finally cut through and he moaned with pain." His cackle of laughter was high-pitched and wild. "The mighty Laird McGinnis at my mercy, moaning at my feet—no better than one of his hounds as his blood spurted from his neck wound."

"Nay, no more!" she cried, turning away from him in horror. "Tell me no more."

Garth laughed once again, and, drawing his dagger, grabbed hold of her flowing hair. "I could do that to ye," he whispered hoarsely, staring into her eyes. "Or better yet, I could carve yer bastard from yer body and throw its bloody remains to the hounds. They'd fight over the pitiful morsel, tearing it to shreds."

"Nay!" she cried out, throwing up her arm as if to ward off his evil purpose, and, indeed, he seemed to have lost sight of his first objective of forcing her to marry him. He raised his dirk over her and she cringed, expecting any moment to see its downward swing, which would mean the end of her life and that of Iain's son.

"Faither!" she cried out, unknowing of what name she called, but Garth started, his eyes growing dark with fear, his dagger halted in its deadly arc.

Suddenly a rush of wind beat against them, blowing Lillias's loosened hair about her head and tearing at Garth's rich doublet and cape. A roaring sound filled the chamber much as when her mother had died; the dagger was plucked from Garth's hand and flung across the room.

The bodyguards turned and fled, throwing open the heavy plank door and scurrying down the corridor, their faces pale with fear. They could use their arms and might against mortal enemies, but they had no armor against this force from another world. They tumbled down the stone stairs and out of the castle, into the sunlight, then turned to look at each other, dumbfounded by all they'd seen. For the rest of the day they hid themselves—huddled in the stables, silent and unresponsive to their comrades jibes. Only when one taunted them that they'd seen a ghost, did they reveal what they'd witnessed, and no one thought to ridicule them further.

Back in Lillias's room, the wind had left them. Garth knelt on the floor, sobbing like a child. Lady Margaret lay on the bed, serene and untouched by all that had happened. Garth's dagger lay forgotten near the door. Slowly Lillias crept over, and, retrieving it, slipped it beneath her sleeve. Its cold, heavy weight was reassuring against her chilled flesh. She stared at the man who'd threatened her so just moments before. He was pitiful in his fear, but she could feel no sympathy for him. He'd murdered her father in a most foul manner. He deserved the agony he suffered now. She left her room and summoned two servants.

"Sir Garth has taken ill," she said. "Take him to his room and summon his mither."

"Aye, my lady," they said, and sidled into the chamber, for they'd already seen and heard enough themselves to be fearful of this room.

"Tell my aunt that Lady Margaret is dead," Lillias said as they led Garth away. He went without demure, no more than a sobbing, fearful child.

When he had gone, Lillias settled back on her chair and waited, trying to sort out all that had happened. She'd heard much about ghosts, but she'd never believed her father haunted Dunbeath. Now she believed.

"Are ye here, Faither?" she murmured softly. "D'ye hear me? Did ye protect me from Garth's madness just now?" There was no answer, no stirring in the dark shadows. Lillias glanced at Lady Margaret.

"Is Mither there with ye?" Again there was no answer, so she had to content herself with the thought that her mother had indeed joined her father in a happier place than Dunbeath had become. A sound at the door made her start and look around. Catriona McGinnis stood there.

"To whom d'ye speak, Niece?" the woman asked.

"To my faither," Lillias answered, rising from her stool and facing her aunt.

"But he is dead," Catriona said warily. Her pudgy face was pale; she did not step into the room, but let her gaze roam about as if searching for someone or something.

"Aye, my faither's dead at yer son's hand," Lillias replied bitterly. "At last, he has confessed his evil deed. 'Tis little wonder he fears my faither's ghost." She could say no more. Garth's horrific description came back to her and she pressed trembling hands against her lips.

"My mither is dead, Aunt. She passed during the night. I beg ye to make arrangements for her burial."

A smile flickered at the corner of Catriona's mouth and was quickly hidden, replaced by a sanctimonious grimace of grief. " 'Tis sad that one so noble should pass like this." She sighed. "I will, of course, see to her burial at once."

Lillias could not utter words of gratitude to the woman

who'd tried to poison her mother—and may have in fact weakened her enough to bring about her death anyway. Saying nothing, she turned to the fireplace and stared into the dead ashes. She was aware Catriona remained standing in the doorway.

"We will bury yer mither in three days' time, as is the custom. That will give all the chieftains and their families time to come to pay their respects."

Lillias's head came up in surprise. She had not expected this gesture on Catriona's part. Still, she could not utter the civil words she knew such a gesture demanded. She remained silent.

"As long as our chieftains must travel here for yer mither's funeral, we will hold the marriage between ye and Garth two days later," Catriona continued.

Lillias whirled to face her then, her head high, her eyes showing her outrage. " 'Twould be a sacrilege so soon after my mither's death. I will not."

"Ye will, my dear," Catriona said evenly. "Ye ha' na other choice." Her small eyes were hard and unyielding. Lillias felt more afraid of her than she ever had of Garth. "I will ha' yer mither's body removed at once and placed into a casket and packed wi' snow brought down from the mountains. Ye had better rest while ye can for ye ha' a heavy time ahead of ye." So saying, Catriona swung the door closed.

Lillias heard the key grind in the lock and sank down on the stool. She was alone and helpless once more. In her agitation, she moved her arm and felt the weight of Garth's dagger against her flesh. She was not helpless, she reminded herself. As long as she held a weapon, she was not helpless.

The day of her mother's funeral was cold and gray for August. Summer was passing and the hint of autumn was in the air. Heather bloomed on the hillsides, its muted shades a poignant reminder of the goodness of the season passing. Lillias stood in the cemetery before her mother's grave and gazed at the gray sky, listening to the pious words uttered by the Dunbeath priest. Garth and Catriona stood on either side of her, their sharp eyes watching her closely lest she try to escape or make an appeal for help to the chieftains and their families who'd come to pay their final respects to Lord Robert's lady. She had never known such despair.

The chaplain finished his sermon; after a quizzical glance at the lady shrouded in black, he turned back to the castle, swinging his censer.

"Come, Lillias," Catriona said peremptorily. She took hold of Lillias's arm in a painful grip, but Lillias shook her off.

"I would stay by my mither's grave awhile," she said in a voice that carried to the other mourners. Catriona cast a furious glance at Lillias, then set her expression in reasonable lines and nodded her head as if in understanding and complete agreement.

"She kinna stay," Garth said in a low voice. Catriona shushed him with a word and turned back to the castle, signaling to the mourners to follow and partake of the food they'd prepared.

As the clansmen filed past Lillias, they murmured words of sympathy and remembered deeds of Lady Margaret's and Lord Robert's. When they'd all passed by, the grave diggers moved forward, and, taking up shovelfuls of dirt, threw them in on her mother's coffin. The sound was thunder and hell to her. Clasping her hands over her ears, she fell to her knees. Suddenly gentle hands were there comforting her, and a sweet voice murmured sympathy.

"Come, my lady. Ye kinna give way like this," someone said, and Lillias raised her head to look at the hooded figure.

"Aggie?"

"Aye, 'tis me," the old nursemaid said. "I should ha' come back wi' her, but she would na let me. She said whatever befell her, she would meet it without the blood of the innocent on her hands. But I've been sore afraid, my lady."

"Oh, Aggie. I am in such hell." Lillias wept.

"There, there, child. I'll come be wi' ye."

"Ye kinna, Aggie. They would not let ye—and ye'd be

in danger, too. Garth is a madman. He killed my faither all those years ago."

"What must I do for ye, my lady? I kinna leave ye here alone." Aggie's voice shook; she smoothed tendrils of hair from Lillias's cheeks. "Tell me what t'do."

"There is nothing anyone can do," Lillias whispered. "I would rather die now than wed that monster."

"Ach, dinna say that, lass," Aggie remonstrated. "Moire tol' me ye're wi' child. Think of the wee bairn."

"I am thinking of him," Lillias cried, raising her tear-stained face to Aggie. "And I think what chance has he in this world of deceit and hatred? Aggie, ye *can* help me!" She clasped the nursemaid's hand. "Bring me some poison, so that I might end this misery."

"Nay, my lady. I kinna," Aggie cried, appalled at Lillias's state of mind.

"Ye must, Aggie, if ye love me at all. I plead wi' ye. I have a dagger, but not the courage to end my suffering that way. Poison would be easy, a kindness. Dinna fail me in my darkest hour." Her voice cracked with pain. Her face was wet with tears, her eyes dark with despair.

"I kinna," Aggie whispered, crossing herself. Her face was pale; her hands trembled with grief. "Dinna lose faith, my lady. We'll find a way to rescue ye."

"Lillias!" Garth's voice was like the crack of a whip as he called to her from the path. He'd turned back to assure himself she would not escape. Now, he squinted his eyes at the hooded figure bent over Lillias and motioned to his guard. "Seize that person."

"Run, Aggie! Get away!" Lillias cried, but the guard was upon them. He took hold of Aggie's arm and turned back to Garth.

" 'Tis but an old woman," he called.

Garth looked annoyed. Glancing around the clearing, he saw that other mourners still lingered. Riding his steed forward, he glared down at Lillias.

"Let me see for myself," Garth ordered, and the hood was drawn back from Aggie's face. Lillias held her breath, but Garth didn't recognize her serving woman. "Be on yer way, old woman," he ordered, and turned back to Lillias.

"Ye're making a spectacle of yerself. Come back to the castle now. I insist."

She had no choice but to follow him back to the castle. She glanced back at Aggie, but the serving woman had moved away down the path, her shoulders bowed, her hood in place, a nameless, faceless old woman who could do no harm. Yet Lillias remembered the strength of Aggie's arm about her shoulders and the fierceness of her gaze. Aggie had saved Lady Margaret once. Mayhap she could do the same for Lillias. She drew strength from the thought and followed after Garth with a lighter step. She was ashamed of her moment of weakness. She must remain strong and be ready for any possibility for escape that presented itself. Entering the castle gate, she raised her head and met the gaze of Lucais Galbraith, who nodded in silent reassurance. She was not alone.

Aggie watched Lillias disappear behind the walls of Dunbeath and drew a quivering breath. Her heart beat with rage and terror for her beautiful, brave girl. She must do something, she thought, and, pulling her hood forward to hide her face, she hurried away. Within an hour she was astride a borrowed horse, on her way—at a full gallop—to Cullayne Castle.

"By God, I'll not stay here another day!" Iain roared, swinging his legs over the edge of the bed. He'd heard Aggie's report and his teeth clenched with rage. "Lilli needs me."

"Yer fever's not down yet, man," Peadair cautioned. "D'ye want t'ha' a relapse."

"Nay, I've had relapses aplenty." Iain sighed. "And they've led us to this, wi' Lillias trapped at Dunbeath and me as weak as a mewling kitten unable t'go t'her."

"Dinna blame yerself," Peadair said staunchly.

"She dinna want to marry Garth McGinnis. She said it only t'save my neck from the hangman's knot. Now she's there at his mercy while I lie here as at my leisure. I should have grabbed a claymore and gone after Garth then." He'd grown more agitated as he thought of Lillias's plight, and now he swung his legs over the edge of the bed, ignoring the flutter of black wings that threatened to claim his consciousness. "I tell ye, we ride today, Peadair. Saddle Lucifer for me."

"And what? Tie ye into yer saddle? Ye kinna walk, man, much less ride."

Iain glared at him balefully. "Aye, I'll ride—wi' or wi'out ye." By strength of will alone, he rose from the bed and stood swaying on legs that seemed to possess no bones and muscles. Duncan Phipps, the castle physician, rushed forward, arms outstretched as if to catch his laird. Iain righted himself and glared at the man.

"My legs are mush, man. What have ye done t'me?" he cried.

"It's what ye've done t'yerself, my lord," Duncan answered tartly. Never had he had such a difficult patient. " 'Tis too soon for ye t'be thinkin' of gettin' up, much less ridin' off t'war again."

"Would ye ha' me leave Lillias to the mercy of that treacherous cousin of hers?" Iain's eyebrows lifted in black points above his blazing eyes.

"Nay, I'd not leave such a fine lady as that to anyone's mercies but my own," Duncan replied. He turned aside to mix an herb in a cup of hot broth. "Drink this, my lord. It will give ye strength to do what ye must."

Iain stopped glaring at Duncan and took the cup he offered. Without complaint he downed the noxious brew and handed the cup back. "I thank ye, man," he said. "Will ye come wi' me to Dunbeath?"

"I think I'd better, my lord," Duncan said, and gathered up his pouch of medicines and knives. Iain grinned at his friend.

"Peadair," he called, more heartily than he felt. "I've need of yer shoulder."

"Ye have it, my friend," Peadair said, and stepped forward to lend it.

Within the hour they were mounted and ready to travel.

Iain's face was set and white, his lips tightened against every jarring step of his horse, but he made no outcry. He was going to find Lillias—and pray God she was safe.

"Will ye stop for a rest?" Peadair asked when they were half gone to the River Lochy.

"Nay," Iain said, without slackening his gait. "I'll have Garth's head if he's touched her."

"Lilli seemed to think she was safe enough. Said she was getting to know how to handle him, whatever that meant."

"Aye, it sounds like Lilli," Iain said. "All the same, man, ye should not ha' left her."

"I told ye, she would not leave while her mither was there."

Despite Iain's protest they were forced to pause and rest. Sweat beaded on his brow and his cheeks were pale from his effort to stay in the saddle. Peadair helped his friend from the saddle while Duncan hurried to build a fire and heat his special brew, which would numb the pain and restore some of Iain's vigor.

"If I dinna make it, Peadair, I charge ye with rescuing Lilli from Dunbeath," Iain whispered when Peadair held the cup to his lips. "Ye must promise me this."

"Ye'll make it, Iain, but I promise to do as ye ask or die in the trying," Peadair answered fiercely, and went off to stand alone in the woods and give way to the tears he would not let any other man see.

A sound made him swing around and stare through the trees. Two riders were moving stealthily over the forest floor; Peadair cursed when he caught a flash of slender legs and a tumble of black curls.

"Mary! What in God's name are ye doing here?" he called, stalking toward her. Mary pulled on the reins and waited. Her gray eyes studied his face, which was dark as a thundercloud. "And who is this wi' ye?"

"Aggie and I are coming wi' ye," she said, setting her chin stubbornly. " 'Tis too late t'send us back."

"Will ye never listen and do as ye're told?" Peadair snapped. All the anger and frustration he felt over Iain's weakened state was loosened on this high-spirited girl. "I'll not ha' a wife of mine riding about the countryside like a gypsy, not knowin' when t'stay in her place."

Mary's face flushed. "I'm not yer wife yet, Peadair," she snapped, "and like as not, never will be. I'll not marry a man who thinks t'keep me in my place. I've come to help Lillias, and ye ha' not the power to say me nay." Her chin went up and she glared at him, so he knew she wouldn't budge. As quickly as his anger came, it left him, so he stepped forward and put a hand on her leg.

"Aye, lass. I should ha' known ye would come. 'Tis dangerous for ye here, but no more so than for Lilli."

At the softening of his tone, Mary slid from her saddle and fell into his arms. They held each other, grateful to be together when their friends suffered such danger.

"How is Iain holding out?" Mary asked finally, wiping at her cheeks.

"Not well," Peadair said. "Come and see. He'll not make Dunbeath." He took hold of the bridle of Mary's horse and led the way back to the others.

"Kin ye not ride on wi'out him and rescue Lilli on yer own?" Aggie demanded, following after them.

"Aye, and that I would," Peadair answered, "but he won't let us. He insists he will go as well."

They came to the place where Iain lay resting, his eyes closed as if he slept. The small fire had burned down to ash. Mary saw at once what Peadair meant, for Iain's face was gray. She thought of Lillias. She longed to plunge along the trail to rescue her friend, but knew she could better serve here.

"Why dinna ye go on to Dunbeath, Peadair?" she said. A feeling of urgency was upon her. "There is little time left. Go, Peadair, I implore ye. Aggie and I'll stay behind and nurse Iain. We'll follow ye when he's able."

"Ye may stay behind if ye wish, Mary McFerris," Iain said, opening his eyes and gazing at her with some anger. "But I'll not be here for ye t'nurse." So saying, he rose from the ground without assistance and turned toward Lucifer. "Into yer saddles, men," he called. " 'Tis time to ride."

"Iain, are ye sure?" Mary cried, but he did not answer. He set spur to horse and without waiting to see if the others followed, turned toward the road to Dunbeath.

They arrived late in the day, when the sun was slanting through the trees, leaving long strips of light and shadow. Uilliam Sinclair and Logan MacCuag had ridden ahead to scout the terrain around the castle. Now they returned and made their report.

"There's a large force of men lodged outside the castle. Once again we'd be outnumbered."

"God's blood!" Iain exploded. "We'll na be deterred by any number of troops. I won't ride away and leave her."

"Nay, Iain, none expects ye t'do that. We'll fight the dirty McGinnis clan until the last breath," Logan assured him, but he exchanged glances with Kenneth Sinclair, who looked grim. In the past weeks, they'd fought with the McGinnis Highlanders and against them, and all knew what fierce warriors they were.

"There seems to be a celebration of some sort," MacCuag said. "The gates are thrown open and the chieftains and their wives are milling about."

Iain looked at Aggie. "The bastard plans t'marry her today."

"Aye, my lord, it seems that way," she answered, and gathered her reins tighter, as if she meant to ride forward into Dunbeath.

"We'll use the secret passage."

"Dinna be a fool," Peadair exclaimed. "Garth captured ye the last time ye tried that. He'll have it well guarded."

"Aye, 'tis true," Iain conceded. "We'll ha' t'think of something else."

He was weary and his wound throbbed from the hard ride here. His head ached so he feared himself incapable of deriving a plan. He wanted nothing more than to sink to the ground and sleep, yet the thought of Lilli so close and in danger, waiting for him to rescue her, kept him on his feet. Taking a corner of his plaid, he wiped the sheen of perspiration from his brow and cheeks. His restless gaze fixed on the woven clan tartan and he looked up at Mary and Peadair.

"Aye, I have a way," he said, and looked at Logan MacCuag and Uilliam Sinclair. "I've need of the McGinnis plaid. Can ye secure one for me?"

"Aye, 'tis easy," Logan answered, glancing at young Uilliam.

"Then go quickly," Iain ordered, and the two men turned back toward Dunbeath, running swift and silent, disappearing at once among the trees.

Iain turned to Peadair and Mary. "Rid yerself of all marks of the MacLeod clan," he said. "We're goin' t'a wedding."

"Man, what d'ye think ye're doing?" Peadair declared.

"We're riding past the McGinnis troops—right up to the castle steps itself—and none will stop us."

"How will we do that?" Peadair demanded.

"We'll be one of Garth's chieftains come late t'the wedding. Mary will be my wife and ye'll be our guard."

"Mary will be my wife," Peadair said possessively. His eyes sparkled wi' laughter, then he looked at Mary and his humor passed. "I'll not take Mary into danger."

"Not even for Lilli?" Iain asked softly.

"Nay, na even then," Peadair said stoutly. "There must be some other way."

"None I know of, man," Iain said impatiently.

Peadair heard his unleashed anger and knew he'd disappointed his friend, but he loved Mary too much to risk her life. As usual, Mary took the choice from him.

"I'll go wi' ye, Iain," she said quietly.

"And I'll go," Aggie asserted.

"Nay, old woman," Iain answered. "We'll do better t'go alone."

"For once, my lord, ye're wrong," Aggie said stoically. "No lady would travel without her serving woman. If ye wish to carry this off, ye must not arouse suspicion among the men. Besides, I have family within the castle. If I call on them, they'll help us."

"Even against their own clansmen?"

"Nay, against Lord Robert's murderer."

"Bless ye, Aggie," Iain said, gripping her shoulder in gratitude. "So it's settled then." Iain glanced at Peadair.

"Aye, it's settled," Peadair said reluctantly. "We succeed or die together."

"Together," Iain said, holding out his broad hand to his friend. Peadair's anger faded.

"Together," he agreed, placing his hand over Iain's.

"Together!" Mary and Aggie echoed, clasping hands with the two men.

They rose and began to prepare for the journey. Kenneth Sinclair and his troops were given instructions to go forward at a given signal and overpower, if necessary, the unsuspecting McGinnis troops camped outside the castle.

Entering the castle was easier than they'd anticipated. Obviously Garth did not expect interference from the MacLeods. They'd been beaten once at the gates of Dunbeath, and, though their leader had escaped, Garth was certain he was too weakened by his imprisonment to offer resistance.

"Now that we're here, what do we do?" Peadair asked.

"Take the women to the castle and see they're safely inside," Iain ordered, his gaze fixed on the priest who'd left the small stone chapel and was crossing the bailey with his censer swinging rhythmically. "I've a need to make my confessions." He melted away in the crowd of people.

Lillias had never thought the moment would come to this, that she must wed her father's murderer. The past three days, she'd pulled the knife from its hiding place and held its point to her heart a thousand times over, but she could not plunge it into her flesh. While there was breath, there was hope, and her son's tiny heartbeat below hers. How could she still that? Now she stood before the fireplace, a bright ray of color in the drab room.

For her wedding, she'd chosen a gown of ivory brocade richly trimmed with braids of woven gold. Her underskirt was of a pale pink silk. Puffings of palest green showed through the slashing of her sleeves. Her hair flowed around her shoulders, held in place by a single woven ring of wild-flowers.

She'd barely glimpsed her image in the mirror Moire had held, for she'd been angered by her own beauty. She wished to appear drab to her new husband. She shivered to think what this night might demand of her. Her restless hands sought out the knife blade and she hid it in the folds of her sleeve. At the moment of her final degradation in Garth's bed, would she find the courage to use it? Again she thought of her son. Had she such a right? Could she not endure the horror of a marriage to her kinsman in order to assure her son lived?

Sobbing, she turned away and huddled on the bed. In her desperation, she thought of Iain and Mary and Aggie. Where were they now? she wondered. Did they believe she'd agreed to this marriage to Garth? Was that why they had not come?

The door was flung open and Catriona stood in the corridor. Her critical gaze ran over Lillias. "As usual, ye're far too pale, Niece, and ye've chosen pallid colors for yer wedding day."

"Aye, I feel pallid today," Lillias answered. Catriona's face creased with anger.

" 'Tis time for yer wedding, my lady," she said haughtily, and with a flurry of red velvet skirts, stalked away. Sighing, Lillias rose and followed her along the corridor and down the stairs to the great hall.

The castle priest had set up his altar before the huge fireplace; the light of the flames cast a wavery reddish glow over the assemblage like a scene from hell itself—and the priest in his long, full robes, with his hood pulled forward, seemed to be Lucifer himself. On legs that seemed to possess little strength, Lillias walked forward. The tables had been folded and placed against the walls, the benches set in rows for the convenience of their guests. Avidly the clansmen and their wives watched the beautiful girl enter the room and approach the dais.

Lillias walked down the aisle and took her place before the priest's altar. Garth was nowhere in attendance. Nor did he come immediately. Lillias waited patiently, losing track of time, until the murmur of the guests drew her attention. Garth still had not appeared and she flushed at this slight against her. Finally she turned to face the congregation. Catriona stood to one side, her lips smirking, a hard, bright glow in her small eyes. Lillias's gaze swept over the rest of the guests and halted at a face that was dearly familiar to her.

"Aggie," she whispered through dry lips.

Quickly the nursemaid placed a warning finger against her lips and Lillias turned away as if searching among the guests for sight of her bridegroom. She couldn't resist a glance back toward Aggie—and this time, she saw Mary wearing the McGinnis plaid and seated among the guests, for all the world as if she were an important chieftain's wife and belonged there. Lillias could not stay a leap of joy and knew it must show in her face. Quickly she turned back to face the priest. If Mary was here, then Peadair must surely be as well. They had come to rescue her. But what of Iain? Why wasn't he here? Was he ill—or worse, dead? She staggered at the thought, and a clansman stepped forward to take her elbow and lend her support.

"Ha' a care, my lady," he murmured softly, and Lillias jerked her head up to look at him.

"Peadair," she whispered. "Ye've come."

"Aye, my lady," he answered stoically, and stepped back, pulling his face into somber lines as befitted the occasion.

"What of Iain?" she whispered, casting a glance at the priest, who seemed intent on his communion cup. "Did he come?"

"Aye, my lady," Peadair answered.

At that moment, Garth entered the room and languidly made his way through the crowd, weaving slightly, so all present suspected he'd already been heavily imbibing of the wedding spirits. He stumbled against one of his chieftains, cuffed the man slightly as if he'd been at fault, then staggered to the altar. He reeked of ale and his eyes gleamed feverishly as he leered at Lillias. Grabbing hold of her, he pulled her close and rubbed his body against hers suggestively. She saw that he was about to kiss her and turned her head away.

"I would kiss my wife," he declared loudly, and grabbing hold of her hair, cruelly pulled her around so he might plunder her mouth shamelessly before their guests. The onlookers gasped their astonishment at this drunken display of lewdness and the priest's knuckles whitened as he gripped his chalice.

"Nay, Cousin," Lillias protested when his disgusting kiss had ended. "I am not yet yer wife."

"Then let's get on with it," Garth ordered. "For I would bed ye before the hour's done."

Smirking, he turned to face the priest and choked on his own breath as he felt the sharp blade of a sword pressed against his throat. His terrified gaze went to the hooded priest. Behind him, his clansmen were on their feet, stunned at this sudden bizarre behavior by their cleric. The guard himself had drawn his sword, but seemed to stand with the priest.

The priest raised his arm and threw back his hood. With an impatient swipe, he divested himself of the robes. A murmur rose in the hall. Lillias felt tears of elation spring to her eyes.

"Iain!" she cried. He had never looked more magnificent with his strong legs braced wide, his broad body towering over them all, his proud, dark head high, his handsome face scowling fiercely as only he knew how.

"Aye, my love, 'tis I." He looked at the congregation. "Tell yer chiefs na t'draw their weapons unless ye're prepared t'die this day," he ordered Garth, "for my troops have overpowered yer forces outside the castle and even now have taken possession of Dunbeath."

"I dinna believe ye, MacLeod. We've fought ye off once, we'll do so again."

"With all yer leaders here inside the hall?" Iain jeered. "And once they've heard our story, will they wish to follow yer leadership? I wager they're good men one and all and none would pledge to follow a murderer."

A murmur rose among the clansmen and their wives.

They looked at one another uneasily, their old suspicions of Garth McGinnis reawakened. They lowered their blades and glanced at one another as if looking for confirmation of the accusations. Iain eased back the point of his sword, although it still rested against Garth's neck.

"Now is yer moment, my lady, t'tell yer kinsmen all ye know about yer cousin."

Lillias turned to face the assemblage. Her chin jutted high with purpose and pride, her blue eyes glittered with anger. " 'Tis true," she said in a ringing voice that carried to every corner of the hall. "Garth McGinnis admitted to me with his own tongue that he led Red Rafe and his men into Dunbeath Castle through the secret passageway so they might overtake the castle. When Red Rafe failed in his attempt to kill my faither, Garth did so himself and sent my faither's head to Cullayne."

There was a howl of dismay among the McGinnis chieftains. They could little doubt what this slender girl said, for she bore the blood of Robert McGinnis himself; it was evident in the jutting jaw, the fierce blue eyes, and proud features.

Lillias waited until the hubbub died down before continuing. "My mither knew of Garth's treachery and fled to a convent. She agreed to my remaining a bride of Iain MacLeod's because she knew I was safer at Cullayne than in my own home." Every man fell silent, ashamed of this fact—that Lord Robert's daughter had been safer in the hands of their enemy than among her own kinsmen. "When Lady Margaret heard I was to return to Dunbeath, she came to warn me of the danger here and was poisoned by my aunt, Catriona. Only through the efforts of my trusted servant, Aggie, and Peadair McDermott and Mary McFerris was she whisked away and saved, but she never regained her strength and died as a result of Catriona's evil deed. And now he has kidnapped me and seeks to force me to marriage with him so he may allay yer suspicions of him." She stopped speaking and let her clansmen absorb all she'd said. Catriona stood pale and shaking.

" 'Tis a lie," she cried. "I dinna poison Lady Margaret. She was frail and died from her ailments."

"Ye poisoned her," Aggie called out. "And I've proof of yer perfidy." She stepped forward. "Here is the wine from Lady Margaret's room. If 'tis na poisoned, I charge ye to sip from it."

Catriona looked confounded. Her darting gaze went round the circle of clansmen as if seeking some support, but there was none. Their faces were set as they waited for her to respond to Aggie's dare.

"Ye ha' only t'drink of this wine t'prove yer innocence," Aggie said, moving to Catriona's side and holding out the small glass bottle. Catriona recoiled as if Aggie held a serpent out to her.

"Drink, woman," Gordon McGinnis ordered, stepping forward, his hand on his sword.

"Nay," Catriona cried in terror. " 'Tis but a trick. How do I know she has not poisoned the wine herself?"

"I would ha' no reason t'poison ye," Aggie said, and all present knew she was a good woman who spoke the truth.

"Drink," Gordon ordered again, and this time drew his sword. "I promise ye, it will be an easier death than what we will mete out if ye've murdered our fair Lady Margaret."

With trembling hands Catriona reached for the bottle and brought it to her pale lips.

"Nay, Mither," Garth cried, and striking Iain's sword aside with his hand, he grabbed hold of Lillias, pulling her before him as a shield.

Iain cursed. He'd been distracted by the spectacle of Catriona's deception—and now Lillias stood in the dangerous embrace of her cousin.

Garth fumbled beneath his clothing and brought out a dagger, pressing it against Lillias's breast. "Dinna charge me, MacLeod, or I'll plunge this dirk into her sweet breast. Tell yer man t'put down his sword."

Iain hesitated only a moment. "Put down yer sword, Peadair," he ordered. Peadair tossed his broadsword to the floor. Iain's own blade followed.

"Good," Garth said. His eyes glittered with a mad light at this evidence of his power over them all. He pressed the blade against Lillias, so she felt its point through her gown and cried out.

"Dinna do it, man," Iain called out frantically. "She's done naught t'ye. 'Tis me ye've a grudge against."

"Aye, 'tis ye and all the MacLeods," Garth answered, "from yer barbaric faither on down. Aye, and my own clan who would turn against me. A pox on ye all." He looked around the room. "Come, Mither. We'll quit this place and none will stop us." He edged backward to the door, pulling Lillias after him. She struggled in his clasp and was rewarded with the prick of the blade against her skin. She felt the warm ooze of blood beneath her bodice and stopped her futile struggle. He had the strength of madness in him. They neared the carved doors of the great hall. Iain leapt down from the dais.

"Stop!" Garth warned. They were near the carved doors of the great hall now and Garth threw them open, without turning around. Fearfully he still faced enemies in the hall.

Lillias was the first to feel the cold wind against her fevered cheeks. A white mist washed around them. Suddenly she was propelled forward out of Garth's clutches and back into the hall with such force she would have fallen if Iain had not raced forward to catch her. Behind her came a scream; she turned in time to see the white-misted fury tear at Garth, pinning him against the door. His eyes were wide and filled with terror such as no man had seen before.

His mouth opened wide in a high-pitched cry that seemed to fill the hall. There was a high keening roar and the white mist thickened, so they could no longer see Garth, but they could hear his scream, wild and more horrific than any Highland cry. Near the door, Catriona stood rooted, her own eyes wide and mad, her rich red velvet skirts whipping about her like a demon's wings.

As quickly as it came, the wind and mist disappeared and Garth McGinnis was revealed, hanging against the wooden door, impaled on his on broadsword. His face was a terrible thing to see, its features rigid with the terror he'd suffered at his death. Lillias could not bear to look. She turned away and hid her face against Iain's shoulder. The clansmen stood, thunderstruck at all that had occurred, then exchanged knowing glances. They'd heard the rumors that Robert McGinnis haunted these walls—and they were certain he had, at last, taken his revenge.

Catriona McGinnis stared at her dead son's body and her voice rose high and reedy-thin in an unintelligible gibberish of grief and madness. Her skirts were torn, her dark hair, of which she'd been vainly proud, was gray and tangled about her fat neck. She made no move to right it. She was beyond vanity now.

"Remove these traitors from these halls," Gordon McGinnis declared. Men came forward to lead Catriona away and to remove Garth's lifeless body. Gordon bowed to Lillias.

"My lady, may I offer my deepest apologies that we dinna recognize yer distress and offer our assistance sooner. We had no way of knowing what a monster Garth McGinnis had become."

"Dinna blame yerselves," Lillias said, turning to face the man, though she still stood within the protective circle of Iain's arms. "Let the past be in the past now—and let our clans live in peace with each other."

"Aye, my lady, we've a mind for that." Gordon nodded. "We've fought beside Iain MacLeod and have seen the steel of the man. We know him to be brave and fair." He paused, and his next words were addressed to Iain. "Though I am next in line to become *Ceann Mor*, I know not what the council will decide. Should I become the next chief, I pledge a truce between our two clans. We are connected by marriage."

"Aye, and soon our two clans will be bound by blood ties," Lillias said, "for I carry the MacLeod heir, and he bears the blood of Robert McGinnis as well."

There was a roar of approval from the assembled clansmen and their wives. Lillias felt Iain's arms tighten around her and she lay back against his chest, knowing she would never stand alone against her adversaries again. She would always have this extraordinary man standing strong and protective at her back. She leaned against him and felt his large hands slid downward over her belly.

" 'Tis only the first of many MacLeod heirs I'll plant there, my lady," he whispered against her ear, and his hot breath sent shivers along her spine.

"I wish for a big family, my lord," she said primly, and was rewarded by his deep chuckle. She laughed with him, drawing courage in the belief that their evil star was behind them and only sunlight would mark their way.

Epilogue

TODAY WAS HER wedding day, and Cullayne Castle had never looked so grand. In the weeks since her return, Lillias and her helpers had worked feverishly to overcome years of neglect, for she was determined that her wedding vows would be exchanged with far more grandeur than the first time. Despite Iain's protests, she'd insisted on delaying the date of the event, for she'd wanted everything perfect, as befitted a powerful earl and his noble-born lady. Unable to deny her slightest request, he'd reluctantly agreed—only after she'd reassured him that she would not wait for their vows before sharing his bed. After all, was not handfasting an accepted custom in their clans?

So it was that, replete from their lovemaking, she'd curled against him and told him of all she had planned for Cullayne and their life together. She wanted him to be proud of his home, of her and their son, at which point, his arms had tightened around her possessively and he'd lifted her on top of him and shown her just how deeply his pride could run.

Later, sliding his hand down the silken length of her delicate back, he'd thought of what he might do to please this fairylike creature who gazed at him with such adoring eyes and carried his child within her slim body.

Without revealing his intentions to anyone, he'd packed Lillias up and carried her off to Edinburgh, where they took passage on the first ship sailing to France. Beathen and

Everard had accompanied them. Beathen had been determined to find new recipes to enhance his reputation as the
castle chef. Superior though Scottish dishes were to his way
of thinking, he'd gone with an open mind, willing to learn
a little of the French culinary mystique as well. In his capacity as castle steward, Everard had gone to help Lillias
choose goods for the castle, and Iain had busied himself
with the prospect of purchasing his own ships. They'd
dined sumptuously, socialized with French nobility, and
made love with wild abandon.

When they had returned to Cullayne, they'd led a veritable caravan of packhorses and two-wheeled wagons laden
with fine furniture, linens, costly spices, exotic perfumes,
and gowns more sumptuous and breathtaking than any
Lillias had ever seen. The wonder in her eyes made Iain
forget the cost of his extravagance, he vowed she'd never
want for a pretty bauble or fancy gown for the rest of her
life.

"For my wife," he'd said simply, but there had been
nothing simple about the dark lights in his green eyes or in
the erotic things he'd taught her that night in the privacy of
their bedchamber. Even now a delicate blush stained
Lillias's cheeks when she thought of their trip to France and
the sensuous abandonment to which she'd lent herself. Just
to look at Iain left her breathless, so she feared her heart
might stop beating and all the joy she felt might explode
within her and she'd cease existing.

At those times, she sought him out and wrapped her
arms around him, so that his men had grown accustomed to
seeing their leader, clad in his leathers or mail shirt, clasping his beautiful lady to him. The past fortnight had been
giddy with wonders and activity, but now, at last, they were
settled into Cullayne and the wedding was but hours away.

"My lady, ye're not ready," Aggie chided her, and Lillias
turned from her daydreaming to smile at her nursemaid, unaware of how her happiness shone around her like the brilliant facets of the finest stone.

"I was just thinking of all we've been through, Aggie,"

she said softly, "and of how happy I am. This day could not be more perfect."

"Aye, 'tis a grand day for the MacLeods and the McGinnises," Aggie agreed.

"Have all our guests arrived?"

"Aye, they ha', and I've seen to it that they're put up in the spare rooms. We even had to use the tower room."

"Oh, no," Lillias cried in alarm. "That won't do."

"Aye, it will—since it's been newly furnished. Sir Gordon McGinnis himself and his lady are there. He said he would not miss the view for anything—and he'll think of his beautiful kinswoman spending her childhood in that room."

" 'Twas not so bad, was it, Aggie?"

"Nay, love. It could ha' been worse. We could ha' been at Dunbeath, under the protection of Garth McGinnis. Dinna I tell ye that Catriona must be kept locked away in a tower, she's that mad?"

Lillias shivered and turned away. "Let's not speak of them today, Aggie. To do so might bring bad luck."

"Aye, my lady," Aggie agreed, and went to straighten a fold of the beautiful gown Lillias would soon don. "Moire came with her new husband, Lucais Galbraith."

"Oh, I'm so glad," Lillias cried, clasping her hands. Her eyes shone. "I'll always be grateful to them both."

"Aye, my lady, and well they know that. They were honored to help ye. Many more of yer clansmen and their wives came than I'd expected."

" 'Tis their way of showing their commitment to the new friendship between our clans," Lillias said. " 'Tis a fine thing that's happened between us."

A knock sounded at the door. "Lilli, 'tis me," a voice called. Lillias threw open the door and embraced Mary McFerris, whose lovely face was unnaturally flushed.

"Lilli, I don't know what t'do. I'm that beside myself."

"What is it, Mary?" Lilli inquired, taking her hands and pulling her into the room.

Mary was clad only in a chemise and petticoats with a shawl hastily draped over her shoulders, cover enough for the short distance down the corridor from Lillias's old room, which Mary had occupied since Lillias now shared Iain's. Mary cast a quick look around. She could never get used to the transformation they'd wrought in this once drab male bastion. Thick padded cushions had been sewn for all the window seats and the high-backed chair set near the fireplace. A thick rug covered the cold stone floor. Fine velvet draperies hung at the windows and rich tapestries covered the bare stone walls, adding color and warmth. Even the bedcovers were of the finest materials and thickly quilted.

Distracted by her perusal of the room, Mary turned to Lillias. "Aye, 'tis a grand room," she said.

"Is that why ye've come running through the hall half dressed, with yer face all flushed?" Lillias demanded. "To congratulate yerself yet again on a job well done?"

Mary's expression fell and she plopped down on the cushioned window seat. "Nay, Lilli, 'tis not for that I've come." She took a deep breath and her plump breasts rose above the top of her chemise. "I kinna marry Peadair today."

"What?" Lillias stared at her friend. "Are ye daft, Mary?"

"Mayhap." The dark-haired girl shrugged. "I kinna marry any man. I dinna ha' it in me to buckle under to a man, even Peadair. Ye know me, Lilli. I like my own way too much—and I'm headstrong and quick-tongued. He'd hate me wi'in a fortnight."

Lillias hid a smile. "Aye, ye're right," she said solemnly. "But I know Peadair is determined to marry and raise bairns. He needs sons to help him manage Castle Cleary now that Iain has appointed him to run it." She glanced at Mary from under her lashes. Mary only sat nodding her head, shoulders slumped. "If ye kinna wed wi' him, Mary, the only decent thing ye can do is find him another wife, for he leaves for Castle Cleary tomorrow. Now, let's see." Lillias plopped on the opposite window seat and pretended to ponder the problem.

"There's Isabal. Nay, she's got her hat set for Everard."

"Everard!" Mary said scathingly. "He's too bookish a man for my taste. I'd take Peadair over him any day." Her face took on a pinched look. "But I'll na have Peadair wed Isabal—she's given to gossiping. Mark my words, she'll turn to a shrew in no time."

"Mayhap." Lillias sighed. "Then what of Ellen Malloch? She's rather long in the tooth, but still of child-bearing years."

"I've heard she snores," Mary snapped.

"Too bad Beitris is not here. She's a bonny lass, and Peadair seemed quite taken by her when first he saw her."

"I'd scratch her eyes out," Mary said. She scowled at Lillias and the two girls fell to laughing, hugging each other in their happiness.

"Oh, Mary. I'm so glad we're sharing our wedding day. Ye must marry Peadair for that reason alone."

"Humpf! There's reason aplenty t'marry that man," Mary said, "but I'll not let him order me about. 'Mary go here, Mary stand there.' 'Mary come t'my bed.' I'll go and come as I wish."

"And ye'll wish, rightly enough," Lillias teased, "especially when he orders ye t'bed."

"I will not," Mary cried in outrage, then her expression softened. "He is so pleasing in bed, Lilli. Is it that way for ye and Iain?"

"Aye, very pleasing," Lillias said, and couldn't repress a blush.

"Ye're wicked to speak of such things," Aggie scolded. " 'Tis time to get into yer gowns. Come now, be quick."

"Oh, hurry, Lilli," Mary cried. "I would not be late for my own wedding." She disappeared down the hall in a flurry of petticoats.

Lillias looked at Aggie and fell into a fit of giggles—until she hiccuped and Aggie chastised her and offered her a sip of wine, which only brought the color to her cheeks more smartly.

She was faint with excitement by the time she stood outside the doors of the great hall. Within, their guests waited, an august assemblage of earls and lairds, of Highland chiefs and their ladies, of villagers and friends, and, more than all, Iain. Briefly she wondered if he would find her as beautiful as she felt.

She wore a gown of the palest green brocade. Its wide skirts had been slashed down the front and trimmed with ermine to reveal an underskirt of silver tissue beneath. Her golden hair tumbled about her shoulders while a small headpiece of autumn heather held a sheer veil. Last, she'd fastened on the fabulous emeralds Iain had given her the night of their first lovemaking. They'd been left behind at Cullayne when Garth kidnapped her. Now she wore them, remembering as Iain had told her she must, their first night of passion.

Mary stood beside Lillias nervously fiddling with her hair. She was finely dressed in a brocade gown of pale pink with a silver underskirt and a veil much like Lillias's upon her dark head. The contrast of their beauty was not lost on the wedding guests when the doors were thrown open and the two women walked down the aisle. Lillias paid no mind to the murmurs of approval and awe. Her gaze was fastened on Iain. He was her world, her very breath, and he stood gazing at her with eyes filled with all the love a woman could ever need.

She was a forest nymph, Iain thought, a special gift from the fairy people. He'd nearly lost her, but he'd won her back, and he would cherish her for always. He couldn't wait for her to make her way down the aisle to him. With long strides he crossed the distance that separated them, and, holding her hand, led her back to the altar.

He didn't know she was drowning in the green depths of his eyes, or that she heard not a word of the wedding vows, although she answered steadily enough. Later she would be able to recall every word, but for now, her every sense was caught up in the man standing before her, the warmth and strength of his hand holding hers, his tall figure and broad shoulders, the green glitter of his eyes, the richness of his brocade doublet.

Dimly she perceived that Mary and Peadair had uttered their vows and that a great cheer had gone up around the hall, but her heart and mind were fixed on the man who drew her into his arms and slowly lowered his lips to hers.

"I love ye for all time, Lilli," Iain whispered, and she heard his words echo forever in her heart.